OUT OF MY HEAD

She glanced upwards from her corner, and stayed to stare, dumbstruck. For there he was – the quintessential Mills and Boon hero; the perfect Tall, Dark and Handsome dreamboat, right down to the curling lip. It was all there: he was tall and rangy, exquisite navy suit draped from broad shoulders to narrow hips, the face was a Michaelangelo wet dream – lightly tanned planes from a broad forehead punctuated by a perfect James Bond comma of floppy black hair. She was fascinated by the sheer cliché of him – he really did have the controlled grace of a panther as he paced slowly up the display of pictures. As for his air of devastating sternness – Mills and Boon would have bottled it if they could. It was unbelievable. It was god-given – here was her hero, in the flesh, before she'd even had to devote more than a few minutes to imagining what he looked like, her work was done for her – every forbidding, thrilling, darkly stunning inch of him was there to be catalogued.

'an up-to-date gloss on the mating game . . . with wit, sex and a way with words.'

Elizabeth Buchan in the *Mail on Sunday*

About the author

Twenty-eight-year-old Susannah Jowitt gave up her job as a political lobbyist to write full-time. Travel-writing and features in newspapers including the *Daily Mail* are the latest in a long line of ways to keep the wolf from the door. *Out of My Head* is her first novel.

Out of My Head

Susannah Jowitt

CORONET BOOKS
Hodder and Stoughton

First published in Great Britain in 1996 by Hodder and Stoughton
A division of Hodder Headline PLC
First published in paperback in 1997 by Hodder and Stoughton
A Coronet Paperback

10 9 8 7 6 5 4 3 2 1

All characters in this publication are fictitious and any resemblance to real persons, living or dead, is purely coincidental.

British Library Cataloguing in Publication Data

Jowitt, Susannah
Out of my head
1. English fiction – 20th century
I. Title
823.9'14 [F]

ISBN 0 340 68055 5

Typeset by Palimpsest Book Production Limited,
Polmont, Stirlingshire
Printed and bound in Great Britain by
Cox and Wyman, Reading, Berks

Hodder and Stoughton
A division of Hodder Headline PLC
338 Euston Road
London NW1 3BH

For the tightest knot of friends anyone could ever wish for . . . you know who you are.

Acknowledgements

As someone who has redefined the boundaries on free-loading, some of my friends and family have also become sponsors. So thanks go to Teddy, Tamsin and especially Philippa Lennox-Boyd for housing me, putting me on the road and bailing me out; my parents for their roof, company and encouragement (Troof and Hun for just being inspiring), Jim and Mollers Dundas, and the Sampsons, for more of the same; and to all those who teased me into turning a party piece into a manuscript – hah!

Huge thanks to my agent, Victoria Scott, for her spot-on advice, championship and the laughs we've had; likewise Kate Lyall Grant, my editor at Hodder and Stoughton; Heather Hodson for her exposé; Alice Boyd for a great author photograph; Sarah Hirigoyen for being such a fun cover model; Candia McWilliam and Geoff Dyer, through the Arvon Foundation, for boosting me at exactly the right moment; Caroline Chapman and all the other readers who had the good sense to laugh at my jokes.

PART ONE

Do you know when I start to panic? It's when the fear creeps up on me from where I least expect it. I can be lying there, trying to get to sleep, just idly picking my toenails, thinking about unpaid parking tickets, and it will come and squat on that thought.

And I'll see it, and recognise it, and that's when the panic attack becomes real. Then time goes into stop-go motion and the thoughts stop, suffocated by the terror. They are just sluiced out, and I've lost control. My heart goes berserk – this veering, knocking thump-thump deafening me, the veins in my fingers and legs throbbing to the beat.

I'm trying to scream, to jolt myself out of it, but you're not here to hear me. If you see me then, you will think I'm under the physical pain of a knife. In my mind's eye I see how I must look – a shape in a bed, blurring with the shakes, sheets being clutched by stiff, clawing hands. On the pillow, a head which no longer has thoughts in it – it's just an arrangement of muscle, hair, eyes and mouth wide open in a silent wail; beads of sweat mixing with wrenched out tears to fall into salty slicks on the sheets. Not a human head, but terror's playground.

Sounds so melodramatic. Sometimes I – the me that was inside that head – will try to come back, to fight the panic, will shut my eyes, try to isolate one sense: sight, perhaps. But behind my eyelids there's no comfort, but all flashing lights and movement; a cacophony of melting shapes and faces. Like a nightmare funfair ride, it's all going too fast and too loud and I can't get off.

I don't throw up, I never do. Dry heaves just tussle with the iron cinch around my chest: a new band taking up the chorus. There are stars bursting behind my eyes, neck muscles screaming, teeth crashing between each retch. Breaking the back of the panic, my body fights to expel the poison of fear.

I don't know, why does this happen to me? Why aren't you here to explain it to me? I need help here. You're my family – why aren't you here?

1

'Bastards!'

Ben and Eva jumped in unison, Eva's coffee spreading out over the assembled newspapers.

'Wankers! Gits!'

'And a good morning to you too, Cockie,' said Ben drily.

'I can't believe it! I can't believe they've done this to me! Why me?' moaned Cockie, stumbling into the kitchen, letters clenched in drooping fists.

'Jesus, you can be a pain in the arse, Milton,' snapped Eva, mopping up the mess. 'What world crisis is it this time?'

'They've only gone and bounced another cheque, and charged me thirty quid for the privilege. Why do they do that? It can't possibly cost them that much to print off a couple of lousy letters and it just sinks me deeper into the mire.'

'Poetically put, now can we just get on with our usual peaceful breakfast? You'll sort something out, you always do,' said Eva.

'Don't worry, I've already had an idea.' Cockie stopped pacing and sat down, peering at Eva through bloodshot amethyst eyes. 'Oh dear, oh dear, do I sense some grumpiness in the air? Is Madam perhaps feeling her age? Has celebrating her entrance into her fourth decade rattled those old bones?'

Eva laughed. 'Fuck you, whippersnapper. It's all your fault anyway – if you and Ben hadn't bought me all those B52s, I wouldn't be in this state. I have no sympathy for your poverty if you waste money on getting me shedded – oh, and Mike will be presenting his bill for having to carry me home last night so add that to your list of woes.'

'Don't remind me,' grumbled Cockie, opening the rest of her post. 'I still owe you for all that, Ben, and for the birthday present and – oh Jesus!' She stared in horror at the letter, then slumped down on the table, head in hands.

Ben and Eva looked at each other in alarm. This was going a little further than their housemate's usual breakfast time melodramatics.

'Cockie?' probed Ben.

She thrust the paper into his hands. 'Doesn't that just sum up my life?'

He read it quickly. 'You spent £150 on a couple of bras and a pair of knickers?'

'Let me have a look at that!' Eva grabbed it and had a look. 'But Cockie, this is your Peter Jones chargecard – I could have bought all this stuff on my staff discount, you moron!'

'Wait a minute, wait a minute – why were you buying this stuff anyway?' pressed Ben.

Cockie refused to look at either of them.

'Oh no, don't tell me,' said Ben slowly, 'no, you couldn't have, even you.' Despite himself, he started to laugh.

'Oh shit,' said Eva, seeing the light. 'You bought lingerie to try and get Sam back? No wonder you didn't ask me to use my discount – don't you ever listen? Hasn't my vast and painful experience of the enemy taught you anything?'

'Steady on, Eva,' said Ben, 'no warlike talk when you're breaking bread with a man.'

'You're not a man, Ben,' dismissed Eva, 'you're our flatmate.' She turned back to Cockie. 'But Jesus, Cockie, sexy bras for that scumbag? You need help.'

'He isn't a scumbag!' fired Cockie. Then, brokenly, 'No, you're right, he is – he's a shit for all seasons. But I just wanted him to be *my* shit.'

She had a sudden knee-trembling image of him as he was when she first met him: shirtless, squinting bad-temperedly out of bloodshot, but still celestial, blue eyes, turning round to pick up a crate of beer, his divine shoulder muscles leaping into a symphony of glorious action. Who would not want such a back? She had and, in her inimitable way, had gone for it. Nothing doing. Several flirts, one successful strong-arm seduction followed by a desert of silence, and, eight months and four days later, she was back where she started. Wanting him. And not getting him.

'Tell you what,' said Eva practically, not wanting to stray into the dangerous discussion area of Sam yet again, 'I'll have a word with the Credit Department at work and see if I can get you a stay of execution.'

'That's more like it!' Cockie bounced back with characteristic optimism. 'And I'll get a couple more shifts at the Whim, and I'll touch Big Bad Brother for a loan and that'll tide me over until – yeah, I thought it all out last night.' She smiled and nicked a piece of Ben's toast.

'Until what? Thought what out?' he said, swiping the toast back again.

'Look, I've got to go to work – just one bite and I'll owe you?' she wheedled, undecided as to whether to unleash her plans on them at this early stage. 'What *is* that smell by the way?'

'Cockie! You gave it to me, you should know! It's my plug-in aromar – rosemary and peppermint to start the day off with some zing.' Eva looked too over-excited for this time of the morning. 'It's great, you know, tablets instead of messy oils and no blackening flames to deal with, or candles to blow out – you just plug it in and let your worries seep away.'

Ben snorted and a look of conspiratorial amusement shot between him and Cockie. 'Give it a rest, you hippy, and don't let Cockie change the subject. I know this look too well – you've had another Big Idea, haven't you?'

'Hey,' Cockie defended herself, 'I'm not saying that all my financial problems are going to be over immediately – actually, it was more the Sam problem that got me thinking of it, to distract me from moping over him.'

'I hardly dare ask,' said Ben heavily, 'what is "it"?'

'I'm going to be rich and – in certain discerning blue rinse and housecoat circles – quite famous.'

Now she had their attention.

'Oh yes?' said Eva, guardedly.

'Yup.' She beat out an imaginary drumroll and flung her arms wide open. 'Mills and Boon!'

'What?' said Ben and Eva in unison.

'I'm going to write a Mills and Boon, maybe even a whole array of Mills and Boons. I can't believe I haven't thought of it already. I had the idea last night. I started one in Oxford so I've already got the bare bones. All I need now is the world-famous Mills and Boon starter-pack, a few lists of satisfactorily florid adjectives and adverbs and an intimate knowledge of sexual euphemisms – "she could feel the heat of his maleness pressing against her" and suchlike – and I'm away.' Cockie was on a roll.

'Wow, you really need help this time,' marvelled Eva.

'Hey, I'm serious this time – it's the perfect complement to my life at the moment *and* it will pay off my debts, *and* I'll have a laugh. I'll have no problem fitting it in – I'll still work at the Gallery in the mornings, then I'll write in the afternoons, and knock off in the evenings except when I'm on at the Whim.'

'Sounds like a breeze,' commented Ben drily, 'but

where does sleep come into this scenario?' He ignored Cockie's attempts to break in. 'Your social life's a maelstrom, you've just told us you're going to take on even more shifts at the Whim and you know perfectly well you can't drag yourself away from the fun and games until well after the last punter, so night kipping is out. I only ask because if ever I come back in the afternoons to dip into your list of Funky Things to Do of an Afternoon, you are nearly always fast asleep.'

'In the bizarrest places,' added Eva.

'Yes, only you could fall asleep while putting on the kettle – which just proves my point . . . um . . . what was my point?'

'That this new idea is crap,' supplied Eva sweetly.

'The point is,' said Cockie, triumphantly regaining the advantage and ignoring Eva, 'I know I can do it, you know I can do it, you're just being a wonderful friend by pointing out the pitfalls. But I'm not stupid, I know the pitfalls, I know that I've had foolish schemes before, but I've got a great feeling about this one – this time it's going to happen!'

And with that, she flashed them a huge grin, picked up her bag and sailed serenely out of the kitchen. Into the silence left behind her came the slam of the front door.

'Amazing,' Ben said, after a moment.

'Incredible,' agreed Eva.

'Absolute unquenchable optimism.'

'Absolute unquenchable lack of grip on reality.'

'Oh, easy, tiger. It's not like she's giving up all her jobs and worldly pleasures to starve in a garret, which, you must admit, given Cockie's penchant for romantic gestures, is a welcome change.'

'Ben,' said Eva sternly, 'you and I know perfectly well that that girl has the self-discipline of a flea – virtually the *only* way she would finish this bloody book would be if she *were* locked up in a garret!'

'Now who's losing their grip? I'm actually surprised,' said Ben musingly, 'that you're being so down on her. I thought I would be the debunker in this scenario, the chucker of cold water on the fire of Cockie's enthusiasm, and that you would be all sisterly support and talk of her finding her inner life direction, realising her latent potential and some such guff.'

'Writing a Mills and Boon is realising latent potential?' Eva retorted. 'Coming downstairs after a grand few hours' reflection and announcing that she is going to be an active accomplice in a publishing culture which just pulls the wool over the eyes of the miserable masses, encouraging them to believe in romantic claptrap – I mean, your average Mills and Boon heroine doesn't have an orgasm – oh no no, nothing so base, so, so, *physical* – no, she goes to the fucking stars, for Christ's sake, she gets transported to a magical plane of consciousness with a hundred violins part of the deal! This is not seeing your life path, this is Cockie blinding herself yet again to reality *and* blinding others!'

Ben was beginning to wish he had not mused out loud. 'OK, OK, the soapbox is very becoming, my love, but I have to go to work, gardens to plant, people to dazzle. What about you? Are you not going to work today?'

'Nope; day off,' said Eva, still feeling righteous.

'Well, have a good one. Bye.'

As the front door slammed behind Ben, Eva lingered over drinking one last cup of coffee. She was startled that Cockie's announcement had aroused her to such indignation this early in the morning. After all, it wasn't as if Cockie hadn't had similarly useless ideas before. To say that she subscribed to the Madcap and Mayhem School of Crazy Schemes would be an understatement and since losing her job, it had got out of hand. Water filters, Amway networking, a Dateline-type scheme to put old people into nursing homes with other, compatible, geriatrics, these were just a few Cockie flirtations. But nothing ever staggered off the drawing board. Cockie would be all hellfire and brimstone, just about to wreak profitable havoc on society as they knew it, but would then get distracted, smothered by the morass of chaos that was her everyday life, or fall in love with yet another unsuitable man. All in all, Eva reflected, Cockie's life made her own seem an oasis of peace and clarity. This was certainly a novel feeling. *She* had always been the one living life on the edge, stumbling from crisis to crisis, extricating herself from disastrous relationships, the big difference between her and Cockie being that she had been either too bombed or karma-insulated to worry about it all.

It's weird, she thought, that not so long ago, I could easily have been attracted to someone like Sam – excessively good-looking, dumb as hell, and dysfunctional in every emotional sense – and yet here I am going out with Mike. Mike was a new experience for Eva's slightly jaded palate when it came to the opposite sex, having run through men at a rate of knots, all of whom were alternative, different, 'whacky'. To end up with someone who made a successful living out of being Mr Average was quite a turn up for the books. Not your obvious choice for a nutcake like me, or vice versa, thought Eva fondly, when suddenly she noticed the time. Dammit, if she stayed slumped at the table much longer she was going to be late for her first massage appointment of the day. Now where the hell had she put that new ambergris oil, she wondered, as she jammed her newest millinery acquisition, a purple silk top hat, onto her head, hefted up the foldaway massage table that was the cumbersome calling card of her out-of-hours career, and staggered through the hall into the sunlight outside.

2

Lurching absently on the crowded bus, Cockie was in a standing-room-only world of her own, her head whirling with purple prose and storylines for the Mills and Boon. Get a grip, woman, she thought, first things first – what should they look like? The heroine was easy – she could be everything that Cockie wasn't – tip-tilted nose, piquant heart-shaped face framed by dancing blonde hair – your basic romantic novel nightmare.

As for the hero, she had planned to model him on her picture of the ideal man – snapping blue ice-slits of eyes, springy silky blond hair a little on the long side, lean of jaw and mean of mouth, with a glint of golden stubble to top the dreamboat off. Well, forget that, she thought, I've just described Sam. She would not give him the satisfaction of thinking not only that he was *her* ideal man but that she was inviting her vast potential readership to share that view. Anyway, I can't have two blond protagonists – the BNP will adopt me as the propagandist for some kind of Aryan Utopia on the Isle of Dogs. No, the hero would have to be a graduate of the Tall, Dark and Handsome School.

'Next stop, St Paul's,' came a bellow, jolting Cockie from her reverie. Dammit, she'd missed her stop. She pushed forward, only to trip over a helpfully placed foot. Pitching forward, she grabbed the nearest lifeline – a rucksack in front of her, attached to someone's shoulder.

Normally in a state of catatonic depression, there is nothing the average London commuter relishes more than a bit of torment and embarrassment happening to their fellow sufferers. Watching the last minute leaper onto the Tube get her shopping bag caught on the other side of the doors gets a laugh every time from the dehumanised mass inside, and this was up there in those lofty echelons of entertainment.

Cockie, unabashed, glanced up at her hapless rescuer.

'Do you need some help?' smiled the owner of the rucksack, eyes sparkling.

'Thanks! Sorry about that.'

Cockie looked closer as she inched past, half convinced that somehow she knew this person, even though the face itself was not immediately familiar. Maybe it was someone famous, recognisable in that split second as you pass them in the street, wave at them cheerily, then realise ten yards further down that you just greeted Hugh Grant like an old mate. But a curtain of hair was now hiding the woman's face so Cockie gave up and pushed on.

As the bus pulled away from the traffic lights, Cockie did her usual flying leap off the platform. She looked back at the bus, still puzzled by the stranger, but there was nothing she could do about it now. Probably knew her in another life, slugs in the same medieval garden, she mused, as she turned to trot up the street.

Arriving at the door of the gallery in a flurry of scarves, headphones and a trailing handbag, Cockie paused to collect herself and sailed serenely through the door, only to trip over the pile of post that she, as gallery gofer, was supposed to pick up and move out of the doorway. No lifeline this time; arse over tit, she pitched onto her hands and knees – just as her boss, Edward, came out from the back. All this falling over was getting a little ridiculous.

'Hi there,' said Cockie breathlessly, 'just sorting out the post.'

'Don't be so keen, Cockie,' Edward said drily, 'take your coat off next time, relax, have a cup of coffee. Let the post wait.'

The imaginatively named City Art Gallery was a two-fold operation. Like any gallery, it displayed paintings and prints for sale. But this was effectively a front for its more profitable activities which involved finding and supplying anything from paintings and prints to lithographs and sculptures, to aesthetically upwardly mobile corporations.

Its heyday had been during the eighties when the quality of artwork in the boardroom had been a deliberate and well-funded marketing exercise and an acknowledged status symbol. In the niggardly nineties such an expansive gesture was generally avoided but a new ethos had emerged. Along with handwriting experts and psychometric testing, corporate art psychology had emerged as a force to be cashed in on in the City. The basic theory was that if you surrounded your employees with semi-valuable, innovative pieces of art, instead of the usual directors' photos and peeling promotional posters, they would feel flattered, part of the team, enriched by their environment.

Less generally accepted – but also used by the City Gallery in its pitches for new clients – was the possibility that having striking, ground-breaking examples of hard work and genius all around them would inspire these overworked, overpaid grunts to come up with something new and similarly innovative in their line of work. Edward tended to tone down this approach with some of the more conservative English establishments, judging that innovation was not something they wanted to encourage.

When Cockie had applied for the job she had initially

thought that this could be a possible career path, using her PR skills, City contacts and research capabilities to good effect. Not for long. Edward and Emma, his assistant, between them had cornered the market on any of the more interesting parts of the job – Edward did the high profile parts; the travelling, the unearthing of unacknowledged treasures, the courting of clients while Emma scurried behind him making sure that the whole glamorous edifice rested on a basis of sound administration.

The job was Emma's life. Having gone to a public school which concentrated only on discouraging such unladylike hopes as a career, she had left at the age of seventeen with few qualifications except an unqualified hatred for hollandaise sauce, embroidery and the Moonlight Sonata, and a yearning to be Important in Something. Over the last few years she had clawed her way into a position of indispensability at the gallery and was not about to let an over-educated Oxford graduate with far superior work experience undermine that precarious hold on power. Cockie was employed as a gofer and a gofer she was destined to remain.

Once Cockie recognised this she was far too amiable to push the issue, retired to her corner, and made them both a cup of tea. Since then they had got on well, if warily. Mind you, a field where many corporations simply bought art by the yard – concerned primarily that the dimensions, not the content, of a painting should fit that particular wall – was not quite up Cockie's street, having suffered the wounds of a thousand compromises in her PR days.

At least, she reflected, as she hunkered in the corner of the front gallery, cataloguing some newly acquired prints, the mindless nature of this job meant that now she would have the opportunity to mull at leisure and create the Mills and Boon in her head. The impossibly star-crossed lives of Allegra and Luke would spring to life from the unpromising loins – she peered downwards at the print in her hands – of the derivative *Rapscallion at Rest* – School of Hogarth – Engraving c. 1780.

The discreet buzzing of the front door being opened brought her out of her reverie. She glanced upwards from her corner, and stayed to stare, dumbstruck. For there he was – the quintessential Mills and Boon hero; the perfect Tall, Dark and Handsome dreamboat, her Luke to a T, right down to the curling lip. It was all there: he was tall and rangy, exquisite navy suit draped from broad shoulders to narrow hips, the face was a Michelangelo wet dream – lightly tanned planes from a broad forehead punctuated by a perfect James Bond comma of floppy black hair. She was fascinated by the sheer cliché of him – he really did have the controlled grace of a panther as he paced slowly up the display of pictures. As for his air of devastating sternness – Mills and Boon would have bottled it if they could. It was unbelievable. It was god-given – here was her hero – here was Luke, in the flesh; before she'd even had to devote more than a few minutes to imagining what he looked like, her work was done for her – every forbidding, thrilling, darkly stunning inch of him was there to be catalogued.

As for the eyes, Cockie couldn't make out their colour but for Luke's purposes they would be green – limpid pools capable of a range of emotions – from the reproach of a wounded animal to the tenderness of Mantovani – or icy splinters narrowed in fury or veiled with the inscrutability of a cat – the possibilities for purple prose were endless. Yes, he'd turned around and – Cockie inched a bit closer – yes! score! the sunlight flashed into eyes that were every bit as emerald as she could have wished: eyes that were . . . now . . . looking in her direction. Cockie came back to earth with a resounding thud.

'Er, you do work here, don't you?'

She wasn't imagining it – there was a definite air of sarcasm there. What an idiot. What a gawping, mawkish moron she must look, staring at him as if he was an invader from the Planet Romance. But she couldn't resist it, even the voice was right – a true chocolate-brown drawl, with just a hint of some non-British accent. It was all too perfect.

'Excuse me, *can* you help me?'

He was getting impatient now. Cockie pulled herself together, stood up, and rearranged her face from village idiot to beaming salesgirl.

'I'm so sorry, I was miles away, what can I do for you?' A feeble attempt at suavity.

'Well, I'm early for an appointment with Edward Boyle and I was just wondering' – he broke off to walk back to the main wall of prints – 'this is quite interesting and, yes, attractive. Could you tell me something about it?'

Cockie suppressed a small sigh of disappointment. Dead set winner on the dreamboat stakes he may be, but there had to be a flaw. Perhaps it was too much to ask that he had any artistic taste but it was a distinct danger sign that he could describe art as being 'attractive'. She walked over to the print he had indicated; it was one of their Top Ten sellers – a deeply pedestrian view of one of the City approaches to St Paul's in the late eighteenth century, containing all the requisite period details such as pompadoured toffs emerging from their carriages, the occasional lady in all her exquisite ruffles, dashing squires on stylised stallions and a general sense of historical hustle and bustle. Nothing for it but to gird her loins and concentrate on the job in hand with some artistic shenanigans.

'Yes, that is one of the most unusual in our very popular series of late eighteenth-century views of the City. Not only is it of excellent quality but there is a slightly satirical flavour to it which makes it stand out from your everyday engraving.'

Oh, this was a mug's game.

'Do you see down in the corner here, almost concealed in the shadows, there is an almost Hogarthian image of a woman – perhaps a prostitute – sitting in the gutter, all rags and dramatic attitudes of poverty, whereas throughout the rest of the picture there are only silks and satins.'

As he leant forward to look more closely at the spot in question, Cockie caught a whiff of his lemon-tanged aftershave, so sharply redolent of the sophisticated sexuality of her imaginary hero that she unconsciously swayed towards him, eyes momentarily glazed as she found herself thinking again how unbelievably perfect he was, how uncannily right for her conception of how a Mills and Boon man should be. Before she embarrassed herself completely and fell on him, his perfectly formed head swivelled and he arched a thick straight eyebrow at her proximity – quite supercilious enough to bring her to her senses.

'Yes, and then there are the dogs,' she said, betraying herself by being breathless.

'The dogs?' There was that eyebrow again. Oh, he was just too James Bond for words.

'Well, they are all maimed,' said Cockie more level-headedly, gesturing vaguely at the scene.

He obviously thought she was insane, but obediently peered again at the print.

'If you look closely, you can see how all the dogs that you initially think are scampering about without a care in the world, are all actually three-legged or missing an ear, starving thin or generally battered.'

He finally saw what she was driving at, laughed out loud and asked in a more intrigued drawl, 'And why is that?'

Before Cockie could dream up a convincing sociological allegory, Emma appeared behind Cockie. Her Attractive

Male Early Warning System was clearly working well – Cockie could have sworn that she'd even had time for a primp.

'You must be Mr Landis – smashing to meet you – Edward will be out of his meeting in just a jiffy.' Already she had inveigled her way between them to gaze bewitchingly into his eyes.

Cockie couldn't help but marvel. True to her background as a well-brought-up young lady, Emma was usually impeccably polite with strangers; polite almost to the point of froideur. But plonk her in front of a man like this – whose looks went well off the Richter scale – and boy, did her hormones rise to the occasion. Suddenly, she was Scarlett O'Hara – reserve flung to the wind, eyelashes batting, all tinkling laughs and flirtatious laying-on of hands. The transformation never ceased to startle Cockie and this time was no exception. Feminists would have had a fit.

'I'm delighted that we could finally lure you here – I gather Edward usually meets you at your offices?'

'Yes, that's right, but apparently he has some large canvases he wants to show me in the flesh.'

The dialogue was hardly the stuff of prizewinning seduction, thought Cockie, but you could almost hear the swish of an imaginary hooped skirt and the flutter of fan as Emma leant forward conspiratorially, hand already on his arm, holding his bemused glance with her own mesmerising gaze, 'In the meantime, could I tempt you with some freshly brewed coffee? Naturally, we grind the beans here.'

'I wouldn't have it any other way,' he smiled.

Cockie perked up from her place on the sidelines – he'd fallen for the routine. Emma twinkled prettily back at him and turned to Cockie, 'Cockie, would you do the honours?'

Despite all her protestations at being happy to have left

PR, Cockie often found it difficult to reconcile herself to her present lowly status. If she had been a slave in her PR days, she had at least been an executive slave – here she was a human hostess trolley, with making freshly ground frigging coffee the pinnacle of her responsibilities.

She tamped the beans savagely into the grinder in the small cupboard they laughingly called a kitchen. At least, she thought grimly, she had the last laugh in that respect. Since she never touched the stuff herself, she made a truly terrible cup of coffee – or so she had been assured over the years by a variety of people with puckered faces and choking voices. She was waiting for the day when one of her coffee victims from either the gallery or the restaurant would come clean and say how revolting it really was.

Things were well under way out front.

'So, Victor,' – behold! first name terms already, thought Cockie – 'you must have a terribly good eye for modern art to be in charge of such a huge project.'

Cockie wasn't staying to listen to such claptrap; silently she put the tray on the coffee table where The Hunk and Emma were now cosily ensconced on a sofa, lingered briefly to see him sip the coffee, wince very briefly at the taste, but thank her with a friendly nod, before she withdrew to her corner and her cataloguing. Just another lamb to the Cockie coffee slaughter.

Actually the little scene before her was perfect for her Mills and Boon purposes. It gave her the opportunity to take notes for her characterisation of her hero – Luke, Luca when he revealed his Italian roots. Not only was this Victor playing the part of the suave charmer to the hilt – although he was hardly getting a word in edgeways – but this would be good material for the inevitable 'heroine-sees-hero-flirting-at-party-with-pang-of-hitherto-unrealised-jealousy'scene. All good intentions of getting on with the cataloguing fled as Cockie grabbed a notebook and began to devise the scenario. For the next few minutes, the gallery echoed to the sounds of Emma's silvery laugh. Cockie was so intent on staring at them, then scribbling, that she failed to notice that, occasionally, as she bent her head to the page, Victor would glance over at her, as if puzzled by her activities. Then Edward came bustling out of his office with Jonty, the framer, in tow.

'Victor! I am so sorry! How long have you been waiting? Why didn't you tell me Victor was here, Emma?'

'Oh, it's all right, Edward, I knew you would be finished with Jonty in a couple of minutes, and Victor seemed happy to wait,' cooed Emma artlessly. But the presence of her boss restored her to her habitual sedateness as he ushered Jonty out, then turned to take Victor back into his office.

Emma immediately came sprinting over to Cockie.

'What a knockout! Victor Landis – to die for! Can you believe that he's so scrumptious?'

'Well, you obviously couldn't, your eyes were popping – still are in fact,' Cockie said unkindly. Then, relenting slightly, she added, 'Although you were certainly making an equal impression on him.'

'Really? Do you think so?'

'Poetry in motion. No doubt about it. In fact, I was taking notes on the brilliance of your technique,' said Cockie drily.

As usual, the sarcasm wafted undetected over Emma's head. 'Yes, I noticed that you were scribbling away in the corner. Actually, I also noticed that you yourself were a little starry-eyed when I came in.' Emma suddenly looked not so much starry as beady-eyed.

'Not for that reason, dummy. You know my moronic heart still belongs to the worthless Sam. No, it's just that he was perfect for . . .' Cockie hesitated.

'Perfect?' There was a definite proprietorial glint now. 'Perfect for what?'

'Oh, nothing, just an idea.' Cockie suddenly decided

not to tell Emma and Edward about the Mills and Boon. Not just because of the aesthetic scorn that would be heaped on her head but because of the inevitable bullying about her concentration on the gallery job.

'Yes, well, hands off because I managed to get Victor to go to the Maurice Ogden private viewing next week.'

'Wow! Quick work!'

'But I couldn't persuade him to come *with* me because he said he might be tied up at work. Talking of work,' Emma glanced at her watch, 'I'd better get in there and do some before they finish their meeting, otherwise Edward will know that we've been gassing.'

She headed back to the office, 'Oh, Cockie darling, would you just clear away the coffee cups?'

Ben stared morosely across his newest garden. It looked, he decided, like the perfect gentleman's garden – all follies, fountains and levées, elegantly laid out in the perfect symmetry of a Louis XIV estate. Yes, a perfect gentleman's garden – as provided by Legoland. For it was tiny and – as the sounds of the street below wafted up – Ben reflected again how barmy it was that he was trying to reproduce Versailles in a roof garden. Instead of the tinkle of exquisite courtly string quartets there was the overhead roar of stacking aeroplanes; no vast chain of waterfall-connected lakes with a menagerie of exotic birds but a duck-less pond; no Marie Antoinette waffling about cakes but . . .

Mr Takahashi stepped out of the glass doors onto the roof and, beaming broadly, came to stand beside Ben.

'I really must say, Lord Ben, how very delighted we are with your work. It is ravishing and so absolutely right.'

It always amused Ben how Mr Takahashi managed to pack into a sentence so many words containing the letters 'r' and 'l' – as if to show off his perfect non-Japanese diction; but what really tickled him was the way his deputy, Mr Hitokawa, did the same thing in a spirit of corporate adulation perhaps, but without the same ability. Conversation with Hitokawa was consequently an excruciating stagger through a minefield of bogged down consonants, planted with enough 'velly's' and 'solly's' for any Carry On movie.

'Thank you, Mr Takahashi,' said Ben easily, 'but please, just call me Ben' – he had rapidly learned that the Japanese found it impossible to be informal but he kept trying – 'I do think the sundial corner looks marvellous.'

'It is truly a haven of peace and relaxation,' murmured Mr Takahashi, 'and an example, I believe, to my more xenophobic countrymen who insist on duplicating our Japanese surroundings here. I like to think that we can promote Japan through the excellence of our company alone without resorting to the affectation of a bonsai tree. It is time to abandon the conservative and nationalist convictions of the eighties. This garden will not only be a place of beauty but will serve to remind us that it is through the marriage of East and West that our goals will be reached.'

'Er, yes. Quite.' Ben got the feeling that he was listening to the first draft of the speech Mr Takahashi was giving at the opening at the end of the week.

Mr Takahashi bowed briefly and went back through the French windows. This was the moment that Ben liked best. This was the moment of peace and a sense of achievement that made the previous months of mayhem and mud worthwhile. Even if the finished product was a little ridiculous, he had at least achieved the feeling of an oasis – a limpid pool of green and quiet striving to keep the stark grey concrete and cacophony of the city at bay. He wandered idly around before settling himself like a sleepy cat on a bench in a sunbaked corner at the end of the roof. He gazed at the sundial, thinking about Cockie's new scheme.

Although he largely agreed with Eva's condemnation of Mills and Boons, Ben couldn't help thinking that it was almost inevitable that Cockie should have found this métier. Even the timing was typical; Cockie always hatched her most ambitious schemes after yet another of her romantic disasters. The girl was an adman's delight; she wept at *trailers* in the cinema; she was reduced to a pulp by trashy books dominated by star-crossed lovers, unhappy marriages and the ravages of war; she was an emotional nut for nostalgia, with a tear-jerk, knee-jerk Pavlovian reaction to certain – generally terrible – music. Ben had once walked into the kitchen while she was doing the washing-up and listening to the soundtrack of *Miss Saigon*. As the strains of schmaltz died away he realised that Cockie was wracked with sobs, shoulders heaving as she filled the sink with shameless tears. Two minutes later she'd be back to her old acrid cynicism, laughing at herself and saying that since there was no real romance in the world, at least she had the sense to fall for the fun part of the whole con. 'If I was thin and could afford Givenchy clothes,' she'd declare, 'I'd be Holly Golightly – a phoney, OK, but a real phoney.'

It was hardly surprising then, that, à la *Breakfast at Tiffany's*, she fell for the rats and the super rats of the population and that when she fell, she plunged. Ben had given up counting how many times she had dashed herself on a man's indifference or, more accurately, his 'lack of commitment'.

Now Cockie had come to grief again – with Sam. Ben hadn't been able to help liking Sam – the guy was so damn charming to men and women alike that Ben could almost see why Cockie had carried her torch so long and uselessly. He remembered the morning after she'd finally had her wicked way with Sam; despite the ravages of a ruinous party the night before, Cockie had been glowing and triumphant, joyously confident that she finally had Sam within her clutches.

Sam, by contrast, had stumbled down halfway through their Sunday morning breakfast ritual of wading knee-deep through a pile of Sunday papers; barely able to speak, glad rags rumpled and reeking of smoke, his flashy good looks blunted by a hungover scowl and bloodshot eyes. While Cockie had prattled on, oblivious to Sam's less than loverlike aura, Ben and Eva had exchanged speaking looks, their hearts sinking as they did some instant crystal ball gazing. That had been months ago and Cockie had only just really got it through her skull that Sam was a No Trespassing zone.

Only a couple of weeks ago Ben had had a phone call from Sam himself, after a night when Cockie had woken everyone in the house by coming in very late, slamming all the doors she could find and playing Leonard Cohen loudly and lugubriously until Eva had jumped up and down on the floor of her room in a screaming fury.

'Ben, me old geezer,' Sam had opened, reminding Ben that sometimes his charm could sink into rather dim condescension, 'I need to talk to you about Cockie.'

'Yes?' Guarded.

'Well, you know, she's a great girl, bags of personality and all that but,' Sam had paused, 'well, man, she's not getting it through her head that I'm not, like, interested.'

'What makes you think that?'

'Nothing specific but she, like, stares. Last night, at 192 – Fred's birthday – I was, like, getting it on with this bird, Esme, and Cockie was just staring at us. Then she, like, comes over and acts like I'm hers, well not quite hers, but like we're an item and that we have, like, a history.'

'Well, let's face it, you have,' Ben interrupted, beginning to bristle on Cockie's behalf and not sure how many more 'like's' he could stand.

'For Chrissakes, man, one lousy night. Not that it was lousy,' he amended hastily, 'but that was, like, months ago and apart from, like, the odd flirt and, oh yeah, I think I snogged her when I was pissed at that Mayday rave a few weeks ago – but other than that I've done absolutely nothing to encourage the girl.' He finished self-righteously.

Ben hadn't let Sam realise that it was then that he had lost his temper, but had merely attempted to clear Cockie's name with a few well-chosen words attesting to her indifference towards Sam, the way her general vivacity and flirtiness could be mistaken for personal interest, and implying overall, that a lamebrain like Sam should consider himself lucky to have had anything to do with such a paragon party-girl.

He had also resolved to have a subtle word with Cockie along the lines of 'that Sam, he's a shit, isn't he? Boring too. Pleased with himself. Best thing you ever did, deciding not to pursue that one any more'. Come to think of it, he mused, kicking a slightly loose corner of newly-laid turf back into place, I never did have that word with her, but from the flurry of planned activity this morning, it looks like I may not have to.

The burning question now was – how long would this particular scheme last? Now that was worth a wager or two, he thought wryly.

3

'And you didn't say anything else to him?' Flo was aghast, his eyebrows shooting up into his bandanna.

Cockie carried on polishing the glasses. 'There wasn't any need. He plainly thought I was barmy and I didn't need to know anything more about him.'

'But you said he was Mr Right, Mr Perfect, Mr Too-Good-To-Be-True . . .'

'That's the whole point,' said Cockie, 'he is perfect, for the book – the way he looked was exactly how I imagined the hero should look, it was uncanny really.'

'Oh right, the book,' Flo said drily, 'the fact that you goggled at him, virtually fell on him, and spouted complete nonsense at him – all this has nothing to do with raging pheromones and all to do with your newly discovered literary talent and a purely academic interest in him? Yeah right.'

'Yeah right,' mimicked Cockie equally sarcastically, 'I know it's difficult for you to understand, since sex is a subtext to everything for you, but I am not quite so one-dimensional and I genuinely didn't fancy him – for a start he was way out of my league and, to be frank, he also seemed quite an idiot.'

'Never stopped you before,' said TJ who had just approached the bar with an order, 'look at Sam.'

'Not fair, TJ, you can't just interrupt a conversation

only to bruise my – what's the word when you hammer steak into flat pieces, Flo?'

'Tenderised.'

'Yeah, bruise my tenderised heart.' Cockie paused, surprised that she was suddenly able genuinely to joke about Sam.

'Well, I have no idea who the *new* idiot is but Table 3 have whipped through their wine like people just out of a health farm and were making throat-clutching gestures as I walked past, so I reckon they need some more.' TJ pushed her order into a glass and sent it down to the kitchens in the dumb-waiter.

'OK, OK. Flo – can I have some more of that Koonunga Valley white – we'll carry on this conversation later.'

'Mmm, I look forward to some more justifications,' he winked wickedly at her, 'do you need another ice bucket?'

'The way Table 3 are throwing it down, I doubt it'll make it anywhere near an ice bucket.' Cockie turned to follow TJ back into the restaurant.

'TJ!' TJ turned and waited for her. 'Have you got a spare corkscrew – I've put mine down somewhere.'

'Ah yeah, there's a surprise – I think Fred's got a spare one,' she pointed to their fellow waiter, patiently explaining the specials to a hen party of giggling girls. 'So who is the new man?'

'Not new man. Artistic inspiration. Flo was just teasing.'

TJ was looking confused.

'Look, I'll tell you later, OK?'

For the next few hours, people poured themselves in to eat, drink and make Cockie's, TJ's and Fred's lives hell. As a restaurant and bar situated opposite a nightclub, the Slim Whim was especially packed out on Fridays and Saturdays – with people determined to get as filled up and watered as possible before hitting the Club Soda – the rave dance place of the moment but which sold neither alcohol nor any food except fruit.

On a warm Friday night like tonight, the Whim was a jumping mixture of flesh on show and suits on the go – the latter ending their week with a blow-out, the former beginning their weekend with a bang. Even the décor was excessive – blood red walls with an overlay of gold spray tussled exuberantly with a carpet and crushed velvet banquettes of the deepest indigo-purple; a dozen different red, gold and purple designs of velvets and silks draped in all directions shimmered and rustled in the aromatic haze of smoke and good living, converging on each wall behind a vast golden boss set with a myriad of not even semi-precious jewels. Florid, torrid brass chandeliers winked and swayed above the revellers while, set over the doorway, blazing brazen torches did nothing for London's pollution but a great deal for the baroque scene inside.

Cockie loved it all. Wearing the Whim's 'uniform' of frill-fronted and huge cuffed white shirt, and crushed red velvet waistcoat, with her own black flares, she weaved in and out of the crowd, flirting with the regulars, rebuffing the over-boisterous, as she took orders and lost orders, delivered food, and dropped cutlery down cleavages, poured her revolting coffee and spilt herbal teas. Camouflaged by the chaos of a Friday night, she was always forgiven by the clientele who loved the food and who couldn't help but be charmed by this laughing girl who salvaged her never-calamitous mistakes and left them feeling like they were the most important people she'd served all night.

'Cockie!'

It was Fred, perched on a stool, yelling across the undulating, ululating bar crowd as Cockie tottered out of the restaurant with an armful of dirty plates. She nodded to show that she'd heard. He gave up trying to be heard – put five fingers on his wristwatch, put two fingers up to his mouth and exaggeratedly breathed in, gestured to his chest, pointed at Cockie, then hunched over with his hands linked in front of him, then pointed at the girl standing beside Patrick, owner of the Whim, at the bar. If you gave him a ping pong bat, he would be a dead ringer for a ground air traffic controller.

'Got it,' she murmured to herself, 'five minute fag break, both of us, hand over my stuff to that new girl.' She nodded again as Fred began to push his way through the crowd.

By the time she herself got to the bar, Cockie's arms were feeling the strain. 'Patrick, I think Fred said we could have a break.'

'Yes, give those plates to Annalisa here and be back in no more than five minutes.'

'Thanks, Annalisa, sorry, I haven't had time to introduce myself, I'm Cockie.' She smiled at the girl as she took the plates.

Annalisa didn't acknowledge her, just made a moue of distaste as her thumb went into the remnants of some hollandaise sauce on the top plate.

'I'm doing the far corner tables: 3, 7, 12, 14, 15; they're all at pretty much the same stage – main course – but 12 has just ordered coffee.'

'Don't worry, I think that I can probably work it out for myself.' The girl turned away, leaving Cockie shrugging and a little nonplussed.

'C'mon Cockie, time is money, let's go,' said Fred, grabbing her elbow and steering her down the stairs to the little office-cum-smoking room next to the kitchens. Felipe, the sous-chef, was already there, puffing on a joint which he offered to Fred and Cockie.

'Thanks, Felipe,' said Cockie gratefully, and inhaled deeply on the offering. 'Fred?'

'Nah, I've got my own stuff for later, thanks.'

'Stuff? What do you mean by stuff?' Fred looked vague and didn't answer. 'Oh, don't tell me you're taking E again?' Cockie said accusingly, handing the joint back to Felipe and lighting a cigarette.

Felipe, sensing a dispute, left.

'Just a tab, to celebrate selling an article – nothing to get your hypocritical knickers in a twist, you puritanical dope fiend, you.'

'Not dope fiend, and not hypocritical – the odd leaf of grass doesn't qualify for either count – but if you want to melt your spine with dubiously procured chemical dust, don't do it anywhere near me,' Cockie said self-righteously, then did a double-take, 'what article?'

'Oh, just a little eight hundred word number on all the controversy about rollerblading in London, for the weekend section of *The Independent*,' bragged Fred airily, lighting his own cigarette.

'You're kidding!'

'Nope. Three hundred smackeroonies – payable to Fred Ellermann, Bright Young Reporter About Town.' He stretched luxuriously, 'Actually, we're doing the photoshoot on Sunday in Hyde Park – you know where they play roller hockey by the Albert Memorial – do you want to come along? You've got a pair of rollerblades, haven't you?'

'Well, yes,' said Cockie sheepishly, 'but I'm not that good. The initial burst of enthusiasm suffered a bit of a setback when I tried to rollerblade to work.'

'Here? Or all the way to the gallery?'

'Here – not that that made a jot of difference. I couldn't even make it to the end of the road. Do you realise that our pavements are like bloody moon craters? Even though I looked like a Gladiator, with all the kit – knee-pads, elbow-pads, wrist-guards: the works – I crashed, and burned with shame, about every ten yards. By the time I'd cut my hand open and smashed my head on a recycling bin, I thought, "Bugger this", and got on the bus in my socks. And don't laugh, you pig, I still bear the scars.' Cockie looked thoughtful, 'Come to think of it, I got some extraordinary looks on the bus – no shoes, bleeding, bad-tempered and looking like I was on my way to star in *Starlight Express*.'

'So that's a no to roller hockey, national fame and exposure then?'

'Much as it goes against the grain,' said Cockie mournfully.

Fred grinned wickedly. 'Well then, I thought I might ask Annalisa if she wanted to come.'

Cockie looked at him sharply, 'Annalisa? The new girl?'

'The very same – I reckon she'd be quite a sight in a lycra rollerblading outfit.' Fred licked his lips exaggeratedly. 'Why, Cockie? Are you jealous?'

'Give over, Mr Ego, back in your box. Actually she is quite attractive – if you like that combination of petite hourglass figure, gorgeous brunette hair,' she smiled, teasing him now, 'sparkling come-to-bed eyes and a lightbulb smile with an on-off switch reserved exclusively for men.'

'Put like that, how can I resist trying it on?'

'Yeah, personally I don't think she's the friendliest of souls but you know what they say, if with one you don't succeed, try try try again with sundry others!'

'Ouch! Touché!' Fred threw up his hands in defeat, laughing. 'Can I help it if you broke my heart by refusing me, leaving me numb to romance, and wedded to the idea of convenient sex? You know what they also say about a filled-with-woe man spurned!'

'Oh nice try, Romeo. Man, you are so full of it! Mind you, I like the idea of me being some sort of heartless Boadicea, with you the cringing woad-painted slave at my feet – I'll remember that the next time I stride through a field of men, wheel blades whirring at my side.'

'Now who's full of it? What a bizarre imagination you have, Cockie my darling. Talking of which, what's this I hear about a book – are you trying to steal my thunder?'

Cockie pulled a face at him, 'Don't worry, Shakespeare, I'll leave the Whitbread and the Booker to you – I'm going for the Betty Trask Prize.'

'The what?' Fred looked blank.

'It's the prize for best romantic novel – mind you, I'm not sure I'll be eligible for that because I'm going to write a Mi—'

There was suddenly a roar from upstairs. Patrick was on the rampage.

'Cockie! Fred! How long does a bloody cigarette take to smoke? It's bloody chaos up here!'

They scrambled to their feet, Cockie taking a last puff, and hurried upstairs. Silhouetted at the top was a Mayan figure of rage – Patrick, hands on hips, every inch of him bristling.

'Calm down, oh Thor, God of War – your loyal staff are here,' Cockie said unrepentantly.

'Yeah, I make that almost exactly four minutes,' said Fred looking importantly at his watch, 'where would you like us to spend the remaining minute of our break?'

Moods were quick to come and go with Patrick. 'Oh stop grinning like jackasses, the pair of you. Heads will roll in a moment, so I would just scarper,' and he watched them with a reluctantly fond smile as they scurried back into the restaurant.

Eva and Mike sat in Wodka, the fragrant vapours of a spectrum of vodkas swirling about them, with eyes only for each other. Even the balalaika muzak that was prompting drunker diners to practise their cossack-dancing couldn't impinge. Eva herself was aware of a face that wasn't hers plastered all over her own mug, a slack, gaping face which was three-quarters dopey smile and a quarter dazed drooping eyes; a martini of love with a dash of pepper vodka. Shaken. And very stirred.

For about half an hour, an Amazon-flow of slow, molten desire had been curling through her, all streams converging hotly at the points of contact with Mike. There was now a conflagration at her left knee, a flame or two through the toe of her shoe where she could just feel his instep, and a forest fire raging between their two clasped hands. She didn't think she had ever felt this intensely aware of all parts of her body; every nerve ending, every follicle was gasping for close bodily contact with Mike's every nerve ending, his every follicle; and the whirlpool sensation in her groin was gaining momentum with every minute. Feeling increasingly like her mind was just a satellite spinning round her recalcitrant fanny, she attempted to concentrate on something other than what Mike's body was saying back to hers; after all, his mouth had actually been speaking to her all this time, albeit a little goofily, while she'd been deaf to little else but her shrieking hormones.

'. . . even Huw noticed that I've been completely out of my head recently and actually asked if I was on drugs. Can you believe it? The funniest thing is that not only was he completely serious but the next thing is, he's asking me if he can have some . . . !'

Never taking his eyes off Eva, Mike laughed happily, unselfconsciously. Instantly, a large hand reached in and clutched Eva's entrails, chucking them unceremoniously into the whole heaving, turgid melting pot of sexual need. It was those damnable eye creases, the perfect teeth, the extra squeeze of her hand; the sheer sexiness of him. It was too much.

Not trusting herself to speak, Eva wobbled up onto her feet, rejected the table between them as too wide for her purposes, floated round it, bent down – though from her tiny height it was scarcely necessary – and solemnly kissed Mike squarely on the mouth, drinking him in like she'd been in the desert for days. She could feel Mike rigid with shock beneath her, but he rallied quickly and for a few seconds they stayed frozen in this unlikely tableau as, inside her, she felt the bursting into bloom of a thousand flowers. Around them the quizzical looks and startled silence of the surrounding diners gave way to a round of applause and good-natured wolf whistles.

'Wow,' gasped Mike weakly, as Eva finally pulled away and reassumed her seat. 'Wow. Wow.'

'Sorry about that,' she Cheshire-catted back at him, 'but I thought I was going to explode with lust if I didn't kiss you.'

'I think I have exploded,' said Mike in a strangled whisper, then choked with laughter as he saw Eva's instinctive, horrified look over the table at his crotch, 'No, you idiot, in my head – you've completely done for me – I'm jelly, all flavours and hardly set. Except for one persistent part of my body,' he had recovered enough to mock-leer at her, 'I'm soft; complete mush. Useless to man or beast.'

'I'll be your beast,' Eva mugged at him, reaching out again to stroke his hand. That touch was enough to silence them again for a moment. Then Mike took a deep breath, suddenly serious.

'Eva, you know, the only drug I'm on is you.' He looked intently at her; she held her breath; the restaurant receded completely now; she and Mike alone in a humming space, suspended in time and motion.

'I know it's only been a few weeks, it's absurd really, you know, I feel like I've been at this bloody table for a century, just trying to think of how to say this to you,' the usually terminally self-possessed Mike was floundering, 'I – we – I mean, this is *It* for me, Eva; no games now, I've never said this to anyone before – well, not properly – well, I, I—'

'—love you too,' said Eva calmly, suddenly serene, and flooded with a clear certain joy. There it was. She'd said it.

'I love you,' he breathed, and between them there shot a glimmering look of communion.

Mike moved even closer, hand winding up a long lock of her blonde hair. 'Will you move in with me?'

Eva flinched.

Oh, it would be so easy to say yes. So blissful to let herself be swept away to domestic bliss in Islington. But now the implications of what they had just said to each other were crowding around her, clamouring over the quiet certainty she had felt a moment ago. Eva was too pragmatic not to see past the romantic haze. Too seasoned a veteran as well. She had had many such offers before and on one occasion had accepted. Never again, she had vowed. Admittedly, he had been a complete nutter but then again, wasn't she? Eva was no longer sure. For so long she had been skating outwards, small chin jutting, determined always to be the rebel, the social anarchist, grabbing convention by the short and curlies and pulling hard.

But her life had changed since she'd moved in with Cockie and Ben. By doing so, she had 'subjected' herself to a material comfort she hadn't known since she'd left home, and to a close friendship with Ben and Cockie that she had never let herself get into in her days on the streets. With them there were no hang-ups, no political shenanigans, no one-up-manships of street cred. With his background, Ben should have been anathema to Eva. She should have thought that Cockie was an empty-headed crackpot, wasting her intelligence through frivolity and redeemable only through the personal tragedies that she had suffered. Mike himself had brought her down to an earth that she hardly recognised, but at the same time he had lifted her up to a new stratosphere. So where did that leave her? Metaphorically mixed for a start. Was she now a normal person? She was in love with Mike – couldn't she do the normal thing and move in with him?

Mike saw the barriers come up in Eva's eyes and cursed himself for pushing too hard, too soon. 'Don't worry, my love, forget I said that. Early days!' And he smiled ruefully, trying to break the tension.

It's incredible, thought Eva, smiling gratefully back, it's as if my body is just taped onto the end of his, like a tied rag twitching on the end of a cat's tail – if he smiles, I smile – it's as simple as that.

'Yeah, early days. It's just that at the moment, since I've been living with Ben and Cockie, I have been truly happy, happily content and every other smug concept that you can think of. It's like I want to be really selfish and keep all my toys around me.'

'Nice to know I'm now a toy boy!'

'Hey, it's so easy to wind you up, after all,' grinned Eva, 'but you know what I mean? For the first time in ages I am disgustingly happy and blissfully safe and the old superstitious Swedish elf in me says not to rock the boat and change any of that – yet.'

'Well, I'll tuck that "yet" away for safekeeping, and concentrate on the more short-term aspiration of getting you out of here and into bed.'

Eva's eyes glowed and her foot travelled halfway up his leg. 'Can't wait, but shall we just drop in at the Slim Whim on our way home? Patrick's a soft touch for free booze on Friday nights and I did mention to Cockie that we might swing by.'

'Whither goest a free drink, there go I. Lead on, MacTonkin.' He stood up and swept her a grand bow.

'You fool. I adore you, you moron.'
'And I you, with knobs on.'
'Save those for later, stud.'
She ogled mischievously up at him, as Mike paid their bill. He tucked the invoice carefully into his wallet and bent down to whisper into Eva's ear, 'Just think about what I said, OK?'

Annalisa, to Cockie's pique, had managed perfectly well in her absence. It was about 11.30 p.m. and chow time at the Slim Whim was reaching a pitch; outside, long lines for the Club Soda were already meandering past the Whim's windows; inside, the punters were winding their way as tortuously down Patrick and Flo's long list of liqueurs. The beautifully illustrated list, handed out as a rolled-up scroll complete with purple ribbon (one of Patrick's more infuriating literal whims for his long-suffering minions to deal with), was one of the last remnants of Patrick's original wish for the Slim Whim to be a high class establishment, and one that was abused with bacchanalian impunity by regulars and ravers alike.

Cockie's hands began to stick to the glasses as she ferried boatloads of Amaretto and green Chartreuse to the baying revellers – 'Fingerprints are just part of the service,' she was explaining gaily to one glazed exquisite when she froze, her stomach and heart leaping up to give one another a firm Masonic handshake.

Across the room, golden hair glinting hazily through the lazy reams of smoke, was Sam, his back to her, and most of his extremities anchored firmly to the unfairly nubile form of the blonde beauty sharing his table. She dumped the glasses of cognac at one table, and, chest thumping, edged closer, wiping her hands nervously on her trousers. Willing herself not to betray herself, she tapped him on the shoulder.

'Hi, Sam,' she said brightly and stopped, as he turned to face her. It was Sam and yet it wasn't, quite.

'Er . . . you're not Sam?' Suddenly it was no longer a question so much as a statement – this guy was looking at her with a friendly gaze quite unlike the irritable squint that Sam usually awarded her with.

'Not guilty, I'm afraid, but you're Cookie, aren't you?'

She stared at him, now completely nonplussed.

'Well, sort of, my name is Cockie. But who – how—'

'I am sorry, I should explain – I'm Sam's brother – Chas. Sam told us about this place and since we're – oh, this is Lara by the way' – he gestured to the fashion plate he was with who gave Cockie a chilly smile – 'since we're meeting them in the Soda later we thought we might check out the famous Slim Whim food'n'festivity first.'

'Them?' As soon as she asked, Cockie knew that she shouldn't have done.

'Sam and Esme – they would have come with us here but they had to have dinner with Esme's mother and stepfather. Sam said that he knew you and to say "hi" from him if we saw you, so "hi" from him!'

Cockie smiled a charming smile, recognisable to anyone who knew her as a rictus grin over bared teeth. 'Say *hi* back,' she tried not to put too much savagery into the words, 'and I'm sorry for mistaking you for him.'

'Oh, it happens all the time – the penalty of being supposedly identical twins – just remember that I'm the good-looking one,' he smiled at her with the ubiquitous charm that was obviously a family trait, 'I'm glad you came over so that we could meet. See you around, Cookie.'

It was the final straw. '*Cockie*. It's *Cockie*,' she said shortly, and moved away, reeling. Ignoring Table 14's bill-writing gestures she stumbled downstairs to the loo, forehead burning with shock and shame as she leant against the cool, cool mirror.

Sam had a twin brother? She had realised that she'd been kidding herself about her chances with Sam, but she couldn't believe that in the year she'd known him, he'd never even seen fit to tell her that he had a brother at all, let alone a twin, for Chrissakes. With the bitter bile of humiliation in her mouth putting her off having a life-saving cigarette, she realised that she couldn't even fool herself that Sam had treated her badly. He just hadn't treated her at all – to him, she was merely 'someone he knew' – a persistent ex-fling who had barely grazed the surface of his life except as a sodding recommendation for a restaurant.

Oh fuckfuckfuckfuck. Sam and Esme? Sam'n'Esme? Since when this natural pairing of names? Sounded like a cheap Cole Porter song title. She could have laughed out loud at the irony of it all – she would have bet her last few quid in the world that Sam would no more have gone out for a cosy Friday dinner with a girlfriend's family than he would admit that he dyed his eyelashes and yet here he was, dining with the Esme 'in-laws'. Oh, the teeth grindingness of it all. She took a deep breath, peeled her face off the mirror and gazed sternly at herself.

'You are Cockie Milton. You are going to be a successful writer of utterly crap books. You are a Mistress of the Universe. You need no man.' What a creed, she thought drily, as she pushed her way out of the ladies', ignoring the bemused glances of those outside.

Back upstairs the frenetic pitch of activity was subsiding. Table 14 had either done a runner, or paid their bill to somebody else, her other tables were soon paid up and just lingering over their drinks, and the general decibel level was becoming acceptable again. Fairly soon, all that was left was the usual assortment of odds and sods – a table of two where the man's seduction hadn't gone quite as planned but where he was waiting until the fat lady had sung her guts out before conceding defeat and going home on his own. On a banquette in the corner, both facing out into the restaurant, were another couple, hardly talking to each other but drinking in the bucolic atmosphere around them, perhaps delaying the moment when they had to return, empty of shared words, to their empty, silent home. Please God, Cockie prayed, looking at them, let me never lose sight of the red blood of life like they have, never fall silent out of fear of what might be said if I spoke.

She finished clearing her table and went over to the bar where everyone had gathered, still high from the night's exertions, footsore and fancy-free, and slumped on the Whim's excruciatingly uncomfortable bar stools, designed specially to deter punters from loitering at the bar and blocking any would-be-profligate drink-buyers behind them.

'TJ – what's the time? Ben and Eva said they'd be here at some point.'

'Just after midnight, so don't panic, they'll be here by the time we've finished eating.'

On cue, Felipe arrived with trays full of food, peering nervously round the doorjamb at the top of the stairs before he came in.

'It's OK, Felipe, there's hardly anyone left to see you,' grinned Fred.

'Unless you count those off-duty immigration officers on Table 7,' added Cockie ominously.

Felipe froze, not noticing carrot soup slopping decoratively into the saffron risotto in his left hand, before he realised the joke.

'Har har. Yes, I think is very funny. I send you and Fred postcards from Chile when they bring me back there, then you laugh,' – the sarcasm was belied by the grin of relief on Felipe's face. As the talented and kind-hearted sous-chef, Felipe – with the rest of the Slim Whim family – lived in constant fear of his illegal alien status being discovered.

'A good night, my flock, especially for an early finisher.' Patrick appeared from the office and went to stand behind the bar, waving a note of the night's takings. 'Now eat, drink and carry on being merry. Flo, I think a bottle or five of Chateau Musar '83 for our loyal minions.'

'Coming right up, squire.' Flo smiled at Patrick, exaggeratedly tugging his forelock, and Cockie felt an unconscious frisson of jealousy race up her spine as she saw the swift look of humming intimacy pass between the two men.

Patrick was so outwardly blustery and old-maidish and Flo so dry and patently wicked that Cockie sometimes found it hard to believe that they were lovers. Flo – short for Flaubert ('would you keep the name "Colin"?' he'd ask) – with his dark, whippet-leanness, his piratical bandannas over his head, and his ethnic waistcoats over a tight white T-shirt and butter-soft old Levis, just looked so unlike the Garrick-tied, tweed-jacketed, soft at the edges Patrick. 'If I stand on his shoulder you can call me Flaubert's Parrot,' Patrick had murmured on occasion, but unlikely as it seemed, the relationship had thrived for over seven years. Now looking at them as Flo leaned back imperceptibly to lean his head for a moment on Patrick's shoulder, Cockie saw such a forcefield of steadiness around them that their surface incompatibility was completely irrelevant.

'Hi chucks! Sorry we're late – no taxis anywhere, so we had to walk – boy, have I worked up a thirst – Flo, save my life, gimme a beer!' Eva was glowing, breathless, hand in hand with Mike who couldn't take his eyes off her. Again, Cockie started to feel a twist of envy before she stamped it down.

'Cockie! You look knackered – hard night at the grindstone?'

'Yeah, my nose is raw again. Patrick, I'm suing you for Repetitive Stress Injury.' Cockie made a face at her boss.

'Hi Mike – you're looking sharp tonight – where have you two been?'

'Oh, it's all reflected glory from this lady here,' said Mike self-deprecatingly. 'She's just taken me to the cleaners and back at Wodka.'

'Bursting with blinis?' asked TJ. 'Would you spew if you watched us eat? I'm bloody ravenous.'

'No, no, go ahead,' Eva said, handing Mike a beer, 'we'll just match you beer for bite.'

As the last punters left the restaurant, the rest of them sat down and got stuck in, wolfing the smorgasbord of leftovers from the Whim's peerless menu. Just as they were sitting back in their chairs, replete, Ben arrived, red-faced and a little unsteady on his feet. Immediately TJ brightened, one hand going up automatically to rake her hair into look-at-me mode. TJ had always had a soft spot for Ben and, with true Australian directness, never minded showing it. This time, however, it was all in vain: Ben wasn't focusing on anyone.

'A beer, a beer,' he shouted, 'several kingdoms for a beer.'

'Would that be a Japanese beer, honey bunch?' Cockie asked slyly. 'We've got some of that Sapporo, haven't we, Flo?'

'Sure have,' confirmed Flo.

'Don't even tease me, you bastards; nothing Japanese, thanks ever so. I've had enough bloody saké to refloat the *Titanic* – I now know why karaoke was invented in Japan, the bloody stuff goes straight to your vocal chords, gives you the most incredible urge to sing – loudly.' He gestured over-expansively. 'I've been clearing my throat all night, ready to burst into "New York, New York" and then having to swallow the urge before old Taka . . . Taka . . . Takahashi died from a heart attack at the breach of protocol.'

'Ben, where have you been?' TJ pulled the now

swaying Ben down beside her on the banquette and offered him a swig of her beer while Flo got a fresh one from the fridge behind the bar. Ben didn't answer, just stared with incredulous relief down the neck of the bottle.

'He's been at the Grand Opening of his garden for that Japanese company in the City, haven't you, you old soak?' Eva leaned past Mike to ruffle Ben's hair affectionately.

Cockie nearly laughed out loud at the look that TJ shot at the oblivious Eva; by rights it should have hissed when it landed.

'So come on, Cockie,' asked Patrick, 'tell us all about this book you're going to write.'

Eva rolled her eyes at Mike.

'Yes, and don't forget to ask her about her new man,' Flo added naughtily.

'New man?!' they chorused, all eyes swivelling to Cockie.

Cockie laughed, holding up her hands for silence.

'Calm down! Relax! There's no new man, Flo's just muck-raking.'

'Plus ça change,' interrupted Patrick.

'Yes well – yes, Patrick, I am going to write a book – a Mills and Boon,' there was a groan of dismay from her listeners, 'which is going to earn me pots of cash,' now there was laughter, 'and provide me with some fun into the bargain. Although,' Cockie was indignant now, 'at the rate I'm going so far, it's going to take six months to get over the justification to my friends stage.'

'There's a message there,' put in Eva pointedly.

'And where does this new man come into it?' asked Fred persistently.

Cockie glanced at him exasperatedly. 'The "new man", as you will insist on calling him, is virtually a figment of my imagination—'

Ben looked up blearily – were things really that bad with Cockie?

'—in that I saw someone whose appearance is perfect for my fictitious hero and that's it – I have only seen him – spoken to him briefly – which is just how I want it because I have no interest in his character, just in using his looks as a basis for the character that I will design for my hero.'

Amongst the hubbub, Ben noticed a new face at the fringe of the circle. It was obviously that of a new waitress and she was looking uncomfortable, out of sync with the easy familiarity that ebbed and flowed around her. She was also very, very pretty, he decided, feeling the solemn revelation of the very drunk. Dark glossy hair fell in two shining arcs from a middle parting, framing a creamy-skinned face, which narrowed to a point at a determined little chin. Lips that were unsmiling now but which even in repose were absurdly Cupid bow-shaped and as pink and as soft as . . . as . . . his descriptive powers failed him but he felt a jolt of excitement that wasn't alcohol-related.

Cockie, almost helpless with laughter, waggled a weak hand in surrender. 'Stop! Stop! I give in. I'll think of a title myself. You're all rubbish – you're sacked. Let's talk about something else. What's new with you, Mike?'

'Well, if you want earth-shattering news, you're probably dying to hear that I cut a voice-over for a new breath freshener this morning which has set new horizons in the radio world.'

'You gave unheard-of dramatic heights to gargling, huh?'

'Yes, Pavarotti would have been hard pushed to out-vibrato me . . . Listerine will surely be looking to their laurels.' Mike smiled at Cockie, his eyes narrowing within a network of laughter lines.

He really was incredibly nice-looking, thought Cockie, glad that she could approve so heartily of Eva's choice.

Curly dark blond hair, smiling blue eyes and a craggy face were not an exceptional package next to the zanily gift-wrapped Eva, but Mike's appeal was in his easy humour and acute sense of the ridiculous. He was an actor, of sorts, who had started off his thespian career as a leading light of several prepubescent shows in the West End; asking for more as Oliver, flirting with a nine-year-old Tallulah as Bugsy Malone, sobbing winsomely as the Go-Between. All went well until adolescence rendered his childish sweetness into something clean cut but ultimately ordinary. Undeterred, he had decided to hang on to his Equity card and his reputation for professionalism and, from Mikey the Moppet he became Mr Average. Soon the new face of the man next door in the lawnmower ad, the staid old-before-his-time father of 2.1 children in the cornflakes ad, the proud owner of numerous saloon cars in numerous car ads became Mike's. Never dull, his affability had worn down Eva's spikiness and occasional abrasiveness until now she no longer felt guilty about being happy, was no longer offensively defensive but positively amiable.

Everyone was talking amongst themselves now and, out of the corner of her eye, Cockie saw Ben extricate himself from TJ's ministrations, smooth down his unruly hair and come round the table towards her. Cockie gave a little stretch and sat back in her chair in anticipation of his attention. But he stopped at Annalisa's chair and hunkered down beside her. Seeing the girl's sullen face come to life as he chatted to her, reminded Cockie that not everyone saw Ben in the same light as she did, as an almost avuncular figure, sounding-board and huggable honey. He was no Victor Landis or Sam Westerfield – neither especially tall nor especially good-looking – but she could see that, for other women, he had 'It'.

He was drawing up a chair next to Annalisa now and, as he turned round to wedge the chair in between hers and Fred's, he caught Cockie watching them and gave her a big wink. She couldn't help but grin back – he had such a rogue's face – a narrow face punctuated by usually half-shut gleaming slits of eyes. When he smiled like now, his long narrow nose, broken out of a dull symmetry, would seem to soften and the slightly thin lips would widen to reveal a surprisingly vulnerable lower lip. It was this lip that had apparently done for TJ. In the course of many fevered chats with Cockie, she had almost named the damn thing and had speculated so endlessly and publicly on the concept of kissing it that even Flo, who loved titillating gossip as much as the next sex maniac, had finally told her to keep her own lips firmly sealed on the subject.

Ben had his back turned to her now and, watching Annalisa over his shoulder unfurl like a flower under his shining attention, Cockie could observe the unlikely romantic effect wreaked by her housemate. Annalisa herself looked like a different person – no longer just grateful for his attention but warming up into flirtatiousness, her large dark eyes sparkling and animated, her smiles revealing cheekbones that even Eddie the Eagle could get a good jump off.

'Guess I missed out there, huh?' Fred broke into her observations, following her stare to Annalisa, 'I don't know how that ugly bastard does it, but they lap it up, don't they?' He was good-humoured in his defeat.

'You'll probably find that he's just trying to include her – but you had your chance, Freddy-me-lad, you were sitting next to her before Ben even arrived – you blew it.'

He nodded, conceding the point, and lit them both a post-prandial cigarette.

'Cockie, I think Mike and I are going to head back to the ranch. Do you want to come?' Eva smiled at her wearily, 'that is, unless you're planning to go over the road?'

'Yes, come on Cockie, let's go shake'n'bake at the Soda!' Fred's evening was clearly just beginning. 'Hey, TJ, are you on for a mad manic march onto the dance floor?'

'Sounds great,' she called back, her Aussie accent sounding stronger backed by alcohol and a long night, 'how about you, Ben?'

'Nah, not in the mood. Another time, my love.' He cocked an enquiring eyebrow at Annalisa, but before he could say anything, Fred broke in, 'Annalisa, would you like to go along? It's a wicked place.'

Annalisa looked at Ben, then past him, at Fred. She looked like she was weighing up the options, thought Cockie a little irritably, realising sleepily that all she wanted to do was bop straight into her bed.

Finally Annalisa nodded to Fred, 'I think clubbing sounds a good option. Are you sure you don't want to come, Ben?'

Ben smiled and shook his head.

'Well, count me out, guys,' said Cockie, standing up, 'I'm bush-whackered – I'll come home with you two, Eva – Ben, are you coming now, or staying on a bit?'

They finished putting their dirty plates in the dishwasher, wiped the tables and, Ark-like, left the Whim in twos and threes.

'Notice how no-one asked us old fogies if we wanted to go?' Flo said wryly to Patrick as they watched them leave. 'Do you think the Soda would charge extra for Zimmer frames?'

4

Cockie looked around her with pride. Less than a week since she'd had the idea and here she was, surrounded by the tools of her new-found trade. All weekend she had buried herself in the latest volumes to come panting, sneering and coquetting off the Mills and Boon press. Averaging an hour and a half per book she had romped through eight of them, leaving her with an aching right arm from hurling them across the room, a head whirling with passionate prose, and a healthy respect for the people who could produce this stuff so skilfully.

Going downstairs to clear her head with a chat to Eva, a fag, and a glimpse at the telly hadn't helped. Half an hour's listening to Eva had clogged her to capacity with even more romantic mumbo-jumbo – that girl was off with the little love fairies, that was for sure – and it took another half an hour of mindlessly watching *Mastermind* for Cockie to extract herself from the land of domineering, chocolate-brown voices, and quivering lower lips. It was all good research, she told herself.

So here she was, crumpled romances on one side, starter pack and reference books on the other, list on the wall above her and a white, white piece of paper in front of her. She glanced up at the list yet again, grinning to herself.

During her trawl of Mills and Boonamania, she had

jotted down recurring 'bons mots'. She had divided them up into His and Her turns of phrase, appearance and for the scenes of sexual contact that had to happen approximately every fifteen pages.

Consequently the wall above was groaning under the hormone-laden weight of words like 'sardonically, silkily, scornfully, snarled, snapped' for Him (why so many 's' words, she wondered) and 'tremulously, bravely, spiritedly, rashly, flushed, gaspingly' for Her. Cockie had it on the best authority that this was the way to start – that every time either Luke or Allegra spoke, she should bung in one of the listed adverbs. One book had even cautioned against recycling them too often, without even a hint of tongue tucked in cheek; 'too much use of one particular adverb, such as "curtly", on one page, can cause the hero to seem one-dimensional'.

God forbid! thought Cockie. So the pre-groundwork rotivating had been done; roll on the premise, the synopsis and the character sketches. She took a deep breath, pen faltering over the page, and thought fleetingly of that stack of unpaid parking tickets tucked hastily into her glove compartment. That gave her the resolve.

'Premise,' she wrote, carefully underlining it. 'Allegra is a twenty-three-year-old personal assistant to an Oxford don who does a lot of TV and column work. Her dearest wish is to study music – piano, harpsichord, etc. The only child of a much older, academic father and long-dead mother – now both dead – Allegra is naïve, unaware of her looks, unused to being on her own, only really happy when playing the piano. In Oxford her personality flowers with independence and exposure to the people of her own age to whom her rather glitzy employer introduces her.

'Luke/Luca is a thirty-five-year-old mature post-grad student in history, the product of an Italian father and English mother. Devastating looking, he is tortured and bleak, with a fine line in scowls and muscles-ticking-in-jaw.' Getting frivolous already; there's an ominous sign, thought Cockie. 'At the beginning we know him as Luke, ostensibly English, misogynist in the extreme and carrying some deeply burdensome secret. That secret is that he is actually Luca Ventorini, multi-millionaire mastermind of one of Italy's largest family-owned industries, whose wife's elopement with a Ventorini cousin ended in tragedy in a car smash, in which the cousin was paralysed and the wife and his unborn child were killed. Luca, in his grief and rage, has vowed to give up all things Italian, including the business, and has resolved to rediscover his English roots. He has also, naturally, sworn lifelong abstinence on the faithless female front. Enter Allegra.'

Cockie paused. Not bad so far. But how was Allegra to enter? Time to conjure up a set of coincidental encounters, all initially disastrous, with Allegra being a dippy tart and Luke being a dictatorial, dismissive, bad-tempered old grump. Luke's supervising tutor could be Allegra's boss, so she could have one encounter outside his rooms, one in the street – maybe some sort of collision involving Allegra on her bicycle.

The phone rang. Cockie considered doing her now perfected impression of their answering machine, complete with beeps, but decided she didn't have the energy so just picked it up.

'Hello?'

'Hello, Cockie? It's Annalisa . . . from the Slim Whim.'

'Hi, Annalisa. How are you?' Why did she feel such an instinctive dislike for this woman, Cockie wondered.

'Yes. Look, I know you're not scheduled to work tonight but we were wondering if you could come in anyway. TJ's off sick so we're a bit short-staffed.'

'Oh, sorry about that, but I'm already busy tonight – have you tried Fred? Or Marco?' Where did she get off, thought Cockie furiously, with all the pique of the old-timer being condescended to by the cocky newcomer; all this talk of 'we' – since when was she a part-owner of the Whim?

'Fred's already working and Marco's not in . . .' she paused. 'Well, OK, if you really can't cancel your plans to help us out—'

'Sorry, no can do,' said Cockie airily but with a touch of steel. This girl was unbelievable, 'I should keep trying Marco, if I were you. Anyway, it's only a Tuesday night so things should be fairly quiet – I'm sure you'll be able to cope if the worst comes to the worst.'

'Hmmm, yes, I'm sure you're right,' said Annalisa reluctantly, then paused, 'Er . . . is Ben there?'

'No,' said Cockie shortly. So that was her game. 'He's working on site in Devon.'

'Does he have a mobile phone?'

'Yes.' There was a short silence and Cockie sighed: why was she such a soft touch? 'The number is 0836 608498. But he's coming back tonight.'

'Great. Well, I might try him anyway. Bye, Cockie.'

She was hardly a wilting flower when it came to pursuing men, thought Cockie almost admiringly. Poor Ben hardly stands a chance. Annalisa may look the part of a Mills and Boon heroine but no sweet naïveté for her. Cockie briefly considered modelling Allegra's looks on Annalisa's undeniable attractions but whereas Victor whatshisname was just a dreamboat face on which to build Luke's character, Cockie felt that she was already less than . . . objective about Annalisa; she was too knowing, too much a man's woman. Nothing like a snap impression, said a tiny voice, but Cockie ignored that.

On an impulse, she picked up the telephone and rang TJ, feeling suspicious.

After several rings, summoning up a picture of TJ struggling up from the depths of her delirium, her sweat-slicked hand slipping off the receiver, she finally answered.

'Huh-huh-hello?'

'A masterpiece,' said Cockie. 'I give you two months to live. That artful quaver, the feverish huskiness – as an expert myself of the tuberculoid twinge, I'm impressed. So, who is he?'

'Cockie!' TJ's normal clear healthy boom drove Cockie's head sharply away from the receiver, 'How the hell are you?'

'By the sound of it, not quite as well as you are. Answer my question, tart.'

'Ah yeah, he's a real spunk – totally gorgeous – I guarantee you'd do the same, my girl. Anyway, how did you know about me being crook? The Whim?'

'How can you sound so Australian sometimes, when you've been here three years? Yes, I just had Annalisa on the phone.'

'Yeah, what a cow – is she the new boss or what? I practically had to produce a doctor's note to satisfy that old Rosa Klebb – although I don't think Ben would agree with that description – did you see the way she was eating him up the other night?'

'Now I see the reason for this bile – yes, I did. That reminds me, how does the spunk's lower lip compare?'

'Lower lip? What are you on about, you flake?!'

'TJ, after listening to constant odes to Ben's lower lip, I think the least you could do for this newest sex-toy is notice his.' Suddenly a thought hit her – perhaps Ben wasn't in Devon after all. 'Unless it is Ben?'

TJ snorted. 'Ah, get out of here, you dag, of course not. Anyway, I've been too busy snogging it – who needs to go on about it when I've got it right here?'

'Fair enough,' laughed Cockie, 'well, I'll leave you to it – is he there at the moment?'

'Yeah – asleep. I've worn him out, I reckon,' said TJ

complacently. 'But I'm feeling a bit frisky now so maybe it's time to wake him up.'

'Forward into the breeches, huh?' The allusion was lost on TJ but she laughed obligingly, used to Cockie's cockeyed literary puns, and rang off.

All thoughts of authorship out of the window now, Cockie chewed thoughtfully at a cuticle. Was it her imagination or was everyone except for her getting it together with someone? Eva and Mike, the dreaded Sam'n'Esme, Annalisa and Ben – she shuddered at the thought of that – and now TJ and the 'spunk'. Even her friend Drew had been suspiciously unavailable lately. That meant she didn't even have anyone close at hand to bitch with about the situation. For a moment she was tempted to put herself into therapy: go shopping and buy the ultimate manslayer of an outfit, but a glance at her watch told her that it was just after five and a bit late to start nursing serious sartorial ambitions, quite apart from the post-apocalyptic aid zone that was her bank account. Cockie sighed – nothing for it but to watch *Home and Away* and *Neighbours*.

God, how I hate Fulham, Cockie thought, as yet another parking space turned out to be for Doctors Only – it was nearly ten o'clock at night and even three streets away from her dinner party she couldn't find a bloody parking space. She turned the corner and there was a space, a mere fifty yards away, separated from her only by a helpful No Entry sign. Bugger that, she thought grimly, turned the Mini round, slammed it into reverse and wheezed up the street. Just as she was drawing parallel she saw she was backing straight into a contender for the same golden opportunity. In a split second she gauged the situation and the distances involved, mentally jammed on an Evil Knievel helmet, and shot backwards into the space, missing the other car by fractions of inches.

Nice one, Milton, she congratulated herself, and straightened up the car. Looking in the rear-view mirror she saw that the other car hadn't accepted the inevitable and moved on but was still there, lights blazing. Uh-oh, she thought, as she saw a door open and a tall dark figure get out. She tried to gather her stuff together but couldn't do it before there was an imperious rap on the window. Winding it down, Cockie was at her most deliberately nonchalant.

'Hi! Sorry! Did you want this space? Hey, all's fair in love and parking, you know.'

'You stupid woman,' the man barked, 'of course I wanted the space – I got here first – do you realise you were driving the wrong way up a one-way street, probably breaking the speed limit, and you nearly went directly into my car? You stupid idiot! Do you ever look where you're going?' He paused. 'Are you completely half-witted?'

He had a point. For Cockie was staring up at him, mouth half-open, eyes wide – to all appearances, not an educationally normal person. The man was a god, an angry god maybe, but a deity all the same. But not only that – it was Him, her hero, her model, her Luca – it was Victor Landis; the same Count-Dracula-on-the-catwalk face, that comma of hair across the forehead. Sap her vitals, but what a turn up for the books.

'What are you doing here?' was all she could manage.

'What am I doing here?' he said blankly. 'Ach, my God, you are deranged. I am trying to park and I would be grateful if you would leave this parking space to me and drive on and please find your own.'

Even in Cockie's dumbfounded state this was too much. 'Wait a minute, who the hell do you think you are?' She scrabbled for her paraphernalia and launched herself out of the car, almost knocking him over as she did so. 'I got the space and I keep the space – that's all there is to it – so hard bloody cheese.' The guy may look like Rudolph Valentino but he was an arrogant sonofabitch.

'Oh but this is completely unbelievable!' He did a good impression of someone trying not to stamp their foot, turned on his heel and swept back to his motor.

He really was unspeakably gorgeous, even if he hadn't recognised her. Even the car was perfect – a low-slung, well-hung bug-eyed monster. BCSD, she thought defiantly, as she went up the street.

By the time she reached Mel's flat, her car stereo, rucksack and bottle of wine were going all over the place. Looking helplessly at the front door, Cockie wondered if her nose would stand up to pushing the entryphone button, or if she could kick it. Nuzzling the buzzer panel with determination but getting nowhere, finally her car keys fell out of her precarious clutch, landing on the doorstep with a shattering clatter, breaking the silence of the street. Cockie swore and, trying not to let everything else slip, bent slowly down to pick them up.

'You look like you need some help.'

Cockie dropped everything. The voice had come from nowhere. By some miracle the bottle of wine didn't break – just rolled obediently to the feet of the man in front of her.

'Jeee-sus!' exhaled Cockie, patting her heart exaggeratedly, 'you gave me the fright of my life. Sorry,' she added in that particularly English way.

'Not at all. My fault for creeping up on you – probably my new DMs – look.' He pulled up the hem of his jeans and proudly showed her the offending rubber-soled shoes, 'Cool, huh?'

'Er – yes.' Yikes, a weirdo.

There was a small silence. Cockie looked up to find the man looking at her intently. She couldn't quite see what he looked like in the gloom, but he certainly looked more potentially cute than lunatic. As he bent to pick up the wine and her keys, Cockie concentrated on arranging the remaining articles in her arms so that she was, in theory, able to swing out at him if things turned nasty. With emphasis on the 'in theory'.

'Right, all set. Can I help you in?' He put the bottle of wine and keys into her spare arm and started to put a key into the front door.

'Oh, you live here!' said Cockie with obvious relief. Anyone who shared a Fulham front door with Mel couldn't be an axe-murderer, she reasoned less than logically.

'Well, sort of.' He held the door open for her. As she passed by into the light of the hall, Cockie looked up at him but could see little against the light except an impression of his eyes sparkling down into hers.

'So, are you going to Mel's dinner as well?' she asked brightly.

'Mel? Oh, Mel. No, no I'm not.'

Cockie was about to feel a small twinge of disappointment when she stopped herself. Christ. Was she so far gone that she had started to imagine romantic possibilities with every stranger she bumped into? She *did* need help.

Then he closed the door behind her and, with his back to her, started rifling through the post on the table by the door.

'Well, thanks for helping me out,' Cockie said a little uncertainly.

'No problem, sorry for giving you such a shock.' He didn't turn round.

Cockie shrugged and headed upstairs, speeding up when she saw the time on the hall clock – ten-fifteen! She kicked hurriedly on the front door of Mel's flat and launched into a spiel as soon as Mel opened it, her face thunderous.

'Can it, Cockie,' interrupted Mel, 'I've heard it all

before. At least I can depend on something more creative from you than "I was kept late at the office" because, let's face it,' her tone turned steely, 'it's not as if you even have a job to clog up your schedule. For God's sake, you just can't go through life pretending to be a ditzy blonde when you're not,' she did a double take as she looked at Cockie properly, 'Bloody hell! You're not even blonde any more!'

'Give a gold star to the woman with eyes in her head,' said Cockie drily, 'and please let me in – I'm barking for a drink.'

Mel's usually unnaturally tidy sitting-room looked almost in disarray when Cockie entered – seven people draped on available chairs tended to take the edge off its impeccable sterility. She saw, with a slightly sinking heart, that it was to be an evening of few surprises. She would even lay bets that the guy she vaguely recognised as being a slightly up-his-own-bum aspiring film director – was his name Mark? – was Mel's matchmake for Cockie. She braced herself and launched forward saying her hello's, then smiled as from behind her came a recognisable voice.

'C-C-C-Cockie! K-k-k-killing to see you! K-k-k-kiss me!' It was loud, it was booming, it was Rowena.

Cockie turned and gave her a smacker on the cheek. 'Hi, chuck. What's with the stutter? P-p-p-pissed already?'

Rowena laughed and threw herself on the floor at Ravi's feet, 'No, no – although you're so late you're lucky any of us are making sense. No, sorry, it's this bad habit we're all into at the office – I seem to have brought it home with me.'

'It's quite c-c-c-catching, I must say. Where's Jacko?'

Rowena was a friend from university days who now worked as a trader in the City. She was a most unlikely City slicker – even taller than Cockie, even bigger boobs and, sickeningly, reed-thin everywhere else – except in her voice – all of which stood her in good stead on the commodities trading floor where, with her bright red hair and buttercup yellow jacket, she was a fixture that her fellow-traders were proud of, even if she was a woman.

'Oh, you know, I'm a TV widow as ever,' she grimaced. Her husband, Jacko – so-called because of his surname, Spader – was a TV researcher who worked on the current hit show, *Drop Your Pants*. 'Jacko's got this great idea that I should apply to be Tommy Pepper's co-host – both too loud, too tall and—'

'—and you're too ginger. You'd look like Chris Evans in drag and you'd frighten off the audience,' said Ravi smoothly, 'but you don't scare me, so hop on my knee, you Titian tasty.'

'Ravi!' Cockie and Rowena groaned in unison.

'No harm in trying,' he defended himself quickly, 'I feel it's my bounden duty to test the resolve of newly married women. Oof!' as Cockie, sitting on the arm of his chair, caught him a good blow in the stomach. Ravi – his girlfriend conveniently based in America – could be depended on for a good letch. It had been the same story since their university days.

'How long have you been married, Ro-Ro?' asked Sarah, one of the coupled girls that Cockie knew only slightly, sliding her hand encouragingly into that of her boyfriend, Dougie.

'Fifty-six days,' answered Rowena promptly and then, ignoring the chorus of 'aaaahs' and 'still counting by the day – how sweet!' went on, 'Fifty-six days as well, since I banned anyone from calling me Ro-Ro, Sar-Sar.'

Sarah drew back offended, but Mel saved any awkwardness by coming in to announce that dinner, overcooked and ruined as it was by Cockie's late arrival, was finally on the table.

'I must be mad having ten to dinner,' she confided to Cockie on their way in, 'it'll be real "Elbows Hold

Back" time – why don't you go in the corner and,' she turned her head round but Cockie knew exactly what she was going to say, 'Mark – why don't you sit next to Cockie?'

Smoothing his goatee, Mark inched in beside Cockie. 'Hello, Cockie, I haven't seen you for a long time – what are you up to these days?'

Cockie held back her groan. 'Well, actually I've just finished making a film in LA,' she ignored the clang as his jaw hit the table, and carried on blithely, 'yes – I was spotted by a talent scout when I was walking down South Molton Street a few months ago and he asked me to audition for the role of Camilla in the movie of Donna Tartt's *A Secret History*. I couldn't believe my luck when I got it but hey, them's the breaks – how's your own film-making?'

'Wh – wha –?' gasped Mark. 'My God, that's incredible, that's unbelievable, that's . . .'

'Cockie,' reproved Hugh, who was now sitting on her other side.

'Yes, you're right, I mustn't tell fibs. The truth is,' she turned back to Mark whose face was beginning to match his hunter-green suede waistcoat, 'I'm not ashamed to admit this – I mean, it was an honest $10,000 – but the name of the film was actually *Jurassic Tarts*.'

'Cockie!' the whole table laughed. As for Mark, the penny finally dropped and even Cockie, busy chuckling at her own joke, stopped as she saw an angry tide of red creep past the goatee and carry on right up to the elongated sideburns.

'Mark, I'm sorry, I didn't mean to tease, but the truth is, the reality is rather different – I was laid off from Bandwick and Parker and I now have two part-time slave jobs which are less than glamorous and not worth talking about at dinner parties so I can never quite resist making up some fantastical claptrap.'

'Coquelicot, will you stop digging your grave deeper and shut the fuck up,' said Ravi sternly from the other end of the table, 'just eat.'

Cockie ate.

Gradually Mark collected himself and began to eat as well. Around them the conversation ebbed and flowed, ranging from the inane to the ridiculous. It was often a source of real disappointment to Cockie that, with her university friends, even a telephone number's worth of supposed IQs collected into one room should produce such a pedestrian exchange of conversational paste.

When Cockie had gone to Oxford, shorn of the comforting ballast of the hard-won popularity and effortless exam results of her school days, she had stolen into her first few days there, a tiny tadpole, wiggling nervously in what felt like a large pond full of intellectually bloated carp. Oppressed by her Bridesheadian expectations of angst-ridden debates in smoky, chilly rooms with smoky, tortured Romeos – and desperate for the oxygen of fun after her last few stifling months with her mother – Cockie had been initially delighted by the talk of sex and beer, sport and beer, years off and beer, essay crises and beer. Hey, she could keep up with this; she didn't need to have mugged up on the subject and, best of all, she didn't need to dip below the carefully preserved surface of her fragile gaiety.

But by the end of the first year she was beginning to feel cheated – beyond the walls of her easily conned tutor's room, was she ever going to discover whether she had an intellect or not? Cockie had always had a sneaking suspicion that all she had was a knack for telling teachers, examiners, interviewers what they wanted to hear; that she had a facility for the intellectual short-cut round real intelligence and that it would take one of these Oxbridge geniuses that she now called her friends, to flush her out as a fraud. It never happened.

Even now, as Cockie peered equally thoughtfully into her plate of paella, listening with half an ear to Hugh and Mark babbling across her, she could not remember a single serious conversation while she'd been at university, except when she and her friends had been so wasted that their logic was only a chemical conflagration in the brain, and their conclusions inevitably to do with the need to find food to feed their munchies. Four years later, she was still waiting for the day when she would be busted.

'Cockie?'

She looked up to see Mark fixing her with that deliberately intent look that was top of his body language repertoire.

'I noticed that Ravi called you Coquelicot a few moments ago – that must be your real name then?'

No shit, Sherlock, she thought uncharitably. 'Yes.'

'So are you French at all?' he asked, persevering.

She relented. 'No, I was the afterthought, a late contender behind two much older brothers with rather grandiose classical names chosen by my father.' Cockie warmed up into the usual anecdote. 'Apparently, by the time I came along, my mother was still into the whole Summer of Love flower child thing, but in a sort of middle-aged hopelessly inaccurate way and basically she got it all wrong. Instead of calling me Daisy or, let's face it, Poppy, she missed the point completely and tried to be original. Of course, by calling me Coquelicot, she ended up with a name that no-one could pronounce and where only French hippies could recognise the initial intention.'

'Hey, Coquelicot isn't so bad; just think, you might have been called Coucou – that's Cowslip in French, in case you were wondering – or something like Ragwort,' chuckled Rowena, waving her empty glass unsteadily.

'No, you just try going to a public school with this name,' retorted Cockie grimly, 'you may hate being called Ro-Ro but imagine being run up to in the street by someone you haven't seen since school who hails you merrily as "Cocklicker"! Try explaining that one to the new boyfriend on your arm at the time. My eldest brother got so fed up with his "tag", Cornelius – imagine what they made of *that* one at school – he changed his name to Robert.'

'My God, I've just made the connection,' interrupted one of the other coupled girls, 'you're Coquelicot Milton, aren't you?'

Cockie nodded.

'Of course, now I remember – you're the Little Opiate – he used to refer to you like that so fondly I was almost jealous. You see, I used to go out with your brother, Gus – oh, years and years ago; you must have been about fourteen at the time. How is he? I must say, you can tell him from me that it may be ancient ancient history, but he was a complete bastard to me! I simply adored him of course – this glamorous twenty-five-year-old turning up to take me out of school, ogling all my friends, and trying to get me to go to bed with him. I didn't, of course,' she smiled naughtily at her boyfriend and went rabbiting on, caught up in her own nostalgia, totally oblivious to the frozen silence around her and the uncomfortable looks of those who knew. Cockie herself, though she could feel her fingernails sinking bloodily into the palms of her hand, was almost tempted to laugh at the girl's relentless clodhopping. It was either that or scream.

Finally the girl – was her name Mivvi or something equally stupid? – faltered to a halt, her blandly pretty features creased in confusion.

'Um, did I . . . ?' she started tentatively.

'I'm sorry, you obviously don't know,' said Cockie calmly, 'Gus is dead, I'm afraid. He died of adult meningitis eight years ago.' She felt treacherous tears thickening her voice and swallowed, forcing them down.

She turned to her hostess, 'Mel, I'm sorry to cast a blight – can I help you with the next course?' Without waiting for an answer she stood up and picked her way out from the crowded, speechless table. In the kitchen, she paused, staring blindly at a poster on the wall, fists clenched. Next door she was just able to hear Mel explaining, '. . . still gets upset . . . one shock after another . . . she's usually very quick to recover . . .'

Cockie closed her eyes momentarily. 'Still gets upset' was such a minutely callous phrase. Then she felt an arm go round her shoulders, and opened her eyes.

'Are you all right, darlin'?' It was Ravi. She smiled wearily and nodded, leaning against his tallness for a long sweet moment.

'Sorry about that,' her voice was muffled against his shoulder, 'it was just that she kept banging on and on.'

'I know, what a dumb bozo. What is her name anyway – Mojo? Milkshake? Something like that.'

Despite herself, Cockie laughed. 'Mivvi, I think. Some sort of ice cream anyway.' She punched him softly. 'You're an idiot, but you're a lovable idiot.'

'Care to find out just how lovable, back at my place?' he grinned, arching an eyebrow exaggeratedly.

'Oh you!' She punched him harder this time and turned away laughing. 'Now, let's get this show on the road. Do you reckon these plates are for the pudding?'

Ben pressed the buzzer, feeling a bit foolish. When Mel had insisted that he drop by on his way back from Devon 'no matter how late it is', he had a sneaking feeling that she would not have bargained on a Cinderella-in-reverse impression. While he was waiting to be let in he glanced at his watch – shit, half past twelve. They'd probably think it was a police raid, for God's sake. Then the entryphone buzzed – great vetting procedure, Mel – and he was in.

Hugh – Mel's banker boyfriend – opened the door

of the flat. 'Ben! Great to see you, my man – Mel! Ben's here.'

Walking into the dining-room, things still looked in full swing. It was obviously a game of two halves, thought Ben wryly; Cockie, Ravi and Rowena down one end, Cockie in full flow, Ravi thumping the table; while at the other end, two obvious couples he recognised vaguely looked like they were being given a verbal rundown of the periodic table by a guy with ridiculous facial hair and a great line in meaningful hand gestures.

'Ben! Perfect!' Rowena hailed him as if it were the most natural thing in the world to see him standing there and held out her arms, 'You can take over where Hugh left off!'

'Sounds interesting,' Ben smiled, sliding in beside her, 'what position were we in?'

It wasn't that funny, but the others fell about, Cockie completely missing the ashtray with what he now saw was a joint. Ben suddenly felt very sober.

'Ben, just get on and roll, will you? Hugh made a complete hash of it.' Ravi pushed over all the paraphernalia of grass.

'Hash!' wheezed Ro and they were off again. Mel, coming in from the kitchen, gave him a big hug and a flagon-sized glass of wine.

'Anyway, where was I?' Cockie still had the anecdotal bit between her teeth. 'Yeah, so she goes down to stay with this guy, still not sure whether she fancies him or not, but trusting his good intentions. He has this tiny cottage near Exmoor and she's sleeping in his bedroom, but she's chaperoned by the rest of the houseparty and he's on the sofa so she reckons she's safe.'

'Famous last words,' interjected Hugh.

Cockie slugged back some more Baileys, eyes glittering, hands unsteady.

'So that night when she goes to bed she starts poking

around in his room. And there in his bedroom cupboards she finds,' Cockie paused for dramatic effect, 'all this *kit* – thigh-length boots, spurs, bits of rope, odd-looking bits of chainmail and even some sort of iron mask. So, of course, she thinks that the guy is some sort of bondage freak – after all she had met him at that leather and lovetoys party,' the others started chuckling at what had obviously been an earlier punchline in the story, 'and for the rest of the night she cowers in the bathroom, convinced that he's pegged her for a willing dominatrix in his dastardly sex games.'

'Stop, Cockie, please!' begged Ravi.

'No, no, the best bit's still to come. The next morning – she's really pissed off after a night proving that you can't sleep in a bath – she's all set to leave then and there when he starts talking about possible plans for the day. He tells them all about this rally that's going on a few miles away,'

Ben knew that the final punchline was near because even Cockie started laughing. 'Get this – the bloke is a Civil War revivalist – whose idea of a cracking good time on a Saturday afternoon is to charge around Exmoor recreating battle scenes, waving a pike and shouting, "For England, Cromwell and St George!".'

'I say, isn't it meant to be "For England, Harry—'

Cockie rolled her eyes at Mivvi's nitpicking interruption and bulldozed on.

'So, of course it transpires that the thigh-length boots, spurs, iron helmet etc were just part of his Roundhead costume and nothing to do with his sexual predilections and far from *him* having the dirty mind and suspicious intentions, it was her – in fact, you could say that the boot was on the other foot!' Despite the groans at her last line, Cockie finished triumphantly, complete with silent drum roll and an invisible crowd going wild. It was, Ben thought, a vintage Cockie performance.

Eventually the evening careered to an end and they left the carnage to an unusually tipsy Mel. Cockie had decided that on balance, or lack of it, it wouldn't be such a good idea for her to drive so Ben and she set off home in his van. The pungent smell of seedlings in the back swirled around them as Ben pulled out of the parking space and headed towards the Fulham Road. Just as he was turning the corner into Munster Road, Cockie suddenly sat up straighter and pointed ahead.

'Look! There it is!'

'What is?'

'That guy's car – that green, spiffy looking thing.'

'Cockie,' pleaded Ben, 'please try to make sense.' He followed the line of her finger, seeing a green TVR, cramped awkwardly into a small space up on the pavement opposite, and listened while she explained about stealing a parking space.

'So let me get this straight,' interrupted Ben, as they set off again, 'you just *happened* to run into the man who is single-handedly the inspiration for your book's hero?'

Cockie nodded. 'Yes, almost literally ran into him too.'

'Jeez, what an incredible coincidence!'

'Yeah, s'pose so.' She didn't seem too impressed by the coincidence but that was par for the course. Cockie's life could often look uncannily like a scene from a Tom Stoppard play, a not-so-controlled experiment in probability where the unlikely becomes repeatedly likely.

'It also sounds straight out of a Mills and Boon – those accidents of meeting that you were talking about the other day, you know, where hero and heroine do nothing but slag each other off.'

'Yeah. Weird. I was just thinking about those this morning.' She yawned and snuggled back into her seat. 'Wake me up when we get home.'

* * *

When they got back to the house, Cockie didn't feel like going to bed quite yet. She said good night to Ben and wandered into the kitchen, thinking about the evening. It was at times like this that she wished she did have a boyfriend – someone to laugh with and to bitch with about the Mivvis of this world. How come someone so . . . dull and inane had a boyfriend, when she, the supposed 'life and soul of the party', was looking at a Gobi desert of sexual abstinence where she might as well not bother having her legs waxed or shaving her armpits. When you'd reached the point of depilatory don't-carishness you knew you'd hit rock bottom.

Was that where she was? Rock bottom? In her half-stoned, light-headed state, staring into her steaming mug of Chocolate Break, Cockie suddenly felt intensely maudlin. And lonely. Any minute now she'd be getting out the damn photograph. Why did that stupid girl have to bring up Gus and all the attendant horrors, when she was teetering on the edge of self-pity anyway? That way lay another panic attack and she was damned if she was going to let that happen again so soon after the last one.

Suddenly angry with herself, she thumped the table savagely. 'Oh, why do I still miss you all so much?' she burst out loud into the silence. And then felt intensely foolish. When would she stop secretly hoping for some kind of answer?

5

The lot of a shopgirl was always a back-killing one, mused Eva, as she kicked off her court shoes and lay down on the floor, looking like a human bookend with her legs propped against the wall, bum pushed right up underneath. But today she'd been forced to hide out here in the storeroom – Mike's invitation to move in with him was preying on Eva's mind like a particularly baleful mantis. Or did mantis pray? And were they mantises?

She was definitely not on the ball, despite having consulted her crystals, fumbled nervously with her Tarot cards, and done her charts over and over – hampered as ever by not knowing her exact time of birth. The trouble was that, having covered all holistic bases, Eva was no closer to being given an answer by a comforting Third Party who could be blamed for her making the wrong decision. I'm just too old and battle-scarred to fuck up all on my own, she thought dolefully, there's got to be some cosmic being out there that's having a slack day; surely they could take time out to give her a sign. 'Go for it!' flashing up on the cash register would be a good start; shame she didn't live in LA for some helpful communion à la Steve Martin with a friendly traffic sign.

Closing her eyes at her own hopelessness, Eva draped herself mentally onto her internal beach, feeling her mind string out into the murmuring of the surf and the rustle of fronds above her. A warm hand – yes, she'd allow

Mike to be there as well – settled on her back and she stretched languorously, letting her muscles expand and relax under this mental massage. Gorgeous, gorgeous man, I can't possibly count the ways, she thought, as she gazed into his image. He smiled, a ripple of crinkles, and leant over to whisper in her ear – oh, the delicious power of daydreams! 'Eva, my little love,' she heard him say huskily, 'it's your turn to do the washing-up and, by the way, did you block the toilet?'

Eva's eyes snapped open. No! Domestic drudgery had invaded even her beach – what had happened to the power of relaxation? But surely that's what moving in with him would be like? Romance ruined by rent, ardour kiboshed by arguments over telephone bills, and boxers drying on every radiator. Sleeping on the same side of the bed every night, negotiating social windows in each other's diaries, asking him to buy her Tampax as he nipped to the shop for that Domestos and oven cleaner that they'd run out of, her finding a pile of his toenail clippings on the bedroom carpet as he ranted at her for using his razor on her legs. Not being able to read if she couldn't sleep. Trying to be one of the lads when he invited his mates round to watch *100 Greatest Moments in Football History* only for her to talk distractedly through the ultimate goal save by Shilton; seeing a polite mask of incredulity slip over his features as he watched her and Cockie rev up to their usual mile-a-minute gossip cruising speed while demolishing that Victoria sponge that she had made for him in a fit of homemaker's hubris. Wanting to make love in the morning as he got up to go for a run. Wanting to make love when he came back and watching him stretch out for the crossword. Not wanting to make love after she'd had a hard day's massaging and he'd been doing Haagendasz voice-overs. Starting to wear pyjamas in bed with each other. Buying an electric blanket together.

Nooooooo! Eva closed her eyes and tried to summon up the beach again. To no avail.

'Eva! There you are!' A short pause. 'Why are you upside down?'

'Cockie! Jesus, you gave me the shock of my life!' Eva rolled over and stood up, smoothing out the creases in her gabardine skirt. 'It's kind of a yoga position, good for ironing out kinks in your back.'

'So Mike's getting kinky now, is he?'

'Fnarr, fnarr. How did you find me in here?'

'Oh, when I saw that you weren't on the floor, I used my nous. This was just the first Staff Only door I saw.'

'No flies on you, eh? Well, come with me to the glove counter and I'll pretend to interest Modom in some hand-stitched leather so that old Hamster-features doesn't cotton on that you're a mate. I'm about due for a break anyway.'

'Just as long as you don't let me buy anything – you know me and the state of my bank account.'

Back at the glove counter, Eva was watching Cockie trying on gloves with all the assumed hauteur of a hardened shopper when, out of the corner of her eye, she saw the unmistakable signs of a shoplifter. She nudged Cockie and rolled her eyes towards the suspect. All the symptoms were there – the deliberate nonchalance as the girl wandered towards a rack of silk scarves, hands fingering a few while her eyes swept a little too slowly, a little too casually around her vicinity. Without once looking at the scarf in question she slid a red one almost imperceptibly off its hanger while simultaneously appearing to examine another one. Cockie and Eva watched, enthralled, as the first, red, scarf was tucked away under her coat while her right hand flicked over the price tag of the other. Then she appeared to blanch at the price and, dropping the end of the second scarf, moved away unhurriedly.

'Now what?' hissed Cockie, itching for action of the 'Stop! Or I'll shoot!' variety.

'Now we have to give her the benefit of the doubt until we can be sure that she is going to leave the store without paying for it. I really should call up the store detective,' said Eva, looking around for her.

'Oh bugger that! Let's do it ourselves – I can always make a citizen's arrest!'

'OK, OK, we'll follow her until I see the store detective.'

They left the counter and ambled casually after the shoplifter, keeping her head, in its black velvet cap worn backwards like a beret, clearly in range. Eva almost groaned as she watched the girl exhibit all the classic signs; after all as the past Princess of Purloining herself, she should know. The difference between them – who actually wore dark glasses inside a department store unless they were a film star or a thief? – was that in Eva's petty-crime-filled past she was clever enough to observe these give-aways in others and make sure that she avoided them herself, hence she had never been caught. It was a skill that she hadn't bothered to mention in her job interview for Peter Jones.

'Why is she wasting so much time? Shouldn't she just try and leg it?' Behind her, Cockie was fascinated.

'No, she thinks – oh, I'll explain later.'

They inched down the spiral staircase, down to the ground floor. As the girl turned the corner below them, shoplights winking in the large lenses of her sunglasses, something about her looked suddenly familiar but then she turned her back to them once more.

She was getting closer to the door now and Eva speeded up their stealthy pursuit, looking around her in vain for a store 'tec or more senior shop assistant. According to their precious book of conduct, this wasn't really her remit. Damn Cockie for being so gung-ho; this could lose Eva her job. Just as the girl was passing the last china and glass display rack, she turned round casually – ostensibly to look at a set of glasses. Eva, instinctive professional, didn't flinch, safe in her shopgirl's camouflage but this strange game of Grandma's Footsteps finally got to Cockie. Wide-eyed, she leapt back, behind a display rack out of sight, realised how stupid she'd been, and laughed out loud. She was out of the hunt.

Eva crossed the few yards between her and the shoplifter as fast as her short legs would allow her and, just as the culprit approached the doors, reached up and tapped her on the shoulder.

'Er, excuse me,' she began in her best stern voice. Quick as a flash, the other girl whirled around, gave Eva a monstrous shove and sprinted towards the big revolving door.

As Cockie recovered herself and came round the corner she saw Eva flying through the air to land spread-eagled on a carefully constructed display of picnic crockery. She stopped, dumbstruck.

'Cockie!' There was a bellow from the bowels of the display. 'For fuck's sake, get that bitch!'

Cockie was off. Like a late starter at the Grand National she shot through the pack of shoppers between her and the doors. A small boy in the revolving door was almost dashed against the glass as Cockie charged through to be spat out on the other side.

Quick glance round Sloane Square. Black beret bobbing towards Lower Sloane Street on the right. Deep breath and Cockie plunged into the traffic, trusting blindly to the excellent qualities of both the pedestrian crossings and her own stainless steel luck. Hop and a skip across that street, steer round old lady with shopping bag on wheels, narrowly avoid small yappy dog on diamante lead, swerve past snogging couple, step on toe of – wow, stunning – man, accelerate past band of sluggish tourists. Cockie was now out of Sloane Square with a clear run down Lower Sloane Street, and – through sweat-misted eyes – up ahead she saw the girl, now running as well – red scarf clutched in her hand, fluttering brazenly behind her.

'Ha!' thought Cockie. 'Gotcha!'

Too late she saw what the girl was running for – a bus, about to leave its stop. With a sinking, thundering heart, Cockie forced herself to run faster but too late. The girl hopped on the bus, doors closing firmly behind her. Cockie got there steps behind, thumped on the doors as the bus began to move off, but the bus driver grinned and shook his head. Bastard. Last chance was at the traffic lights, just turning red. On she lurched, lactic acid singing in her legs. Got to the lights, banged on the doors again.

'You can bang all you like, love, I can't open between stops!' came the answering yell from inside.

'But . . . but . . .' Cockie tried to force the words out between gasps, 'thief . . . thief . . . on board.'

'Yeah, right!' he hooted, smiling again.

Double bastard. This was hopeless. Cockie walked unsteadily along the side of the bus. There was the culprit, hat pulled down over her face.

'Oi! You! You're a thief!' Cockie did her thumping routine again, shocking the girl into looking up, her sunglasses sliding down her nose as she did so. For a moment, they looked at each other in equal surprise. Then the lights changed and the bus moved off, leaving Cockie breathless, stunned and stranded in a sea of hurtling, beeping traffic.

Eva was dusting herself off, torn between picking up the shattered debris behind her and apologising profusely to the apoplectic floor manager. Past the gaggle of curious shoppers gathered round, she saw Cockie trudging towards her.

'Excuse me, Mr Simkins – Cockie! Did you get her?'

'No. Silly cow got on a bus.'

'What?!'

'You heard.'

'Why didn't you follow her in a cab, you idiot?'

'Oh, for God's sake, Eva.' Cockie couldn't be bothered to say any more. Then she noticed the wholesale destruction around Eva – the splintered remains of a picnic hamper, shards of plastic glasses and once delicately patterned crockery, a wooden display pedestal listing drunkenly.

'Cor, quite a trashing you've got here, Eva,' she grinned. 'Ten out of ten for effort.'

'Fuck off and die. Sorry, Mr Simkins. You didn't hear that. Cockie, I think you'd better go.'

'Is that all the thanks I – OK, OK,' Cockie backed off, 'I'm outta here. Just one thing though – did you recognise that girl?'

'No, of course I didn't – well, now you come to mention it . . . something about her . . .' Eva looked thoughtful.

'I think, I'm not sure at all, but I think it may have been . . . Annalisa,' said Cockie slowly.

'Annalisa? Annalisa from the Whim? Nah! Can't have been. Even for you that would have been too much of a coincidence!'

'Yes, you're probably right. Oh well, catch you later – as it were. Have fun!' Cockie winked as she turned away.

Eva pulled a face at her departing back and turned to the hapless Mr Simkins.

'Right. Where were we?'

Ben was at the bar, assuming the pose. If Rodin had been in the same bar, taking a tea break from the afterlife, he would certainly have recognised this pose. For late dates or tardy clients alike, Ben had perfected the comfortable, absorbed in a book look; thin fingers clasping a delicately formed brow, elbow propped on the bar, other hand flopping loosely off it. Once, before hitting upon this solution, Ben had been waiting for Cockie in a bar, had caught her eye when she came in and had then had to go through the agony of watching her trip over handbags, send drinks flying and step on a thousand toes in her self-conscious hurry to reach him with her excuses, all the while pulling 'Sorry-I'm-late' faces at him. This way, because his eyes never lifted from the book in front of him, he never had to catch the eye of his guest as they came across the bar or restaurant, saving them both that embarrassment.

It was a necessary defence too, Ben thought to himself, in a place like this; wall to wall self-consciousness; the myriad sparkle of a thousand eyes flicking round over each and every jam-packed shoulder; the beatless yap of a sea of smalltalk. The Atlantic Bar, still the Place To Be Seen and Not Heard – not his idea of a first date venue but as per usual he had gone blank when she asked him where they should go, ceding gracefully to her suggestion that they come here. He took a niggardly sip of his £3.50 beer and squinted back at his book. Finally there was a tap on his shoulder.

'Ben! Ever so sorry I'm late; bloody tube!'

Ben swivelled gracefully off the stool and stood up. 'Annalisa, don't worry about it, I was late myself. How are you? Would you like a drink? Wow! You look incredible!'

She certainly did. Dressed to kill in an armour of silver low-slung hipsters and a steely grey top, fastened round her neck and leaving about as much sun-tanned flesh on show as was legal outside Soho. Ben took a thirstier gulp of his beer.

'Thanks,' said Annalisa, speaking coolly over the din. 'You don't look so bad yourself.' She met his slightly googly-eyed stare with an unblinking gaze of her own;

then, not dropping her eyes as her irresistibly bowed mouth parted, she licked her lips and slowly smiled.

Holy cow, thought a part of Ben that was still thinking, holy flipping cow. This was certainly a different girl to the shy waif at the Whim. He couldn't decide whether to feel flattered or nervous by this full-on treatment, so mentally he just lay back for the ride.

'How about a couple of tequila slammers?' she asked. 'If you're up to it?' she added, tapping his thigh teasingly.

'Ye—!' Ben cleared his throat and tried again. 'Yes. Absolutely. Good idea. Arriba arriba.'

So far he'd only spouted complete nonsense, he thought ruefully, only too aware of losing his usual poise. It didn't seem to matter though – a few slammers later, and he was the wittiest man alive, regaling Annalisa with loud anecdotes that had acquired a new lease of life, watching her fall about with laughter on every cue. A few more and they were both falling about, rocking back and forth on their respective stools, hands clamped on each other's thighs . . . for balance, of course.

'Annaleesha. Oops.' Ben chuckled. 'Annalisa. Shall we go and have some dinner somewhere?'

'Somewhere over the rainbow,' she sang, running a long-nailed hand up the inside of his thigh. Ben gulped a cartoon gulp, imagining a Hanna-Barbera head of steam coming out of his ears.

'We could go to Bistro 190,' he battled on manfully.

'Yeah. Sounds great. Let's go.' Annalisa stood up decisively and leant past him to stub out her cigarette. As she did so, her top rode up her midriff and Ben, gazing hopefully at the gap, saw a glint of metal from her stomach. No, surely not.

'You – you – you've had your belly button pierced?' he spluttered, feeling his own retract in mingled fascination and horror.

'Navel-piercing is really in at the moment, although, to

be honest, I only had mine done because my boyfriend dared me to. But now I like it. Why? Don't you? Here, have a touch.'

'Boyfriend?' gasped Ben, as she guided his fingers to the small silver hoop protruding from her belly button.

'Ex,' Annalisa purred, glancing up at Ben, as she slid his hand downwards. 'Very much ex.'

Feeling any vestiges of independent thought going up in smoke behind the fiery trail of his fingers, Ben struggled to regain some control over the way things were going.

'Come on. Time to leave.' He snatched his hand away and pulled her up almost roughly, elbowing his way out of the stifling bar, Annalisa wallowing obediently in his wake. Once outside, he ignored the queue of people still waiting to get in to the Atlantic and crushed her into his arms, taking control as he bent his head to hers. But she gave as good as she got – opening his mouth wider with hers, plunging her tongue in and wrapping it around his, hands going immediately round his hips, grinding her own into his.

'Ooh,' she giggled, when they finally came up for air, 'you Tarzan, me Jane.' She moved her hands up his back, under his shirt. 'But we've got too many clothes on for that, haven't we?' She leant back in his embrace, hands coming round to caress his stomach, the innocence of her look up at him belied by the tiny thrusts of her pelvis into his.

Ben gave in. 'OK, OK, you win,' he said with mock reluctance. 'Forget dinner. Let's get a cab. Your place or mine?'

'Yours is closer.' She spied a vacant taxi and, putting two fingers in her mouth, gave an ear-splitting blast. Ben wasn't the only one to clutch his head in disbelief but he was certainly the closest. But it worked: the taxi sliding obediently up to them.

'Ebury Mews, please,' said Ben, as he held the door open for Annalisa.

'Oh, and can we stop at an all-night pharmacy, please?' added Annalisa, and pulled Ben in right on top of her. Ben, extricating himself momentarily from her small but perfectly formed cleavage, gave her a questioning glance.

'Why?'

'Well, I'd lay bets that you don't have any condoms at home, do you? Or any with a decent sell by date?'

He gaped at her, resisting the temptation to bury himself in her breasts again.

'Oh, it's OK, I found out from Fred at the Whim that you hardly ever actually sleep with all these women that you flirt with' – she suddenly sounded alarmingly sober and clear-headed – 'so I knew I was going to have to make a bit more effort than usual. But I'd run out myself so . . . hope you're not shocked.'

Ben was speechless. Speechless and powerless, as the taxi gathered speed.

'So how many jobs do you have?'

'Hmmm?' Cockie, intent on adding up her bill, didn't look up at this unexpected salvo.

'You do work at the City Art Gallery, right?'

'Uh, what? Yes.' Why did Fred always hide the bloody calculator, she raged, tussling with the service charge, still not looking up.

'Right . . . well, yes. I thought so. Good.'

Something about the voice, peevish now, was familiar. Thirty-eight pounds and 80p. There. At last she looked up, only to see her questioner walking away from the end of the bar, black head held high in righteous indignation that she had ignored him. Something about the back of him twanged a small chord of memory. Dead sexy too.

'Earth to Cockie. Table 8 want their bill some time

before the next millennium. What's up? You have an unnaturally thoughtful look on your face.'

Cockie turned away to face Fred. 'Mental arithmetic. Does it every time. Now if you would just occasionally let us at the calculator, life would be so much simpler.'

'But then there'd be no fun. There's nothing I like better than to make a woman struggle.'

'Yuk. Let me pass, you chauvinist sadistic braggart.'

'Big words, Cockie! Been working on the Mills and Boon?'

There was nothing you could do when Fred was in this mood, as he had been all night. The tips had better be worth it because tonight was turning out to be a huge bore – business was brisk but not so the wit. She'd been irritable all afternoon, snapping at Ben as he got ready for his hot date with that silly thieving cow, and reining in her temper with difficulty at all the usual idiosyncrasies displayed by the Whim diners. Like that table, she ranted inwardly, looking across to Table 10: a load of wankerbankers, all clicking their fingers and keeping poor old TJ running back and forth with endless bottles. Prats.

Cockie gave her table their bill and went through the usual credit card swiping. As part of the eternal mysteries of waitressing, her surly, lacklustre service had garnered her a higher than usual tip so she was feeling more cheerful, when TJ suddenly cannoned into her.

'Here.' TJ shoved her order pad into Cockie's hands. 'You take Table 10. I've had it with those arrogant drongos. One more fucking Antipodean crack and I'm going to spew . . . I'll show them how God created the duck-billed platypus with my own bare hands.'

'But TJ—'

'No, fair dinkum, Cockie, I took two tables off your hands when you had that hangover last week and,' she wheedled, 'you'll be so much better at giving them what for – I'm just too mad at them to make any sense.'

'Oh God,' sighed Cockie, 'why did I get up today? OK, who are the worst offenders or are they all wankers?'

'Pretty much, but the two at this end are really giving me strife.'

'No problem. Leave them to me. I think,' Cockie twinkled wickedly at TJ, 'that a Deadsea Dickhead could just be in order.' She was beginning to feel more cheerful just at the prospect, 'Oh, the joy of ridiculing somebody . . . bliss!'

'Yeah. Righto,' said TJ a little uncertainly.

Cockie darted behind the bar, reached up to pull two scrolls out of a labelled wine rack, checked that they were the right ones and marched with martial stride to Table 10. On her way, she grabbed a couple of the liqueur menu scrolls for good measure. Careful not to muddle them up, she gave each of the first two to the offenders targeted by TJ and passed the others down the table.

'Right,' she said briskly, 'since you've driven TJ off the deep end what can I get you all to drink?'

There was a small silence as a couple of them looked expectantly at the ringleaders, waiting perhaps for them to come back with a quip. None were forthcoming, however, as these two stared in disbelief at what they were reading, one going slowly redder, one going slowly whiter as they got to the bottom of the scroll.

'Perhaps I could get you both a fortifying brandy?' said Cockie gently, suppressing the inward 'Ha!' that the Deadsea Dickhead always provoked. They nodded dumbly, those adjacent to them gazing at them in mild astonishment.

'Ah, I will have a Kümmel, please,' came a loud voice from the other end of the table. Cockie looked up and dropped her pen straight into the lap of the red-faced Dickhead victim. Simultaneously she had recognised both the voice of her earlier inquisitor and the face of her inspirational hero. Victor Landis! Again!

'Hello!' she exclaimed, covering her confusion by bending down to retrieve her pen from the pinstriped crotch of the now purple-faced man. 'You do pop up all over the place, don't you? How was your parking this time?'

Victor Landis didn't even drop his smile, just looked slightly puzzled. There was nothing more annoying, thought Cockie, than a cheap jibe that didn't even register. 'Kümmel, was that? A man of taste at least. What about the rest of you?'

'You're not going to believe this, Flo,' said Cockie as she gave him the drinks order, 'but Mr Perfect Hero is sitting right here in the Whim.'

'Mr Per – bleedin' 'eck – the guy who's the schmooze muse for your Mills and Boon?'

'Nice choice of words. Yep, the very same – sadly, he's one of those idiots on Table 10. You know, shoot your mouth off, flash your wad types.'

'Sounds saucy,' mugged Flo, squinting across to the restaurant area.

'Well, I suppose with looks like his, you can't expect a personality to match.'

'Hang on,' said Flo, 'he's not the one on the banquette right at the end – the unbelievably dishy one with black hair?'

'Er – yes, that's the – shit! He's looking straight at me – how embarrassing, he must think I fancy him.' Cockie whirled round to face the barman, her back to the restaurant. 'Flo, I don't know, this is all getting a bit weird. I mean, I keep bumping into him and now suddenly he's here? In the Whim? It's a bit strange, don't you think?'

'Cockie,' reproved Flo, 'a certain phrase involving mouths and gifthorses springs to mind here. Go for it, girlie – I would, if he weren't straight and I weren't married. And remember, tell me all the dirty details!'

'Such moral guidance, Monsieur Flaubert,' laughed Cockie as she took the tray of drinks from him, 'but being a masochist, I'm still hankering after the fading ideal of Sam.'

'Oh God, change the record, my sweet,' Flo rolled his eyes. 'I get the cold shudders just thinking about that creep.'

But Cockie was gone, insult unheard.

Cockie and TJ were on a break.

'Oh, by the way,' asked Cockie, puffing absently, 'how is the spunk?'

TJ patted away the smoke. 'Playing a bit hard to get actually. He won't even give me his home number. He says that his last girlfriend really blew him away when she dumped him and that now he's too—'

'No! I don't want to hear it!'

'—emotionally bruised,' finished TJ.

'Aaargh! That phrase again! It hath a dying strain!'

'Well, I nearly died, I can tell you, especially when he went on to say that, yeah, of course, if he could commit to anyone—'

'He would commit to me!' they chorused.

'Well, you,' amended Cockie, 'although he sounds like one of many that I know. Why is it that men have just updated their excuses? It used to be that they "weren't ready to settle down" – now even they have cottoned on that they've outlived that one and what do they do? Come up with an equally awful line! It's that dread word "commitment" – as if that were our Holy Grail: what happened to "going out" with someone, having a laugh, making whoopee?'

'Yeah, men think that once they've slept with you once or twice and, gorblimey, taken you out for a feed, it's on with the shackles, do not pass go, do not collect £200, go straight to jail.'

'Unimaginative creatures, the lot of them,' agreed Cockie.

Felipe's head appeared round the door. 'TJ, I hear Patrick on war road upstairs; he look for you to take bill from big payers on Table 10.'

'At last! They're going,' sighed TJ, standing up. 'I'd better get a decent tip after all this.'

'I think after the Deadsea Dickhead treatment, you'll be impressed by the generosity of these kind people,' deadpanned Cockie as she got up to follow her.

Sure enough there were a couple of tenners in it for TJ when she came back from collecting their bill.

'I forgive them!' she carolled happily. 'Here, Cockie, here's a fiver – you earned it.'

'My pleasure, treasure,' said Cockie, exaggeratedly kissing the note. Then she froze as, out of the crow-like flurry of dark suit jackets being put on, she saw, emerging towards her, the tall figure of one Victor Landis. In two strides he was right there before her, a perfect smile flashing across his perfect face.

'Please tell me, I'm so curious, what did you give Andreas and Martin to read before?'

'To read? Andreas and Martin?' stalled Cockie.

'You know, those rolled papers – what did they say? They certainly worked – I have never seen those two shut up so quickly.'

'Well, why don't you read one for yourself. Flo!' she yelled across the bar, 'chuck me a Dickhead.'

'Quoi? Anyone in particular?' asked Flo, gesturing at the late night habitués propping up the bar.

'No! A Deadsea Dickhead.'

Victor deftly caught the scroll as Flo threw it towards them, and unrolled it. 'Why Dead Sea? Oh I see, because it is a scroll – sorry.' He looked down, started to chuckle and began to read passages out loud.

'Being loud and abusive may be synonymous with fun

in your tiny brains but your surrounding diners and staff do not agree . . . ha! We are not impressed by big noise and big wallets . . . oh, this is funny . . . if you cannot be more sophisticated guests of the Slim Whim, then please leave . . . perfect.' He rolled the scroll back up and looked at Cockie piercingly.

'Now, are you going to acknowledge that we have met before?'

'Are you going to acknowledge defeat on the subject of parking spaces?' riposted Cockie.

He frowned. 'What is this talk of par—oh! That was you, stealing my space the other night?'

Cockie bobbed a curtsy. 'Yours truly.' She ignored clearing-up signals from Patrick and TJ.

'Mine?' he questioned. 'Oh, I see. Well,' cue that smile again, 'I forgive you. There! Is that not magnanimous of me?'

'About as magnanimous as I would be if I forgave you your taste in friends,' retorted Cockie. Why am I flirting with this guy, she wondered, or more to the point, why is he flirting with me?

'Oh, they're just people I work with,' he said with a careless wave, 'as from now I have forgotten them.'

'Lucky that, since they've gone without you anyway.'

He looked round. 'So they have. Well, in that case I have now fired and forgotten them!' he laughed, with a glint in his eye.

'Oh, quite the big cheese, huh?'

'No, I am only kidding. At Silverman Bone, there are very few big cheeses – I am just one of the many big – shall we say – yoghurts.'

He laughed again and Cockie laughed with him. TJ, hovering close to eavesdrop, rolled her eyes at Flo, lurking on the other side. This was priceless.

'We-ell,' Cockie drew the word out reluctantly, 'my boss is going to disembowel me if I don't clear up soon, so I'd better go while he's still sharpening the knives.'

Victor did another glint. 'We shall carry on another time . . . ?' The proposition lingered a little too long to be casual.

'Yes!' said Cockie quickly. 'Why not? Yes!' Stop gabbling, you fool, she thought, amazed at herself.

'Well, how about—'

He was interrupted by a veritable explosion of activity, as a strange man barrelled in between him and Cockie and swept her into his arms.

'Cockie! My darling love! Let me look at you . . . gorgeous as ever and look at those heaving boobs. Are you all right, my sweetling, you look a little flushed? Just pleased to see me, eh, you wee devil?'

He held her out before him before crushing her to him again, as Victor stepped back in astonishment.

'Och, I've been trying to get hold of you for as long as the moon has been in Jupiter. I know, you won't believe me but I have—'

'Drew! Drew! Stop!' cried Cockie breathlessly, trying to extricate herself from his bearhug. 'You can't just barge in here – this is Vic—'

'No time for that – my taxi's waiting for me – I just wanted to know – do you still love me?' He looked at her piercingly.

'Oh, for God's sake, Drew.'

'Och, please!'

'Oh Jesus, of course I do, but—'

Victor's face tightened as Drew interrupted her again. 'Good, because I need you – how about lunch tomorrow: special occasion; I'll take you to – are you working at the Gallery tomorrow?' Cockie nodded, bemused. 'Well, in that case I'll take you to the Savoy.'

'Drew!'

'It's only five minutes' walk if you jog. American Bar

– one o'clock – be there if you care!' And with that he was gone, as quickly as he had come, leaving a stunned Cockie, a speechless Victor, and Flo and TJ crouching weakly behind the bar.

Victor was the first to recover. Gone was the flirtatiousness of that short moment ago. He was back in moody hero mode again, all hooded eyes and furrowed brow.

'Well, as I was saying,' he said politely, 'it was nice to meet you properly. Please send my regards to Edward at the Gallery.' And with that he turned on his heel and headed for the street. For a moment, Cockie almost let the opportunity slip completely.

'Victor!' she called as he reached the door. He turned and lifted his beguiling eyebrow once more. 'See you soon?' she finished lamely. He waved a hand and was gone, the back of his head flickering in the light of the torches outside. Cockie felt almost bereft.

Then there was an explosion behind her, as TJ and Flo could hold back no longer.

'Classic,' wheezed Flo.

'What a beaut!' cackled TJ.

Bereft swiftly transformed into furious.

'Do you think it's possible just once, just bloody once, to have a private conversation without every fucking harpy in this place eavesdropping and adding their tuppence worth?' Cockie demanded. 'I'm sick and fucking tired of being free entertainment for you lot. And as for Drew – I'm going to kill him, stupid clodhopping moron.'

'You provide the entertainment, woman, we're just the appreciative audience,' crowed Flo.

'And don't call me woman!'

'Overreacting, Cockie!' carolled TJ.

'Are we to assume that yon Tall Dark and Handsome is no longer just material for the book, then?' asked Flo, as archly as only he could.

'Oh fuck off, both of you – and that goes for you two

as well,' finished Cockie, as Patrick and Fred approached, agog. 'And don't ask me to clear up, Patrick, 'cos I'll only break plates. Over heads.' She grabbed her bag from beneath the coffee counter, poured her tips out of her glass, and stomped out, every pore shrieking indignation. Flo and TJ exchanged knowing glances, Patrick and Fred ones of confusion.

'Hmmmm . . .' said Flo thoughtfully.

Cockie was still furious the next day as she strode up the Strand to the Savoy. Drew was going to get a hefty kick up the backside for barging in like that, but mostly now she was angry with herself. Last night she'd tried to rattle off a few pages for the Mills and Boon, but every time she'd tried to write about Luke, Victor's face had intruded, not as inspiration but as distraction. She couldn't quite believe that she was so annoyed that their burgeoning flirt had been curtailed by Drew's entrance – surely she wasn't falling for a total stranger, and an unrealistically beautiful one at that? Hadn't she explored all the possibilities of that scenario with Sam? Yes, she had and no, she wasn't going to again. But, let's face it, she told herself glumly; propositions of any sort weren't exactly coming in thick and fast. I will kill him, she promised herself, as she approached Drew in the American Bar.

'This had better be good, you jerk.' She sat down and took stock. Beside the table there was an ice bucket containing a bottle wrapped in a thick white napkin. Champagne? At lunch time? In the Savoy? But Drew was Scottish . . . she frowned suspiciously at him, alarm bells ringing loudly. His cherubic face, all big eyes and glossy curls of hair, displayed only sweet innocence.

'Of course it will be. Why are you in such a mood, sweetie?'

'Didn't you stop to think about what you were interrupting last night?' His genuine look of surprise was answer enough. 'The closest I've come to being asked out on a date by someone other than you, that's what.'

'What, with that pinstriped mannequin?' Drew rallied scornfully. 'Och, surely not.' He went on before she could protest. 'Anyway, far more importantly, how do I look?'

Reluctantly, she looked him over. Biased as she was against him, she had to admit that he looked good: shirt of an intense powder blue, tucked into soft looking chinos in a buttery yellow, all tidied up for the Savoy by a crisp well-fitting blazer and finished off with suntanned bare feet slipped into neatly battered brown suede loafers.

'Pretty spiffy,' she conceded. 'Very Ralph Lauren,' she added more dampeningly. 'Why?'

'Because I wanted to look so delicious that when I ask you this question, you won't have the heart to turn me down.'

Cockie was mildly intrigued.

'What question?'

Drew suddenly looked very serious, almost pleading. He reached across the table for her hand and gazed intently at her.

'Coquelicot Milton, the only girl in my heart. Will you be my wife?'

6

Cockie burst out laughing. Great gusts of air went round her system then gave up the ghost. Drew didn't say anything. Then, just as suddenly, Cockie stopped; narrowed her eyes at him and took a couple more gulps.

'What,' she demanded, 'are you on, Drew? What are you talking about? What's your game?' She started chuckling again.

Drew struggled to maintain his solemnity.

'I'm asking you to be my wife and all you can do is snigger?' he said dolefully. 'Well, thanks a lot, Coquelicot.'

'And will you stop calling me bloody Coquelicot! What is going on? And don't even try to tell me that you've done a one-eighty on your sexuality because—'

Drew snorted. 'God forbid I "do a one-eighty" – whatever that is. OK, OK, I give in – let me explain. You see, I have to go to a wedding and at that wedding I have to be married.'

'Wha –?' goggled Cockie.

'Just shut up, you. I have to be married because I told a client that I was married and it's her nephew that's getting married.'

Cockie couldn't wait for Drew to reach the words 'clarity' and 'coherence' in the great dictionary of life.

'Just a minute: why did you lie to your client and why do you have to go to her nephew's wedding?'

'Because she's a total homophobe and being married was the only way I was going to get this enormous contract – I mean, it's huge – and, och, this is impossible: why don't I just start from the beginning?'

'Good thinking, Batman,' said Cockie wisely, and sat back to listen. It was eye-widening time as he unfolded his tale.

He had, Drew told her, heard about this ripe plum of a contract up for grabs from a rich Cit's wife. It transpired that, to stop her from being bored, her husband had given her a hotel, tucked away behind the Ritz, and had told her to do with it what she wanted. Drew had done his homework and had found out that this woman – the Hellhag, as he referred to her – was pathological in her hatred for gays but wanted a man to be her decorator so that another woman wouldn't steal her thunder.

Confused? Drew asked Cockie at this point. Heavens no! she batted back, goggling. So Drew had girded his loins, so to speak, jammed on a wedding ring and had pitched for the job. This was why he had been so incommunicado these past few weeks – swags, testers, interlining and underlay had been draping themselves round his head as he battled to come up with the Dream Scheme and Quintessential Quote to suit the Hag. By means fair and foul but all of them imaginative he had wriggled his way into her good favour.

'You slept with her?' interrupted Cockie, horrified but impressed.

Difficult, Drew assured her, given the wiring of his circuits – not that she hadn't hinted that she was prime for a little upholstering. But he'd dodged that pitfall by stressing how happily married he was and had finally heard the night before that he'd got the job – all twelve suites, dining-room, cocktail bar – the lot. Hence his exuberance in the Whim, he concluded, leaning back in his chair, beaming, and hence the champagne now.

'Cor.' Cockie sipped obediently. 'Well, I can see why the job was worth all the palaver. Easy Street, here we come!'

She looked Drew up and down consideringly. She knew better than anyone how convincingly straight he could be; after a crush on him that had lasted two summers, it took an outing to the film, *Maurice*, and a gentle guiding chat engineered by Drew afterwards for her to realise that even at her most bombshell she was never going to get anywhere with him. Coming out of the closet two years earlier had been a late and virtually imperceptible event for Drew: no sudden hydraulic links to his wrist or voicebox had accompanied his emergence, and many of those who knew him were still none the wiser. He was as he always had been: a soft-spoken, molasses-eyed gorgeously packaged guy.

'But I still don't get why I have to marry you?'

Drew looked sheepish. 'You don't actually have to marry me, you just have to pretend to be my wife for one day – at this wedding.'

'Whose wedding? Remind me.'

'Hellhag's nephew.'

'Why do you have to go? Why has this woman invited her decorator to a family wedding?'

'Not decorator, interior designer, puhleeeze, Cockie. And she didn't invite me: this was one of my scams to get myself into her good books, when it looked like she might be giving the job to someone like John Stefanidis. She mentioned that her nephew was getting hitched so I did a bit of sleuthing, and found out who the blushing bride was.' Drew grinned wickedly.

'Then it was easy as pie to crash the engagement party, convince this rather dim lass that we knew each other from way back, and wangle an invitation to the wedding out of her.'

'But why?' asked a muddled Cockie.

'Because then, you numbskull, I could go back to Auntie and say, "What a lovely coincidence, Mrs Hellhag, that my old old friend Flavia is getting married to your charming nephew – see you at the wedding!" She thinks, "What ho, a good egg indeed," and then, as well as being blown away by the lyrical brilliance of my designs, she is reassured by my impeccable connections and the fact that I'm virtually one of the family. Otherwise she'll sack me as a liar and a sham.' He looked at Cockie beseechingly, puppy dog eyes on full wattage.

'Whew.' Cockie didn't appear to weaken. 'What a tangled web you've woven – all for the sake of your career. Even for that size of job it's quite a tall order – to pull the wool over so many people's eyes.' She looked thoughtful. 'Why so driven, hon? Are things that bad?'

'No, no, not at all,' Drew rushed to reassure her, 'business is booming but, don't you see, this project is a whole hotel – with total artistic control going to me, Drew Fraser, new name in town, eight-page spread in *Interiors*, that sort of thing. Forget the odd bijou pad in Chelsea, a restaurant in Islington – this is W1 – the Big Time! With this job, it's all going to happen – and then,' he went on grimly, 'then I can write to dear old Daddy and tell him that his banished bender of a son has done more in five years in the den of vice that is London than he has done in his entire boring narrow little life, and that he can stick his pathetic little family business up his bum—'

'Instead of telling you what not to stick up yours,' said Cockie quickly, trying to defuse this sudden turn of conversation.

'Cockie! Don't be so crude!' exclaimed Drew sternly, but a twitch at the corner of his mouth gave him away.

Suddenly they were both giggling like naughty children, worsened by the appearance of an impeccably haughty Savoy waiter asking them if they required anything.

'His is cute,' observed Cockie, as he walked away from them.

'His what?'

'His bum.' And they were off again, co-conspirators.

'Och, you're disgusting,' choked Drew, 'flirting with a waiter who's so obviously mine for the taking – are you not getting your oats, my little man-eater?'

'Well, frankly, no. For a brief eyeblink of a moment there, things were looking up, but then you blundered in, you creepoid.' Cockie told him about the non-starter that might have been Victor.

'And what does Ben have to say about this Victor?' asked Drew.

'Ben? What does Ben—? No, Ben is too busy playing sack races himself. You should have seen him this morning – God, it was so funny – he was virtually cross-eyed, while this harpy he's sleeping with – or not, judging by the bags under his eyes – purred away, lapping up her cornflakes like it was Whiskas Deluxe with clotted cream.'

'Mia-ooow,' drawled Drew. 'Don't tell me, she's thin, small-breasted and petite?'

'Of course, aren't Ben's flirts always?' scorned Cockie, then she paused, leaning forward conspiratorially. 'OK, four walls stuff this: do you think I should tell Ben that I think she's a thief?'

'What?!'

She quickly told him about her abortive chase through Peter Jones, culminating in her suspicion that it was Annalisa.

'So, what do you reckon? Do I shop her?' she finished.

'Cockie!' Drew stared at her, looking almost ruffled. 'Have you totally lost your senses? Unfounded accusations will only do one thing: drive Ben straight into her arms! And he'll hate you!'

'Oh Mr Melodrama, calm yourself,' laughed Cockie, then she realised that this was a Serious Drew Face. 'Drew! I looked straight into her face – that's hardly unfounded! And why should I care what Ben does with her?'

Drew just raised an eyebrow.

Cockie ignored him. 'So, has all this careering around—'

'Arf, arf.'

'—turned up a new Romeo in your life? Everyone I know is getting hitched so why should you be any different?'

Drew looked shifty.

'Drew? Reticence? From you? No!' Cockie was intrigued.

'Och, shut it, Cockie. Yes, I am involved with someone. It's early days yet.'

'That's never stopped the usual crowing—'

'Cockie, will you belt up? Anyway, this time it's different . . . I think I'm in love.'

For once, Cockie resisted the impulse to tease him. Manfully, she consigned all those other times when he'd said exactly the same thing into the rubbish bin of her memory and tried to carry on as if this were a new conversational sortie. Time to dig.

'Wow! You've fallen in love! That's amazing! Tell me all!'

'No. As I said, early days, so let's just leave it at that. There are complications, of course – when aren't there?' said Drew ruefully.

'But who—?' asked Cockie, spade still poised. 'Drew, look at me!'

'Leave it out!' He still wouldn't meet her eyes.

There was a short pause. Cockie opened her mouth to apologise for prying, but Drew beat her to it, looking up with a mischievous grin and speaking quickly, 'OK, when we are man and wife, I shall feel able to trust you with my damp and dark secrets.'

Cockie seized the straws of frivolity gratefully. 'Hey, I don't remember agreeing to be your wife – you didn't even go down on your knees: what sort of a lame proposal was that?'

'No, petal, I will not stretch the knees of my new chinos for anyone,' he declared, camping it up shamelessly.

'Vain old queen.'

'Well, that's no way to talk about your husband!'

'Drew! Get serious for a moment! I can't do it! I can't go to a wedding where, knowing my luck, I'll probably be recognised by someone I know and be sprung immediately—' and Cockie went on to list the top ten reasons why this idea was damper than the dampest squib.

'Humbug,' rebuffed Drew stoutly. 'For a start, you didn't even come to my launch party in Chiswick the other day which could otherwise have been a problem because the groom, Julian, was there.'

'How did you explain your "wife's" absence?'

'Och, you're a good wife who had to go home for your niece's confirmation, or something.'

'Oh great.'

'Anyway, the bridal couple are a good five years older than you and are deeply buried in the City lifestyle, so that narrows the field of overlapping friends and, furthermore, they are both twenty-four carat nouveau riche, sheikhs of the shagpile; these people would buy their groceries from Harrods if they could be sure to have the Harrods logo embossed on each and every apple!' he finished triumphantly.

Cockie wasn't impressed. 'So? I may not have that kind of cash but I'm not entirely trapped in my spiral of genteel poverty, you know, I do get out and about occasionally. I have been known to eat cake even, on occasion.'

'Cockie.' Drew had a hidden ace. 'The wedding is in Penge.' He paused artfully. 'Or is it Crouch End?'

It was the ace of spades. Despite her anti-snob colours,

Cockie had always been fascinated by the suburbs of London, or more particularly, by the awfulness of their names, and Drew knew that she had always sought a raison d'être for investigating her prejudices.

'Hmmmm . . .' she stalled for time, 'just tell me the plan for getting away with this then?'

'I have a plan,' intoned Drew solemnly, 'a plan so cunning—'

'That if it had two ears and a tail, you could call it a weasel!' they chorused.

Cockie stared at the last page she had written, impressed despite herself by the progress she had made. Allegra and Luke hated each other already, he'd crushed her lips to his once and Allegra was well on her way to suspecting Luke of not being entirely English. She glanced at her watch – half eight – too late to join Rowena, Jacko and the rest of the crew at the Hole in the Wall, too early to do anything else. All at once Cockie felt lonely and unfulfilled, knowing that she needed something to fill the gap in her life. Hmmm.

As if by magic a picture popped into her head. Doughnuts! Of course! It was late night opening at Sainsbury's and she needed comfort food like a Bloody Mary needed Tabasco. If she could get the defibrillators on the Mini, she could just make it . . .

Despite her new financial strong will – doughnuts, and that was her lot – it started badly when she grabbed a trolley out of pure habit. Immediately she started to feel the usual euphoria of supermarkets: the thrill of the open aisle was calling her, the wind of pumped-out baking smells was in her hair, and the trolley in her hands trembled and side-stepped like a skittish mare. Trust her to go for the one with the broken wheel.

She glanced at her watch – ten minutes until closing time. It was clear that the only way to avoid the lure of the tempting wares on either side of her and to make it to the bakery at the other side of the store was to go there at speed – but with the top crossover route still blocked, the backroads were her only option.

Wheeling her trusty steed around, she was off: down Herbs and Spices, taking a racing line through the corner of Crisps and Savouries into the middle crossover aisle. Racing past Cereals, she saw up ahead at Frozen Vegetables, a traffic jam of chatting mothers, small children littered inconveniently around their feet. Scattering them might have involved casualties so she nipped up by Frozen Poultry, gauging that the crowds at the top may have thinned out at this, the Delicatessen stage. She was right, but they were thick again at the milk pallets so she clipped down Preserves at high speed, losing control of her dodgy trolley wheels as she took the corner too narrowly and crashed into someone walking up that aisle, goods and chattels stacked high in his arms. At the moment of impact, Cockie realised who it was and wanted to do a pound coin impression and roll under the nearest counter. It just couldn't be. It was.

'You! You! You idiot!' He was flabbergasted, staring with growing incredulity at her face, and then down at the remains of his shopping, most of which was now in Cockie's trolley, except for a sad-looking avocado doing a roadkill impression on the floor. 'You! Always you!'

'Yes, me,' said Cockie a little impatiently, 'though why you couldn't put your stuff in a trolley like any normal person is beyond me.'

That's right, Cockie, the best form of defence is offence.

'What?' Incredulity to rage in one easy facial movement. 'So now, you are saying, it is my fault that you crash into me, that you make me to drop all my goods, that, that—'

'"Make me drop", Victor, not "make me to drop",' said Cockie snidely.

'Ohhh!' He gave up, just clenching his fists and glaring at her.

Cockie glared back, then turned on her heel to make a grand exit. Grand wasn't quite the word that sprang to mind as, in seeming slow motion, she slipped in some egg yolk dripping down from the trolley, flung out a hand for balance, swept four jars of SunPat Extra Crunchy off the shelf and slammed to the ground, nose coming perilously close to the guacamole mess on the floor.

There was a short moment of pure, stunned silence as Victor stared down at Cockie, and Cockie gaped at the floor. Then she looked up and caught his look. Cockie's nostrils flared with the effort, Victor's lips tightened, but it was no good. At the same moment they both grinned at each other helplessly.

'Here.' Victor proffered a hand down to Cockie, his hair falling across his forehead as he did so. 'Let me give you a hand up.'

Cockie found herself gazing into the impossibly emerald depths of his eyes and suddenly couldn't find it within herself to ridicule either them or his offer. 'Thanks,' she stammered, holding out her hand, and for a moment actually believing that she needed helping up. Once up, he didn't let go, but drew her closer, conspiratorially, 'Why don't we just leave this stuff and make a run for it?'

Cockie grinned. 'Good thinking, maestro, but let's not run – I learnt from a professional that it's much less suspicious just to walk away from the scene of a crime.'

Victor looked at her quizzically, as they strolled nonchalantly down the aisle. 'Nice friends you must have, Cockie – that is your name, isn't it?'

Cockie was suddenly reminded that they hardly knew each other and gently pulled her hand away from his. 'Yes, that's right.'

In a minute, they were outside the store.

'Look,' said Victor, turning to face her, 'let us start again with each other. Victor Landis, and I am delighted to meet you properly.' He stuck out his hand.

Cockie actually blushed. Even at the time she could hardly believe it, but blush she did. 'Cockie Milton,' she replied, narrowly avoiding demureness, 'and the pleasure is all mine,' just managing to inject some more Cockie-like irony. Then she clapped a hand to her forehead, and swore. 'Oh, bugger it!'

Victor looked alarmed. 'What is it?'

'Doughnuts,' she told him. Alarmed changed to non-plussed. 'I forgot – the whole point of me coming to Sainsbury's was to buy some doughnuts, and I forgot to get them. Dammit, it's too late now.'

'Well,' said Victor decisively, 'since my shopping is now an impromptu omelette in there, and you did not get your doughnuts – why did you have a trolley for doughnuts only? – why don't you let me take you out to dinner?'

Then, before she could answer, he looked at his watch and cursed. 'Forget that – I'm sorry, I have to be back at work for a conference call at 9.30.'

'Oh,' said Cockie, at a loss.

'But what about dinner tomorrow night instead?' he offered briskly, obviously in a hurry to be off.

'Will there be doughnuts?' teased Cockie, desperate to regain the initiative.

'Absolutely. Doughnuts for all. Will you be working at the City Gallery tomorrow morning?'

Cockie nodded.

'Well, I will call you there and we'll set it up. Shall I walk you to your car?'

'No, no,' she assured him, 'I'll be fine.' She was damned if she was going to let him see the way she'd parked the Mini diagonally in the space, in her hurry to get into the store.

'Until tomorrow then.' He leant forward gracefully, picked up her hand, then turned away.

Cockie was too immediately bemused by a wave of that lemon-tinged aftershave to react immediately to the fact that he had kissed her hand. Kissed her hand? She stared at it in disbelief, and then after him. What – or who – was happening to her?

7

Eva felt old. Like an elderly, indulgent parent, she was watching her children paddle around their own little stormy tea-cups. She herself was feeling remarkably secure: having told Mike last night that she definitely wasn't ready to move in with him. But look at her housemates! Floundering, both of them. Eva tuned herself back into the conversation.

'So what time did you get back from Soho House?' Cockie had another munch of toast.

'God knows,' groaned Ben, 'feels like about five minutes ago.'

'Poor Benny-boy – she's wearing you out like a pair of old socks!' teased Cockie.

Ben opened his mouth to retort when the door opened and in came Annalisa.

'Be-en,' she pouted, 'I thought you said you were going to bring me breakfast in bed?'

Eva and Cockie exchanged startled glances. Ben? Breakfast in bed?

'Right away, Annalisa – I hadn't forgotten,' replied Ben, hardly able to peel his eyes away from this thoroughly tousled sex-bomb that by some miracle had condescended to be half-covered by his humble sheet.

'Oh well, I'm up now, I might as well join your cosy little threesome – morning, you two.'

Annalisa swept into the kitchen and sat on the table

with her feet in Ben's lap, back roundly turned to Eva and Cockie on the other side. Cockie was very tempted to laugh at the helpless expression on Ben's face; it looked like he was conscious of Annalisa's rudeness but, like a wasp caught in honey, couldn't do anything about it. At that moment, she heard the soft 'whump' as the post fell through the letter box. Ben obviously heard it too and seized the opportunity to extricate himself from Annalisa.

'I'll get the post,' he said, standing up.

When he came back, he sat at the head of the table and dished out their letters.

'Look,' he laughed, holding up an expensive looking white envelope, 'here's a stiffy addressed to "Lord Ben Hyde and his gorgeous sounding housemates" – who can it be from?' He ripped it open and whistled. 'Cor lumme, get the sparklers out, my lovelies – you shall go to the ball – Red Lester's having a carnival party, down at Slake.'

'Red Lester? You mean, the rock star, Red Lester?' breathed Annalisa.

'Yup, Ben did his gardens for him,' Cockie informed her, 'but Ben, how come we're all invited?'

'God knows, except that I probably talked about you when I was down there the other day, also, from the look of the invite, it looks massive – carriages at dawn and all that guff – but not only that – we've been asked to bring partners as well.' He grinned at Eva and Cockie. 'Parteeee!'

'Let's have a look at that,' demanded Annalisa and took the invite from him. '"Lord Ben",' she said slowly, reading it off, 'you never told me that you were a Lord.'

''S really not important, Annalisa, I never use it,' said Ben uncomfortably.

'Well, you obviously do in your business, otherwise Red Lester wouldn't know, would he?' Annalisa pointed out logically. 'So what does that make you, the son of an Earl? Son of a Duke?'

'Something like that,' agreed Ben. Eva came to his rescue.

'By the way, Cockie, what were you wittering on about when I came downstairs? Something about the Perfect Man?'

Cockie responded to the save-Ben lifeline. 'No, I just had the strangest encounter last night.' And she told them about meeting Victor. 'And then the Mini broke down on the way back from Sainsbury's and while I was waiting for the AA, I decided that I've just got to concentrate on the book and that I haven't got time to involve myself with a man who is too gorgeous by half and who will certainly break my heart – again. So then I decided I wouldn't go on this date.'

'But it sounds to me like this guy *is* the book, and that this is all perfect material,' teased Eva.

'And if he's so gorgeous, how could you resist him?' asked Ben a little helplessly, gazing over at Annalisa.

'Well, I'm not so sure I can now, because I ended up having sex with him all night.'

'What?!' Even Annalisa was gripped now.

'Well, only in my dreams,' – the others laughed out loud – 'but you don't understand – not only were they the dirtiest dreams I've had in ages – and they kept coming, all night – so did I but that's not important right now – but the point is that in each one, Victor was trying to persuade *me* to go to bed with *him*. God, I felt so powerful!' she finished, grinning naughtily at her housemates, while Annalisa just gaped at her.

'That,' gasped Ben, 'is classic. Cockie, you just have to go out to dinner with this bloke – let's face it, the signs are good!'

'Yeah, just fuck his brains out and then he won't have the strength left to break your heart!' hooted

Eva. 'I'm almost jealous – can you leave some for me?!'

'Well, Cockie, if you ask me,' said Annalisa more cautiously, 'if you think that this guy is out of your league, then maybe it is a good idea not to get involved with him at all and then—'

But that decided Cockie. 'No, you're right, I should go for it – what the hell, right? As Gus used to say, ubique carpe omnes et omnia.'

'Seize everything, anything, anybody,' said Ben in response to the puzzled looks all round, 'or something like that.'

Suddenly Cockie stood up and walked over to the calendar. 'Oh God, I nearly forgot – how could I?'

All at once her voice was anguished and then as quickly she took hold of herself, and went on calmly, 'Er, Ben, Eva – look I'm sorry to spring this on you but could you – it's the anniversary of Mum and Dad this Saturday so could you, you know, make yourselves scarce? I'm sorry that it's such short notice and that it ruins your weekend—'

'Cockie, shut up,' said Ben gently. 'Of course we'll go – I was going to take Annalisa to Kew on Saturday anyway.' He ignored Annalisa's surprised face.

'And Mike and I were going to spend the weekend at his place so it's no problem for me either,' added Eva quickly, 'it's a kind of "let's take the pressure off" weekend after all the heavy duty chats last night.'

'Thanks, guys.' Cockie put her plates into the sink and stared out of the window for a moment. Outside, everyone's back garden was coming out of the shade, geraniums glowing as neighbourhood cats wended their careless way. For once she could hear the cheerful chirrup of birdsong over the usual grind of traffic through Pimlico. It was the sort of day that celebrated life in a heartless way, the brightness allowing no gloom.

'Okey-dokey.' She turned round, face carefully transformed into a careless smile. 'Let's hitch up the wagons – Eva, are you going to catch the bus with me?'

When they'd left, Annalisa pulled a face at Ben. 'Whatever was Cockie going on about? If it's her Mum and Dad's wedding anniversary, why does she have to chuck you out – and what's this about going to Kew – I don't want to go round a mouldy old garden.'

'Belt up, Annalisa,' said Ben, standing up to clear the remaining bits and pieces off the table.

'Well, I just think it's a teensy-weensy bit selfish, that's all.'

'Annalisa!' She jumped in shock, as Ben's hand slammed down on the table. 'Cockie is the least selfish person I know – if you must know, this Saturday is not her parents' wedding anniversary – her parents are dead! This is the anniversary of the car crash that killed her father outright and her mother six months later. Within eighteen months, she lost her favourite brother to adult meningitis and then her parents – can you even imagine what demons she must be carrying inside her?'

He stared at her, breathing fast. 'No, I don't think you can. I don't think I can, for that matter. But as far as I can see, she only allows herself any self-pity just one lousy day a year and this year that's on Saturday. So just leave it.' Annalisa quailed under his glare, then he turned his back on her to do the washing-up.

'Ben, I'm sorry,' she stammered, while shooting a considering look at his back, 'I wasn't to know – how was I to know?' She paused, 'I mean, Cockie's usually ever such a happy person, you know,' – silly, attention-grabbing cow more like, she thought inwardly – 'you'd never guess that she had such a deep side to her.'

'No, you're right, she's very good at burying it,' said Ben grudgingly.

'Ben?' Annalisa's voice had thickened. 'Will you forgive me for being a nasty cow?' If he wasn't so cute it wouldn't be worth grovelling so much, she thought, thinking of his eyes that could widen into hypnotic pools of the palest silvery grey, fringed by the most surprisingly long dark eyelashes. She threw in a little sob for good measure.

Ben turned around to see one perfect tear sliding down Annalisa's peerless cheek and, against his better judgement, found himself weakening. 'Look, forget it, my sweet, it's no big deal,' and he turned back to the sink.

When no more sympathy looked like coming, Annalisa tried another tack. 'Well, you could always let me make it up to you,' she purred.

'What?' asked Ben absently.

Annalisa's voice behind him was like liquid silk. 'Well, how do you feel like another breakfast?'

'No, I haven't really got time, thanks all the same,' said Ben, turning round. He gaped, closed his eyes for a second, then looked again. No, he wasn't hallucinating. Suddenly, his sheet had become a tablecloth and laid out on top was truly a feast for the eyes, an utterly naked Annalisa.

'Would milord like today's special?' asked the vision demurely, raising herself up onto her elbows.

Any doubts about her character were swamped by a chorus of hormones, screaming 'Yes! Yes!', any thoughts about all the things he had to do that morning drowned out by the drums of approaching rumpy-pump. With a gleam in his eye, and not even bothering to wipe the suds off his hands, Ben stepped forward.

'Well,' he said drily, stroking soapy hands up her legs, 'they do say that Fairy is gentle on dishes – and my oh my, are you a dish!'

The setting sun seemed to bathe Cockie's attic room

in a warm, rosy light, turning the slovenly mess into romantic disorder. Downstairs, Ben put on that Romeo and Juliet overture that she loved so much; through the skylight drifted the improbably sweet fragrance of the next door neighbour's honeysuckle. It was truly a night for romance. And here she was, getting ready for her First Date with Mr Romance without the smallest clue what to wear. Cockie sighed heavily. Then her eye alighted on her one pair of feminine shoes, your bonafide slappy stringbacks, as Rowena always called them. How about going for the feminine angle for once? She did yet another ransack and let out a yelp of triumph.

Ten minutes later a most unlikely-looking Cockie tripped downstairs. If life had been fair, Ben would have whistled when he saw her, would have walked round her, saying admiringly, his eyes eating her up, 'Wow, you look fantastic. Any man would be proud to have such a beauty on his arm. Where did you get that slinky black Empire line dress!'

But life was not fair, and Ben would probably think that an Empire line was something to do with the Maginot defence system, thought Cockie, as she had to kick him into opening his eyes from his trance position between the two speakers on the floor.

'Ben! Ben!' she yelled. 'What are—' she shook her head and stepped over his prone body to turn the stereo down. 'That's more like it. What are you doing tonight? Re-enacting Lust's Young Dream with Annalisa?'

'Nah. Snooker night with the boys.'

'Great. Do you feel like giving me a lift to Tante Claire down Royal Hospital Road – it's sort of on your way.'

'Tante Claire, huh? No wonder you're all dressed up: you've got somewhere to go. Very posh, I must say.'

'Do you think so?' Cockie preened, twirling slightly.

'Yeah, fifty quid a head if you're lucky. He's definitely out to impress – obviously wants to sleep with you on the first date.' He neatly avoided a left hook from Cockie. 'OK, let's go, love-priestess, your chariot awaits.'

In the van, Cockie suddenly got the jitters. Why did everyone assume that she was just going to bonk this guy straight off? Eva this morning; Emma at the gallery had, in a rare moment of pithiness when she'd put Victor's call through to Cockie, called her a thieving tart; and now Ben. Drew, when she'd rung him to crow, had immediately offered to bring round condoms. Even in her dreams, her subconscious – foul-minded traitor that it was – had set the ball rolling, and had cast her firmly into femme fatale mode. And this get-up – was it really romantic with its gossamer lines . . . or was it just a dressed-up invitation to undress?

'Ben,' she said, losing her nerve, 'can we go back, please? I've forgotten something.'

'You're kidding,' groaned Ben. 'You complete dipstick.' But he obediently did a U-turn in the Belgrave Road.

'Won't be a sec,' promised Cockie, darting out of the van. Sure enough, a blink later and she came running back out of the house.

'We came all the way back just so that you could change?' scorned Ben, as she got in.

'Uh-huh.'

'Well, don't mind me, Lady Penelope, I'm just the chauffeur . . . but why? Before, you looked almost seductive; now you'd better hope that he has a schoolgirl fixation.'

'Fuck off, Ben,' trilled Cockie, 'I feel more comfortable like this, so lay off.'

Good, she thought, even Ben noticed the difference. She glanced in the side mirror. Now that she'd added the fashionably shrunken white T-shirt, she'd gone from lady of the vamp to trendy waif, shoestring straps now snaking over white cotton, not just the hills and valleys of her flesh. Maybe not right for Tante Claire but right for her.

Finally they were there.

'Would milady like to be collected later?' said Ben, tipping an imaginary cap.

'Actually, yes. Yes please.' That would fit in with her plan not to be a sure thing, thought Cockie.

'Cockie, I was kidding! Make your own way home, you lazy tart!' leered Ben.

Cockie took refuge in her new found calmness. 'Well, that lost you your tip. Good night Ben, pot your balls well.'

Ben, marvelling at this new unleavened Cockie – when did she not rise when being teased? – watched her go. He had to admit that she looked good, even with the added T-shirt. Surprisingly sexy, he thought . . . and very tall, as he watched her dwarf the doorman. Cockie never wears heels, he grumbled to himself – who is this guy?

Half an hour later, Cockie was thinking much the same thing. If she had been nervous on the way to the restaurant she was now a Molotov cocktail of embarrassment and fury . . . where the hell was he? Her napkin, starting life as a triumphant fan, was now compacted into a small ball of damp anxiety. She had memorised the wine list, decided which waiter she would sleep with, and was now dreaming up a scene in the Mills and Boon where Luca was castrated by wild boars. Where the hell was he?

'Miss Milton?'

Oh God, it was the maitre d' – here to tell her that Victor wasn't coming. She nodded miserably.

'A courier just delivered this for you.'

He handed her a small package, wrapped in white tissue paper and topped with a green cellophane bow. She thanked him and opened it. Inside was a short typewritten Silverman Bone compliments slip . . . and two doughnuts. 'Victor says that he is so sorry but he is stuck in a meeting and is going to be late. In the meantime he hopes that these will ease your hunger and maybe delay your departure.'

Goddammit, now she was floundering – how could she remain cross when she was so flattered? Just as she was deciding whether to eat them or keep one as a souvenir – could you press a doughnut into a photo album? – she was tapped on the shoulder. She lifted her head and felt her stomach do a gravitational overload. There he was, six foot many inches of otherworldly magnificence, repentance reeking out of him. Late he may be, but he was far too delicious to be in the wrong. She must have been early.

'Cockie,' he started in a low voice that rang all her bells, 'do you hate me? I wouldn't blame you if you just wanted to walk straight out of here.' He took both of her hands in his and sat down opposite her.

'No, no, no,' Cockie assured him, heart flopping like a dying fish, inwardly cursing herself for appearing so eager. She tried to pull herself together. 'I need to spend a bit of time with you so that I can get a good likeness on the wax doll that I'm going to stick pins into later tonight.'

'Oh well,' he laughed, 'make sure you get my best profile then. Now, what are you drinking? White wine? Well, I think the very littlest I could do is to get us some champagne – I wonder, do they have Laurent Perrier here?'

'Yes, they do – No. 26, I believe. Er, good short-term memory,' she explained in response to his startled look. 'But I'd have thought you came here all the time.'

Victor gave the order to the waiter and turned back, again taking her hands in his, 'No, this is the first time. I wanted my first time to be romantic, so I have waited.'

Green eyes bored into hers as he waited for her to reply. What could she possibly say? If Sam had ever said such things to her, she would have laughed it off, would have pulled her hands away in embarrassment, with the cynical part of her not believing a word of it.

Up close, he looked tired, the filmstar perfection of his looks smudged into a heartbreaking vulnerable beauty. Cockie couldn't believe that all she wanted to do was smooth away the faint etchings on his forehead, Tipp-Ex out the blue shadows under his eyes, press her lips to the sharp edge of his cheekbones. Out of her head went words like hard-nosed, trenchant, cynical and forthright and in romped fluffy bunnies bearing placards saying things like compliant, starry-eyed, soft-centred, love at first sight. Was she possessed? What could she possibly say?

'What is your accent?'

The god of inanity smiled a satisfied smile.

Victor laughed, perfect teeth stretching out a white flag of amusement. 'What a crazy girl you are! And I thought I had no accent!'

'Well, only really when you're angry,' reasoned Cockie more level-headedly.

'My father is Swiss and my mother Turkish, but I've lived all over Europe and we generally spoke English at home, and I was educated here and in the States—'

'Oh, thank God you don't sound American!'

He looked at her enquiringly. 'You English are so often rude about Americans – I myself found them to be—'

'No, no! Don't get me wrong, some of my very best friends are—' No! She wasn't going to fall into that trap! 'But my sister-in-law is American and she's enough to put anyone off 250 million people at one fell swoop.' Wasn't there some sort of rule about not being bitchy on your first date? Shit. 'Look, don't mind me – just keep the exotic accent!'

'For you, madame, anything. Doughnuts, accents, whatever you want. Ah, here's the champagne,' he held up his glass. 'Here's to my stunning dinner partner.'

'Oh, is someone else joining us then?' joked Cockie weakly.

'No, she's right here.' Another emerald probe. 'We had a rocky start but I'm glad that we finally made it to here. Here's to rocky starts!'

'Ain't no mountain high enough,' stumbled Cockie, holding up her own glass. Violins started up in her head. This was it, she was lost. She had no idea how it was that this Playgirl centrefold was gazing adoringly into her eyes (she herself could only ever seem to gaze into someone's *eye*) but she wasn't about to complain. For a few minutes someone up there had obviously taken a shine to her and to cavil would, after all, be churlish.

Three hours later, Cockie knew what was happening to her. She had been drugged into a romantic novel. Maybe this wasn't actually happening at all – this was just the great god, Mills, and his consort, Boon, giving her some handy tips for writing up the Perfect First Date. Well, it was working: the judges were holding up 5.9 score cards across the board; Victor was flawless.

Together they had gambolled up a staircase of mutually overlapping anecdotes, until they were both exhilarated by the tit for tat of tales. Neither waiters nor their surroundings had broken the strange circle of intimacy around them; more champagne had appeared as if by magic, with Victor just seeming to rub the old bottle, even the table seemed to have shrunk, bringing them closer together over the ambrosial food that Cockie enjoyed more from the way it looked as it went into Victor's mouth than from the taste of her own. She had listened spellbound as he told her tales of derring-do and screwing-there in the international banking world of Silverman Bone, although she would have failed the short written test for attention to detail, so glittering were the depths of his eyes, so lean and tender his hands over hers, so mesmeric the changing planes and angles of his face.

Cockie knew that she was no longer breathing the same air she had woken up to that morning; she had been flown first class into a high place where the air was a heady cocktail of champagne and pure oxygen which kissed every pink tingling inch of her skin. Where she thought and acted like a romantic heroine, where she could see reflections of her eyes in the stars surrounding her. A small part of her brain produced a sickbag at this point but the rest of her was clamouring for more. She had hardly noticed when they left the restaurant to walk along the Embankment; had hardly drawn breath as they talked on and walked on.

London at night was some parts shimmering black, some parts light and white, Cockie mused tipsily, a black tie city – occasionally dazzling with jewels, able to pass muster at the most demanding of gatherings but, like any garment always worn on occasions of the highest excess, slightly trashed all over. And here she was, with the man of her dreams, also slightly trashed.

'London!' said the man of her dreams.

Cockie jumped – could he read her mind as well? 'You remind me of London,' he went on, 'you have an attraction unlinked to elegance—'

'Hey!' bridled Cockie.

'No, no, but you see, like London, your energy and all the different, contrasting parts of you make your own very individual beauty—'

'Carry on, I like this part.'

'—as well as a distinctive style. Don't, whatever you do, let anyone change that style – the way you dress – so smart, and yet so informal—'

Score! thought Cockie.

'—the ideas you have, the way you express yourself so strongly, your attitude to life and career – it's so wonderful, so you! The first time I saw you in the Gallery, I noticed you – in the corner, acting so strangely – and I said to myself – this girl I want to know.'

During all this delicious nonsense, Cockie's mind had spun away a little, into a delectable vision of Victor and her attending the ballet, him in white tie, her in big jewels and biker boots, but this last comment brought her back to earth.

'Rubbish!' she denied stoutly. 'You were flirting your socks off with Emma.'

'But I noticed you,' he said sternly. 'If I flirted with Emma at all it was a polite response to her, but I noticed you. And I could tell that you noticed me.'

'Hey, whatever you say,' said Cockie, thrown. 'But from what Emma says, she definitely had her dibs on—'

'Cockie, sometimes you talk too much,' said Victor, 'I was getting all ready to do this,' and suddenly Cockie found herself being kissed very hard, 'until you reminded me that this is the first date, so I really should not do that, should I?'

'No, no,' said Cockie, pulling his head very firmly back to hers, 'let's not be a stickler for the rules.'

'Eva! Eva! Eva!' yodelled Cockie, as Eva opened the door, swearing her to eternal hell for waking her up. She grabbed Eva by the waist and span her round in the narrow confines of the hall, 'What a night! What a fandabidosi glorioso megatuf top top top night!'

'Oh Jesus, I don't suppose this can wait till breakfast? No, I didn't think so,' said Eva as Cockie opened her mouth even wider. 'Let's go into the kitchen.'

'OK,' she said when they were both nursing cups of tea, 'what happened? In less than one minute.'

As Eva had hoped, Cockie rose to the challenge.

'OK, OK, oh, where to start? OK, went to Tante Claire – great food, very square – he was late and I was thinking about cutting off his gonads but there was a cute waiter and he was so sweet, he sent doughnuts by courier and we drank champagne by the lorryload but the weird thing is I didn't get pissed the whole night – it was as if I had my fairy godmother with me to avert any crisis – I hardly said anything embarrassing all night and he loved all of my stories and it was like we really connected which is so ridiculous when you think about it—'

'Why?'

'Well, he's so fucking gorgeous he makes my eyes hurt. And he's really successful at old Silverbum's. And seeeeriously rich, from the sound of it. Anyway, where was I? Then we both had Kümmel – bit of an in-joke – and then we went for a walk—'

'Ah-ha! Here we cut to the action!' leered Eva.

'No, but it was so romantic, like the spell was still holding – we held hands, for God's sake. He's got such nice hands, Eva.'

Eva pulled a distinctly anti-schmaltz face.

'No! You'd go to town on them, talking of which – he compared me to London,' – Cockie ignored Eva's questioning look – 'and then he said that I was talking too much which was kind of corny but worth it for what happened next!'

'Yes?'

'He kissed me!' There was a short pause.

'And?' prompted Eva.

'And it was so lovely,' sighed Cockie, 'I kept forgetting to close my eyes because I just wanted to remind myself that I was swopping juices with the ultimate hunk.'

'Nicely put,' said Eva drily, 'and then?'

'Well, I was just wondering how I was going to have the strength not to invite him home—'

'What?'

'My new vow of celibacy. Well, not to be a sure thing, anyway – when he suddenly looked at his watch and said that it was time we went home. So I just thought that he'd assumed that we were going together and sort of gave in without a struggle—'

'You don't say.' Eva rolled her eyes.

'Then he hailed a taxi and gave my address and a tenner to the cabdriver, then he kissed me really tenderly and said that he couldn't wait to see me again, put me in the cab and waved goodbye. I was gobsmacked!'

'So am I,' said Eva. 'You mean to say that I've sat here all this time, at nearly three o'clock in the morning and nothing more than a quick snog happened?'

'But it was so romantic – he didn't just assume that sex was on the agenda; it was like a real date, you know, in the good old days. I felt so – so courted. Flattered, really.'

'You know, I had thought that writing this bloody Mills and Boon would at least keep your hopeless notions on the written page but truth seems to be slushier than fiction so I give up. Mind you,' Eva added, getting up to pin an imaginary medal on Cockie's chest, 'congratulations on finding the last saint in London. Are you sure that after plunging to the depths of Sam, the giddy heights of this perfect gentleman might not prove a bit much? As for this vow of celibacy, dare I even ask?'

'Eva?' said Cockie dreamily, having not listened to a word she had said, 'Do you believe in love at first sight?'

It was quiet in the little mews house as the shadows lengthened into a heat-hazed afternoon. The photograph was nothing more than a blurred snapshot, with the dated clothes and hairstyles of a decade before. A seated, middle-aged man and a woman, her face turned to someone off camera, were dwarfed by a young man behind them, who leant over them towards the camera, clasping their shoulders affectionately and laughing unselfconsciously into the photographer's lens. She wasn't even quite sure why she always turned to this photograph above all others. Perhaps it was because this was how she remembered her brother and parents. Gus – a vibrant and dominant spirit of merriment, her parents blurred and faded in her own memory. Her eyes filled with tears as she battled to bring her gentle, academic father into the front of her recollection, but she couldn't. His loving, amiable presence in her life was cast into the shade by the sharper image of her mother. Not her mother as she had been during Cockie's childhood – busy, brisk and sometimes intimidating but also exciting and thrilling. No, Cockie could only ever see her mother as she had been in those last few months between the crash and her death, as her fading kidneys etched their lethal lines on her face. It was not a pretty picture and not one that Cockie allowed herself to visualise often. Her fingers clutched convulsively at the photograph. It was getting dark now, nearly time for her to bring her vigil to a close. Too many hours and she found it difficult to turn off the memories, too few and she felt cheated of her annual chance to mourn. This year, she'd been better than some years, distracted even.

'OK, Mum, Dad, Gus,' she whispered, tears blurring the now shadowy lines of the photograph, 'time to go. From now on, I promise, it's back to happy-go-lucky Cockie and no more grief.' She wiped her eyes and took a deep breath. 'Until next year.'

PART TWO

This time I swear I am not going to lose control. As the fog of fear rises to blur my mind, I grit my teeth, curse at myself to breathe deep, keep my eyes open, fix them on a point of reference in my room. It does no good, of course; by this time, I should know better than to try.

They say that drowning can be quite pleasant if you give yourself up to it; you can be lulled by the criblike waves, heartbeat slowing to the lullaby rhythm of the undertow, salty blood cooling to merge imperceptibly with the chill of the salty water. But if you struggle, as I always do during the panic attacks, you choke and thrash, capillaries popping behind your eyes. So it goes this time, but when I come out the other side, this time I am angry – just as exhausted but also bloody furious. Why this time? Why this night? Why this month – a month after the anniversary – a month with no significance, and, usually, a month with no nightmares?

Of course, sitting at your bedside for all those months taught me that nothing is ever quite as it seems. When I hated you for being alive but prayed that you wouldn't die; when I resented you for keeping me from living my life, but fought so viciously when you tried to send me away; when I thought I understood you, but you confounded me with every breath from your battered body; when your slow slippage away leeched every impulse of life and joy from me, yet within weeks of burying you I was dancing on your grave. There seems to be no rationale for how any of us act, or how we should act.

I hate you still for only being a mother to me when you hardly had the strength to be alive, but most of all, I hate you for not following through, for not being a mother to me now so that I could come to you and say, why?

This is one of the times when I really need an explanation. Why do I feel like I'm living out my own Mills and Boon, where my written story only mirrors the unreality in my own life? Why do I feel a tight kernel of loneliness even when I am with the man of anyone's dreams? What do I want if it's not him? Why are you not here to help me? Why are none of you here?

8

'More poppadoms?' asked the waiter resignedly. 'Are you ready to order now?'

The five girls looked blank, then looked hurriedly at their menus.

'Just two minutes, please,' said Rowena, 'promise. And yes, lots more poppadoms.'

'But do you realise,' said Mel, going back to their conversation, 'this is the first time since we've all known each other that we've all had boyfriends at the same time – doesn't that qualify for some kind of toast?'

'What? Celebrate the fact that we're all mugs?' grimaced TJ. 'Anyhow, I don't have a boyfriend. Jules and I, we're just,' she put her hands up to simulate speech marks, 'seeing each other, taking it one day at a time—'

'Practising coitus non-committus,' laughed Rowena.

'Yeah, and every other bloody fancy way of saying that I'm just a stupid dag he can rely on for a lay every time he comes round,' said TJ. 'Mind you, we have great sex so it's fair dinkum.'

'I remember sex,' said Cockie thoughtfully, 'that's what I used to think about all the time before I met Victor.'

'What?!' chorused everyone, except Eva who was kept regularly updated.

'Cockie! You and Victor have, according to you, been behaving like Romeo and Juliet without the family feuds for a whole month and you're telling me that you haven't been to bed with him?' demanded Mel, checking Cockie's pulse.

'Right choice of words there, I'm afraid. Forget getting to that deliciously sticky juncture where you can either part your legs and hurl yourself down the primrose path of pleasure, or you can keep your knickers on, look soulfully into their eyes, say no, no, no, I'm not that sort of girl and then give them a blowjob.'

The hovering waiter, unnoticed by them, thought that all his Christmases had come at once.

'I haven't even been to *bed* with Victor – as in, in his bed. I haven't even been to his flat – not that I think he'd know where it was, because he seems to spend all the time he's not with me at that bloody office – and do you know the worst thing?'

The others shook their heads, agog.

'It's only when I'm not with him that I think this lack of sex is weird: when I'm with him, the violins are always playing super loud, and we're too busy cooing romantic things to each other to think about anything so base as bodily juices. We've practically snogged each other's faces off but nothing more, not even a fumble. Now that is weird, but it's like whenever I'm with him there's some kind of spell on me that makes me completely forget about sex.'

There was a stunned silence.

'And all this from the girl who, only a few short weeks ago, swore herself to celibacy,' said Eva drily. 'Quite a table turner that, being denied sex instead of denying yourself. Shucks.'

'Well, maybe it's love,' said Rowena. 'It does happen, you know!' as everyone turned on her with catcalls. 'It doesn't have to depend on a multiple orgasm and him bringing you a cup of Earl Grey afterwards.'

'Helps though,' TJ snorted, 'especially the Earl Grey.'

'Oh, come on,' cried Mel, 'when was the last time

any of us had a multiple orgasm, let alone the cup of tea?!'

This time, the whole restaurant listened in.

'What is a multiple orgasm?' choked Cockie.

'Come to that—'

'As it were!'

'—what's an orgasm?' finished Mel.

'I tell you though,' said Cockie, when they'd recovered slightly, 'we ought to take notes. I've never heard anyone faking it as well as Annalisa.'

'Annalisa – Ben's girlfriend?' asked Rowena.

Cockie, Eva and TJ pulled faces.

'Not so much girlfriend as sextoy,' dismissed Cockie, 'but this girl has watched *When Harry Met Sally* and then worked on her own routine, I tell you. We're talking yodel country here – screaming, shouting, moaning, whimpering – the whole shebang.'

'Oh arf, arf,' deadpanned Eva.

'And my poor Benito probably doesn't suspect a thing,' said Mel. 'Nor does Hugh. Aren't men innocent little lambs? Can't you just see them out on a lads' night like this, trying to outboast each other. "Yeah, it was the most unbelievable sex ever, we're talking female ejaculation . . ." I mean, yeah, right.'

Cockie and Rowena glanced at each other. Mel was clearly even drunker than they were.

'I mean,' Mel ploughed on, 'do you think men ever wonder about sex from a woman's point of view with each other or is it just one big brag with them? Look at blowjobs!'

'Not my usual vantage point!' said Eva.

Mel laughed. 'No seriously, do you think they ever even mention the gag word?'

At the next door table, an old buffer, dining alone, quietly put his knife and fork together and waved for his bill.

'Gag?' TJ joined in the fray. 'Tell me about it: they should just try breathing when they've got a rolling pin flattening their tonsils!'

'Rolling pin? Now who's bragging?!' Cockie managed.

'Breathing?' retorted Mel, ignoring her. 'Who cares if you can't breathe? The only thing he's worried about is if you're doing all the fancy business, the Mr Whippy licking and so on – I mean, don't you just hate it when it gets to the point when he's practically holding you by your ears – as if you're going to fall off otherwise and your ears are the rudders – left a bit, right a bit.'

Rowena was now chewing her napkin.

'Yeah, and how do you stop him doing all that . . . bucking?' TJ gasped.

'Stop. Please. Stop,' groaned Cockie. 'Oh Jesus, my stomach muscles. Please. No more. I'm too young to die.'

At last the waiter could get a word in edgeways and they ordered.

'But doesn't this all just come back to my theory that we always want what we don't have,' started Cockie.

'Oh God, this old chestnut,' groaned Rowena.

'Just let me finish,' Cockie said with a hint of steel. 'We always want what we don't have, but once we get it we don't want it – right?' She looked around and everyone nodded.

'And?' said TJ.

'So, although I wanted Sam, if I'm completely honest, I craved the devotion and attention that Sam couldn't – or wouldn't, bastard – give me. But now that I get that from Victor I find myself questioning it. It's like we want gentlemen who don't push for sex but as soon as we meet someone who does think with something more than his dick we doubt them and ourselves, ask ourselves why they aren't ripping our clothes off – "what's wrong with me, aren't I sexy enough" and all that.'

'So you're saying that deep down we all want bastards?' asked Eva, trying to clear her way through the rhetoric.

'Well, that's easy enough,' said TJ, 'all men are bastards.'

'But the point is,' Cockie said excitedly, lightbulbs coming on all round her head, 'that we can only appreciate that we want bastards when we've had the perfect man and got bored of him. We think that the eternal hunt is for those rare good and sensitive men but, having found them, they are just the catalyst to send us happily back to the bastards.'

'So the good men are the means to the end, who are the bastards,' puzzled Mel. 'So where are all of us in this equation?'

'Well,' said TJ, 'Ro is married so she's out of the game—'

Rowena rolled her eyes.

'—and you and Hugh seem to have been going out since the dawn of time. I'm definitely nowhere near finding the nice guy in the first place. Eva? Is Mike a bastard or a boring gent?'

Eva smiled. 'Mike is my perfect partner – and I've been shafted by enough bastards to know. And he's kind and sensitive – who else would have been so understanding about my refusal to live with him? I mean, we're happier than ever at the moment. So I reckon that blows a hole in your theory, Cockie. Perhaps you'll have to rethink.'

'Oh, that's OK, I never thought it out in the first place,' laughed Cockie, 'I just made it up as I went along. Just for a bit of a laugh, really. You must have realised that. I mean, for all my talk, I'm just as nuts about Victor, and he could very well turn out to be a bigger bastard than Sam ever dreamed of, so that blows a hole in my theory for starters!'

'Milton, you are so full of crap,' said TJ, chewing into her balti chicken.

'No, I'm not,' said Cockie, getting indignant despite herself, 'just think of it as a defence policy. Imagine every scenario and then you won't get any unpleasant surprises.'

'Surprises don't have to be unpleasant.'

'In my life, they invariably are,' said Cockie without thinking.

'Oh,' said Eva, nonplussed. 'Yes. Well. Anyway . . . surely you can never think of every scenario?'

'Wanna bet?' challenged Cockie.

'C'mon guys,' said Rowena, 'can we at least change the record from men? Do you realise that whenever we have a girls' night out, whichever way we turn, we always come back to talking about men.'

'Can you just imagine how big-headed they would be if they knew that even when we're not with them, we can't stop talking about them,' giggled Mel.

'If you heard what we were saying about men, and you were a man, would you be flattered?' asked Eva bluntly. 'Insulted, embarrassed, maybe. Big-headed, I think not.'

'Fuck,' intoned Ben solemnly. 'What to do? What a to do. What am I going to do? Fucked if I do, not fucked if I don't.'

He looked up. 'What do you think, Fern? Do you think I should turn my back on a sure thing; regular sex, great bird on my arm, intellectually undemanding company, and return to my former peaceful, if monastic, existence? No? Barmy? You're right, why over-analyse every situation? Just go with the flow, as the actress said to the Bishop.'

'Ben, I think you're meant to whisper sweet nothings to plants, not tell them bad jokes. I don't know – you're as bad as Cockie – you with your plants, her with her dogs – what do the two of you have against human interaction?

Look, Cockie and I are off to the flicks; do you want to come?'

'Thanks, but I think I'll give it a miss.'

Eva looked hard at Ben, prone on the floor of the small greenhouse, with his head invisible inside a mass of greenery. 'Are you sure? You sound a bit down. Do you want to talk about it?'

'Wow,' said Ben, propping himself up on his elbows so he could raise a derisive eyebrow in full sight. 'Even for you that was pretty good. What, do you want me to be the guinea pig for some new counselling course? Some La-La Land psychobabble crap designed to make the counsellor feel better and who cares about the counsellee? Thank you, but no. Caring I may be, but sharing's not my bag.'

'Right, well, fuck you too, you pompous arsehole!' Eva's own ready temper flared up to match his. 'Forgive me, your lordship, for interrupting what is obviously a far more efficient communication than you could ever have with a person. Reserve me a yucca for the next time I'm depressed.' And she slammed out of the greenhouse, window panes shuddering as she left.

Ben sighed and sank back down amongst the plants. Down here in this verdant world, his sense of sight swamped by the scents and rustling sounds of his beloved plantlife, was where he thought best. He regretted his dismissive outburst, half-wishing that he was able to talk about his problems in the effortless way that Cockie and Eva could, but they were girls; that ability came with the territory. He could no more imagine his close friends advising him about his lovelife than he could imagine going for a pint with his plants. Each had their function, and that was just the way it was.

'Heigh-ho,' he said out loud. 'Time to grovel.'

He stood up and left the greenhouse. Going into the kitchen, he surprised Eva with a bearhug from behind.

'Sorry, sorry, sorry. A hundred lines for Ben, "I must not take the piss out of Eva's beliefs, I must not take the piss".' Yes, he was a past master at grovelling.

Eva wriggled out of his grasp but smiled reluctantly. 'You call this an apology?'

Ben swept a deep bow. 'I lay my humble self prostrate so that you may trample all over it to your heart's content.'

'Sounds good to me.'

'So, Ben, are you coming to the movies?' asked Cockie, who'd just come in.

'Yeah, what the hell. Let's go.'

'Bright lights, big bucks and no parking in the West End, or easy parking and cheapo cosiness at the Clapham Picture House?' Eva picked up the paper.

The doorbell rang.

'I'll get it,' Cockie stood up.

'Wait, I'm sort of expecting Toby to send over a selection of cuttings from the nursery – I'll come with you.'

Before Ben opened the door, Cockie, out of habit, glanced out of the window beside it. What she saw there was enough to make her grab Ben and pull him to the window. There stood a vision. Cockie's incredulous gaze travelled up from the low-heeled navy courtshoes, over the well-pressed navy bermuda shorts, widened a little at the upturned collar of the navy blue and white striped shirt, her eyes closing altogether for a second at the discreet string of pearls hanging round the outside of the collar. Top it all off with the inevitable velvet navy Alice band, smoothed over bobbed blonde hair and the pearl studs nestling in delicate pink lobes, and the picture was complete.

'OK, so who sent me the Sloanagram?' murmured Ben to Cockie, as he turned back towards the door just as the doorbell rang again. He opened it.

'Hello?'

'Hello,' stated the girl firmly. 'I'm terribly sorry to bother you, but does Eva Tonkin possibly still live here?'

'Eva? Er, yes, she does,' Ben said slowly, thinking that this couldn't possibly be a friend of Eva's, must be someone from Peter Jones.

'Oh, marvellous, I've tracked her down. How do you do,' she stuck out her hand, 'I'm Eva's sister, Laura Tonkin.'

Eva's sister. Ben, and Cockie behind him, goggled.

'Ben Hyde.' Ben said weakly.

'Cockie Milton,' came a choking voice from behind him.

'Er . . . is Eva in? Should I perhaps come back later?'

'Who was it at the door? Why are you both just standing there? C'mon, guys, let's vamoose.' Eva came bustling into the hall. Ben and Cockie stood aside wordlessly, allowing her past them. Eva froze when she saw the girl in the street outside.

'Laura!'

Ben looked at Cockie. Time to withdraw from a touching family reunion.

'Laura!' Eva said again, hardly able to believe her eyes. 'What the fuck are you doing here?'

'And then it was absolutely classic – there were Ben and I thinking that this was so sweet, long-lost sisters falling into each other's arms – not a bit of it, Eva just turned on her heel, slammed the door in the poor girl's face and stormed back into the house. So then there was another ring on the bell – and Laura's voice through the letter box telling Eva that this was so unnecessary, couldn't they let bygones be bygones and Eva chanting mantras in the kitchen and Ben and I caught in the crossfire, both with a bad case of the nervous giggles, not knowing what the hell to do.'

'Did you know that there were any bygones?' asked Drew, brown eyes sparkling.

'Bygones? We didn't even know that Eva had a sister! She's kept very stumm about her whole family background – I knew that she left home straight after school but she would never tell me why and after a while I never thought to ask. It didn't seem like it was a big deal, funnily enough.'

'So now what?'

'Well, after a while, Ben thought this was ridiculous so he let Laura in and told Eva that they had to talk this out.'

'Oooh, Ben showing his strong and masterful side – that I would have liked to see!' camped Drew.

'Yes, it was quite a revelation,' agreed Cockie. 'Anyway, we never did find out what the huge drama was but Eva eventually calmed down and asked Laura what she wanted. Well, little sis turns out not to be backward in coming forward and asks Eva if she can stay with her for a few days while she starts her new job and looks for a place to live. Eva didn't exactly have much choice in the matter – she could hardly chuck her own sister out, could she? – so now we have the girl living with us! Blast from the past to houseguest in one easy movement.'

'So it's all sorted out?' said an almost disappointed Drew.

'No! Not at all!' cried Cockie, drawing the attention of most of the surrounding Fortnum and Mason tea crowd. 'What I want to know is – what is this big family mystery? And how come Eva's sister is a deadringer for Princess Di with a cutglass accent like you wouldn't believe?'

Drew moved the teapot out of the flightpath of Cockie's expansive gestures.

'So?'

'God, you can be dense sometimes, oh husband mine. You *know* Eva – ee bah gum comes much higher in her vocabulary than OK-yah – and the amount of grief she's given me for being so complacently middle-class would turn anyone capitalist – and suddenly it transpires that she comes from the perfect two-Volvo family herself—'

'Hang on a sec,' interrupted Drew, 'did you just say "husband"? Does this mean you've agreed to the scam?'

Cockie shrugged. 'You know me, I can't resist any opportunity to rip people off – that's what annoys me so much about Eva; she's always the one that's purer than the driven, honesty in everything, being in touch with yourself and all that crap – what –?' Suddenly she was enveloped in an enormous hug, scones flying as Drew lunged at her.

'You treasure! You honey!'

'Drew! Easy, tiger!' Laughing, Cockie pushed him away. 'Anyone would think I've just accepted a proposal of marriage.' They grinned, complicitously. 'Well, if you're determined to change the subject from Eva, how about a few ground rules?'

'Uh-oh, I smell trouble.'

'Well, if I'm going to do it, we have to be completely confident about this foolproof plan – I want to know everything about everyone involved – total low-down on their background – I mean, who are you going to know at this wedding?'

'Well, there's my esteemed employer, obviously, and her nephew, Julian, and the blushing bride, Flavia, who, as you know, thinks that I'm an old, old friend. Oh, and a couple of nip'n'tuck friends from the Hellhag's coven. That should be about it.'

'What about her husband? Won't he be there?'

'Er, yes. Yes, obviously he'll be there. Yes.'

'And what's he like? What does he do – something in the City, you said.'

'Oh, he's OK – yes, he's a big noise at some American bank.' Drew looked at his watch. 'Look, I'm going to have to get back to the site now, check that the builders haven't screwed up.'

'Great idea,' said Cockie. 'I'll come too. I'd love to see this hotel I'm laying my life on the line for. It's just round the corner, isn't it?'

Drew stared at her. 'Have you lost your mind? What if the Hellhag turns up? You – I – we're not ready to be married in public yet!'

'We'll wing it,' said Cockie blithely, 'and she's hardly likely to turn up at,' she looked at her watch, 'six o'clock at night – isn't she a lady who cocktails?'

'Oh God,' said Drew.

As they came up the street towards the hotel, Drew looked at Cockie and stopped. 'Well, you don't exactly look like a nice Scots girl called Caroline, that's for sure, more like a Salome.'

'What do you mean?' Cockie looked down at herself, and laughed. 'Oh, I see – the veiled look – what do you think?' She twirled round – all the gauzy layers of loose cream silk trousers, sea-green silk shirt, cream waistcoat and deeper green silk scarf wafting obligingly up around her.

'Yes, it's a good look – makes you almost fragile – still stately, but fragile at the same time. You know, I really do like the new hair – blonde always made you look a wee bit . . . obvious.'

'Oh, the art of the backhanded compliment,' growled Cockie, 'for that I may just have to do the Dance of the'– she plucked at her clothes – 'well, Four Veils – in front of all your builders.'

'Too late; they'll have gone home – and believe me, I'm immune!' laughed Drew as they went in.

'You see, the idea is,' said Drew as they stood in what he laughingly assured her was going to be a bedroom suite, 'that we almost halve the number of rooms, making twelve enormous rooms, hence all the building work. Individuality! Familiarity! A home from home but with knobs on!' Drew's fists punched the air with each phrase.

'After all, living up to our prospective clients' homes is quite a task. Each room will be completely different from the next: this one, for instance, is streetside, with lots of light so this will be the Egyptian Room – papyrus colours, all white, cream, and beige – but the plasterwork's a bit dodgy so we'll have pleated walls and a tented ceiling, bamboo furniture with this incredible boat-like bed I found in Chester, of all places, and Egyptian bits and pieces.'

'Isn't bamboo out now?' asked Cockie, trying to sound clever.

'Who cares?' crowed Drew. 'This isn't about fashion – this is about each room making a totally unashamed statement – "I'm the best! I am so comfortable, so in tune with your needs, that you are never going to want to leave!"'

He pulled a speechless Cockie into the corridor, and up the stairs, punching open each door they passed, with a rapid-fire commentary.

'This one: Galerie des Glaces takeoff: loads of mirrors, white and gold panelled walls, fake Louis XIV furniture, gauzy curtains, very filmstarry – this one, very much a laird's room – heavy mahogany furniture, rugs on the floor, shaded candlestick lamps, dark dark blue and gold fleur-de-lis curtains with a fantastically OTT pelmet, and loads of military gold braid – all very plush, a bit of a mishmash, but very severe, clean lines.' He sprinted up to the next floor and paused for a moment. 'No, let's go straight up to the penthouse pièce de résistance.'

On he raced, Cockie puffing in his wake, wondering if she was meant to be showing a more active reaction to this onslaught. Suddenly Drew froze, nearly braining her as he stuck his hand back for silence.

'Wha—?' began Cockie, but stopped, mainly because the offending hand was now clamped firmly over her mouth. She glared at Drew over the gag and tried to bite it. Drew rolled his eyes and pointed upwards with his free hand. Then she heard the tinkling of laughter. She pushed his hand away. 'Hellhag?' she mouthed.

Drew nodded. Suddenly the voices grew louder and they shrank back against the wall.

'But Nikki, darling, this trompe l'oeil room will be just the cutest!' came an American drawl.

'Oh yah, absolutely, and I should think you'll have the most super fun doing it up,' added a voice that was vintage Kensington.

More silvery laughter and the chink of glasses. 'Here, I knew the builders hid some whisky somewhere up here. Yes, it's mine, all mine,' tinkled a voice that was, Cockie couldn't help noticing, pure Surrey, 'and Jonathan's paying for the whole thing, may he rot in his silly office for ever!'

Drew and Cockie raised eyebrows at each other, then slowly turned to go back down the stairs.

'But, sweetie, you must have a decorator?' said the American.

They froze at this, unable to resist listening. 'Oh yes, ever such a darling little man called Drew Fraser.'

'Never heard of him,' dismissed La Kensington. 'Why ever didn't you say, my pet? I'm sure I could have persuaded David, that's David Hicks, to take on your little project.'

'Thank you, dahling,' said Nikki more stiffly, 'but I am very happy with Drew. He may be new but he's frightfully talented and ever so nice.'

Drew pulled a Mr Universe pose. Cockie tried very hard not to giggle.

'Anyway, I wanted a new name so that I could launch him as my own discovery and be able to boss him around.

I mean, what other designer would let the owner have all her own ideas for the décor? Dearest Drew knows that I am the artistic inspiration and that he is really just carrying out my orders.'

The other two laughed. Cockie restrained Drew from going upstairs to beat her up. 'How clever you are, Nicolette,' came the saccharine tones of the American, 'and what a sap this pet decorator of yours must be.'

Cockie clung to Drew.

'Oh no,' said the Hellhag, 'he's lovely – the sweetest Scottish lilt and' – she lowered her voice, so despite themselves, Cockie and Drew leant forward to hear what came next – 'such a hunky body. I can hardly keep my hands off him.'

Drew buried his face in Cockie's neck.

'You mean . . . ?' breathed the other two in unison.

'Exactly!' she trilled. 'He's not queer! Happily married, sadly, but not a poofter. I can't tell you how relieved I was when I found out.'

'How thrillingly unusual,' said the Kensington voice speculatively. 'That alone will get the gossips through the door to have a look. Have you met the wife?'

'Oh no!' said Nikki hastily, 'she's probably some ghastly Glaswegian housewife with an unintelligible accent. Now look, drink up – I do so want to show you the basement where I'm trying to persuade darling Marco to open another restaurant.'

Cockie tugged at Drew's flexed arm and pointed downstairs urgently. They crept downstairs, letting themselves out quietly onto the street.

Drew was silent as they walked up to Piccadilly. 'What a cow, what a worthless, scraggy bag'o'bones,' he said under his breath. '"Yes, I just adore having him to boss around."' He stopped suddenly and grasped Cockie's upper arms. 'I tell you one thing, Coquelicot Milton, you and I are going to knock their stinking socks off at this wedding. I am personally going to design your outfit and hang the cost. We'll show them!'

Cockie gulped nervously.

9

'It just seems a shame that you have to move out so soon after coming here,' said Mike as he watched Laura pore over the *Evening Standard* classifieds. 'You appear out of the blue and disappear again almost as quickly, before I even have a chance to get to know you. What's the deal?'

Laura glanced up, stroking one recalcitrant frond of blonde back under her velvet Alice band, one hand twitching her peach cotton skirt back over her knees.

'Goodness, how melodramatic you sound, Mike! Anyone would think that there was something frightfully cloak-and-dagger about me coming up to London – some secret bad blood between Eva and me.'

'Well, she's hardly brought out the fatted calf for you, has she?' mused Mike. 'Not that I mean to sound disloyal,' he added hastily, 'but it seems—' he tailed off.

Laura looked at him closely for the first time. She smiled. 'It's all terribly simple, I'm afraid. Chalk and cheese, that's Eva and me, always have been. Especially nowadays. I'm far too staid and boring to compete with her . . . image. So it's not really a marvellous idea to inflict my company on her too long – all I want to do is keep the peace.'

She paused. 'Eva really hasn't told you much about me, has she?'

'Laura, I didn't even know Eva had a sister!' exclaimed

Mike, completely forgetting that he had been sworn to secrecy about this. 'I don't know the first thing about your family.'

'But I thought you and Eva were so close?' puzzled Laura, looking concerned. 'I'm sorry, I didn't mean to pry,' she added.

'Don't worry,' said Mike heavily, 'I thought we were close too. Close enough to live together even.' He stared off into space.

'Really? When?'

'No. She refused,' said Mike absently, then snapped to. 'I mean, we both agreed that it wasn't a great idea for where we are in our relationship right now.'

'That sounds like counsellor Eva at her best,' laughed Laura, 'but what do *you* think?'

Mike suddenly realised how personal the conversation was getting. He couldn't believe how easy Laura was to talk to.

'I'm sorry, I'm nosing again,' she grimaced. 'I am awful. Tell you what, would you help me sort out the wheat from the chaff in these flat adverts? My head is spinning from all the jargon.'

'Yes, sure,' smiled Mike.

When Eva came in from work five minutes later, she saw Mike leaning over Laura, one hand on her shoulder, as they scrutinised the classifieds together.

'What the—' she started furiously, then stopped as a pair of candid blue eyes, so like her own, gazed up innocently at her.

'Hello, halfpint,' said Mike, scooping her into his arms. 'Mmm, I just love the feel of that PJ polyester slithering over your body!'

'Hard day on the shopfloor, sis?' smiled Laura. 'Poor you, you look fagged out. Mike and I have just been mooching about together, so let us pamper you.'

Eva clutched on to Mike convulsively. 'Don't worry,'

she said stiffly, 'I'm fine. How's the flat-hunting going, Laura?'

Looking up at Mike, she saw that the mood ring on her thumb had changed colour completely.

Cockie sneaked a look at the perfect profile beside her, noble brow pursed in concentration, strong-fingered hands looped around the spokes of the steering wheel and resisted the urge to pinch herself. Which lamp had she rubbed to get herself this prize? Even in the depths of her most wishful fantasies she hadn't pictured herself in this situation: riding shotgun in this leather-reeking sex-mobile, all smooth knobs and indecent roars, snarling as it flung her round corners to the strains of REM on the CD player. With her belly-button slamming into her spine and the scent of burning rubber still lingering in her nostrils, she was beginning to realise that this wasn't just the Perfect Man's Perfect Accessory. This was pure testosterone.

Just then they came out onto a stretch of straight road and, on cue, back came the hand, first to the gearbox to slap them up into fifth gear, then settling itself again on her right thigh. Cockie instantly raised her leg slightly, so that the hand couldn't feel the spread of thigh on leather and sighed slightly. The muscles in her leg were already killing her from that earlier stretch of the A3 – keeping up with perfection was proving to be tiring.

'A penny for your thoughts, beautiful?' There was an emerald flash as he glanced over at her, and his hand tightened its grip.

'Ten quid and it's a deal,' quipped Cockie, still reeling from the 'beautiful'.

'Sorry?'

'Oh. Nothing. I wasn't really thinking about anything – just about how I love this car.'

'She's gorgeous, isn't she? The transmission is so smooth, the—'

Cockie smiled. Thank God Ben wasn't here – normally she would have rolled her eyes at the personalisation of a machine and he would have busted her for sure for making Victor's gaffe an exception. She tuned back in.

'—so even on the iciest roads, you don't have to think about cadence braking! But you have seen nothing yet – the cars at this rally will all be beautiful, stunning, masterpieces.' Victor grinned heartstoppingly at Cockie and, with one sure movement, he lifted his hand off her thigh, picked up her right hand and brought it to his mouth. He kissed it. 'Just like you.' He kissed it again.

Cockie had that Barbara Cartland feeling yet again, the butterflies in her stomach flying up to join in a celestial beating of wings. She watched her hand creep round to stroke his chiselled jawline, and wondered at herself.

'Mmmm,' he crooned, 'that feels good.'

Get a grip, Cockie told herself, unable to quip back at all and about to dissolve into the cowhide. She gently removed her hand and cast about desperately – how could she feel like this towards a man who spouted such garbage at her? How could he possibly be sincere?

She pouted into the side mirror to see if she'd had a Schiffer makeover without being told. No, just as she thought, all was quiet on the transformation front, just her attempt at a fetching Björk-like imitation hairstyle tumbling less than attractively over her forehead. It was the only note of reality in this increasingly spellbound situation. It's probably the Mills and Boon's fault, she thought. Only a mind steeped in romantic tosh could be falling for such baloney. Still, this whole trip was great material – dynamic hero sweeps easily impressed moll off to glamorous classic car rally, for equally classic displays of wealth and machismo combined. Perfect.

* * *

Ben Hyde, aspiring landscaping guru, had had enough. His peaceful working Sunday in his supposed bachelor pad had steadily been shattered by a stream of female racket – first Cockie on her way to her car rally, then Eva shouting at Mike, and now someone had seen fit to turn on some godawful Sunday afternoon musical at full volume on the kitchen telly. Ben Hyde, leisure consultant, had a better idea. Maybe it wasn't too late to catch up with Lenny and the others in the pub.

On his way out, Ben went into the kitchen to fetch his wallet, but stopped short as he stepped in.

'Annalisa! What are you doing here?'

Annalisa smiled and turned down the volume on the TV; she'd known that *Showboat* would flush him out. 'That girl, Laura, let me in but said that you weren't to be disturbed – she's bossy, isn't she? – so I thought I'd wait in here. Any longer, and I was going to come and seduce you away from your boring old work. So, do I get a kiss?' She draped herself against him, lips plumped and waiting.

Ben was amazed how little he was pleased to see Annalisa, how resistant he was to the now familiar wave of sexuality pumping out from her luscious body.

'Actually, I was just off to catch the lads at the pub,' he dropped a dutiful kiss on her lips, eyes focusing on the clock behind her, 'and I'm already late. But maybe I'll see you later.' He moved away from her to pick up his wallet. Without even thinking about it he had left off the usual question mark.

Congratulating himself on building up to a safe exit, Ben could hardly believe his eyes when an unabashed Annalisa just looked at him through narrowed catlike eyes, while unwinding a deep red silk scarf from around her neck, and said as slowly as if talking to a simpleton, 'You won't see me later, you'll see me now except that you won't see me, because I'm going to take you upstairs and I'm going to blindfold you with this scarf . . . and then I can guarantee that you won't be worrying about being late for your mates in the stu-pid, bor-ing pub.' She stepped forward and, putting the scarf around his hips, pulled him into her own swaying pelvis.

Ben the sex-blinded walking groin couldn't help but get a hard-on. Ben the newly cured head couldn't help but laugh. This did not go down well.

'Well, fuck you, Mister Snooty Git,' Annalisa erupted.

'Oh, calm down, I'm just not in the mood and I really am late.'

This was clearly too much. 'I come all the way down here, wait while you finish drawing your shitty little trees, and now you're sending me home?'

'Now, look—'

'Well, that isn't how you treat a girlfriend – you just take me for granted and it's not bleeding good enough!'

Ben felt a familiar noose tightening around his neck – Miss Independent Sex Chick was showing her true colours, trawling out the age-old guilt patter – why did women always change the goalposts? Now he would never get to the pub.

'Annalisa, Annalisa,' he said soothingly, but got no further as she suddenly changed tack.

'And what's this?' She plucked a piece of paper from the table top and shoved it towards him.

Bemused, Ben looked at it. 'It's a telephone bill, Annalisa.' She'd definitely lost her marbles.

'No, you fucking moron,' she hissed, 'what's this?' She stabbed at the top of the page, where there was a note in his handwriting.

Ben read out slowly, '"Cockie, my own sweet darling love – any chance of a few groats going BT's way?"' He looked at Annalisa. 'So?'

'"Cockie, my own sweet darling love"? Oh, you make

me so sick. I just knew that you two had something going!'

Ben tried to hold on to his departing temper. 'Sarcasm. Have you heard of sarcasm, Annalisa?'

'You can be as condescending as you like, you git, but you know and I know that you're in love with Miss Stupid Flower Name—'

'Oh for fuck's sake—'

'All that crap about you feeling sorry for her because her parents died and how she's such a tortured soul – it's all a con, isn't it, Ben? Unless she's got you sucked in so bad that you don't even realise that all you—'

'Right, that's—'

'Sucked you in, Ben! She sucked you in!' Annalisa capered tauntingly in front of him. 'She's about as emotionally wounded as a steamroller – the way she galumphs around, thinking that she's so great, so funny – but you fell for the Little Orphan Annie routine, didn't you, Ben? What a mug! She just has to be the centre of attention, that's all. What a cosy little set-up this is – I can be your girlfriend, but Cockie's way ahead of me . . . she can be your fragile flower for you to protect!'

Ben saw red. 'Shut. Up.' He grabbed her by the upper arms and shook hard. 'Just shut the fuck up, you twisted little bitch. I don't have to explain myself to you – you're not my girlfriend – we're just screwing each other. You have no idea about me or Cockie. You're so shallow yourself, you're so see-through, you can't even imagine anyone else existing on different levels.'

'Oh, Ben the psychiatrist now?' taunted Annalisa. 'Ooh, I'm impressed. Put me on your couch, big boy, and show me the error of my ways – no, no, if you show me your "different levels", I'll show you mine – how about that? So how many levels does your precious Cockie have? What happens after total show-off, big-headed, and did I mention, badly dressed?'

Even as she spoke, Annalisa knew that she had gone too far and she hated herself for losing her usual cool. 'I'm going to go now before I say things that I'm going to regret – you'll have to crawl back to me, your Lordship, if you want to see me again.'

Ben was also trying to regain his poise. 'Things you regret? Me crawl to you? Christ! Oh, just get out, Annalisa.' She glared at him. 'You're boring me,' he added cruelly.

Annalisa got up to go but wasn't going to let him have the last word. 'You're a pompous arsehole and a fake, Ben. As for me . . . really, my sweet, I don't give a shit.' She blew him a kiss and sauntered out, red silk billowing behind her.

Ben stared after her and laughed weakly. Eva appeared in the doorway as she said this, narrowing her eyes at Annalisa's scarf. 'What was all that about?'

'I think I'm meant to feel like Scarlett O'Hara,' said Ben faintly.

'What?'

'"Frankly, my dear, I don't give a damn!" has just been updated to—'

'Oh! I heard that – what a terrible parting line!'

They looked at each other and had to laugh.

'I assume that was a *parting* parting line,' probed Eva, 'it sounded like a kind of terminal ding-dong.'

'Yup, 'fraid so. I think the silly cow got it into her head that Cockie and I are having some wild affair.'

'You're kidding? All that was the green-eyed monster? About you and Cockie? Ha! She really was stupid, wasn't she?'

'Yes, criminally inane, I'm afraid.' Ben felt a stab of guilt that Annalisa was so quickly relegated into the past tense.

'Just wait till we tell Cockie about this – she'll do her nut!' giggled Eva.

'No, don't tell Cockie!' Ben's tone was sharp.

'Why not?' demanded Eva, her interest piqued.

'Oh, she never liked Annalisa anyway and she'll just get impossibly conceited thinking that she had a role in our break-up. Anyway, what were you and Mike arguing about earlier?'

'Oh, nothing much. Just a tiff,' said Eva, suddenly thoughtful.

Maybe this wasn't such good material, after all, thought Cockie. This car rally was not living up to her romantic expectations. She was bored, bored, bored. Victor and his cronies were practically making love to the car Victor had come to see, an AC Ace 1961, apparently, crawling over it, stroking it as reverently and as passionately as Cockie wished Victor would stroke her. Granted, it was a sporty little number with its wide-mouthed tree frog face and toothpaste tube lines but she couldn't see the big difference between it and the multitude of other sports cars revving throatily around her.

She'd even mugged up on it by looking it up in a classic car magazine and had her little patter off by heart – the trouble was that no-one was showing the remotest interest in giving her a chance to show it off. She'd watched a couple of races but she didn't really get it – the cars weren't going that fast, and she couldn't seem to get a viewpoint that showed her a decent part of the track. She also felt the alienation of being one amongst a crowd of enthusiasts. Altogether she wasn't particularly wide-eyed and bushy-tailed to be seen as Victor's groupie.

'Hey, Victor!' she called, as Victor crouched down to take a look under the damn car. 'Don't forget to check on the straightness of the parallel tube chassis. And look out for a probable crack in the body at the lower leading edge of the rear wings – although this is usually caused merely by normal chassis flexing.' That'll show him, she thought.

Sure enough, Victor came striding over, leaving the other guys gaping at Cockie's spiel. He pulled her towards him and said admiringly, 'You are the most surprising woman, Ms Milton, you almost take my breath away.'

For a brief delirious moment, Cockie really did feel like a Modesty Blaise character – a breathless ingénue, draped against the muscular frame of her hero. Just complete the fantasy with a kiss, she prayed silently, closing her eyes like the best of romantic heroines. Again he came up to scratch, dipping his lips briefly to hers before patting her gently and moving away.

'There. Now you will probably get very bored if you stay around here because the guys and I are giving the AC the toothcomb treatment so why don't you go to get yourself a cup of tea? They usually serve them in the flying school over there.' He tapped her on the bum. 'And thanks for the chassis tip; even though I had already checked it, it is good to know that you are keeping up.'

There had to be a downside to being a glamorous moll, thought Cockie resignedly. After generations of careful breeding and a peerless education, she had evolved into something that was patted and tweaked like a piece of dough. How far had she come.

When she'd got her cup of tea, she wandered outside the flying school. Ever since they'd arrived, she had vaguely noticed the buzzing overhead but, too busy trying to get her head round the ground-based vehicles, she had not paid much attention. Now, as she sat back, face turned up to the sun, she saw, through her eyelids, a noisy shadow cross the sun. Curious, she opened her eyes and squinted upwards. Now that looked like fun, she decided, watching what seemed like a tiny craft flickering and skittering around the skies – there was an apparent lack of control that appealed to her.

Her parents would never let her come and watch Gus fly, their view being that with an audience he would show off to the point of lunacy and beyond. As an awe-inspired teenager, however, she had listened to him telling tales of aeronautic derring-do to various breathless girlfriends or backslapping mates. Now she could see for herself what it was actually all about. If only she could have a go at it herself, she mused, as the bi-plane she had been watching came in to land, bouncing fraily from one wheel to the other on the green swathe that was the runway.

She looked behind her to where Victor was still getting his rocks off on his car, and a scheme occurred to her. It would be fun and there was nothing wrong with a little one-upmanship. What the hell, it was worth a try. She got up and walked a little hesitantly over to the petrol pumps where the candy-striped little plane had finally come to a halt. Then, as she watched the lanky frame of the pilot unfold himself from the rear cockpit, resolve tightened its mischievous grip on her dithering and propelled her towards him. Stifling an urge to call him Biggles, she ignored the ridiculous leather helmet and goggles and launched herself into it.

'Er, I'm sorry to bother you, but I wondered if it was at all possible to – well, I noticed that you had an extra, well, a passenger, cockpit, and I've always wanted to – but you've just finished, you won't want . . .' she tailed off, feeling quite hopeless.

Underneath the goggles, his lips widened into a smile. 'Yes, of course I'll take you up; any excuse to show off my new plane.'

Within seconds of the plane being filled up again, Cockie was being bundled into the front cockpit without so much as a demurring peep from her faceless pilot, her head enveloped in an identical leather condom, torso wrapped round by a rough, crumpled tweed coat he had extracted from a tiny locker behind his own seat. Lowering herself into what seemed more like a hole than a cockpit, she tried not to impale herself on the joystick or to step on the various spokes and wires that she was assured were vital for him to control the plane.

'Do you need some help?'

Cockie suddenly felt his hand plunge between her legs. Not wishing to appear uncool, she yelped nonetheless.

'Don't panic, I'm just doing you up – you see, all the straps clip onto this one spoke here in the middle, here, here, here. There, all done.'

'Er, right, yes, I see.'

Busy pulling her stomach in, trying to get her boobs out of the way and generally trying to retain her composure, Cockie started to babble nervously.

'You know, my whole life at the moment seems to consist of people asking me whether I need help. It's the first question any stranger ever asks me – I mean, a girl could get paranoid. Do they know something I don't? Perhaps I do need help? I mean, I know you were only, well, you know what I mean.' Oh shut up, you idiot, she berated herself.

'Don't worry about it,' he said calmly, 'flying often makes people nervous. You'll love it when we're up there.'

Now Cockie really began to feel chicken. What was she doing sticking her head out of a canvas-covered loo roll, with only two puny slices of wood, silk and wires meant to keep them up, all piloted by a faceless stranger she'd just picked up in full view of Victor? She must be completely hatstand. Or else he was. Why had he needed so little persuasion to take her for a spin? Any normal person would have balked at her undeniably brazen approach. Oh God. Serial murderers had been known to have stranger modus operandi than dropping their victims out from an open plane at 10,000 feet. Where the fuck was her parachute?

Now fully in the right frame of mind for her debut flight, Cockie was thrown into panic by her kidnapper's loud yell from behind, 'Clear ahead!' then a staccato burst as he powered up the propeller. But suddenly through the earphones clamped over her ears came a calm, compelling and oddly familiar voice.

'Right, can you hear me? Just check that your mouth-piece works.'

'Er, yes I can hear you. What would you like me to say?' asked Cockie, hearing a stranger's voice say the same words into her ears. 'Cor, it's weird hearing your own voice like this, innit?' Full marks for sophistication with that comment, she thought disgustedly.

'You'll get used to it soon; anyway, you've got a nice voice. I'll just be setting up our flight details with the control tower while we taxi over to the start of the runway, so we'll be out of touch while we do that, OK?'

Cockie nodded then said hastily, 'Yes, OK. Wilco. Whatever.' Oh, God, she was babbling again.

Finally they were in place at the start of the runway. Cockie had now resigned herself to her fate and was almost enjoying herself trying to work out who the voice in her earphones reminded her of. Even when the engines rose to a roar and they started trundling forwards with some purpose, Cockie was too busy flipping through a mental filofax of men in her past to panic. Then the staticky chat between pilot and tower stopped as they really gathered pace and Cockie realised that they were trying, and as far as she could see, failing, to take off. Eventually, when they were close enough to the racing track for Cockie to see the whites of the cars' markings as they skibbled past, they lurched unevenly off the ground, then down again, then, reluctantly, agonisingly, they were up, over the telephone wires, engines screaming, climbing up to the sun.

'We'll just gain some height,' said the intimate voice in her ear, 'then what would you like to do? Fly around on a little tour to get your bearings, then do some aerobatics?'

'Yes! Both! Everything!' shouted Cockie wildly. 'This is unbelievable, I'm not scared – but I mean, not at all – this is just wicked!'

'OK, OK, calm down!' There was crackly laughter through the headphones. 'I knew you wouldn't be scared. Just stick with me, kid, let's ride these skies!'

For the next few minutes, Cockie was in a roaring cradle of sensation, dipping over Goodwood Racecourse with its cake wedge racestand poised over the downward sweep of the valley, squinting briefly down at the sinuous grey curves of the tiny racetrack below before they were flying up the coast, inlets green and soggy after the retreating tide, everything two-dimensional and so orderly from this sanitising distance. Despite the roar of the wind, the screech of the engines and the crackle of static in her ears, Cockie felt silently suspended between the blue-washed calm above and the colour-by-numbers landscape below. At the whim of her unknown pilot, she nonetheless felt all-powerful, able to embrace as far as the eye could see inside her circled finger and thumb.

'Magical, isn't it?' said his voice, quietly threading into her head, reading her thoughts. 'Makes you feel invincible on a day like this, with heaven and earth an eye's blink apart. Mind you, they always are, people just seem to make the gap bigger with their noise and posturing. Up here you can hear the silence of this waiting place.'

'Who *are* you?' Cockie asked curiously, but her question was drowned out by static. She tried to turn around in her seat to look at him, but her straps were too tight.

'Aerobatics now? Ready to go upside down?' he called over the hissing. Cockie gave him a thumbs-up.

The joystick between Cockie's legs came back, and before she could really do anything except book some space in her mouth for her heart, the world had tilted over her head, the sky becoming a distant patchwork of green and brown, nothing but a blue bowl beneath

– or above – her feet. She didn't even want to think about what her stomach was doing but as they reached the zenith of the flipover, Cockie could feel only giant invisible hands pulling down her cheeks so that wedges of face hung off her jaw then shot up to her forehead to join the veins pounding there. It took Cockie a few milliseconds of yapping excitedly into her microphone to realise that they were now upside down and that she was dangling, separated from a plunging death only by a few measly leather straps. That flush of fear swamped all other sensations from her mind, leaving her hanging in a humming bubble, one thought revolving in her head.

Her hands, still resting in her lap because of some strange G-force, plucked gently at the clip holding all the straps together. She was so close to being able to resolve everything. It would be so easy: one turn and she could be free; she was one step away from an unimaginable fall that could reunite her with a family that had never left her but were here, waiting for her . . .

'Don't do it,' said a gentle voice as clearly as her own thoughts, 'nothing's that simple.'

The words reverberated in her pounding head. Under the helmet, her scalp prickled with shock. Cockie was electrified.

As the plane taxied to a halt back where they had started, Cockie fumbled quickly with her harness, still confused by her feelings up there. What had she been thinking of? Had she really been about to undo her straps? Did that count as a suicidal impulse? Surely even she couldn't be that much of a drama queen. Pulling off her helmet, goggles and headpiece in a rush of claustrophobia, she felt an invigorating blast of fresh air breeze through her hair.

'What do you think? Was that fun? Do you want a hand?'

'No, no, I'm fine. Thanks.' Cockie stood up and started to clamber out. 'Do I know you?' she asked abruptly.

'I don't know,' he laughed, 'do you?' and he pulled off his helmet.

Cockie stared at him, average smiling face, indeterminate thirtysomething, sandy hair blowing in his eyes – a totally ordinary, totally unfamiliar face. Oh well, so much for the conspiracy theory. She stepped beside him on the wing and jumped down.

'Well, I can't thank you enough,' she grinned up at him, 'that was easily the most fantastic thing I've ever done, it was utterly brilliant, fab, amazing—'

'My pleasure,' he said, and swept her a bow, Cockie's bemused glance following the movement as his hand grazed his shoes. Then she froze. He was wearing DMs. She stared back up at him, remembering Mel's dinner party. That voice and those DMs. It couldn't be. Was it him, the mysterious next door neighbour? As she gaped at him, the breeze blew the hair out of his eyes and, just for a second, they sparkled down at her, before the sun came out behind him, throwing him into silhouette and causing Cockie to squint and look away.

'I, I – Gus?' she stammered. 'Sorry, no – I didn't – yes. Bye. Sorry. Bye.'

'Wait!' he called, jumping off the wing. 'Why do you keep calling me Gus?'

Cockie turned and gaped at him.

'While we were flying upside down, you were babbling into the headset, I thought to me, but you kept talking about Gus and your Mum and Dad.'

'I, I—'

He looked at her carefully. 'You know what you were saying to me before we went up, about needing help?'

She nodded, still unable to speak.

'Well, obviously I don't know anything about what's

going on in your head, but it sounds to me like you're all worked up about this Gus guy. I'm no shrink, but I reckon you just need to get him out of your system. You never know, just relaxing about things might help. Flying's my way of relaxing, perhaps you should find your own way. That way, you won't need help.'

Now he looked embarrassed. 'Sorry, I'm interfering, aren't I? My wife always says it's my worst fault.'

'No! Thanks, thanks for the advice,' stammered Cockie, with just a momentary twinge of disappointment that he was married. 'I'm just sorry I wittered on—'

'Cockie!' She span round to see Victor waving and yelling at her from the fence separating the airfield from the car field. 'Cockie, what the hell are you doing?'

'Don't tell me that's Gus,' commented the pilot drily.

Cockie turned back to him, and smiled. 'No, that's my, er, boyfriend.'

'Now he doesn't exactly look the relaxed type,' he joked, as they watched Victor vault the fence and start to run towards them. 'I'd better clear off – he looks like he's after my blood!'

'I doubt it – homicide might just threaten his career prospects!' Cockie quipped back, hardly able to believe that she was taking the mick out of Victor. Before she stopped to think about it, she reached up and kissed the pilot quickly on the cheek. 'Thanks again for the wise words, I really do appreciate them.'

'No problem. Bye now.' And he strode off.

'Cockie!' Victor's face was a study.

She ran over to him. 'Victor! I've been flying – loop-the-loops, upside down, the whole works – I even flew the plane myself for a few minutes – did you see me waggle my wingtips? Oh, it was fantastic!'

Victor was staring at her. 'Did you know that guy?'

'No, I just sort of launched myself at him and asked him if he'd take me up.'

'Are you totally mad?' He was aghast. 'You put your life into the arms of a complete stranger?'

'Hey, I never complained about your driving, did I?' teased Cockie. 'And I really don't know you that well.'

'Sometimes, I think you are very strange,' he said seriously. 'Anyway, I wanted you to be there when I took the Ace for a spin – that was what we came down here for, no?'

'Oh, so that I could cheer you on prettily from the finishing line?' said Cockie sharply. 'Why didn't you just tell me to wear hotpants and lobotomise myself before we came, maybe then I wouldn't have been so bored.'

'Clearly you are bored,' he retorted, 'if you're prepared to go off with a strange man in some flying toy without even telling me. Who was he, anyway, this pilot of yours?'

'I haven't a clue,' said Cockie quite truthfully.

'You did not even find out his name? But you were kissing him!'

'Oh for God's sake – yes, that's me, love 'em and leave 'em without even being formally introduced – shock horror probe!'

'You are acting like a teenager,' he bit out. 'We are leaving now – unless you want to fly some more with your precious Mister X?' He turned and stalked off.

'Victor?' called Cockie. 'You're not jealous, are you?'

She could hardly believe her luck. If he was, then her strange encounter had certainly done some good . . . maybe Victor really was as keen as he said . . .

10

'Well, my choice of play was simply disastrous. I thought I'd impress him with my intelligence and my street-smartness, so we went to *Oleanna* – you know, that play with David Suchet about political correctness and the woman student crying rape on the male tutor?'

'Yes, I've been meaning to see that for ages. But I wouldn't have thought it was quite sugar daddy seduction material.'

Emma grimaced. 'Well, I didn't realise quite how . . . how strong it would be, or how it left you wondering who was right, you know, it was kind of – oh, what's the word?'

'Ambiguous? Ambivalent?' Cockie suggested.

'Exactly. So when we came out I thought that since Peter was the crusty sort, I'd better take the man's side so I started banging on about the evils of political correctness and how the student was an awful little tart who deserved everything she got. Big mistake. He took completely the opposite view, thought that she was right to do everything she did – I think that the quote was "marvellous actress – jolly pretty too" which should have shut me up – and that David Suchet was a crass pig of the highest order for hitting her. So then I got frightfully cross and started saying how feminism would only ever succeed if we were able to see past such obvious assumptions and realise that sometimes a woman could be big, bad, and in the wrong, rather than always being the helpless little victim – why are you laughing?'

'Oh, I'm sorry, Emma, it's just that it's such an unlikely picture – you up on a bandwagon virtually burning your bra at the table – him cowering in the corner, bleating about damsels in distress – what next? Did you storm out?'

'Oh bugger that,' said Emma gleefully, 'I wasn't going to give him the satisfaction. No, I settled down for the rest of the meal, ordered the most expensive things on the menu, insisted – with a lot of batting eyelids—'

'You don't say,' interrupted Cockie drily.

'—that we had the best champagne in the restaurant, followed by some rather fine Armagnac then got my revenge as the bill arrived and I watched Peter go green at its size, by asking the waiter if the "darling little watercolour" above Peter's head was for sale and if so, would darling Peter like to buy it for me. Darling Peter, of course, couldn't lose face in front of the waiter and duly bought it for yet another fifty quid. Golly, you should have seen his face! Funnily enough,' finished Emma, 'he didn't ask if he could see me again! So that was that.'

'Hey, I'm impressed,' said Cockie, relieved that things were back to normal between her and Emma.

The phone rang and Emma picked up. 'Hello, City Art Gallery – oh, hello, Victor, how are you?' Her face darkened. 'Yes, of course. I'll put you on hold.'

Cockie stood up, cursing Victor's timing.

'Despite ringing you twice already,' said Emma tightly, 'it seems that loverboy still wants to talk to you.' She dropped the receiver into Cockie's hand. 'Don't be too long, I need to check the front till with you before you leave.'

'Hello, Victor? What now? God, you're useless! Yes, Hebden St Mary at five o'clock – yes, yes, I know.' Cockie looked up to see Ben leaning on the door bell. She looked pleadingly at Emma, who got up, with a bad grace, to let him in.

'Look, Victor, I've really got to go – Ben's about to be towed away. No, it's not on the main line, you have to change at Exeter – oh, for Christ's sake, it's not that difficult, surely? No, Ben, no!'

Ben was standing in front of her, hand descending inexorably towards the telephone.

'No, Victor, I wasn't shouting at you, I've just got to go.' She pulled a long-suffering face at Ben and made winding up motions. 'Look, you dumkopf – what? Dumkopf – yes, German – yeah, multi-lingual when it comes to idiots.' Cockie smiled fondly at the phone as Ben made strangling movements. 'Look, why don't you just get to Exeter and we'll pick you up there at 4.30? OK, OK, see you then.' She blushed and hunched closer into the receiver. 'Yeah, me too. Mmmm, till tomorrow. Bye.'

'If you've stopped billing and cooing to your bloody boyfriend, can we go now?' said Ben testily.

'Keep your hair on, sweetie, I'm ready when you are,' said Cockie, grabbing her bag, and following him out to the van.

'Do you realise I've never even met Victor?' said Ben, after a few minutes' driving. 'Why is that? You've been going out with him for quite a few weeks now.'

'Oh, don't you start. It's rare enough that I get to see him, between the Whim and his bloody work schedule, let alone anyone else.' She ticked points off on her fingers. 'He doesn't like to come to the Whim, because he thinks Patrick and Flo are weird and because Fred always takes the piss out of him; he's been away on some roadshow all week—'

'I thought he was a banker?'

'Yeah, a roadshow is apparently when you go round Europe or whatever, selling your rights issue or whatever, to all these different countries – oh, who knows, who cares? Before that, naturally enough, he was too busy preparing for the roadshow to spend,' she drawled, '*quality* time with me. Can you imagine? He'd take me out to dinner, and then go back to the office – even at weekends. Last Sunday, after that car rally he dragged me off to, he didn't even have time to drive me home, just paid for me to get a taxi back from Silverman's—'

'Aaah, how tough for you.'

'Yeah, well, life's too short.' She didn't add that it had been her flying jaunt that had made them so late. 'The trouble is,' she sighed, 'he's so gorgeous and comes on so strong when we are together that I'd forgive him anything when I'm with him. It's strange really, as if I'm under some sort of spell and I only remember to get pissed off when I'm apart from him.' She trailed off and gazed out of the window.

Ben wished that he hadn't asked. A lovesick Cockie was always too much to take.

'Well,' he said briskly, 'I'll meet him tomorrow – I'll see if I can see the magic then.'

'Yes, a rock star's party – orgies and drugs with the glitterati – who knows what will happen?'

'Don't get too excited – when in Devon, Red's more Lord of the Manor than Mick Jagger,' said Ben a little brusquely, 'and I don't think his wife and kids will stand for much in the way of orgies.'

'Spoilsport. Let me keep my fantasies for a little while longer.'

Story of your life, thought Ben sourly, and revved the van in frustration at the Friday afternoon traffic. Cockie didn't notice the change in atmosphere and leant forward to fiddle with the stereo.

'I do love the way you have this crumbly old van with this state of the art CD machine – what have you got in the stack?'

'It's not a crumbly old van,' retorted Ben, 'what? Have we suddenly turned into a car snob now that we're so used to being squired around in a TVR?'

'Idiot!' Cockie teased, 'I much prefer this old heap, if truth be known.' Ben felt an unaccountable glow of pleasure. She sniggered. 'After all, just think what a leap forward my lovelife with Victor could take if he had this van – cushions in the back, and all. Phwoaarr!'

Ben was silent.

Eventually they pulled up outside the Whim. Eva and Mike were there, talking to TJ and a man Cockie didn't recognise. As soon as Eva saw them she kissed TJ on the cheek and headed for the van. TJ waved at Cockie and Ben and pulled the guy down the street after her.

'Hi-de-hi, campers!' trilled Eva, as she and Mike climbed in the back to subside on the cushions. 'Ben, you've got a flipping forest back here!'

'Orange trees – coming-to-stay present for Red's new sunroom.'

'Mmm, they smell gorgeous.'

'Hi there,' said Cockie, 'did you have a nice lunch with TJ? And who was that guy with her – was that the new boyfriend?'

'I think boyfriend's putting it a bit strongly,' said Mike drily, 'he looked kind of terrified to be seen with her.'

'Charming. What's his name?'

'Oh, what was it? Jules, or something nancy like that,' said Eva. 'Mike's right, though, he seemed a bit of a prat to me.'

'I didn't exactly say that.'

'No wonder TJ wouldn't come to Red's party with me,' said Ben, 'I didn't know she'd found herself a boyfriend.'

Cockie looked at him, aghast. 'What a condescending thing to say! You didn't tell me you'd invited TJ?'

'So?'

'So, it's a terrible thing to do – it's completely leading her on!'

'So?'

Cockie was white hot. 'That's so fucking cynical – just because you're not getting your rocks off with Annalisa, you just turn to the next available woman, knowing that, for some ungodly reason, she carries a torch for you and so you're likely to score with her – without having to make any effort!'

Eva tried to break in. 'Speaking of An—'

'You make me sick,' raged Cockie. 'It's just so bloody lazy of you. What happened to your old legion of girlfriends, anyway? You used to have heaps of perfectly amiable bimbos – you could have invited any of them without raising TJ's hopes – what happened to Tiffany, Bugsy and all that crowd?'

Ben never took his eyes off the road. 'Shut the fuck up, Cockie. As we have just established, I have nothing to do with your lovelife, so you can just keep your sticky little beak out of mine—'

'Look, shut up, you pillocks,' interrupted Eva more determinedly, before they crashed. 'Cockie! You'd never believe the gossip from the Whim.'

Cockie glared at Ben, then swivelled in her seat to look back at Eva. 'Yes, what was this big meeting? Patrick rang me at the Gallery and tried to get me along – but Edward was pissed off enough that I wasn't staying later anyway, what with the Silverman's job reaching feverpitch, so I didn't even dare ask.'

'Don't worry, Fred apparently couldn't make it either – but TJ said that it was OK. Anyway, where was I?'

'Patrick telling you about—' prompted Mike.

'Shut up, Mike! You'll give away the punchline, you idiot.'

'Well, pardon me for living.'

'OK, you tell them – you're the public speaker round here.'

'Just get on with it!' cried Ben and Cockie together. They looked at each other and laughed, spat forgotten.

'Well, TJ was saying how the atmosphere at the Whim this week has been really strange.'

'Yes,' said Cockie, 'very tense.'

Mike quietly unpacked a folder from his bag and settled into his cushions to read.

'Well, apparently there's been some major till-pilfering going on and Patrick has been spying on all of you lot to see who it could have been.'

'You're kidding!' exclaimed Ben. 'The sly old dog!'

'With Flo's help, of course,' added Eva. 'Isn't it quicker to turn left here, Ben?'

'Shut up and get on,' begged Cockie. 'How much was nicked?'

'Not sure, smallish amount of notes each time I think. Only Patrick, basically, would be eagle-eyed enough to spot it, but altogether it added up to quite a bit. Anyway, he decided to call everyone in today – TJ said it was like when you watch Poirot, you know, at the end, the – oh, what's it called?'

'Dénouement?' suggested Ben, neatly cutting up a dawdling BMW.

'Exactly.'

'So, who was it?' asked Ben.

'Well,' said Eva, suddenly hesitant. 'It turns out that it was, um, Annalisa.'

'What?' said Ben.

'Of course!' sighed Cockie simultaneously.

'What do you mean, "of course"?' demanded Ben, instantly suspicious.

'Well, I shouldn't have said "of course",' amended Cockie. 'I mean, just because she's a shoplifter doesn't necessarily mean that she's also a thief.'

'A shoplifter? What?'

Cockie rolled her eyes at Eva, deciding, finally, to tell all to Ben. 'And I wasn't absolutely sure that it had been Annalisa on the bus,' she finished, 'until Eva saw her wearing the very same red silk scarf.'

'Eva! You're in on this too!'

'Yes, Ben, I'm sorry, I saw her wearing it the day you split up, funnily enough.'

'Ha-bloody-ha,' said Ben gloomily. 'If I remember rightly, Annalisa was going to tie me up with that silk scarf. Jesus, bondage with stolen property – what else did she have in store for me?'

There was a short silence, then Eva and Cockie couldn't help but laugh.

'Give it up, you insensitive berks,' Ben growled at them. 'How would you like it if your ex turned out to be a reincarnation of the – the – Kray Twins? I mean, Christ, only I could go celibate for months and then pick out a bloody psycho!'

'Ben!' cried Eva and Cockie.

'OK, maybe psycho's a bit strong, but only a nutter would nick things so close to home, then wear the evidence for you all to see it.' Ben's voice started to wobble with laughter. 'Not just a thief, but a dumb thief. Anyway – just one question – why didn't you tell me you knew she was a thief? Fine pair of friends you are.'

'Can you blame us?' retorted Cockie. 'What would you expect us to say? "Oh, by the way, Ben, we know that you're utterly besotted with this girl but we have totally unfounded suspicions that she shoplifted one measly scarf – which is, we know, totally irrelevant to your relationship but we just thought we'd ruin the illusion . . ." I mean, talk about shoot the messenger!'

'Rule Number One,' added Eva, 'never interfere in someone else's lovelife.'

'OK, OK, but I was not besotted with her!'

'Oh, puh-leeze!' chorused Eva and Cockie.

'Sexually enslaved is not the same thing as besotted! I mean, I never respected her mind!'

'That's a really crap thing to say,' Eva said forthrightly. 'What a fucking caveman!'

Mike pressed his fingers into his ears. It often staggered him how these three could bicker so amiably and so irrelevantly, for so long, without tempers being lost or banter exhausted. Even in his fringe thespian world he had rarely come across people who loved the sound of their own voices as much as this little gang did.

'Still the tickling lust devours,' he muttered, 'Long stretches of my waking hours. Busty girls in flowered scanties, Hitching down St Michael panties. Easing off—'

'Mike, what are you on about?' asked Cockie, bemused. 'Don't tell me that's the script for an M&S ad?'

'No, no!' interrupted Eva. 'Didn't I tell you? Mike is rediscovering his thespian roots. No longer is he content with being Mr Bisto – the smell of the greasepaint is once more upon him . . .'

'Shut up, Eva.' Mike hardly looked up.

Cockie turned and looked quizzically at a bootfaced Eva. 'Well, I think it's brilliant of you, Mikey; when can we come to see you? Can I be your Stage Door Johnnie?'

'Oh, that's the best thing, Cockie,' Eva said, 'you can't see him – this launching pad to superstardom is not only a farce but a *radio* play . . . "Welcome to Listen with Grandma Hour. Adjust your colostomy bags for some real entertainment, and let me present Mike Richardson in *Habeas Corpus*, a serious Pulitzer-Prize-winning study into outdated humour and laboured lavatory wit, studded with such sound effects as the twang of knicker elastic."'

'Belt up, Eva, what *is* your problem?' said Cockie. 'I don't remember much aesthetic pretension about your own performance career, let alone any words of more than one syllable.'

'Thank you, Cockie, but I can fight my own battles,' said Mike calmly.

Cockie gave up.

'Actually, mate, it's all coming back to me – I remember Laura saying something about it when I was helping her move house.' Ben was in diversionary mode. 'Well, anyway,' he went on, unintentionally putting the cat back amongst the pigeons, 'Laura certainly seemed very starstruck, so at least you've impressed one of the Tonkins, even if it isn't old sourpuss here.'

'Yes, that'd be right,' raged Eva, 'Laura is always impressed by Mike. "Oh, Mike, do it again, just for little me, oh, Mike, you're my hero—"'

'Eva, grow up,' started Mike long-sufferingly.

'Oh, don't tell me you haven't noticed; she practically goes down on her cord-skirted knees every time you walk into the room.'

'Cockie, Ben, I apologise for what I'm about to do,' said Mike firmly. He leaned over, pulled Eva towards him, and kissed her extremely hard.

Ben, looking in the rearview mirror, glanced at a wide-eyed Cockie – placid, steady as a rock, Mike?

'Now, just belt up,' Mike said, lifting his head but not letting go of her. 'You know you're being an A1 neurotic drama queen but we're all bored of it so, for the last time, give it a rest. I'm tempted to tell you to sort your hormones out, or smell some soothing oils or get in touch with your biorhythms.'

'Oh!' gasped Eva.

'But I know that you'd bite my head off so just cuddle up and shut up, you daft brush, you.'

There was a silence while Eva looked as if she couldn't decide what to explode with first.

'Would it annoy you even more if I told you I loved

you when you're in a rage?' whispered Mike in her ear.

She could see him now, impatient head above the smaller slower Devonians. Instead of calling out to him, she gave herself the luxury of watching him for a few moments. Closer up he looked tired, dark shading under his eyes and a hint of gauntness under his tan pushing his handsomeness into a beauty less arrogant and more breathtaking. Then he saw her, and smiled at her . . . an honest-to-goodness, bring-out-the-bunting beam of a smile which ignited the green fires in his eyes, waved his glittering teeth like a banner and caused Cockie's heart to jump beats like a cheerleader. She grinned back at him automatically, foolishly, then she was in his arms, nose pressed into the small horse of a Ralph Lauren polo shirt, senses reeling under a triple whammy of fragrant cigar smoke, travelling soap and the usual cartilage trembling aftershave, only noticing him dropping his bag on her toes because it weighed a ton.

'Hello there,' he said, looking down at her.

'Hello,' Cockie said, almost shyly, fingers reluctantly sliding away from the cotton-clad muscles in his back. 'C'mon, we'd better shift it, Ben's waiting for us in the van.' She bent down to pick up his bag, and tugged at his hand.

When they were outside, Victor stopped short a few yards away from the waiting van. A faint wrinkling marred the usually perfect profile of his nose.

'We're going in . . . that?'

Ben saw them. 'In your own time, Cockie!'

'Don't be a car snob,' she told Victor forbiddingly. 'It's got the same stereo as yours. Here, give me your briefcase, I'll go in the back, you ride shotgun with Ben.'

'Hi, you must be Ben,' said Victor, carefully dusting off

the front seat. He stuck out his hand. 'I am pleased to meet you, I have heard a lot about you.'

Must be a bit tricky trying to click heels in the passenger seat, thought Ben irrepressibly.

'Well, although it is Cockie's habit to pick up unfortunate strangers as they get off trains, I'll have to assume that you're Victor.'

'Ben!' frowned Cockie.

'No, it's good to meet you,' he said smoothly. 'And I've heard a lot about you too so you'd better not blow the myth.'

As Ben and Victor lumbered through some typical male sparring inanities, Cockie lolled on the cushions in the back, secretly relieved that this meeting, delayed for so long, seemed to be going . . . amiably. She looked at their two heads, backlit by the blaze of a Devon day on full wattage: Victor so defined: black hair trimmed into a no-nonsense short back and sides, with just that dangerously cute lock flopping down over the knee-liquefying profile; the picture of clean-cut perfection in his eye-co-ordinated dark green Polo shirt, mysteriously uncreased pale chinos and diving watch nestling amongst the springy dark hairs on his wrist.

Ben, so different, less daunting, with his bright and mustard yellow paisley shirt, flapping over an ancient Funkadelica T-shirt, half-tucked into much washed and faded blue cotton bermuda shorts. Gleaming golden in the sun, his auburn hair went every which way and loose, pushed out of his eyes with an impatient hand as he negotiated the narrow roads that led back to Slake Manor, his hooded, quicksilver eyes narrowed in concentration. Next to Victor's full-on movie star looks there was no denying that Ben was, by comparison, ugly but . . . Cockie decided . . . not quite. Where Victor was a solid, dominating presence, drawing all eyes, Ben was less corporeal, a mercurial presence whose mobile, narrow face and glittering eyes made you want to look more carefully at him beyond that first glance, pin him down like a butterfly.

As they pulled into the gates of Slake Manor, Cockie imagined the view through Victor's eyes, as she had seen it herself only a few hours before, she and Ben in the front, a subdued Mike and Eva in the back, all of them preoccupied with their own thoughts after a big session the night before in their bed-and-breakfast.

'Wow.' Eva and Cockie had spoken in unison, Eva's blonde head dipping into the front seat.

'Wowee-zowee,' repeated Cockie.

'You did all this, Ben?!' crowed Eva proudly. 'Stop the van so we can have a proper look.'

Ben nodded. When he had come down a few weeks before, even he had been blown away by the change time and nature had wrought since those stubby beginnings eight years ago.

Below the road, the hillside fell away in a swathe of moorland, down to a lake fed by a river flowing from left to right, allowing them an undistracted view of the landscape opposite, as the valley rose the other side. The house itself was set halfway up the hill, at the top of an enormous flight of stone steps, themselves arranged in terraced 'stair' formation, so that on each giant tread they could see an ornamental flowerbed flanking the staircase. On the outer edges of these beds, nature took over: a mixture of young and new trees, some aflame with the very first beacon calls of autumn. At the bottom of the valley, the lake looked timeless, two ancient oaks standing sentinel at each end, but the new dam at the right end told a different story to the careful observer. On their side of the lake, a ha-ha separated the banks of the water from a field in which grazed spry-looking sheep. To the right of their viewpoint, they could just see the drive snaking up the hill through the trees, past a block of outbuildings to the back of the house itself. Up travelled their eyes; up a steep-looking hillside thickly planted with new trees, up to a Grecian temple folly.

This time for Victor, Ben paused again at the top of the hill. In the late afternoon sun the house itself blazed with a special golden luminosity, competing more strongly with the heat-hazed landscape around it. Now that she had seen it all up close, Cockie could really see the skill of landscaping the different terraces on either side of the stone staircase so that the further away from the house, the less ornamental, more natural the design. Just as the formal parterres right outside the house seemed an extension of the architectural details, so did the wilder, more tangled beds down by the lake seem more at home.

'Nice house, but I expected it to be bigger,' said Victor. 'Shall we go on now?'

'Bosoms,' said Ben helplessly, nearly falling off his stilts.

'Ben!'exclaimed Cockie, coming down the stairs into the stable yard.

Victor swung round to give Ben a suspicious glare. With his hair brilliantined into a middle parting and his leopardskin vest, he looked enough the part of the circus strongman for Ben not to persist. At least he looks like a complete tosser, Ben thought defiantly.

'Hardly backward in coming forward, is she?' said Eva drily, coming out into the yard, complete with turban and crystal ball.

Some days, Ben tried to remind himself, Cockie looked like a dog. But on others Cockie pulled a whole warren of rabbits out of a hat, and managed to look so stupendous that you couldn't remember any past flaws. This was one of those times. His eyes lingered almost painfully on her long, long legs, encased by shiny, black, thigh-length boots. He winced as his inspection travelled past the infinitesimal cycling shorts, up to the miracle of engineering that was contorting her already curvaceous torso into proportions that were surely impossible to uphold like that.

'I'm sorry, Cockie my love, but really, have you no mercy?' groaned Ben. 'Where did you get the outfit anyway – the tails? And the topper?'

'My bro lent them to me – I had wanted to come as a poodle trainer but he wouldn't let me take the dogs so I lumped it with this lot – it's his Hunt Ball kit, dontcha know – given on pain of death that I don't do anything to it.'

'Don't worry,' said Eva, 'everyone's going to be so busy spilling things down that corseted cleavage that the rest of the outfit's not going to get a look in.' She looked at Victor, 'Hey, strongman, you can shut your mouth now!'

Ben glanced at him. Victor did look a little shell-shocked. At least he and Eva were accustomed to Cockie's sporadic emergences into party animal extraordinaire. This guy had obviously never seen anything like it. Nor could he remove his eyes from the magnificent half-globes of flesh that Marie-Antoinette would have been proud to have teetering over the edge of her best frock. Ben felt almost sorry for him.

'So how do you know Red Lester?' Victor said to Ben, as they walked over to the party. 'I mean, how did you get the job you did here?'

'I didn't know him, actually. About eight years ago, I read an article about him buying this house and I knew the family who used to own it so I knew there was huge potential here.'

'So you used your contacts. Good for you.'

'No. No, I didn't, actually,' started Ben testily but stopped as they rounded the corner of the house to the new sunroom. Ben's heart swelled with a pride that wasn't confined to the garden unfolding fragrantly before them. Red Lester and his wife – both dressed as clowns – greeted Cockie and Victor like old friends, and Cockie batted back the easy greeting like a pro; Mike was chatting amicably to a group of people with famous faces that Ben remembered from Red's other parties; Eva was immediately claimed from his side by some fellow crystals freak with whom she had been communing all afternoon. These were his true friends: chameleons, at home in any situation, quite unlike the carefully labelled and filed circles of people that he also counted as his friends, as long as they never strayed from their allotted spheres. For a short moment, Ben felt dangerously smug.

It wouldn't last.

Red came bouncing over to him, almost tripping over his outsized shoes.

'Capability, me old soak, how the hell are you?'

'Thirstier than this afternoon, thank you, Red.'

'Get the boy a drink,' he shouted to a minion, then turned back to Ben. 'Fucking taller too, eh? Great costume, man!'

Ben stood upright on his stilts, striking a flamboyant pose in his purple velvet suit and huge stovepipe hat. 'Impressed at the lengths I go to to please you, buana?'

'Get outta here,' Red leaned closer, looking like he was talking into Ben's belly button. 'The birds lived up to their advance press too, that Cockie's a stormer – good on you, mate!'

'Nothing to do with me, I just live with her.'

'Well, you're a fool. In my day . . .' The rock star sighed. 'The boyfriend seems a bit straight for that little cracker but, I don't know, women! Suckers for a pretty face, eh?' He gazed fondly at his wife, a still stunning forty-year-old.

Ben followed his look. 'You've done all right for yourself and since when were you a pretty face?'

Red played an exuberant air guitar. 'Music, boyo, food of love and all that. She fell for my melodies – simple as anyfink!' He noticed a security guard waving at him. 'Gotta go, see you in a mo.'

Ben couldn't help laughing at the thought of the serene, classy Mrs Lester being wooed by the sweat-soaked screams of Red Lester and the Big Cheeses. After a year of living on top of them recording a particularly thrashful album, the best decision, in Ben's opinion, that these boys had ever made was when they refused to play at their own parties. 'Busman's holiday, or what?' Eric, the drummer, had grumbled.

To his surprise, Red came straight back to him. 'Listen, man, they've had a spot of bother down at the front gate.'

'Oh? Do you want me to go down there and help out?'

'No, no, mate – it's just some bird and her bloke – anyway, it's too late, they're already in – on your invitation!'

'What?! Jesus, Red, I'm so sorry – as you know, I didn't have the invite but I just thought I'd left it somewhere at home.'

'No hassle, couldn't matter less.'

'But who?'

As he said this, Ben saw the look of horror on Cockie's face as she glanced behind him and his heart sank. Slowly he turned round to see his worst nightmare coming out of the door of the sunroom. Him being the tallest person in the room by a good two feet, she spotted him immediately and waved.

'Hello, Ben, sweetie,' she trilled across, 'this looks like a great party!' She turned to the man beside her and snuggled up to him, 'You remember Fred from the Whim, don't you? Fred and I have been having such fun together so we thought we'd drop in here – after all, we just happened to be in the neighbourhood, didn't we?' She screamed with laughter.

Ben's heart found new sinking options. Annalisa . . . Annalisa and Fred . . . both, judging from the calibre of jokes and their glittery eyes, coked off their boxes. Time, he thought, to climb off the stilts; something told him he needed the sort of drink that would need two hands and his full attention.

Eva hadn't been able to believe her eyes. Annalisa and Fred! What a tangled web: the last real contact she'd had with Fred was when he'd been pestering Cockie to be the ultimate Frankie and Johnny combination and now, here he was, draped incoherently over Ben's ex-girlfriend. Against her better inclinations, Eva was beginning to have a grudging respect for Annalisa. Thieving bitch she may be, but it took balls to gatecrash the party of one of Britain's biggest rock stars, and to be so brazen about it, charming the Redman himself so that he didn't throw her out and looking like . . . that.

Eva, unused to being outdone, was so stunned herself that she could only guess at the effect that Annalisa was having on the men. Silver Barbarella boots were laced up to the knee; a minuscule mauve and silver spangled leotard arrangement of a sequinned G-string framed a silver ring in her navel; Gaultier-like cones of silver took the place of a top, and that head-dress . . . it had to be three feet worth of ostrich plumes and other, coloured, feathers, all sprouting high from a sequinned skullcap. Whether the whole ensemble was inspired by a Rio Mardi Gras street float, Come Dancing or Madame Jo-Jo's, Eva wasn't sure but yes, one thing was certain: this girl had gold-plated cojones.

Apart from worrying sporadically about Ben, who had sloped off in the direction of the bar with a determined look on his face that she knew well, Eva herself was having the time of her life, and was even admitting to being a little starstruck. Her days bashing up the electricity meter in a Brixton squat seemed a Jurassic age ago as she and Imran went into the dinner tent, followed by Sting and his wife, and chatting to Liam Neeson as if it were the most prosaic, everyday occurrence.

Gallingly, Eva the iconoclast was feeling cheated of targets for bile and condemnation. She looked around for Mike and saw him a few tables away, talking animatedly to a well-preserved lady also dressed as a fortune teller. Eva caught his attention and widened her eyes in a 'cor lumme' gesture, body code that she and Mike both understood well. Mike smiled back at her, shook his head, and turned back to his conversation. Snubbed, Eva thought indignantly, but I'm the one who does the snubbing. I'll teach him, cheeky bugger . . .

For the rest of dinner, Eva dug deep into her visible flirt repertoire, resurrecting old chestnuts like the tossing of her waistlength blonde hair – to the alarm of passing waiters, hapless people sitting behind her and innocently placed candelabra – and gazing burningly through the plastic web of her false eyelashes. Never were palms read so intently, cranial analyses delivered so feelingly, karmas so touchingly explored. Surrounded by dinner companions who went from a bemused interest in her alternative beliefs to an interested bemusement in her bodily alternative, Eva was enjoying herself. And if a tiny voice inside her said that maybe it would have been more interesting to stop performing and to find out something real about a group of heterogeneous people the like of which she was probably never going to see again, then she had another drink to drown out that voice. Nor did she look at Mike; she didn't need to, she was having a high old time without him.

At last dinner was over. Eva was having a surprisingly sensible conversation with an initially taciturn young man (when, she asked herself, had she started to use that term?) on her left, when, finally, Mike came over.

'Mike,' said Eva gaily, 'meet Leo – Red's son.'

'Hi, Leo.'

'He's training to be a doctor so we're having a total dingdong about homeopathic medicines – I think I'm losing on points, damn his gorgeous eyes.'

'No, I was just saying that it's naïve to think of conventional drugs as manmade – therefore dirty – chemicals, and homeopathic drugs as somehow natural and therefore pure, when they're all chemicals – obviously,' said Leo earnestly, blushing at the attention.

'You see,' challenged Eva, 'it's words like naïve that totally crush me!'

If Mike was surprised at Eva being so flirtatious instead of her usual dogged campaigner, he didn't let it show.

'Well, Leo, I hope you don't mind if I interrupt you and take Eva away.' He turned to her, tucking a recalcitrant wisp of hair under her turban, 'My love, would you like to dance?'

Oh, the swell of relief that two tiny words could produce. Eva realised that, like a lovesick teenager, she had been waiting all day for some sign of his unaltered affections. Now that wilting blossom in her breast perked up once more, revived by the flood of released self-confidence.

'Yes,' she said simply, the crystals around her neck and wrist completely out-dazzled by the glow from her eyes as she looked up at him. 'Catch you later, Leo.'

As they walked through the fragrant sunroom, now rechristened the Orangery by Susie Lester, Eva grabbed Mike's arm, 'Hey! I've just had an idea – didn't Ben say something about a walled garden that was Red's fantasy and specially designed to smell wonderful? Let's go and find it!'

'Eva, it's pitch dark! What about our dance?'

'It's nearly a full moon, our dance can wait and anyway, Ben said that flowers smell even better at night – look, there he is, let's ask him where it is.'

Ben was looking a lot more cheerful. A lot more unsteady too, even off his stilts, his eyes almost half-closed, hat off, and auburn hair all over the place, but his lips curved up in an easy smile, hand wrapped firmly around a glass.

'Hi, kids,' he greeted them. 'What a swell party this is, eh?' He tapped out a little dance step. 'Have you heard,' he sang, 'amongst this clan,' he twirled Eva round, 'you are called the forgotten man? Hang on a sec,' he giggled, 'wrong sex, you must be dear Blanche.'

'Yes, Ben,' said Eva, humouring him. 'Now, tell us where the—'

'Have you heard?' He was off again. 'About dear Blanche? Got run down by an avalanche—'

'Game girl, though,' Mike joined in, 'got up and finished fourth—'

'Well, did you evah—'

'Ben! Mike!'

'What a swell party this is!' they finished triumphantly, doing a most un-Sinatra like high five.

'What's the joke?' asked Cockie, passing with Victor.

'Come on!' Eva grabbed Cockie's arm, 'let's all go to the walled garden!'

'We were about to go—'

'Capital idea.' Ben had just seen Annalisa and Fred entering the Orangery, both looking wild-eyed, Annalisa rubbing her nose. 'Look who's coming.'

The others followed his gaze.

'I had such a blow-out with Fred before dinner,' said Cockie grimly, cracking her whip. 'The only good thing about having been the object of his lust that time is that I think I've frightened him out of mentioning this party in any piece he ever writes, no matter how tempted the coked-out little sleazeball is.'

'Oh, let's not waste time talking about them,' said Ben airily. 'Follow me, troops.'

Outside, everything was blanketed with that velvety darkness peculiar to summer and so unfamiliar, Eva mused, to Londoners accustomed to an opaque orange veil day and night. Any rural peace was being shattered by the dance music and the whistles and tinny janglings of the fairground that Red had set up on the other side of the house, but as they headed into the woods in the opposite direction, even that faded into a background pulse. Eva, tucking her hand around Mike's elbow, threw her head back to look for the moon in the gap above their heads, seeing autumnal clouds scudding past it, reminding her of when, in her other life, she and a boyfriend, reckless on acid and speed, had navigated their car along a country road, heads looking out of the sun-roof, using only a similar gap in the trees for guidance. A whiff of remembered exhilaration puffed up her spirits even more.

'Here we are,' said Ben up ahead, his voice sending ripples through their silence. 'Now, can I remember the way in?'

As she and Mike caught up, Eva saw that, in front of Ben, there was a high hedge and behind that, a little way back, an even higher wall.

'What do you mean?' asked Cockie, then, peering, 'Oh! A maze. Wicked!'

'Did you not build this then?' asked Victor.

'Christ, no! Hedges this high and this thick take bloody centuries of cultivation – but having said that I really should know the way through. Durr!' Ben hit himself on the side of the head. 'Fuck. That hurt.' He stepped through the entrance and turned resolutely left.

'Anyone got a ball of string?' Cockie grinned, following Ben.

Ben was obviously sobering up in the fresh air, because he led them through without a fault, opening an arched wooden door with an exaggerated rise of his eyebrows and a finger to his lips. As Eva stepped through, she could have sworn that there was a change in temperature – a sweet warmth saturated with a gathering tumbleweed of scent wrapped itself around her, each new flare of her nostrils unravelling a new tendril of honeysuckle, lavender and spice, a sensual body of recognised but unnameable fragrances. Beside her, Cockie too was standing, rapt, head flung back, breathing in deeply; next to her, Victor's perfect profile slashing the night sky as he looked down at her. Behind Eva, with his hands on her shoulders, Mike was still and, as she tipped herself back to look at him, just as tightly woven into the web of sensual sensation. And, grinning with pride and satisfaction at their reactions, Ben, to the side of all of them, the sorcerer of this spell. Her sweet Ben, tall velvet hat back askew on his head, sartorial splendour of his purple velvet suit outshone in the gloom by his black and white striped T-shirt and looking even more like the Cat in the Hat, long gangly legs with flapping flares.

Then the moon came out fully, flooding the garden with a silvery wave.

'Wow,' gasped Cockie.

'Fuck me,' whispered Eva. 'Sorry,' she added, to no-one in particular.

No-one bothered to reply; they were all gaping. Out of the darkness sprang an enchanted grotesque sight, dwarfing them and robbing them of speech. All around the tall walls was a profusion of activity; plants tangling, draping, climbing, tumbling, weaving in and out of each other, colourless in the monochrome light, dark studded by light blooms, pale shivering leaves laced with dusky boughs. But all this just surrounded the centrepiece of the rectangular space, the meaning of which Eva was only just beginning to realise.

'You see,' Ben murmured into the hush, 'we already had an avenue of espaliered trees on either side of a fairly wide path but they were rotten at each end so we chopped those out, keeping the ones in the middle, then built a trellis across the top, half vine, half wire-mesh, to make a table top. Then we built very basic chair seats, cutting out and painting the seat-backs, in each of the trees – much like building a treehouse with a ladder down to the ground – then Red got some wire sculptor to make the wire teapot, cups and saucers and, hey presto—'

'The Mad Hatter's Tea Party,' Mike whispered.

'It's incredible,' said a stunned Victor. 'Like a film set—'

'Or a really major duty trip,' Cockie added. 'Are you sure you've only ever smoked dope, Ben?'

Eva thought that Cockie had a point. Towering over them, like some spooky kids' dream, were gargantuan carved silhouettes of the March Hare, the Dormouse, Alice – six place settings in all – a giant dinner party going on above their heads; what sort of mind had the imagination to create this mise en scène from an avenue of half rotten fruit trees? She gave Ben a cautious awed look, only to receive a reassuring wink in return.

'Shall we take our places?' he asked, with a bow.

'What, sit up there?' asked an astonished Victor. 'Is it safe?'

The others ignored this nicety, scrambling up the ladders set discreetly into each trunk, discovering the gap in the vegetation from which they could emerge sitting on a surprisingly comfortable platform, knees tucked neatly under the 'table'. Victor soon followed suit.

'I feel like I'm in a highchair,' laughed Mike, banging an imaginary knife and fork on the leafy surface, 'but I can't even see the ground.'

'Ben, this is just so . . . wicked,' breathed Cockie, leaning over from her Alice seat to tousle his hair, 'you are a clever lad!'

Ben was obviously beginning to feel uncomfortable with all the adulation. 'Well, let me tell you, it's fucking crap during the day, which is a bit of a shame.'

'Why?'

'Imagine sitting up here, trying to have a picnic or whatever, with a small army of ecstatic insects going nuts over all the grapes – when I was down here a few weeks ago to sort out some final details, Rosalie – Red's youngest sprog – was trying to have a birthday party here – the first time anyone except Red and Susie have actually used it—'

'Actually up here?' Mike asked.

'Yeah, but before they could get anyway near it, Susie Lester had a bloody army up on ladders spraying the whole caboodle with enough insect repellent to kill The Swarm and all its relations—'

'So a lot of bug spray then?'

'Shut up, Cockie, and give us one of those fags. So when the kids arrived there wasn't a bee or a wasp or any creepy-crawly for miles around – huge sighs of relief, pats on back all round until one of the kids' faces swells up like a balloon, and she starts convulsing.' He pulled deeply on his cigarette. 'It turns out that she's allergic to the bloody insect repellent—'

The others laughed.

'Total disaster – screaming mums running about on the ground, screaming kids falling out of the trees, Rosalie having a tantrum, Susie frantic – and me and Red at the bottom, killing ourselves with completely inappropriate laughter.'

Eva finally finished rolling, and lit the spliff. The moon had disappeared now, leaving their visual senses to be swamped again by the fragrant assaults of jasmine, lily, spiced notes of mulled orange, ginger and vanilla; musky honeyed smells rolling up from below and around them. For the next few minutes there was a companionable silence with the distant throbbing of the music the only undercurrent, and the only movement the slow passing of the smoke.

'Mmmm, this is great,' crooned Eva after a while. 'So what did you plant to create such a scented paradise, Ben?'

'Nicotiana alata grandiflora,' murmured Ben, 'abronia umbellata, lilium formosanum, hosta plantaginea,' each unfamiliar syllable was licked over slowly and deliberately, an elixir of unfamiliar sounds weaving itself languorously around his listeners. 'Angelica archangelica, lippia citriodora, hedychium coronarium, lavandula and rosmarius officinalis, petunia myctaginiflora, lindera benzoin, camellia trichotomum . . .'

As if in a dream, Eva saw Cockie's hand, small and white in the dimness, slowly describe a path through the air to caress Victor's face. His own dark hand came up over hers. Trapped by the mesmeric effect of Ben's incantation, Eva could not turn away her gaze nor could she feel any surprise that Cockie was being so unusually demonstrative in front of them.

'Dianthus plumaris, mathiola incana annua, nicotiana sylvestris, thymus herba barona, lonicera heckrotti, lilium regale . . .'

With heightened sensitivity, Eva detected a change in Ben's voice. As he paused, she dragged her heavy head round to look at him. Now he too was staring at Cockie and Victor, the two of them hardly moving but locked into a tableau so charged that they might as well have been naked.

'And loads of other things, equally boring,' Ben finished, his brisk voice breaking their trance as effectively as any therapist's snapping fingers. He glanced at Eva and hoiked his thumb over his shoulder. She nodded and looked meaningfully at Mike, who understood immediately.

'Oh, are you going?' asked a surprised Cockie, as they began shinning down their respective ladders.

'Hey, don't let us disturb you,' Ben said airily. 'We'll see you guys later. C'mon Mike, Eva, let's hit the fairground.'

It wasn't until they were quite a way from the walled garden that anyone spoke.

'I am bloody starving,' said Ben suddenly. 'Tell you what, I'm going to run up ahead and see if there's any food for grabs – I was too pissed to eat at dinner – and I'll catch up with you at the Big Wheel.' He started jogging away from them. 'Catch you later then.'

'Bye, Ben,' Eva said, Mike silent.

At last they were alone, she thought.

'At last we're alone,' she said, snuggling up to Mike, and sliding up a tiny hand to fondle his dear face. He turned to face her, gently removing her hand to clasp it between his.

'Was that a spontaneous gesture, or just what you thought you ought to do, having watched Miss Romance in there do it?' he asked, almost conversationally.

Eva jerked her hand away. 'What?'

'You heard me. It doesn't matter.' He gave her a hug.

'Look, Mike, we need to talk—'

'Eva—'

'No, just let me finish. I know something's gone wrong, somewhere, and it's my fault. It's all tied up with Laura – I know you think I'm an irrational bitch when it comes to my sister – but there's something I haven't told you—'

'Eva. No!' as she tried to speak again. 'Look, my love,

not at a party, OK? I don't want to know any deep dark secrets – and there's nothing wrong between us, OK? I love you.' He grabbed her hand again. 'Race you to the bumper cars.'

The moment for telling had gone. Eva didn't know whether to feel relieved or cheated.

'Alone at last, huh, Ben?'

Ben knew that it had been too much to hope that he could have avoided Annalisa all night. He felt too drunk to attempt his usual diplomacy.

'Piss off, Annalisa, go back to loverboy and crash some other party.'

Annalisa smoothed her hands over her silver breast-shields. 'Oh, you're ever so peevish tonight, your Lordship.' Her eyes glittered. 'Are you quite sure you don't want to play?'

Despite himself, Ben couldn't take his eyes off her body, his intoxicated hormones rising to the occasion. Every poisonously delectable inch of her was so close, so available.

'You're such a tart,' he said with difficulty, feeling his head spin.

'All the better for you to eat me,' she breathed, ostrich plumes swaying towards him, her hands whispering up his thighs.

'Jesus,' Ben gasped, 'I will not fall for this.' Yet along with the hairs on the back of his neck, his hard-on was rising.

Annalisa looked at him consideringly. 'OK,' she said abruptly, 'have it your way.' And she turned and walked away, her tight, shiny buttocks clenching and unclenching around the sequinned G-string.

'Don't,' said Ben hoarsely, involuntarily.

She paused, but didn't look back.

Ben cleared his throat. 'OK, Annalisa, you've got—'

Then he stopped, frozen. Behind her he had seen Cockie and Victor step into the marquee. Suddenly, he was sober again.

Annalisa saw them as well and turned round to face Ben, her face cold. 'They make a lovely couple, don't they, Ben? Look, they can hardly keep their hands off each other.' She came back to him and put her arms around his unyielding neck. 'Just think, Ben,' she whispered, 'they're going to screw each other tonight, Eva and Mike are going to screw each other, I'm going to screw, oh, someone – and what about you? Oh, I know who you want to screw.'

And she closed in on him, insistent lips on his, her tongue snaking around his gritted teeth, hands going unerringly to his groin. Over her shoulder, Ben's eyes were wide open, seeing Cockie look over at him, frown and look away again into Victor's eyes. Ben closed his then, fists clenched at his sides. Finally, Annalisa stepped away, licking her lips. She smiled victoriously and waved mockingly at him.

'Bye, loser.'

There was absolutely no possible way she could get to sleep. Envisaging herself and Victor in all the sexual positions she could imagine wasn't helping, but that was all his fault. Was there ever a more provocative man? Cockie's face creased into a vast smile, thinking of the things he had said to her that night. Was there ever a man more gorgeous, more drop dead, more dreamy, more godlike, more hunksome, more romantic, more deliciously arrogant, more, more *phwoarrr* . . . Cockie buried her head in a pillow and just stopped herself from squeaking with glee, drumming her heels on the bed instead. She had to get out of here.

Swinging from the top bunk, slipping as noiselessly as she could into a pair of jeans, Gus's old cricket sweater and a pair of clogs, she crept out of the room, then cluttered down the stairs into the stable yard. Quarter of an hour later, croissants and apples filched from Red's kitchen and tucked into the lap of her jumper, Cockie was in the folly at the top of the hill, settled in a deckchair. The morning was at the brightest point of dawn – impudent beams bursting over the horizon beyond the eastern end of the stables, the sky that way the palest gold, behind her still a moody blue. Various feathered friends were exacting a noisy revenge for the night long interruption of their slumbers, and the air was so clean, so sharp with the joy of nature that Cockie could almost feel it bite her kiss-bruised, party-battered face. It was one of those perfect mornings. Cockie, in the preliminary stage of an inevitable hangover, was determined to enjoy it to its full extent.

Closing her eyes, she saw Victor as he had been the night before, muscled chest gleaming in the warmth of the walled garden, dark eyes boring into hers, hands either side of her face.

'There is something very special between us, Cockie.'

Then, when she hadn't answered. 'Don't you agree?'

'What? Oh! Yes! Oh yes!' How could she have told him that she'd been marvelling too hard at the feel of his hands to concentrate on what he was saying?

'There is a key in that door, I saw it as we came in so we could lock it and—'

Lock it! Lock it! Her very being had shrieked.

'—then I could kiss you—'

Kiss me! Kiss me!

'—and we could make love here and now in this beautiful place—'

Rendered speechless by the cacophony in her body, as her hormones did a victory lap around it, she just squeezed his waist and hoped she wasn't going to spontaneously combust.

'—but I won't let myself do that.'

There was a burning silence.

'Wh-wh-what?'

'I'm not going to let myself make love to you because I feel sure in my heart that we should wait for that right moment; that moment when, instead of just wanting to, we have to; that divinely appointed moment where we will know each other.'

The romantic writer in Cockie couldn't help noting down this little speech. The rest of her just thought that this man was on serious drugs. And he hadn't even had any grass.

'What if I thought that this was the right moment?' she asked weakly, 'I mean, "wanting to" works for me.' She dared herself to move a little closer to him, hands creeping round his back, under the leopardskin vest, to rest lightly on the cool muscles there.

'Oh, don't tempt me,' he groaned, 'I can't quite believe that I'm saying this myself – but it's like, I don't know, I'm caught in a spell when I'm with you, which makes me see more clearly that this is the right thing to do.'

Her Bullshit Detector was going off the scale by this time, but at the same time this was so close to the enchanted bemusement that had entranced Cockie all along that she stared at him, a thousand ludicrous suggestions flitting through her head. Mickey Finns in their drinks? Had they been hypnotised? Maybe she should give up the Mills and Boon. She should definitely think about giving up the spliff.

Even now, as she lay in the sunshine, she was trying to account for their unusual restraint. The trouble was that when she wasn't physically near him, his will no longer dominating hers, she was going nearly mad with frustration. After Sam, she had thought she was familiar with the concept of sex deprivation, but that had been a poor relation to this fiend champing round her body, pummelling vulnerable parts like her knees, heart and loins into a simmering pulp, and chewing out the more decisive lobes of her brain so that she became a simpering, trembling wreck.

Maybe this was love. It didn't bear much resemblance to the poetic ideal, but then she'd never exactly been the Lady of Shallott so why should love be any different? In any case, she had to make a decision: go along with Victor's Divinely Appointed Moment theory which now, in the warm light of day, sounded even more like tosh and balderdash, or go for it herself, steel herself to those bewitching green eyes and choose her own damn 'special' moment. Yes, cut through the romantic twaddle with a short, sharp seduction.

On that appealing thought she smiled – and promptly fell asleep.

'Cockie, my love, wake up!'

Swirling up from a deep sleep, she heard this tender exhortation filtering through the last moments of her dream and, without knowing it, she smiled so languorously and squirmed so provocatively in her deckchair that her waker narrowed his eyes and drew closer.

'Hey, earth to Cockie, come in please!'

Cockie opened her eyes wide and saw him leaning over her. A jolt of lust coursed through her so strongly that she nearly grabbed him there and then. Then she realised who it was and, for the first time in years, she blushed the sort of blush that could heat a Third World country for months.

'Hello,' she said weakly.

'Hello,' replied Ben.

For a moment they stared at each other, Cockie seeing the reflection of her own eyes in his intent silvery irises, hoping that he couldn't guess what she had been thinking. It must have been that she thought he was Victor.

She'd certainly been having some very . . . provoking dreams about someone.

'Victor was nearly sending out the search parties for you,' he said, as if reading her thoughts. 'How long have you been up here?'

She twisted his watch around, hands a little nervous on his wrist. 'Cor, it's one o'clock – I've been up here since dawn.'

'Great tan you've got, though.'

He held out a hand, and she scrambled out of her chair. Two apples fell out of her lap and rolled down the slope. They watched them go and looked at each other, Cockie finally remembering to pull her hand away. All at once, she remembered Ben and Annalisa together last night, how they had looked, and the sudden kick of revulsion deep in her guts when she had seen them.

'In this valley, they'll probably both be apple trees in a couple of years' time,' laughed Ben, breaking the sudden suggestion of tension.

Cockie started, and pulled herself together. 'And won't that play merry hell with your landscape planning?!'

'So nice that you care, my love! C'mon, the party's not over yet – Red was dropping hints this morning that Royalty was dropping in for lunch.'

'Lawks-a-mercy, I'll have to change into a frock!' Cockie gestured dramatically at herself.

Ben looked at her as well, taking in the tiny sleeveless T-shirt, the loose jeans, and all at once she felt self-conscious about the amount of sunkissed flesh on show, still blushing.

'And brush up on those curtsying skills!'

'Yes, my lord.' Cockie made a creditable bob.

'Cockie,' said Ben, looking almost pained, 'whatever would I do without you?'

'Wh–what do you mean?'

'Without you I would only have the faintest idea of what an idiot really was – oof! Hey! Don't hit me!'

'Plenty more where that came from, buster, so watch your mouth.'

'Charmed, I'm sure.'

11

'So, it's your big day, Drew – how do you feel?'
Drew groaned and dropped his head into his hands. 'I must be totally loony – why oh why did I say I'd do this?' As ever, under pressure, his Scottish accent became more pronounced.

'Look, come into the kitchen and have a calming cuppa. I'm sure Cockie will be ready eventually.'

Ben shepherded Drew through, and put the kettle on. He had the feeling that this was going to be a long morning. Drew paced up and down the length of the kitchen.

'Well, this paintjob in here worked out all right, didn't it?'

He didn't wait for Ben to answer. 'Jesus Christ! What is wrong with me?' He held out a hand. 'You see this hand? Steady as a rock.' He waggled the other one up. 'Ah, but this is the hand I shoot myself with.'

'Drew, you're gabbling.'

'Ben, so would you be!'

'Look, you got Cockie into this by your own free will,' said Ben testily. 'If you want to pretend to be married – which is very un-nineties of you by the way, Gay Pride and all that – then that's your problem, but don't worry about Cockie – she'll pull it off.'

'But—'

'The point is that she's a born grifter!' Ben was getting

impatient with Drew's cavilling. 'Cockie could fool the Pope himself that she was a Saint – persuade Stevie Wonder that he's been white all along – make the youth of today vote Tory—'

'OK, OK, point taken,' grumbled Drew. 'If you'd just listen to me instead of being a one man Cockie Fan Club, you'd know that I don't doubt her ability to carry this off – it's me – what if *I* cock it up? Then I'll not only shaft myself but will totally humiliate Cockie as well; och, I couldn't bear that!'

'Oh, I shouldn't worry about humiliating Cockie,' said Ben, 'she's a tough old bird, it would take more than an unmasking at Crouch End to rattle her cage.'

Drew looked at him. 'Sometimes, Ben, you don't know Cockie as well as you think you do,' he said pointedly.

Ben's eyes narrowed into gleaming slits. 'How dare – I think the point here is that I know Cockie better than you do – I certainly wouldn't put her through it in the first place, but at the same time I know that this *particular scenario*' – he emphasised the words – 'will not upset her.'

He went on furiously, 'I am the one she comes to, I am the one she confides in – I know what makes her tick so, so . . .'

By this time, Drew was looking at him in astonishment.

'Ben,' he interrupted, 'why are you jealous of me?'

'Jealous? What are you on?' For a moment Ben glared at Drew, then his face cleared and he laughed. 'God, it did sound like that, didn't it? I'm sorry, mate; don't know what came over me – Eva would probably say that it was my biorhythms or something.'

He turned away and busied himself with teabags and kettle. 'It's all none of my business anyway. Have you met Victor, by the way? And does he know about today?'

'I met him briefly in the Whim and no, he doesn't

know. Apparently he's away for the weekend in any case, so Cockie didn't think it was worth spreading the secret any further when there was no need. It seems,' Drew added, looking consideringly at Ben, back still turned, 'that Victor's the jealous type too.'

'Ho, ho,' said Ben irritably.

It wasn't doing any good, decided Cockie. No matter how many times she looked in the mirror, it wasn't going to get any better. She kicked the mirror for good measure but nothing changed. Eva came in while she was still rubbing her toe.

'Don't ask,' said Cockie grimly.

'Cockie, get your act together! Drew's downstairs wearing a hole in the kitchen floor – why is he so worked up? I think it's deeply suss. If you ask me, there's more to this than just a lousy job. Anyway, if we're going out for this champagne breakfast he was banging on about, we've got to get a wiggle on.'

Eva grabbed the bag Drew had brought round and peered inside. 'Now, you've got the dress on, tights on, knickers on? I hope so, otherwise you're in trouble – that dress is seriously short.'

'Eva! That's what I've been trying to tell you – it's obscene: I hate wearing skirts at the best of times and this hardly even qualifies as a skirt! Fucking pussy pelmet is what it is!'

'Well, it would be, wouldn't it,' Eva giggled, 'Drew being an interior—'

'And look at this back!'

'It's a very nice back – you're very brown.' Eva relented. 'OK, OK, so three straps don't exactly leave much to the imagination but it certainly looks spectacular.'

'Oh really?' said Cockie grimly. 'Well, check out the front – talk about two sliding bowls of Boobe Surprise.' She tapped the side of her head. 'Dur! Hello Drew!

Backless dress means no bra, no bra means black eyes for yours truly!'

'Simple . . . you just glide all day—'

'In these heels? Forget the black eyes – I'll be too busy worrying about breaking my legs.'

'Well, put them on – in fact put it all on and we'll reappraise the situation.'

Eva emptied out the bag and, two minutes later, Cockie was head to toe Drewified.

'Isn't it horrendous?' Cockie appealed to Eva. 'Only a bloody man would dress a woman like this – I thought gays were meant to be empathetic to a woman's needs.'

Eva found her tongue. 'But Cockie,' she breathed, 'you look . . . fantastic . . . Jackie O. eat your heart out . . . you look . . . gorgeous . . . completely unlike you.'

'Exactly. Completely unlike me. More like a prize turkey. The only redeeming feature is that because of this ridiculous hat the most I can see at ground level is from about toes to waist so at least there's not a hope in hell of anyone recognising me.'

She had a point. Unless you were looking from Eva's lowly standpoint, all of her face except a heavily lipsticked mouth was obscured by an enormously brimmy hat that would have been a dead ringer for Audrey Hepburn's in *Breakfast at Tiffany's* were it not for the whirlpool stripes of gold and black straw. Hanging from her ears and round her neck were a pair of earrings and a necklace fashioned out of several huge, old gold coins.

Even the rest of the accessories were *just so*: the shoes – black and gold woven stripes balanced on four-inch spike heels; the softest black kid gloves and a handbag that Eva noticed covetously was the finest little black Bill Amberg that money could buy. The whole effect was of a deliberate chic so distilled that it was nearly one hundred per cent proof.

Cockie was right; no-one would recognise her.

'Fuck me, but you're tall,' Eva giggled, craning her head back fully to take in the extra fourteen inches between her and Cockie. 'You are going to dwarf Drew – I wonder if he realises this? God, what wouldn't I give for Victor to see you like this!'

'Cockie! Come on! We've got to go,' came a yell from Drew downstairs.

'This reaction I can't wait to see,' said Eva, emptying out Cockie's usual rucksack, picking out fags, money and matches and jamming them into the new minuscule reticule. 'Ben and Drew are going to do their nuts.'

'Here's to the most beautiful wife a man ever had!' boasted Drew, raising yet another glass of champagne.

'I would take that as a compliment except that I'm the only wife you are ever likely to have,' teased Cockie. 'Oh, and by the way, I'm not wearing these dark glasses as well – did you borrow them from Bono or what? – I couldn't see a thing through them and nearly fell over twice just getting out of the car, not to mention not seeing Cat do her best to ladder these blasted tights. Why couldn't I wear a nice trouser suit, Drew baby? Hubby love? Sweetness?'

'Because we've got to show old Mother Friedman that you are no Glaswegian housewife and that you can knock the socks off whatever haute couture dog's dinner she's dragged on to her scrawny little frame. Where is Cat, by the way?'

'Don't worry,' said Ben, 'I saw her wreaking only the tiniest amount of havoc over by that flowerbed.'

It was two hours before lift-off and the four of them were sitting in the garden of an anonymous suburban hotel. Drew had insisted that Ben and Eva come along to launch Cockie with a little moral support, bribing them with the promise of champagne.

'If only she were better behaved,' said Cockie wistfully,

'she would make the perfect accessory for this outfit.' She gestured at her hopelessly sophisticated heavy gold brocade bolero jacket and they all looked over at Cat, a golden springer spaniel happily eating grass and the odd petunia.

'Why Cat?' asked Eva suddenly. 'The name, I mean. I know you've told me before but remind me . . .'

'Nothing very clever,' Drew answered, 'it's short for Chatelaine – in a roundabout way – because she's the only lady in my house and in my life – before I met my sweet wife, of course,' he patted Cockie on the hand. 'I really can't get over how stunning you look, darling – what do you think, Ben?'

'Oh yes,' said Ben, getting up and walking towards Cat, 'quite the little chameleon,' he tossed over his shoulder.

Cockie, who hadn't missed a single expression of his since she'd walked into the kitchen back at Ebury Mews, when Drew's cries of admiration and ecstasy hadn't distracted her from the fact that Ben only narrowed his eyes and said nothing, began to feel a tad sick.

'Drew,' she began, 'I'm not so sure I can pull this off—'

'Nonsense!' said Drew stoutly, completely over his earlier jitters. 'You're letter-perfect, *Caroline* – but if you want to go over it all again, then that's fine.'

'Just talk me through this double agenda angle,' suggested Eva, 'and Cockie – have some booze and belt up.'

'OK,' started Drew, 'we've been married a year, having known each other since I first came to London.' He started, clapping a hand to the pocket in his waistcoat, 'Christ! I nearly forgot: the ring – here, Cockie, bung this on.' He handed her a plain gold ring and turned back to Eva.

'Then, at the wedding itself, we have to show everyone that we are married but drop hints of strain, enough to suggest future divorce which gives me a get-out clause if I ever meet any of these people again. But at the reception we have to concentrate on convincing Nikki and, er, family, that we are happily married, and forget about the divorce hints.'

'Clear as mud. But I don't get it,' Eva pondered, 'why the change of plan at the reception? Wouldn't it be just as helpful for the, er, Hellhag to think that you were getting a divorce as well? Surely she's not going to think that you're gay just because you get divorced? Huh?'

'Look, it's fine by me, Eva,' interrupted Cockie. 'I think it'll be quite fun: total bitch in the church, sparkling wifely ornament on Drew's arm afterwards, for the benefit of this horrendous-sounding woman. Anyway, Drew is worried that if he's no longer married, she's going to get the hots for him, isn't that right, mi esposo?'

'Yup.'

'No, it's not that, is it, Drew?' said Eva. 'I can tell when you are lying – there's something else, isn't there, Drew?'

There was a telling silence. Cockie looked at Drew, eyebrows raised.

'Well?' she demanded. 'Out with it.'

'It's nothing really,' said Drew weakly.

'Drew!'

'Och, every word I've told you is the truth, I swear! I just missed out one detail . . .'

'Uh-oh,' said Eva.

'Go on,' said Cockie.

'Well, I told you that I'd met someone . . . someone special, didn't I? I just omitted to tell you that he was married—'

'Oh, Drew, you stupid, fucking masochist!'

Drew looked down at his hands. 'To the Hellhag.'

'What?!' both of them shouted together.

Drew looked Cockie straight in the eye. 'I am having an affair with the husband of my client. This client is rabidly homophobic – for the simple reason that she didn't know about her own husband's bisexuality until a few years ago when she caught him in bed with some guy.'

'Oh wow.'

'Now I'm really confused,' gasped Eva.

'I know,' said Drew, sighing heavily, 'it is a wee bit twisted. You see, I initially pretended to be married because I knew that Nikki wouldn't employ anyone who was gay; what I didn't know was she not only hated gays but was afraid that her husband would seduce any homosexual man he could lay his hands on—'

'With good reason, as it turns out!'

'Och, shut your trap, Eva. Anyway, I thought it would all be no big deal once I got the pitch accepted – then I met him and I knew, and he sort of guessed and one thing led to another—'

'You can spare us the details,' said Cockie drily.

'But you see, then the fact that I was "married" became much more important because Jonathan believed it as well. He doesn't get involved with anyone who is "out"; being with married bisexuals like himself gives him a camouflage, and cuts down the chance of him being caught out by the Hellhag.'

'So you put up with this?' asked a scandalised Eva, more shocked by this than the rest of the incredible story. 'You're pretending to be married because otherwise your boyfriend will drop you? Jesus.'

'I'm in love,' said Drew simply, 'and I think it's worth it.'

'Hang on a sec,' Cockie said slowly, 'this means that I have to – oh no! No way!'

'What?' asked Drew.

'There is just no way on this God-given earth that I am going to try and convince your lover that I am your wife!'

'Why not?' said Drew, leaning forward to fill up

Cockie's glass. 'You know me much better than Jonathan does—'

'Well, that's really sad,' scorned Eva.

Drew ignored her, '—and, apart from anything else, he really wants to believe that I'm married because he loves me.'

'That, at least, is so blindingly clear.'

'Och, get back in the knife drawer, Mrs Sharp. He loves me and doesn't want to give me up but he's got his position to think of – he's a seriously big cheese at this swanky American bank in the City which prides itself on its respectable family-orientated corporate identity – he's got kids, for Lord's sake—'

'Oh Drew!' wailed Cockie.

'I know, I know,' he defended himself, 'but they're all grown up – they're from his first marriage—'

'He's been married *twice*?!'

'Who has?' Ben sat down, with an ecstatic Cat lolling belly-up in his arms.

'You don't want to know. It really is sickening,' mused Drew, 'the way that dog turns into a drooling little hussy when you're around, Benny-boy.'

'Oh, he's used to that, aren't you, my sweet? Look at Annalisa.' There, thought Cockie, revenge for his complete lack of support. Ben raised his eyebrows but said nothing. She felt foolish. 'Sorry, that was bitchy.'

'Yes,' Ben said equably, 'it was.'

'Put it down to nervousness,' said Drew, 'my wife is having a wee touch of the jitters.'

'Ben, Drew is having an affair with his client's husband,' said Cockie, for maximum impact.

'Complicated,' agreed Ben, tipping his head and submitting to a thorough ear clean from the adoring Cat.

'Well, don't you think that I'd be mad to go through with this charade?' demanded Cockie impatiently.

'Why any more mad than before?'

'Why? Because, well, because . . .' Cockie was spluttering.

'Look, it's patently obvious that you are going to do it, Cockie,' interrupted Ben. 'You're dolled up to the nines, you're due to be there in twenty minutes which would be a short notice pull-out even by your standards, and you've never yet pulled out of a scam, so why the histrionics now?'

'I think,' he crooned, nuzzling Cat's silky golden head, 'that Miss Milton just wants some attention, doesn't she, my beauty? Well, who could possibly comply with that when the Queen of all Dogs is here?'

Cockie looked levelly at him. 'Not attention, Ben. Reassurance perhaps. Silly me.'

Drew couldn't decide whether it was genius or lunacy which had led him to ask Cockie to be his wife rather than hire a professional imposter for the job. She was fulfilling the requirements of Phase One as if to the manner born and this was all very well and good, but on a more immediate, fundamental level she was being a total bitch. From the moment they had left Ben and Eva drowsing boozily in the sunshine, along with the gloves, Cockie had slipped on an obsidian hauteur that was utterly convincing and totally hideous. Even now, she was passing judgement on the outfits and hats in the surrounding pews in a crystal clear whisper.

'That girl,' he heard someone mutter behind him, 'is so rude.'

Cockie heard it too, and without so much as an amused gleam in her eyes, turned to him.

'Surely in the House of God, one could be more imaginative – don't you think, darling? "Godless", maybe, "a veritable Jezebel": better, exhorting the Lord to turn me into a pillar of salt would be terrifically impressive but . . . "rude" . . . oh dear me, no.'

'Co-Caroline!' Drew stuttered. He leant closer, finding

he had to strain upwards to whisper into her ear, 'if you don't cool it just a wee bit, my sweet, we are going to be divorced before we even leave the church . . .'

Without doing anything so obvious as flinching, Cockie – his adorable, laughing, affectionate, clumsy Cockie – managed ever so slightly, so slightingly, to pull away, leaving an inch of icy froideur between them.

'I do so hate it when you hiss at me,' she informed him calmly. At that moment, the organist moved up a gear as the bride entered the church.

'Oh God, another mangled version of the Arrival,' she enunciated scornfully. 'Let us pray that the bride is worthy of the title of Queen of Sheba.' She turned her head as Flavia passed. 'Then again, maybe not.'

Drew needed no excuse to sink to his knees, bury his head in his hands and pray.

Finally, after an interminable service, they were outside the church, with Cockie, towering over him, looking supercilious but thankfully muted. Drew, on the other hand, was trying not to whimper as he nursed the perfect stigmata in his left foot where Cockie had buried her right heel in response to his more urgent pleas to shut the fuck up.

'Drew my sweet!'

They both turned to face this greeting.

'Nikki, it's quite lovely to see you,' charmed Drew, leaning forward to kiss his employer. 'Hello, Mr Friedman,' he added politely to his lover, disguising the shock of lust and pride he always felt when he saw him. 'How's life?'

'Good, thank you, Drew,' Jonathan said easily. He looked pointedly at Cockie who had, Drew noticed curiously, gone quite still, staring from her lofty height to beyond the Friedmans' heads.

Drew pulled her forward. 'May I introduce my wife, Caroline? Caroline, this is Nikki and Jonathan Friedman.'

There was a pause.

'Nikki is, of course, my boss at No. 42,' Drew added hurriedly, wondering frantically why Cockie hadn't said anything. Don't blow it now, he entreated her silently.

Cockie suddenly came to life. 'Yes, of course, I've heard so much about you, Mrs Friedman.'

Drew started visibly.

'I feel that I almost share him with you since you are working together so closely on the hotel. I can't wait to see it; Drew says that you have such exquisite taste that he feels almost *de trop*.'

While his boss twittered and preened under this onslaught of gush, Drew reeled. Instead of her usual clear speaking voice Cockie had unleashed these oozing words in a deep purr, pitched at least an octave below her usual voice and laced with the faintest suggestion of his own Scottish lilt. What was she up to?

'Come on, Drew,' Jonathan's voice interrupted his stunned reverie, 'I'd like you to meet our most recent bright spark from the office. I dragged him here under the false pretence that we are going to do some work later but I think you'll find him a useful contact – he's very involved in our current corporate art refurbishment.'

He turned around to the young man standing behind him. 'Hey, Vic, come and meet the designer who's doing my wife's hotel. You can talk to him about arty things.'

Looking at him, Drew knew suddenly that he had met this guy before. Hot on the heels of this came the realisation of who he was. The reasons for Cockie's furtiveness were immediately clear . . . Drew went hot and cold with the knowledge that he and Cockie were about to be busted, sprung, seriously blown out of the water. His brain kept flinging up a succession of clichés at him but one thing was abundantly clear. They were history.

'Drew Fraser,' said Jonathan, 'meet Victor Landis.'

* * *

'Shit shit shit shit shit,' said Cockie.

'Yes,' replied Drew, hands white-knuckled on the steering wheel.

'Buggerfuck, buggerfuck, bugger—'

'Quite.'

'I just can't believe it, I just can't fucking well believe it.' Cockie dropped her head into her hands. She came up teary-eyed. 'I can't believe he didn't even recognise me!'

For a moment they stared at each other, then they erupted.

'Score!' whooped Cockie, giving Drew a high five.

'Bloody incredible,' marvelled Drew, 'you were bloody incredible.' He started the engine and roared away from the kerb.

'You were absolutely fantastic in there,' he went on after a minute, 'although I thought I was going to have heart failure when you looked up at the video man during the prayers—'

'Well, the guy was sticking his camera in my face and we were meant to be praying!'

'Yes, but to say, "What am I supposed to do? *Wave*?" was almost beyond the call of duty; that lass sitting next to you so nearly hit you, brass knuckles were coming out of her ears.'

'Did I overdo it then?'

Drew glanced at her. 'No, my darling, you did good. You did brilliant.'

Cockie pulled a face. 'You know, I *can't* believe he didn't recognise me,' she said, her voice more plaintive now. 'I'm supposed to be his girlfriend; I'm supposed to be so special to him that he won't even sleep with me until the moment is just right.'

She looked at Drew. 'It's OK, you can close your mouth, I can't believe I fell for that either.'

'No, no,' Drew hastened to reassure her, 'I can't believe

that you are taking the fact that Victor is at this wedding so calmly. Don't you think it's the most bizarre coincidence that he's here at all? I don't know, I think that's the spooky part – talk about small world! I'm not surprised that he didn't recognise you – you can't see yourself – I certainly wouldn't – and with that voice! Are you now going to have to speak like that for the rest of the day?'

'Hey! It was the first thing I could think of! Talking of small worlds, I'm sure I've seen the bridegroom before. Anyway, let's just get a handle on this. Your lover is my boyfriend's boss at Silverman Bone; I have to convince your lover that I am married to you while my boyfriend, who presumably doesn't know many other people here, is likely to be hanging round only a few feet away . . . is that about right?'

'Uh-huh.'

'Fine. Just fine and dandy. No problemmo. Easy-peasy-lemon-squeezy.' A thought occurred to her. 'Did Victor recognise you?'

'I'm not sure, he sort of squinted at me so I gibbered on about how we must have met at Flavia's engagement party bla bla bla. Anyway, let's not push it; I'll keep away from him wherever possible.'

'In fact,' he slowed the car down, 'what are we doing? This is all too risky – let's just give the reception a miss: we've made our point about being married; I can just say that you felt ill or something.'

'Yes, maybe you're right.' Cockie was silent for a moment. 'No, bugger it, let's see it out. If Victor Landis is so up himself that he can't notice his girlfriend five feet away, that's his problem, not ours.' She lifted her chin. 'Fuck it, I'm going to enjoy myself.'

Drew looked over uneasily. 'Cockie? You're not going to do something reckless, are you? Something *I'll* regret in the morning? We are talking my lovelife and my career here, remember?'

'Oh pish,' said Cockie, hardly reassuringly.

'This was a good idea, Benny-boy – it's almost as gorgeous as it was last weekend,' Eva lay back down on the bench outside the pub, somnolent with steak and wine, eyes closed against the sun. Then she sat up again. 'Oh! I completely forgot – I got the photos back – the photos of Red's party.'

'Supersmashin',' said Ben, absently tickling a burping Cat. 'Let's have a butcher's.'

He flipped through the pictures. 'Nice one of the house . . . very picture postcard grin here, Eva . . . aaah, you've taken lots of the gardens, you groupie you . . . Cockie and the Perfect Man . . .' He paused. 'So, what do you think of Victor?'

'Well, you called him the Perfect Man,' Eva teased, 'so you must have a fairly high opinion of him!'

She saw that the photo he was looking at was of Cockie and Victor entwined on the lawn after Sunday lunch at Red's.

'Yeah right.' Ben paused. 'I haven't got much of an opinion really. He seems OK. Very good-looking. Gorgeous car, oodles of cash. Presumably gets paid the GDP of a small country by Silverman's. No, I can certainly see what Cockie sees in him.'

'Cor – I'd hate to hear you say anything nasty about someone.' Eva sat up straighter, put her elbows on the table between them and gave him the full benefit of her best Paddington Bear stare.

Ben refused to rise. 'I'm hardly going to say that I fancy the pants off him, am I? We're just very different people – he looks like a film star, I look like a dog – no offence, Cat – he's a fully paid up suit, I'm a gardener. As long as he makes Cockie happy, he's—'

'Ben! No more of this martyred rubbish,' snapped Eva. 'What a complete crock of shit. You know as well as I do that Victor Landis is an A1, one hundred per cent, undiluted, pure and simple prat!'

Ben laughed out loud. 'Eva, *you* are a two-faced, lily-livered, yellow-bellied con artist. I've heard you giving Cockie a ton of girlie advice over the last few weeks but, strangely enough, I never heard you giving that particular opinion about a fine, handsome, upstanding, high-earning, amusing – no, that's going too far – interesting, well-meaning specimen of macho pride like our Victor.'

He grinned at her and paused. 'Of course he's a prat.'

'Arrogant dickhead.'

'Lounge lizard.'

'Money-grubbing corporatist.'

'Overweening flash git.'

'Humourless hunk of bland.'

They looked at each other, smiling. For the first time in a week, Ben nearly felt cheerful.

Things were going suspiciously well, thought Cockie, as she escaped undiscovered from the feeding frenzy of the Hellhag's cronies. She glided away as gracefully as she could in her damnable heels, clasping Drew's arm more out of a need for balance than from conjugal affection.

'Caro, my sweet, this is my old friend, Flavia,' said Drew, with a wicked champagned twinkle in his eyes, 'and her husband, Julian.'

'Oh Drew,' giggled Flavia, a bride who had more than a suggestion of hatchet about her vaguely rectangular face, 'it does sound funny when you say "husband" like that – did it give you a thrill when you first called Drew that, Caroline?'

'More than you could ever guess,' said Cockie truthfully in her assumed purr, moving effortlessly into the small talk that was the essential passport into conversation with newly-weds. Talk of 'beautiful flowers in the church . . . so lucky with the weather . . . oh, a surprise honeymoon destination? How very romantic!' flitted inconsequentially back and forth.

'Who would have thought our little Drew could have such a wonderful wife hidden away?!' Flavia said with an arch little smile.

Cockie felt Drew's arm muscles tense and squeezed imperceptibly back.

'When we come back from Location X, we must have both of you to dinner, mustn't we, Jules?' She looked adoringly at her groom, who was gazing rather fixedly into his glass.

Jules! Alarm bells rang in Cockie's mind. She knew that name; she couldn't see the face now because of her hat, but she had recognised it as it came down the aisle in the church – she'd seen it once for sure . . . she'd been sitting in a car . . . no, in Ben's van . . . he'd been walking down the street towards them . . . and had then been pulled away, laughing, by . . . TJ.

Shit! This was Jules, TJ's 'spunk', the boyfriend who 'wouldn't commit'. No bloody wonder. Cockie's mind was reeling under the implications of this final Chance Encounter of the Hellish Kind when a familiar voice came to join the party.

For the full nightmare effect, it could only have been one person.

'Flavia, Julian – Jonathan sent me over to tell you that they're doing the bridal pictures outside now.'

'Whatever you say, Victor!' carolled Flavia. She leaned forward to speak mock-confidentially to Cockie who was locked solid to Drew's trembling arm, never more glad to have such an enormous hat concealing her frozen face. 'My uncle-in-law says that Victor is the best thing that ever happened to Silverman's – he's got so many talents!'

'Your uncle, Jules, is a wonderful man but he is a little

too impressed by my eye for art,' Victor laughed easily. 'I keep telling him that I am also making the company millions a year but he will keep talking on about the corporate art refit that I am overseeing.'

He sounded, Cockie thought with dismay, positively oily. Oily enough to outslick the Exxon Valdez.

'Mmmm,' she murmured, feeling that she had been called on to respond, 'it all sounds very impressive. I rely on my husband to make all the artistic decisions, don't I, darling?'

Inanity was surely the easiest option at this juncture, she decided; just follow Flavia's lead. She could recognise an expert in the bimbo field when she saw one.

'Ta-ta for now then,' trilled Flavia, 'see you during the speeches.' She pulled the silent Jules after her.

'He doesn't say much, does he?' Cockie muttered to Drew.

'Oh, he is often the life and the soul,' said Victor, 'but today I think he is prepared to be second fiddle to Flavia.'

His voice sounded closer, thought Cockie nervously, not daring to peep out from under her brim, even with The Fly sunglasses firmly in place.

'I don't think we were actually introduced outside the church, even though I wanted to be – my name is Victor Lan—'

'Caroline Fraser,' growled Cockie abruptly, 'and this is my husband.'

'Drew Fraser,' said the spouse in question, with a terrifying quaver that Cockie knew well. The bastard was about to laugh, she thought furiously. Ha-bloody-ha.

'I have to say that is the most incredible hat that I have ever seen,' said Victor. 'It is very spectacular . . . and, er, very big. I will just have to take your husband's word for it that there is just as spectacular a face underneath, no?'

He was flirting with her! And in front of Drew! Something inside Cockie flipped, all safety switches blown at the fuse, women and children abandoning ship all over the place.

Disengaging herself gently from Drew, she pulled off her hat with one hand, her sunglasses with the other and gave Victor her best, blazing, fuck-you beam of a smile.

'Spectacular?' she spoke clearly in her own voice. 'Why not judge for yourself?'

Just as quickly she jammed the hat back on her head and grabbed Drew by the hand. 'Now I really need some of that fresh air you were promising me, darling.'

And with that, she stalked off as best she could in her precipitous shoes, Drew flailing in her wake, and the image of Victor, gaping like a landed fish, etched permanently into her mind's eye.

Outside, an afternoon of the utmost limpidity awaited them, unlikely green swathes of fairway, with the occasional flash of Fair Isle, rolling in a manicured way into the wooded suburbs beyond, the very air soaked with a bucolic haze.

Cockie and Drew subsided onto a considerately placed garden bench.

'I was standing there, watching him talk to you and I thought, "No, she wouldn't, she won't blow it. For me, she'll keep a lid on that temper. She's too intelligent not to have weighed up the pros and cons of revealing who she is, she'd do that for me", then – kazzamm! Off you peel, bold as brass.'

Drew's voice faded away to a rumble as he buried his head in his hands. '. . . life flashing before me . . . fame and fortune . . . dreams snatched away . . . that eight-page feature in *Interiors* . . .'

Cockie took her hat off again, and massaged her head wearily. She had no idea what to say to Drew, how to comfort him.

'The Hellhag will have seen the whole thing,' she said slowly, 'she'll be told by Victor that her decorator is a con artist with an imposter wife; she'll then realise that you're gay when she tells Jonathan and sees him looking so shocked – there'll be a public humiliation – Nikki will knock Jonathan's lights out, Victor will deck me, you won't be able to work out whether to take out Nikki or Victor or just slit your own wrists – oh God,' she added brokenly, 'the last scene of *Hamlet* will have nothing on this. Bodies everywhere . . .'

The shoulder she was anxiously patting gave a sudden convulsion.

'Oh Drew, Christ, Drew, I'm so sorry – oh shit – please don't cry; I was just exaggerating, I'm sure Jonathan won't even find out and if he does and he still drops you then he obviously wasn't worth falling in love with in the first place—'

'Cockie!' Drew lifted up his curly brown head. 'Will ye just shut your trap?!' He drew in a long shuddering breath.

'Yes. Yes, of course,' said Cockie contritely. Then, looking closer, 'Hang on a minute . . .'

Tears squeezed themselves out of Drew's screwed-up eyes. 'I have never,' he started, gasping for air, 'heard such a load of total and utter,' he doubled up momentarily, as if in pain, 'a load of complete and utter shite . . .'

'You bastard!' Cockie launched herself at him, gloved fists flying, 'You're laughing! You're bloody well laughing!' All contrition vanished into the ether. 'And I was being so nice! You bastard! It's all your fault – I'd still have the most beautiful boyfriend in the world if it wasn't for this stupid bloody scam. Oh!'

Drew was too weak to defend himself. 'I'm sorry, I'm sorry, I'm sorry – what can I say? Ow! That bloody hurt! Och, I don't – hey! Stop that!'

Cockie found herself being smothered into Drew's chest as he muffled her fists with physical proximity.

'Don't even think about making me laugh,' she said into the region of his shoulders, 'we are in serious shit here and you have got to think of a way to get us out of it.'

Suddenly, she felt Drew stiffen.

'Shit is right,' he murmured, 'and here comes the fan.'

'What?' Cockie pulled away from him and turned around. 'Oh.'

'Cockie. A word please.'

St George, complete with large jousting staff, would have been handy at this moment. If Victor had been a Mills and Boon hero at the start, now he was one with bells on. Towering darkly over her and Drew, like a hurricane with a name; pale of face, beetled of brow, ice-splintered of eye, even – she was sure – a muscle ticking angrily in his jaw; he made looking angry a statement of romantic style.

Despite herself, Cockie was impressed. Judging by the spellbound look in his eyes, Drew was too. She also respected his courage in grasping the nettle by confronting her. *Her* first instinct was always to turn and run. Admiration made her unusually passive.

She got up, hat in hand. 'I'll catch up with you, Drew.' Then, with a flash of the usual Cockie, 'Keep an eye out for any strangling motions: feel free to intervene at that point.'

'Cockie,' warned Victor.

Drew stood up and pulled her close. 'Er, try not to tell him everything, my sweet,' he whispered. 'You know, keep it simple.'

Cockie nodded.

When they were out of earshot of the clubhouse, Victor cleared his throat. 'Shall you tell me what is going on?'

She didn't dare correct his grammar.

'It is clear that you are having an affair with that man – or is it me you were having an affair with? – but why did you have to pretend to be his wife? Or maybe you *are*' – menacingly – 'Caroline?'

At that she could only burst out laughing. 'Whoa! Easy, tiger!'

This didn't go down particularly well. She pushed on.

'Look, I *am* pretending to be Drew's wife, otherwise Nikki will sack him!' There, that was simple enough.

'Nikki? Mrs Friedman? Drew is the decorator for No. 42?'

Cockie nodded to each question.

'But why?' he stumbled on. 'Why married? Why you?'

'Well, I'm his best friend.'

'Yes, I saw that just now,' Victor interrupted grimly, 'and how many other best friends do you embrace so fondly? Ben too? Maybe I'm just one of a lot of men for you?'

'Oh, for God's sake, Drew is gay, thickhead.' Victor, she noticed crossly, even looked gorgeous with a jaw halfway to the floor, as he gaped again. 'Yes, gay – so now do you see?'

Victor's eyes bulged, and he brought his hand up to his forehead as if to push back some eruption from his frontal lobes. 'No.'

'You must know how the Hell – how Nikki feels about gays?' Cockie appealed. 'Well, there was no way that Drew would've got the job if she'd known he was homosexual and then, when he did get the job, it became all the more important to hush it up because of Jonathan.'

'Jonathan?'

'Yes,' Cockie rushed on, relieved that Victor seemed to be getting the picture, 'because Jonathan would stop going out with him if he knew Drew was single.'

'Jonathan? Jonathan and Drew?' gasped Victor in a strangled croak. 'My boss Jonathan?'

'Yes,' said Cockie shortly. 'Please try to keep up – this may be long-winded but it's the truth so it's the best apology you're going to get' – please forgive me, Drew-baby, she quailed inwardly – 'Jonathan will only keep seeing Drew if he's married which does sound—'

'Stop! Stop! There is no way, no way on earth, that Jonathan is homo – I would know! I work with him day and night! You know I do! I would know!'

'Well, you don't know, and you can take it from me that he is.'

Victor started. 'Take it from you? I would be mad! You are saying nothing except lies! You are being caught by me and you lie!' Victor blustered. 'You speak—'

'With forked tongue? Oh, give me a break with the broken down English when you're angry,' snapped Cockie blisteringly, that safety switch having gone again. 'It is so fucking corny when you do that! In fact, everything you do is corny, you homophobic, Eurotrash windbag of pulp fiction sleaze!' That was good, she thought. 'I don't have to explain anything to you – I owe you nothing, so run off back to your wankerbanker boss man – about whom you know *so* much – and ask him yourself if you don't believe me. Oh bugger it, I give up!'

Too wound up to think about making a dignified exit, she whirled around and ran back to the golf club, hating the way her high heels sank into the green as she did so.

Since she'd put her hat back on it was just her luck that Cockie should run slap bang into Drew without seeing who was behind him.

'Drew! Where the hell did you go? C'mon, let's vam—'

'Caroline!' interrupted Drew urgently, 'Mr Friedman was just saying that he'd like to meet you properly.'

'Oh!' Cockie shot her head up, remembering the low drawl just in time. 'Hello, Mr Friedman!'

'Please, call me Jonathan.'

Shit, Cockie thought fleetingly, this was getting like a farce. Any second now, Victor was going to come gaybashing round the corner and blow the whole gaff.

'I've heard a little about you from Drew but you'll have to fill me in on the rest, dear Caroline – may I call you that? – do you realise, for example, just how talented your husband is?'

On cue, Victor came pounding into the room behind Jonathan. Seeing the three of them standing together, he stopped, narrowing his eyes.

'That trompe l'oeil room at No. 42 will get us talked about in all the papers – you mark my words – but of course, you must know about all that sort of coverage from Drew's earlier jobs, eh?'

Please, please, please don't be a more complete creep than you already are, Cockie silently begged Victor, getting a crick in the neck, so that she could continue imploring him with her eyes. He glared at her, then at Drew, then at Jonathan. Then he walked past them, long legs flashing in time to the quickstep beat of Cockie's heart.

'Don't you?' pressed Drew's lover.

'What? Oh yes, I agree!' she beamed exaggeratedly at him, then saw the look on Drew's face and rushed to retrieve her mistake. 'I mean, I agree that this will really put Drew on the map – I've always had such faith in him that I felt that it was only a matter of time!'

'Well,' said Jonathan a little bumptiously, 'I'm delighted to have finally met you. I must say we were beginning to think that you were a figment of Drew's fertile imagination!'

Well, bugger me, thought Cockie, so that's that. Even without Victor, they'd been busted.

'I see now how stupid that was,' added Jonathan.

Drew and Cockie nearly fell over.

'Your wife is a great credit to you, Drew,' he said meaningfully, 'just as Nikki is to me.'

'Excuse me, miss,' piped a small voice from below Jonathan's stunning statement. Cockie felt a tugging on her hand and, looking down, she saw a tiny boy hopping on the spot with impatience. 'Please, you have to come with me!' he insisted, eyes dancing.

'Wha–?' Cockie looked helplessly around, and back to the little boy.

'Go on, darling,' said Drew, seizing any chance to get Cockie away from his lover, 'he's probably doing it for a dare. Humour him!'

'OK, my sweet, but can I tell you that this particular figment of imagination is going to clobber you when we get home – then there'll be physical evidence that you've got a wife – all over your face.'

'Husband-beater,' said Drew fondly after her, as she was dragged away.

They had reached a small space in the crowd when the child stopped.

'Too many knees,' he said succinctly, 'pick me up now.'

Awkwardly, Cockie bent down, strangely obedient, and gathered him into her arms. He could not have been more than four years old and she was instantly swamped with that perfect wave of baby smells – Johnson's powder, baby soap, and the indescribable distillation of pure human fragrance that was young young skin. She hoiked him up on her hip, hugging him closer and felt his chubby arms entwine themselves around her neck. For a long second or two, she stayed like that, oblivious to the populous, smoky swirls around her, caught in a spell of smell and warm, trusting weight.

Entranced, she then felt the boy, whose face had been

nuzzled into her neck, look up and stiffen alertly. He began to struggle against her clasp.

'Too tight. Too tight. Let me down now.'

She did as he asked, still bemused, and followed him obediently, as he grabbed her hand and plunged into the crowd again. Suddenly he stopped so quickly that Cockie, head dipped and bent double so that she could follow the twisting little body, nearly tripped over him and, unseeing and ankle-less over the knife edges of her shoes, put out a hand to save herself. It landed on a chest – luckily for her, a strong, manly one – and Cockie felt the strangest temptation just to collapse on it like a fainting young miss, until she recognised the tie and sprang back as if burnt by the contact.

'Oh! You.'

'Pretty lady,' said the child proudly.

'Yes,' Victor commented absently, his eyes fastened on Cockie's which she had, despite her best intentions, raised to his face.

'I am sorry,' he said simply.

'I'm sorry too,' said Cockie stiffly, her palm going damp in the child's grasp. 'I should have told you about this from the start.'

'I should have told you that I was coming here.'

There was a small pause.

'Why didn't you?' said Cockie, to fill the gap.

'I'm sorry?'

'Tell me that you were coming?'

'Because I didn't know myself – I had been invited but I thought that I was going to have to work all weekend – then Jonathan said to come out here and we would work together when it was over.'

'So like a good boy, you jumped when he said to, and came?'

'He's my boss,' said Victor as stiffly as her, 'naturally, I do what he tells me.'

'Well, I wish that I could drag you away from your work as easily,' fired Cockie, 'at least now I know who and what your priorities—'

'Hey!' said a commanding little voice. 'You pick me up now.' The boy tugged at Victor's coat tails. Cockie was about to tell the pesky little brat to sod off but, almost absent-mindedly, Victor bent down and picked him up, just as Cockie had done minutes earlier.

He spoke over the child's head. 'You cannot accuse me of—'

'Please don't fight!' said the boy clearly.

He twisted round in Victor's arms and gave Cockie a long look from sparkling eyes. Cockie stared back, wondering why everyone she met seemed to interfere in her life, even a demanding little tyke like this.

'All better now,' said the boy, and blinked.

Cockie's gaze shifted and now she took in the complete tableau of Victor and the child. Even when she denied feeling broody, Cockie was always a sucker for men and babies in close conjunction. Perhaps it was the contrast of hard with soft; straight planes with rounded; machismo with a child's fearless vulnerability, but she melted inside every time she saw a good-looking man hold a good-looking baby, and this mise en scène was straight out of an ad for Eternity. As she feasted her eyes on the toddler's round, little face tucked into the angles and shadows of Victor's neck, his cherubic complexion standing out against the tanned dark-jawed face above, one small hand resting trustingly on Victor's Hermes tie, a great weight seemed to lift off her and she began to understand what this was all about. With the look of a new-born baby focusing for the first time, she met Victor's own arrested stare.

'Yes,' she said hesitantly. 'All better now.'

12

'But don't you see?' asked Cockie. 'I suddenly had this big revelation that the whole thing is predestined – Victor and I are fated to be together.'

Ben rolled his eyes. 'Have you been over-doing the evil weed? Spending too much time on your own? I mean, give me a break. You bring me down for a nice weekend in the country with your brother and then start babbling supernatural nonsense at me just because you've got a captive audience. Cheap move, Cockie.'

'No, please, just humour me on this one, for one minute.'

Behind Cockie, Ben saw her brother, Robert, and his wife leave the house and set off across the garden away from where they were sitting in the fringes of the wood. Vandal and Visigoth watched them go, weighed up whether they wanted a walk, and decided against it, Vandal resting her black woolly head on Ben's foot. He settled himself more comfortably; it looked like he was in for a true Cockie-style philosophical discourse.

She kicked self-consciously at a tussock of grass. 'I think someone somehow has cooked this up for me, and is sending all these people to help me, push me in the right direction.'

'You mean, some kind of guardian angel?'

'I don't know about angel, but yes, that's the gist. Look, I know this sounds completely mad but some weird things have been happening to me lately and I have to come up with some sort of explanation.' Cockie looked up uncertainly.

One thing was for sure, thought Ben, he wasn't going to shut her up, no matter how much rubbish she was spouting. It felt like a million years since she had last confided in him like this, and he welcomed the return of the old intimacy between them – even if it was at the expense of Cockie's sanity. Since Red's party, he himself had been guilty of avoiding her, except when his masochism couldn't keep him away, like that hellish day last weekend when she'd done that wedding scam. She wasn't the only one who'd had a recent revelation.

That moment, supercharged by the number of times he had replayed it in his head, when Cockie had opened her amethyst eyes on top of the hill at Slake Manor, and looked into his . . . that split-second of electric communion between them when he had seen himself reflected in her pupils, before they shrank into pinpricks in the bright sunshine, taking that tiny image of himself with them, and with it his heart, locked for ever inside her, no longer just his own.

It was in that instant that he knew that, for the first time in his life, he had given himself, to her. Then, drenched by the backwash of cold reality, he had told himself that he had already lost her, to another man. The man that Cockie had now decided she was fated to be with. Victor. Mr Perfect. Mr Romantic Hero. Mr Successful. Mr Pin-Up. To say that the other man held all the cards was an understatement, to rail against the Powers-That-Be was patently useless since here was Cockie explaining that they were the ones who had set her up with Victor in the first place. It was time to be a good loser and be a good friend and a good listener and . . . maybe, just maybe, the deck would fall his way after all.

'OK,' he said, mentally girding his loins. 'Let's forget for a moment that we are normal, well-adjusted people and build a case for this supernatural involvement. What do you mean, weird things?'

'Well, taken separately there's nothing special but taken cumulatively it just all seems strange. For weeks and weeks now, everyone I've met has asked me whether I need help.'

'What, like "Can I help you off the bus?"' Ben couldn't help teasing.

Cockie didn't rise.

'Well, it's funny you should say that – the first time it happened it was on the bus!' Cockie exclaimed. 'I was on my way to the Gallery and I caught this girl's eye and I thought that, somehow, I knew her. You know me, and my memory for faces – and you know, *she* asked me whether I needed help. And ever since then I keep bumping into people who have that same something about them – this constant offer to help me and a look in their eyes that makes you look closer and wonder, really wonder, what they're up to. It all culminated with that guy at Goodwood airfield – you know, the pilot?'

Ben nodded.

'Normally, I wouldn't go in a car with a stranger, let alone an aerobatic plane, yet I asked him to take me up and again, it was as if I knew this person who was with me up there, who was talking to me through the headset. Then, when we landed, I made him take off his helmet. And I thought I recognised him as this guy who, surprise surprise, had offered to help me out at Mel's flat a few weeks ago – there was that same something in his eyes and he was wearing the same DMs—'

'DMs?' Ben confined himself to raising one eyebrow.

'I know, I know – everyone's got DMs, but he'd made such a point about them when I met him outside Mel's door that I thought he was a bit of an oddie. And this pilot was also wearing them.'

'Right.' Ben sneaked a look at his watch.

'I know, I know, it's tenuous, but he made such a point about, well, counselling me about Mum and Dad and Gus—'

'You told him about them?' Ben stared at her.

'Well, apparently I was talking about them up in the air but, you know, it was as if he already knew something about me and them, and all my hang-ups. Come to think of it, actually, he didn't seem too keen on Victor as this cure for my problems so perhaps you're right, perhaps this is all just baloney.'

Ben liked the sound of this pilot more and more. 'Certainly doesn't sound as if you're unanimously "fated to be with Victor,"' he said carefully.

'Yeah, but there are just too many coincidences – do you remember that night at Mel's, telling me that you thought it was an incredible coincidence that of all the people in the world, I had nicked Victor's parking space, provoking that sort of corny confrontation, Mills and Boon style?'

'Uh-huh.'

'Well, the Mills and Boon coincidence thing has got way out of hand. Virtually every time I write about Luca and Allegra—'

'Who? Oh, your characters,' said Ben, allowing himself to be confused for a moment.

'Yes, nearly every time they have any sort of coincidental meeting – without which Mills and Boons would collapse – something similar happens to Victor and me. Just one tiny example: in the book, Allegra answers an ad for a research job which involves archiving at an old house in Tuscany and, lo and behold, the house belongs to Luca, from whom she has just parted acrimoniously.'

'Sounds good,' joked Ben.

'Yeah, yeah. You know Victor has this totally dysfunctional family with pots of cash and different branches all over Europe? Well, it turns out that Victor's mother has an old villa near Padua and has just advertised for a researcher to do her archiving. Victor even joked that I should take the job – and I haven't even told him about the book, let alone little plot details! As for him turning up at that wedding at all – and Drew's lover being his boss – not only is that too much of a coincidence for anyone's liking but I also mentioned that in my book.'

'What?!'

'I couldn't resist using the scam as material, except that it was much more low key – Allegra is with her brother, Luca is there through his English relations but the point is that Luca assumes that Allegra is there with her lover, just as Victor did, and gets madly jealous, just as Victor did – for no reason, in either case!'

'Hmmm. Have you ever thought that the reason that Mills and Boons are so popular is because they do reflect human lives? Admittedly, they're exaggerated but you're treating this whole scenario like people who believe in horoscopes, or UFOs – just picking out the relevant bits to suit your case. This isn't *The X-Files*, Agent Scully. Come back to earth, my love.'

Cockie wasn't listening. 'So, anyway, that little boy was the final straw when it came to doing my head in.'

'You said it,' said Ben. 'You're a loonytoon. You forget that I have little brothers and sisters – kids are always being meddling little monsters – and anyway, in what way can a toddler be some sort of guardian angel? Granting you three wishes if you rub his finger paints jar?'

'Oh shut up, I'm serious about this,' pleaded Cockie. 'Anyway, it wasn't so much the child himself, although he did have that same sort of *sparkling* look in his eyes – no, it was more the way Victor and I behaved when the kid was around that was weird; as if all gloves were off, no more games or any social conventions about how one behaves in a certain situation.'

This was all getting a bit much. 'So what happened?

Did you ever find out who the little boy was?' Ben said abruptly.

'No, I didn't but then again we left soon after. Victor and I had a row about two minutes after the kid ran off, because I wanted him to leave with Drew and me, and he said that he had to stay on to do some bloody work with Jonathan – once everyone had gone home.'

'So after all that—'

'Yeah, after all that we parted – what's the euphemism? – on uncertain terms and Drew and I went home.'

'Look,' said Ben hesitantly, feeling a similar need to get things off his chest, 'I know I must have seemed a bit offhand with you that day, but I do admire you for carrying the whole thing off, very few people would have had the nerve or panache.'

Cockie wrinkled her nose. 'I don't know about panache.' She paused. 'Actually, for all I complain, I had a complete ball. Is that a terrible thing to say? After all, I couldn't have wreaked more havoc if I'd tried, could I?'

'Rubbish,' Ben assured her, 'there wasn't any real fallout was there?'

'We-ell, there was just the teensiest bit of fallout . . . when I told the bridegroom, Jules, exactly what I thought of him for carrying on with TJ, but I suppose I was decent enough to do that in private. We did get some strange looks when we came out of the billiards room together, though . . .'

'I don't want to know,' groaned Ben. 'I'm afraid . . . very afraid! Well, OK, but everyone believed the scam, didn't they?' He grinned suddenly. 'Even Victor! Your Perfect Partner, chosen for you by the powers-that-be, taken in by a little disguise – yep, sounds good to me!'

Cockie made a fist at him. 'Oi! Watch it!'

Their emergence from the right side of such an intense conversation made them both light-hearted.

'Put 'em up, pardner!' challenged Ben, raising his own

fists. For the next few minutes they sparred jokingly, Ben humouring Cockie by letting her land an unprecedented amount of punches. Soon the dogs, sensing that this horseplay was better than anything they could sniff out, romped over to join in. Being almost half the size of their human protagonists and twice as nimble, chaos ensued rapidly. Cockie, going for a lunge to Ben's midriff, tripped over Visigoth and went flying, but not without bringing Ben down as well. Vandal, perceiving great licking potential, dived gratefully into the fray. Ben, not sure whether he was tickling through the wool of Cockie's jumper or the wool of Visigoth's coat, felt a double assault; wet dog tongue under his chin, human fingers on his ribs.

'Ow!' came Cockie's laughter-muffled voice. 'That was my tit! Gerroff!'

Ben froze and whipped his hand back. 'Sorry,' he stammered.

'Ouf, I can hardly breathe.' Cockie extricated herself from the tangle of bodies, human and canine, and flopped on her back on the leaf-covered ground.

Fool, Ben berated himself savagely, that was total overreaction. He too lay flat and stared up at the blue sky, washed now by the slight chill of the encroaching autumn. Vandal, never one to pass up a human cushion, came and sat contentedly on top of him, black muzzle resting trustingly on his chest.

'Have I ever told you how much I love your dogs?' Ben said when he could trust himself to speak normally.

'Not as often as I tell myself that I do,' replied Cockie, nuzzling Visigoth's soft yellow ears, 'why else do you think I ever come here?' She laughed. 'How I love to hear the preachings of the converted! When I think how you used to slag off all poodles before you met them, I'm amazed that we ever became friends at all, let alone best mates.'

'Best mates?'

'The best,' said Cockie, reaching out blindly for his hand. Ben steeled himself not to snatch it away when she found it.

What a bloody bad idea to meet Laura for a last-ditch attempt at a sisterly drink before she got on the train, thought Eva, shivering in the rattling, bleak carriage. Stop torturing yourself by replaying the whole conversation, she commanded herself, it's undoubtedly what Laura would have wanted you to do. But she couldn't stop herself.

So many lies, so much poison spilling from that frosted pink mouth. Tales about Mike taking her out to dinner, subtle innuendoes that Eva was going to lose him, just like she'd lost everything she'd ever held dear. The same old not so merry-go-round.

Despite herself, hot tears sprang to Eva's eyes. She had loved Laura so much when she was born, competing with her mother to hold her, bathe her, cuddle her. When her mother had gently suggested that perhaps a five-year-old wasn't the best wet nurse, Eva had puffed herself up and announced that of course she was the best – she was so close to her in age that she would know what Laura wanted when she cried. She had never been able to understand siblings who fought with each other; she and Laura had always been so close, even with their age difference, throughout all the years of moving around the world following each posting of their father. But then, so imperceptibly that even now Eva couldn't put a finger on when, things had changed. The champagne of their childhood had soured into the vinegar of their teenage years until that final day. Never again, she had vowed then, would she be so easy to hurt, by Laura, or by anyone else, because never again would she love anyone so unreservedly.

That was the trouble with vows made when you

were eighteen; passionately made but eventually broken, diluted by a rosy-tinted nostalgia. Now, twelve years later, God only knew what Laura was reporting back to her parents, probably some poignant tale of not being welcomed by her long absent sister, being denied a place to stay and suchlike. Eva steeled herself to ring them for the first time in eleven years – carrying on this feud was only suiting Laura's purposes – and made a mental note to do so when she got back from this weekend.

Her heart quailed a little at the thought of this weekend. 'This is no big deal,' Mike had assured her, 'it's my father's sixty-fifth birthday so I'm going back for that and I haven't seen you all week so thought we might as well go together – no big deal!'

Having only a poisoned memory of her own parents, a very slight acquaintance with Ben's laissez-faire and terminally vague parents and with Cockie being an orphan, Eva wasn't very experienced with the older generation. Ho-hum, she braced herself mentally, and told herself to keep thinking that nothing could be as bad as that time she had been a snake, naked except for body paint, slithering around all the cast members as they read lines from *Paradise Lost* in eliding banshee wails. Now that had been mortifying, especially since they'd all been naked as well and she'd fancied Adam rotten, wrapping herself around him more zealously than even she had planned. As far as she could remember, it had gone down a storm with the audience . . . all eleven of them.

'Meningford, Meningford – change for Sleningford, Bleningford and Little Teningford,' intoned the station speaker where they were stopped. Something about Meningford rang a bell, she mused, hadn't there been a character from the Canterbury Tales – another stunning production by the Castor and Bollox Naked Company – from Meningford?

Meningford! That was her stop! Shit a brick! Eva leapt

up, grabbed her bag and flew to the nearest door. As she scrabbled at the door catch she could see Mike on the other side of the gate, with a well-preserved man who was presumably his father. She stopped to wave and as she did so realised that these doors opened from the outside. Needless to say, this window was jammed. To her horror, as she tugged at it she felt the train begin to rev up. No! She tugged harder and pulled an agonised face at Mike – so near and yet so far. Despite every prayer she could hurl at the jammed window, she felt the train lurch off its brakes and inch very slowly away.

'Help!' she bellowed at the living dead sitting right by the window. One of them looked up.

'It's no good, love, they won't open when the train's moving. That one's jammed, anyway.'

'Well, why the fuck didn't you say so earlier?' Eva gasped. She ran to the next door, opened the window and leant out to open it. Of course the man was right, damn his piggy little eyes, and with the rising momentum of the train she couldn't make it open.

'Mike!' she yelled out of the window, seeing him vault over the gate and come running towards her. 'I can't get out! I'll see you at the next stop! Sorry!'

He nodded and gave her the thumbs-up then dwindled behind her. She couldn't believe what had just happened and sank onto the banquette, clutching her head with shock. 'Shit. Fuck.'

'No need for that kind of language, dear,' said the same commuter corpse, 'and you won't be getting off at the next stop neither – this train doesn't stop there – it goes straight on to Benenden which is two stops behind that.'

Quite unfairly, Eva wanted to deck him. 'Well, that's just fucking great,' she announced flatly, 'I'm fucking dead so, with respect, I think there is a fucking need for that kind of language,' and she slumped back into her seat.

'Well, I think this Victor sounds like a top-notch fellow,' said Robert gravely. 'Earns a lot, good prospects, from what you say he's a good-looker – Cockie, I really don't think you can complain.'

He forklifted another mound of goulash, rice and peas up and managed to get nearly all of it into his mouth. Ben glanced at Cockie, seeing her wince none too subtly, and frowned at her; her brother's way of eating was unfortunate but Cockie's reaction was always excessive.

Ben himself liked Robert – he was clever, successful, bluff and often amusing. If he treated Cockie like a wayward teenage daughter instead of a sister then it was hardly surprising: he was fifteen years older and, since their parents had died, had been the closest thing Cockie had to a father. Perhaps if he and Ariana had had children it would have been different, he mused now, looking over at his hostess. Mind you, the thought of it . . . in the way that had made him charming par supreme to middle-aged women all over the world, Ben tried to imagine Ariana in bed, but gave up, shuddering at the thought. On the subject of Robert's wife, he and Cockie were in perfect accord; she was a raddled, overgroomed, bitter pill of a woman, who was enough to prejudice you against Americans for life. Just looking at her cold little eyes, made up to look like two crows smashed into that powdered white cliff face, was enough to send a little shiver up his spine.

Even for Saturday night supper with just the four of them, she was dressed up to the ninety-nines, bony shoulders poking out of some black lacy number, a choker of pearls clasped round her skinny chicken neck, one wing of her dead straight unlikely black hair held back coyly with some jewelled clip.

'If it weren't for the dogs,' Cockie had confided to Ben and Eva once, 'I don't think I would come home at all. It's not even my home, after all; old Banana always makes sure I know that I'm staying in one of the "*spare*" rooms, by changing which one I sleep in every time.'

From observing this family for six years, Ben laid the blame for Robert and Cockie's continuing estrangement squarely at Ariana's door. As far as he could see, she never missed an opportunity to poison Robert's mind against his sister, always leading him back to his old view of Cockie as a feckless, irresponsible teenager who couldn't be trusted to know her own mind or handle her own affairs. At any moment where he and Cockie might share a view or a laugh, Ariana would inject a deliberately provocative note designed to put them at loggerheads once more.

'If I've told you once, I've told you a thousand times, Robert,' Cockie was saying now, 'I'm not complaining, I was just trying to explain that I'm more interested in what forms a man's character than in the outward things.'

'Isn't that typical of Cockie, darling,' – as usual, Ariana's accent made it sound more like 'khaki' – 'trying to convince us that she isn't influenced by the fact that this wonderman drives a TVR motor car and earns more money in a month than we do in a year. Still the little idealist!'

'I wasn't aware that you earned anything, Banana?' Cockie snapped. 'So why do you say "we"?'

'Oh Robert, do stop her calling me that name – when *are* you going to grow up, Coquelicot?'

'Cockie,' reproved Robert, 'don't be unnecessarily provocative. It's so boring.'

Cockie gnashed her teeth but stayed silent. From the day Ariana, a glamorous American divorcee, had been introduced to the family as Robert's fiancée, she had put Cockie's back up by stating baldly that her name was not pronounced Arianna but Ariarna. 'As in banana?'

a sixteen-year-old Cockie had asked politely. Since her sister-in-law's sense of humour was on the small side of a very small thing, the name had stuck ever since as a fail-safe way of annoying Ariana.

'So when are we going to meet loverboy?' enquired Ariana winsomely.

'Oh, we're not lovers,' said Cockie airily. 'There has been no exchange of bodily juices as yet – well, apart from the fact that he's the most terrific kisser but that's only "making out" isn't it, Ariana? And there's you always thinking that I'm a complete tart – well, don't worry, I'm planning a sexual marathon with him pretty soon so I'll keep you posted.'

'Right, I've had just about enough of this crap,' Ariana snapped. 'I think it's time we left these guys to their brandy,' she stood up. 'Come along, Cockie – I have to write Mom and Dad but I'm sure you'll find something mindless and asinine to watch on TV.'

'Oh, for God's sake!' Cockie exclaimed. 'Dividing us up is archaic anyway but when there's only four of us, it's just bloody daft – in any case, I want some brandy.' And she stayed exactly where she was.

Robert lost his temper. 'Stop being a spoilt brat, Cockie, and do as Ariana says – I've got some accounts to discuss with Ben anyway, if you remember – I'd also like you to remember that you are a guest in Ariana's house. I simply won't have you being so rude to her.'

Cockie flushed and stood up. 'Oh, don't worry, Robert, I'll go – I get the hint.'

She picked up the brandy and headed for the dining-room door, then turned back. 'And if you think I could ever forget that I am only ever a guest in this miserable house, think again, brother. Thanks to you and your wife I am constantly reminded that I have neither a home nor a family!'

There was a small silence when she'd left. Vandal lifted

her head, saw who had gone, and followed Cockie. Visigoth slumbered on oblivious. Robert sighed heavily and looked at Ben.

'Looks like brandy's off, old man. How about some port?'

'Sounds great. Thanks Robert.' Ben, unsure whether it would serve anything if he went after her, stayed put.

Robert sat down and poured out two hefty glasses of port.

'Why is it that I never know what to say to my own sister?' he mused rhetorically. 'I'm nearly forty years old and I still don't have a bloody clue what goes on inside her head. What makes her say things like that? Why is she quite such a drama queen? I've tried so hard with her in the past but when she hardly ever comes home and is so poisonous and immature when she is here, what am I supposed to do? I can't let her go on behaving like that to Ariana, can I? And yet, I just feel like blubbing my eyes out when she says things like that.'

As touched by Robert's uncharacteristic unburdening as he was appalled by the man's blindness, Ben steered a safe course. 'Well, I'm sure that she only said that in the heat of the moment.'

'Bloody hothead,' Robert agreed affectionately. 'I'm sure I don't know where she gets it from – my Ma and Pa weren't the emotional type, especially not with us – Pa didn't really rate infants, just waited for them to be well-read enough to argue back with him – and although Cockie was such an afterthought I doubt they were much different with her, especially since my mother was quite the little businesswoman by then. Mind you, Gus was always fond of the histrionics, so she shares that with him.'

'What was Gus like, exactly?' asked Ben. 'I'm sorry, that's unbelievably nosy of me.'

'No, no, long time ago, my boy, doesn't bother me

at all.' Robert paused. 'Gus? Well, I know this isn't Cockie's opinion – she idolised him, of course – and one shouldn't speak ill of the dead and all that – but I thought he was a pain in the arse, if you'll excuse my French. Devastatingly good-looking but an absolute flibbertigibbet, always chasing after the girls, never did any work, dropped out of Cambridge – or was he thrown out? Can't remember. Permanently broke – but always managed to wheedle enough cash out of my parents to bail himself out and then some. He was bloody charming, though – that's what always saved him.'

He held his port up to the light consideringly, then gulped some more down. 'I'll never forget him coming to see me when I was doing some extra accountancy exams and asking for a loan. Well, as Cockie has no doubt told you I am the original pinchpenny so he must have known his prospects weren't good, but whether it was because I was distracted by my revision or what, I don't know, but he got the loan out of me, no questions asked, and a few days later, I heard that he'd used it to put towards a quarter share in a blasted aeroplane! I ask you! But he loved flying more than anything else, and three months later he was dead, so I suppose I'm glad I made his last few weeks happy.'

'Was Cockie very devastated when he died?' Oh, asinine question, Hyde, Ben chided himself.

'Completely. Utterly. Much more so than she seemed to be when my parents died. We thought she'd never recover, actually. She used to have the most terrible nightmares – well, attacks really – when she'd scream the house down, not crying, you understand, just this awful wailing, almost a keening sound, like an animal. And she'd rip her hair out and retch like blazes but never actually throw up. It was horrible.' He shuddered.

'I'm sorry,' said Ben, 'perhaps we shouldn't—'

'You see, she never saw through him the way the rest

of us did. To her, he was just the most glamorous thing ever, who spoilt her rotten when he didn't have anything better to do, who called her pet names and encouraged her to follow him around like a blasted lapdog. So when he suddenly collapsed with some disease that she'd hardly even heard of and then died two days later it was as if,' he paused, 'well, I suppose it was as if the lights just went out.'

To his horror, Ben felt a lump come into his throat.

'But it was amazing, you know,' Robert went on after a moment, 'for a couple of weeks – well, we were all shell-shocked – but it was as if Cockie had actually gone with him, or at least as if the spark that had been so bright in Cockie had been snuffed out as well, and the only time she really came to life was in the most awful, horrific fashion, during those night-fits of hers. And then, suddenly, one morning, she just came bouncing down to breakfast, all bright and breezy and announced to my parents that she wanted to go to some party in London that night and could she have some money for some frock or other. It was simply amazing: I remember my father talking later about the resilience of youth and how the young can process their grief so much more efficiently than we could, and I must say I think he was right because we never heard her having those night attacks again.'

He stood up and gazed blindly at the portrait above the empty fireplace. 'Even when the car crash happened eighteen months later, she was . . . so strong, as if Gus's death had forged a resilience within her. I was working in America at the time so I had to go back there after a few weeks, but Cockie took my father's death in her stride and nursed my mother every day until she too died seven months later. I came over as much as I could but I'll never forget how calm Cockie seemed then, almost unnaturally calm, as she dealt with my mother. She and Cockie had never got on before, not close anyway, and before she died, Ma was a complete bi— well, she wasn't a good invalid and gave Cockie a terribly tough time. Cockie was just on her wavelength, though; that's what I remember thinking – I can't explain it but it wasn't as simple as Cockie being sympathetic towards her – Good God no, sometimes they went at each other like cats and dogs – but as if she had some inkling of what my mother was going through – not the physical pain but the whole agonising separation from life.'

Robert rubbed his hand across his face. 'Christ! I'm spouting complete mumbo-jumbo – I am sorry, Ben old chap, how did we ever get to talking about this – how terribly maudlin I've become. Frightfully embarrassing – I do apologise.'

'No, no, it's all my fault for opening up the subject,' Ben assured him.

'Well, we've polished off the port at any rate, so if I were you I would trot along and see what's become of that brandy. We'll take a look at the accounts tomorrow – I'm far too sozzled to make any sense of them now.'

'Can I bring you back some brandy?' offered Ben. 'We could make a night of it – just for a change!'

Robert smiled and waved his hand at him. 'No, no, not tonight thanks – I think I'll nurse what's left here, talk to my Vizzy Dog and then hit the sack. Good night Ben, you're a good man.'

'Night.'

Just as Ben reached the door, Robert spoke again, his speech now slightly slurred.

'You know, Ariana's a lot more perceptive than any of you realise.'

'No, yes, I'm sure.' Ben stammered.

'No, please, don't apologise, I know exactly what you and Cockie think of her and I don't blame you, but for me she's perfect. Always loved her, y'know. Anyway, she can be very sensitive . . . when she met Cockie for the first time about a year after Gus's death and then again after my father died, she said that she thought that Cockie hadn't got over her grief, that she was repressing it all inside her, and that she should see some grief therapist. I couldn't see it at the time – still can't, really – and a therapist seemed rather an extreme, well, rather an American solution, but I was willing to give it a try. Cockie went berserk, of course, accused Ariana of interfering, bla bla bla, and has hated her ever since.' He looked intently at Ben. 'I'm only telling you this because, well, I think – I think you probably know why . . .'

Ben didn't dare guess what Robert was muddling his way towards. 'Er, yes, probably.'

'Good. Enough said.' Robert was suddenly brisk. 'Always liked you, Ben – mind you, you're the only friend Cockie ever brings here—'

'Ah, you forgot Eva!'

'Please, spare me . . . ghastly hippy.'

'Robert . . . you promised . . .'

'I wonder if this Victor character will now join you in that privilege, eh?' Robert twinkled at him.

Ben paused. 'With the greatest respect, Robert, I neither know nor care.' And that, he told himself, was as big a lie as he had ever told.

'Look, don't worry about the train business,' Mike assured Eva, 'it just meant that everyone was pissed by the time we got back, so the party went with more of a bang. You were great, you had them eating out of your hand. It was all just bad luck – sue BR is what I say!'

Eva later blamed it on the alcohol and a long, lousy day, but for no good reason, a red fog of anger swept up inside her at these words.

'Why are you always so bloody reasonable?' she spat at him. 'Just for once in your measly life, be *honest* even if it means making a few ripples – dare to be different,

Mike! Just because you make your living from being Mr Boring in the ads doesn't mean you have to be so, so fucking mild in real life – you can say the truth without hurting someone, you know, you could just say, "Eva, only a complete tosser would fail to open a train door. You're a total bimbo but I love you anyway."'

Mike stared at her as if she were a rabid dog. 'Maybe because that wouldn't be me talking,' he murmured.

'What?!' It was Eva's turn to stare at him.

'Look, never mind, just come into the den and let's have a drink.' He turned away, not looking her in the eye.

Eva began to feel very afraid.

'I'm sorry, sweetheart, I've had a really shitty day, what with one thing and another but I shouldn't take it out on you – you know I didn't mean it, it's just that I met Laura for a drink before I came and you know how that always puts me in the foulest mood.'

'So why do you go on meeting her?' he asked mildly. 'Not that I see anything wrong with her, but you obviously have a bad case of sibling rivalry, so why put yourself through it every time?'

'Sibling rivalry?' she hissed. 'It is nothing to do with fucking sibling rivalry, you condescending arsehole! Is that what she told you it was? Did she spin you that little tale over your dinner at Bibendum?'

'Shush, you'll wake my parents up,' he frowned repressively at her. 'Of course she didn't tell me – it's perfectly obvious – and what's this about Bibendum? You know I've never been there.'

Somehow the fact that Laura had been lying after all, didn't make Eva feel any better – in fact, she was well aware that she was losing control of the situation. She took a deep breath.

'It's not obvious, actually, but I see that I—'

'Look, Eva,' he interrupted, 'we need to talk. Every time

we see each other we seem to argue – going round and round in circles – about your sister—'

'Which is why I need to give you an explanation about Laura and me,' she retorted. 'Don't you see that I get so annoyed with you because you just don't know Laura the way I do? I can't stick seeing you being taken in by her, and if that makes me bad-tempered and hell to be with, then I apologise but you'll see why!'

'Eva, we're not babes in the wood and I don't think Laura's the problem here—'

'But she is! For Christ's sake, will you listen, Mike? When I was eighteen years old and Laura was only thirteen, she told me that I was illegitimate, that I was born to my mother before her marriage and that the man I had called my father all these years had adopted me when I was three years old. She was, she said, the only child my parents had had between them, and that my father had always resented my bastardy. I went straight to my mother and asked her if this were true and she went berserk, accusing me of snooping through her private drawers and of trying to pass the buck onto my sister who was, she said, far too young to do such a devious thing. But eventually she calmed down and said that, yes, it was true. Now, it was a shock but I was a big girl, I had just got into university and had a happy life and I knew, no matter what Laura said, that my father – my adoptive father – loved me as much as I loved him, so I just got on with my life.'

Eva paused, and looked levelly at Mike. 'But she didn't stop there. One day I came home from school early. My Dad was on leave at the time and was spending a few days at home, so I thought I'd get home early to see him. I hung my coat in the hall – oh, I was a good girl in those days – and heard Laura speaking to them in the kitchen. Something made me hang back, so I heard the whole conversation from outside. She was telling them that I now hated my father because he wasn't my real father, that I thought my mother was a whore for giving birth to an illegitimate child and that I was determined to find my real father and live with him instead.'

'My God,' murmured Mike.

'Just remember that this was a thirteen-year-old girl dreaming all this up,' Eva said tightly. 'Of course, everyone was going to believe her. Anyway, I went charging into the kitchen to clear my name, but before I could get a word out, my father just came over to me and walloped me, right down to the floor. "That's for calling your mother a whore," he said. I remember seeing my school badge which had disappeared weeks before, lying in all this grunge under the fridge, and thinking that things couldn't get much worse. Then he picked me up and slapped me again, and said, "And that's for all the years of love and support I gave you." My mother just sat there and watched the whole thing with this look of total betrayal on her face – as if the jury had already condemned me. And Laura? She wasn't quite gloating, not quite: she was sitting there with this look of suppressed excitement on her face, and this terrible, tiny, nervous smirk.'

'Is that when you ran away?' asked Mike gently.

'Oh no, I was in far too much shock to think of that, and, at that point, far too deep down sensible to do it – I still thought that somehow the whole mess would be cleared up. I was sent to stay with my Gran – my adoptive grandmother – while my mother got over the shock. I'd been staying there for a few days when a letter arrived from my father. It was a typewritten letter, for God's sake, not even handwritten, saying that since I wanted to know who my real father was, he thought he'd better tell me. He said that my mother had been raped—'

'Jesus!'

'—and had never wanted to keep me once I was born.

But by that time she'd met my father, who was posted over there, and he had persuaded her that she should keep it and love it as he would, and three years later he kept his word and adopted me. He then went on to say, in this letter, that if he'd known how ungrateful I'd be when I grew up, he would never have given her that advice, that anyone who threw away sixteen years of love did not deserve to be called his daughter and that neither he nor my mother ever wanted to see me again.'

Eva took a deep breath. 'That's when I ran away.'

She looked steadily at Mike. 'Now I don't want sympathy or pity or anything like that: this all happened a very long time ago, and I'm well over it, but now you must understand why I hate Laura and why, even though she was so young, and it was so long ago, I can't really see reason where she's concerned.'

'Why did you never tell me anything of this before?' said Mike sadly, staring intently into his drink. 'I thought we were meant to be close, open with each other. Isn't that what people are when they're in love?'

'Telling someone that you are the illegitimate by-product of a rape isn't exactly easy, you know.'

Look at me! She screamed silently at him. Tell me it doesn't matter! Tell me that you love me!

Mike got up and gave her a gentle, oddly impersonal hug. Eva gazed up at him with frozen, guarded eyes.

'None of that makes the slightest difference to me,' said Mike softly, 'you must realise that.'

Eva sagged against him in relief. Everything was going to be all right.

As he crept into the sitting-room, Ben's head was reeling with port and the story he had just heard. Having built up a picture of Cockie as a strong noble martyr to grief, he was a little taken aback to find her lolling on the floor by the fire, chuckling merrily at the telly and, by the look of it, a few glasses down the brandy bottle.

'Bloody hell, you were ages – what on earth were you two talking about?' she hailed him. 'You've missed about twenty minutes but I love this film so you'll just have to shut up and watch it with me.'

'What's on?'

'*The Tall Guy*. I couldn't believe my luck when I saw it was on.' She patted the rug beside her. 'Come and sit here with me – Banana must have chosen the furniture in here because I can never get comfortable anywhere else but the floor.'

Ben did as he was bidden and Cockie handed him her glass.

'Yikes, your hands are cold! That dining room is bloody perishing, isn't it? Here, let me rub them.'

Ben wasn't complaining. In fact, as Cockie snuggled into his arms so that they could both watch the telly comfortably, and they settled in to watch the film, he allowed himself to sink into the intimacy of the embrace. Hey, I can dream, he told himself.

Involuntarily, he thought back to that first time with Cockie – back in her first year at Oxford when he was still a fully paid-up, over-testosteroned member of the Whamming, Bamming and Thanking School of Thought. He and Cockie had met at her college's Christmas disco, smouldered at each other across the dance floor, and indulged heavily in the cut-price beer, before succumbing to the undergraduate's idea of foreplay – juvenile crime. In their case this had involved delivering flowers – well, uprooted bushes from the Master's shrubbery – to all her friends, before falling into bed and wrestling with their clothes and each other in Cockie's unfeasibly small bed. The bin outside the door – Oxford semaphore for 'Do Not Disturb' – stayed there for the next day and night while they rumpled the sheets, ate toast in bed and generally revelled in the sexual freedom that being at university, without parents or commitments, could provide.

On the Sunday morning Ben had left to play football, never imagining that Cockie's fantasies had projected to the point where they patted their grandchildren fondly on the head from his'n'hers rocking chairs. For him it had been a self-contained fling, bridging the fun-filled gap between end of week tutorials and Sunday sports; for Cockie it had been the warm-up to the main event; a beautiful relationship where they would be the First Couple of Oxford, free spirits sparkling together, independent apart but better together, emotionally relaxed but deeply committed.

The next couple of weeks had been agony for both of them – he trying to be firm but friendly, she trying to be irresistible but dignified – even now Ben winced at the memory. It had taken months for them to dredge a friendship out of the wreckage that time, making Ben even warier now. The last thing he could do was fuck up again.

All too soon, they were watching the final few minutes. The fire had sunk down to a few embers, leaving the room dark but for the light from the TV. As he watched Jeff Goldblum pick Emma Thompson up and spin her round, Ben's arm tightened involuntarily around Cockie. She turned her head round and looked at him questioningly. For the longest second, they gazed at each other, film forgotten as the world retreated to a tiny space around them, vibrating with the minute tension he had unleashed.

Now! Ben told himself frantically. Go for it now! Seize this chance! As if still rooted in a fantasy of his own making, he saw Cockie's lips part, felt her warm, sweet, brandy-scented breath pat unevenly on the soft skin of his neck. Deep in the shadows of her eyes, deep purple in the dimness, he imagined he saw his answer and hardly daring to breathe, heart threatening to burst out of his chest, he lowered his head towards hers. Then – put there by some devil intent on mischief – a picture of her and Victor in Red's walled garden, locked in almost this same embrace, flashed through his head, making him check momentarily. It was enough. The spell was broken. Cockie blinked and smiled at him – not a promising smile but her usual friendly grin – and suddenly there was no communication from her eyes.

'So what were you and Robert talking about for so long?' she asked softly. 'I'm sorry about my little outburst – I hope that didn't mean that you were discussing me . . . ?'

Before he could help himself, Ben must have let something slip by his expression, for Cockie suddenly pulled away.

'You were, weren't you?'

'Sort of,' he conceded lightly, 'a bit of family history, that's all. Nice guy, your brother – he thinks the world of you, you know.'

He smiled nervously but it didn't wash. She suddenly pulled up close to him again, and looked him intently in the face, frowning.

'Is this pity I see in your eyes, Ben?'

'What? Not at all! Why should I—' he blustered.

'It is!' she said furiously. 'How dare you? Oh God, you've had the whole sorry story from Robert and you've decided how tough brave little Orphan Annie here has had it – well, fuck you!'

'Cockie—'

'No! I won't have it! I know you mean well, but I will not have our friendship built on some kind of misguided noble sentiments from you. Yes! My brother died! Yes! My parents died! So. Fucking. What. Why can't anyone believe that it doesn't have to rule the rest of my life and it certainly doesn't have to rule the way people see me? I'm so fucking sick of being psychoanalysed and I won't be by you of all people! So just drop it!'

'Look, Cockie—'

'I said DROP IT!'

Ben spread his arms wide. 'OK, OK, consider it dropped.' He smiled broadly, praying that she'd fall for the Ben-at-his-most-casual act. 'You little termagant, you're so damn touchy – I was only trying to be nice. Remind me not to make that mistake again! Jeez!'

It worked. 'You – nice?' she joked back. 'Nah – too unconvincing – it wouldn't have lasted long!'

'You can talk, you've never even asked me about my childhood problems!'

'Ben!' she warned, but followed it up with a smile. 'Anyway, your family's much too boring – I've never seen such a happy domesticated little unit – yuck!'

Ben had never loved her so much as he did then. The trouble was, he realised with a sinking heart, his timing was way, way off.

As Cockie tiptoed up the first flight of stairs and floated past the closed door to Eva's room she heard telltale sounds coming from inside. Petrified with embarrassment, she hovered at the bottom of the stairs, suddenly painfully aware of how squeaky the next flight of stairs up to her room in the attic was. This was a seriously bad idea, she thought, hating the idea of Mike and Eva being able to hear her hearing them making love. She and Ben would just have to do without cigarettes, she decided, turning to go back downstairs. Despite herself, she listened to the sounds again, and frowned. It sounded more like someone was . . . taking her courage in both hands she tapped softly on the door. 'Eva? Are you all right?'

There was silence then the door was opened.

'Oh, Eva . . . you look terrible.'

The small woebegone figure facing her gave a weak

laugh. 'Why don't you speak your mind, Cockie?' Then her face crumpled. 'Cockie . . . he chucked me!' Turning away from her, Eva stumbled back to the bed. Literally stumbled, as she stepped on a shoe, lost her footing in the tangle of clothes on the floor and pitched forward, missing the bed completely and ending up face down in her laundry basket, long hair spread from east to west. Cockie gripped a hand to her mouth, willing herself not to laugh, knowing that sometimes there was a line across which one should not joke, and came to sit on the bed.

'Things cannot get worse,' said a muffled voice from the laundry basket. Eva got up on her knees and shook her hair out of her eyes. 'I don't want to laugh. I have never felt less like laughing in my life,' she said.

'Oh Cockie,' she wailed, turning to her, 'it was so humiliating – I unburdened the whole story on him about Laura and my dad and everything, you know?'

Cockie hugged her, nodding understandingly as if she knew what Eva was going on about.

'And then he said that none of it made any difference and' – her gasps and shudders increased for a moment – 'I was so relieved, I thought everything was going to be all right!

'And then . . . and then he said that it made no difference because it wasn't the facts of my story but the effect that it was having on our relationship that was damaging.'

'What did he mean?'

'He said that Laura's turning up had shown him that there was something wrong with our relationship if I couldn't tell him about a whole chunk of my life. That I was obsessed with Laura being this evil force in my life, and that until I was free of her, he couldn't see any future in our relationship, he couldn't see how he could ever fit in.

'And then he said that I had to stop blaming everything

bad in my life on her, that I had to exorcise her from my heart and mind before I would be free, and then I realised that he really was chucking me.'

'I can't believe it!' Cockie commiserated.

'But Cockie, it's so unfair!' Eva howled, 'I'm the one that spouts the psychobabble – not him – how dare he? There he was, wittering on about wanting different things from life, how he didn't think that he lived up to my romantic ideal, that I took him for granted, that at this point in his career he wanted stability and support, not a girlfriend who thought that he wasn't achieving enough and who shied away from commitment at the slightest excuse. You know, all the usual whitewash tripe.'

'He said all that?'

'Yes. Bastard.'

'Yes, but well-scripted bastard,' said Cockie thoughtfully. 'You don't think that maybe, just maybe, he was telling the truth? That he'd composed a long list of grievances and thought that he had to make a stand?'

Cockie was proud of herself; Eva would never guess that she was clutching at straws. Sure enough, one pink watery eye looked up from her shoulder – in it was the faintest dribble of hope.

'I doubt it,' Eva said weakly. 'Anyway, he knew I loved him. What more did he want?'

'No, no, hang about.' Cockie was getting into the sort of pitching stride that Emma and Edward from the Gallery would have recognised. 'If you think about that weekend down at Red's, which was the last proper time that I saw you together, you were being a real stroppy cow with him – teasing him about that radio play, getting at him every time he opened his mouth – you even seemed quite relieved when we were all put into those dormitories and you didn't have to share a room with Mike, then when—'

'Cockie,' Eva sniffed and gulped, 'you're supposed to be on my side!'

'Sweetness, I am, don't you see? All you have to do, if I'm right, is convince him that you love him for himself, not for the idea you think you should have of him.'

Eva suddenly sat up away from Cockie, looking at her with something approaching awe. 'That's it! Cockie, you're a genius! Being with Mike meant that I was starting to relax all my old defences and ideas, and I think it freaked me out. You're brilliant!'

Oh God, prayed Cockie, please don't let me have given her false hope.

She stood up. 'Look, I'm going to get a cuppa and a fag – I take it that you would like both of the above?'

'You bet,' said Eva thoughtfully, 'then we can talk about how I'm going to get him back.'

'Attagirl.'

'Oh, Cockie!'

'Yeah?'

'There's a message on the machine from Victor.'

'What does he say?'

Eva managed a bleary but convincing twinkle. 'I think you should listen to it. At least someone's lovelife is about to take a turn for the more romantic!'

Cockie was thoughtful as she went downstairs. There was nothing like witnessing other people fuck up their own lives to make you want to avoid doing the same. She had to stop worrying about the details, the probably imaginary oddities about her relationship with Victor.

She pressed Replay on the answering machine.

'Hello Cockie,' came Victor's voice, sounding more accented than it did in real life, 'it is Sunday morning – please phone when you come home – no matter what time, I will be awake, and waiting for your call. In the meantime, here is a poem that I have read recently which says something of my feelings for you, and which I hope will be an apology for the empty time I have spent away from you.'

Crikey Moses, thought Cockie inelegantly, pressing Pause for a moment to catch her breath, poetry? So long longed-for, so daunting now it was here. Here goes.

> '*When in disgrace,*' started Victor's voice – good grovelling start, she thought –
> '*with fortune and men's eyes,*
> *I all alone beweep my outcast state,*
> *And trouble deaf heaven with my bootless cries.*'

I just can't quite believe that I'm having Shakespeare quoted at me down a telephone line, thought Cockie.

> '*Haply I think of thee; and then my state,*
> *Like to the lark at break of day arising*
> *From sullen earth, sings hymns at heaven's gate;*
> *For thy sweet love remembered such wealth brings*
> *That then I scorn to change my state with kings.*'

Cockie leant against the wall.

'Oh my Good God,' said Ben, who had come in halfway through, 'the guy's a total nutter.'

Cockie turned dreamy eyes up to his. 'You just have no idea about romance, whereas Victor is the sort of man who is stylish enough to do this without embarrassment.'

Ben was obviously nettled. 'You've been reading too many magazines, my sweet. Anyway, it's easy to spout that sort of rubbish into an anonymous answering machine – in the real world, you say this sort of thing face to face if you're really *romantic*.' He put a dopey emphasis on the last word.

'Well, let's give him a chance to do just that, shall we?' said Cockie, rising to the unintended bait. 'This is finally it; this will be the Big One – I can just feel it.' And she reached out for the telephone.

13

Cockie was on her eighth cigarette of the day, and it wasn't even lunchtime. The amount of booze that she, Ben and Eva had plied themselves with the night before could be seen in her more than usually bloodshot eyes, the tangled hair, and the slackness of her jaw. Drew thought she had rarely looked better. With an air of suppressed excitement about her, she looked like a kettle about to come to the boil as he watched her jiggle nervously in front of an arrangement of what looked like children's potato drawings.

'Did he say all four, or just one of them?' she muttered to herself, the hand holding the cigarette swooping down and up to her mouth like a gloworm on speed.

'Look, girlfriend, will you just settle down and stop hyperventilating. Why are you so jumpy, anyway? Did you go to Silverman's this morning or what? Is that what this is all about?' Drew suddenly looked alarmed and sat up straighter.

Cockie flopped down on the sofa beside him and grinned briefly. 'No, don't worry – well, not really – well, yes, sort of, but not exactly.'

'Och well, clear as mud,' said Drew drily.

'No, I did go to Silverman's – have you ever been there? It is the most unbelievable place – we're talking major *Fountainhead* territory here – these enormous grey steel pillars, with these tiny little bankers tippy-tapping their way through shiny marble football fields—'

'Cockie, get to the point – I'll take notes on the décor later.'

'Well, the long and short of it was that, as luck would have it, the canvases we were delivering were destined for the corporate finance floor, so I saw both Victor and Jonathan—'

'Oh no!'

'—but neither of them saw me, so relax, loverboy! Don't worry – your bloody marriage is still in place!'

Drew wagged a finger at her. 'Temper, temper, Miss Milton.'

Cockie sighed and closed her eyes, hands reaching blindly for another cigarette. 'God, you're camp today, I'm not sure I can cope. Go away.'

'Not until I find out what's making you smoke like a runaway train, lassie.'

'Tonight,' said Cockie, drawing in such a deep lungful, the cigarette nearly burnt out, 'tonight I am going to sleep with Victor for the first time!'

The dramatic impact of this statement was rather blown by Emma arriving back at that very moment.

'Cockie! Why are you lying on the sofa? What if I had been a customer?'

'Well, you're not and anyway, I'm chatting up a potential customer here.'

From her position on the sofa, Cockie watched Emma's face split into a delighted smile as she took in how cute Drew was. Right on cue, down came the eyelashes and the chin, up came the pout and the libido.

'Well, I think I can probably take over from here, thank you, Cockie.' She shrugged off her coat. 'You couldn't take this for me, could you, darling?'

Cockie grabbed the coat with murderous intent. Drew, spotting this, broke in before Cockie lost her job, 'Actually, if you don't mind, I was just asking Miss Milton here if she wouldn't mind coming out to lunch with me.' He rushed on before Emma could interrupt. 'It's just that I'm doing up this hotel – the old Hyperion in Duke of York Street – and Miss Milton was coming up with such very good ideas for some of the artwork that I thought she might like to see the site and then we could discuss some schemes over lunch.'

There wasn't much she could say to that. Cockie handed back her coat with a big smile, and passed on the necessary messages and queries to a suddenly tight-lipped Emma and within a minute they were out on the street.

'So, why are you so nervous?' said Drew, when they were in the pub. He put the drinks down and sat opposite her.

'Oh, y'know, stage fright,' said Cockie vaguely, lighting yet another fag. The truth was, seeing Victor in his native environment had not been what the doctor ordered. Black hair combed ruthlessly back, stern and forbidding in his exquisitely draped dark suit, broad shoulders thrust forward pugnaciously as he strode past her (she, shrinking behind a large canvas) tossing orders behind him to the secretary trotting prettily in his wake, it hadn't seemed possible that he could be the same person with whom she had exchanged promise-laden sweet nothings on the telephone the night before.

'Well, I think it's great news that you're finally going for it. About bloody time too – this saintly abstinence didn't sit well with you. Does he know what's in store for him, or is he just a wee sacrificial lamb?'

'Well, I hardly told him to pencil "sex session" into his diary,' Cockie snapped. 'We're having dinner, that's all.'

'Let me guess – at his place?'

'You bet,' said Cockie, with a flash of the old balls-breaker showing through. 'He made the mistake of asking where I wanted to go.'

'That's my girl,' leered Drew. 'So, what's the plan?'

Cockie collapsed like a punctured balloon. 'Oh, I don't know,' she wailed, 'I suddenly feel like such a novice! If it wasn't for that three stab wonder with Sam—'

'Sam's rubbish in bed?' breathed Drew. 'How fascinating!'

'Yeah, lean and mean in more ways than one. Anyway, if it wasn't for that, I could qualify to be a Born Again Virgin twice over which hardly fills my confidence cup to overflowing – I mean, what happens if I've forgotten how to do it?'

'Well,' Drew said practically, 'do you actually want to sleep with Victor?'

'Do I want to?' Cockie repeated blankly. 'Of course I do, I mean, he's gorgeous and sexy and . . . and, well, he's mad about me – not many of them around.'

'But how much do you like him?' Drew pressed.

'Like him? Of course I like him! We have great chats about all sorts of things – I mean, he's led an interesting life, traipsing around Europe and America; we do interesting things together – like going to that car rally—'

'Cockie!'

'Well, how can you quantify liking someone?' she asked defensively. 'You either do or you don't – how can I really know? Really? I've been on a handful of dates with him with nothing more physical than some great snogging, but every time I'm with him there is this unbelievable sense of intimacy between us – like with no-one else I've ever known—' She broke off, thinking of one recent exception in front of the television the previous weekend, and blushed. Drew looked intrigued.

'Do you think you love him?'

'Love? I don't know!' Surrounding drinkers turned to see what was going on. More quietly she went on, 'Who knows when they're in love?'

'*I* know.'

'Oh bollocks, how can you be in love every five minutes? Chopping and changing from one bloke to the next and always insisting that this is It, this is the Real Thing?'

Drew leaned back, offended. 'If you're going to take that sort of attitude then I'm—'

'Drew, I'm sorry! I shouldn't have said that – you're probably right but I personally don't have any certainty of when lust, liking, loneliness – whatever – when they all coalesce into this mythical love *thang*!'

'Boy, are you cynical,' Drew whistled.

'No,' grimaced Cockie, 'worse; hopelessly romantic – always wondering if there isn't something better round the corner.'

'In which case, I don't think you are in love,' stated Drew forthrightly. 'Do you get the feeling that we're going round and round in circles here? Crisp?'

'Yes, you're right. Yes please.'

They crunched in silence for a moment or two.

'Now,' said Drew, 'let's cut to the action – what are you going to wear?'

Cockie told him.

'And have you got your condoms?'

'Drew!'

'Cockie!' mimicked Drew. 'Well, have you?'

'Oh God, somewhere, but they're probably way past their sell-by date by now.' Cockie giggled, 'Can you imagine the embarrassment if I got one out and it crumbled like Miss Haversham's dress?'

'Well, buy some more. And remember to brush your teeth properly, and wash your hands thoroughly – the amount you're smoking you'll need to get rid of the smell.'

Cockie lit another to spite him. 'Ja, mein Führer – any more top tips? And don't worry, I'll wear clean knickers!'

'No, don't wear any,' leered Drew, 'you'll feel sexy all night and it won't half blow his socks off when he finds out!'

For the first time that day, Cockie laughed properly.

'Oh!' she gasped, 'if only I dared!'

'So,' Cockie said brightly, 'how do I look?'

Eva flung herself on the bed. 'Wowee-zowee,' she said finally. 'You'll knock 'im dead, honey.'

'Do you really think so?' asked Cockie nervously, hectic patches of red on both cheeks. 'Ben?'

Ben stared at her, the remnants of his heart careering dully against his ribcage. Gone was his crazily dressed Cockie of all colours. In her place was a beautiful, soignée, towering stranger, clad from head to toe in black, her glossy chestnut hair piled up on the top of her head in some complicated looking arrangement.

'Ben! Say something before your eyes pop out!' teased Eva.

'You look fantastic, my love,' he said huskily, and then in a heavy attempt to return to his usual banter, 'and if he doesn't think so, then I'll knock 'im dead for you!'

'Thanks, darling,' said Cockie, sitting down in front of the mirror, and picking up some makeup from the bed, 'but I'd like to see you try,' she added absent-mindedly. 'Victor takes his boxing almost as seriously as he does his cars.'

Ben turned to look at the photos on the wall before she noticed his clenched fists.

'So where is he taking you?' Eva turned onto her front, propping her chin on her hands. 'Tell me, tell me – the suspense is killing me!'

'Oh, he's just cooking me dinner at his place.' Studiously, she avoided looking at either of them, concentrating on applying mascara.

'Oh, I see,' drawled Eva, 'it's that kind of date. Well, about bleeding time too, I was beginning to wonder if Victor was gay—'

Cockie nearly put out her eye. 'Oh my God!' she choked, 'you don't think—'

'Just kidding! Jeez, you're uptight – of course he's not – blimey, I know you're crap at reading the signals, but I can tell a non-starter at fifty paces, and he's OK! I promise you!'

Cockie fanned herself exaggeratedly. 'Phew! I think twice in one lifetime would have made me permanently celibate!'

'But celibate no longer, huh?' said Eva slyly.

'Who knows? It's all in the lap of – Ben!'

'What?!' Ben whirled round.

'Will you stop pacing up and down like that? You're making me even more nervous, if that's possible.' Cockie blotted her lips carefully on a piece of tissue paper.

Ben subsided on the bed next to Eva, and gazed up at the ceiling, masochistically unable to tear himself away from this conversation. 'Sorry, it's just that I was thinking that it's amazing how seldom I come up here—'

'Makeup!' Eva cried. 'That's what is so different about you! You're wearing makeup! I don't think I've ever seen you slap on more than a slash of lipstick!'

'So what? It's just because I've gone back to my natural hair colour – makeup doesn't look so odd any more, that's all.'

'Tell that to the Marines,' snorted Eva, 'it's Victor's influence! Typical fucking male ego: even though he says he likes you for being different and for being individual, the simple truth is that he's been grooming you up. Since you've been going out with him, you've been getting more and more smartly dressed and tarted up. Well, you've lost your individuality; now you look like exactly what you are: a snazzy City girlfriend.'

'Eva! Can you just be a bit more bitchy?!' gasped Cockie.

Eva's face fell in on itself, and she burst into tears. 'I'm sorry, I don't know what came over me,' she sobbed, 'take no notice of me – you look fab, honest! God, I'm such a cow.'

Ben gave her a hug. 'Yes, but you're a very well-loved cow – who is especially prized for her ability to roll joints so do us a favour, love, and skin up. I think we could all do with one.' Boy, oh boy, could I do with one, he thought.

'Hear, hear,' agreed Cockie feelingly, winding a thick choker of dull silver ball bearings around her neck.

Ben started. 'Hey!'

'What?'

'I gave that necklace to you!'

'I know, I love it – what's the problem?'

'Oh. Oh. Nothing,' said Ben.

'Jeez, you two!' Cockie glared at them in the mirror. 'You're both doing wonders for my nerves here – will you just chill out and light up that spliff, or piss off.'

Ten minutes later, she was ready, and they were stoned.

'I'm ready,' said Cockie.

'I'm boxed,' replied Eva.

'I'm going,' giggled Cockie.

'I'm gone,' said Eva, then cracked up.

Please, please, please, begged a small voice inside Ben, please don't go, please don't sleep with that tosser, please don't leave me, don't wear my jewellery for him, don't change.

'Don't,' he said hesitantly.

Cockie looked up from what she was doing, her enormous lavender eyes fixed enquiringly on his. Then he saw what she was putting so surreptitiously into her handbag, and his heart quailed.

'Don't do anything I wouldn't do,' he said weakly. So that was that. Inside him, that tiny voice mewed, and faded.

Short pop quiz, Cockie said to herself, as she rolled like an empty bottle from one side of the black cab to the other. Do I feel sick with excitement, sick with nerves, or just plain sick? The calming, trivialising effects of the grass were now beginning to wear off, leaving her light-headed, with that dry feeling around the sockets of her eyes. Her fingers closed longingly round the spare joint that Eva had pressed into her hands before she left. Clear your head, clear your head, she commanded herself, leaning forward to open the window, otherwise Victor will think you're a nutter. Red rag to a bull really, she smiled to herself. Maybe she should act on Drew's advice. What the heck.

Trying to be as subtle as possible – an achievement marred only by flailing wriggles and the odd squeak – she pulled up her skirt to hoik hold of her pants and pull them down. Brazening it out by holding the taxi driver's stare as he almost drove into the river she tucked the offending lingerie into her handbag, fingers brushing past the condoms as she did so. Oh God. She had thought her heart would fail completely when Ben saw her putting them into her bag.

A wave of apprehension drenched over her as she thought about what she was heading towards . . . with Victor, for Heaven's sake, her original Luca inspiration – she couldn't go to bed with a character in a book, could she? Shivering, she suddenly wanted to tell the driver to turn back – this was all wrong, it was as if she was about to seduce a Toontown heart throb . . . but it was too late, the cab was even now pulling into Redcliffe Square.

'What number, love?'

'Oh, number 4, I think. Hang on a sec. Let me have a look.' What a slapper, she could hear him thinking, knickerless, and she doesn't even know the address of her fancy man. I don't know, young people today.

'Yes, number 4.'

When she'd paid him, had rung the buzzer, and was standing, looking up at the tall building, she remembered that she was wearing a wrapover skirt – with no knickers. The potential for the two halves parting at any given point during the evening ahead was huge, making her a dead cert for doing a Sharon Stone impression. But it was too late; Victor's disembodied voice came from the entryphone.

'Cockie? Is that you? Come up! Top floor.'

'Top floor,' confirmed Cockie heavily. It bloody would be. No chance, then, of arriving looking cool, calm and even remotely collected.

Walking up the first flight of stairs, Cockie became aware of strange sensations gripping her lower body; the friction, as her thighs rubbed together while climbing each stair, together with the unfamiliar eddies of cool air swirling about bits of her that were usually covered up were all combining to produce some . . . interesting results. Suddenly she felt plain, honest-to-goodness horny, just wanting to get this over and done with. Damning all the consequences, she hitched up her skirt and ran the rest of the way, arriving at Victor's door in a fragrant rush of swirling clothes, gasps and flashing eyes, to see him waiting there, looking like the stuff of which sex fiends' dreams are made.

'Cockie!' Victor exclaimed delightedly.

Still caught up headlong in her sexual rush, Cockie just flung her arms around him, and kissed him glowingly on the lips. All credit to him, Victor responded in kind, scooping her up so that her head was on a level with his and kissing her back. Bang, kazzam, and here we go, shouted her hormones, flipflapping crazily through every bloodcell – we're back and we're going to have some fun!

'Come on,' Ben said abruptly, 'let's get a takeaway delivered, watch a vid and get completely and utterly smashed.'

Eva rose to the occasion. 'Yes, I've been miserable for well over twenty-four hours and that's all any man deserves.'

'Hey!' bridled Ben. 'Easy with the man-hating talk!'

Having given her a drink, Ben went to do the necessary telephoning, leaving Eva still sprawled at the table. Who was she kidding? She muttered miserably into her elbow. How much longer could she keep up the bravado? Perhaps it was because to keep breaking down in front of Ben and Cockie went so against the grain. She was the strong one of their little threesome, tough as nails to Cockie's soft-hearted fecklessness, cynical to Ben's idealism and tact. Of course, the upside was that no-one was being cry-on-my-shoulder sympathetic: that would have undone her completely. She took a deep swig from her beer, blanking out that awful, sorrowful but firm look on Mike's face as he led her to the abyss and pushed her off alone. Thirty years old and as alone today as she had been the day she ran away from Gran's . . . Eva reached out for the whisky.

'Hey, go easy on that or we won't have room for the curry,' cautioned Ben lightly, as he came back into the kitchen. Then he saw the look on her face, and, for a moment, his own reflected the pain there. 'Fuck it,' he smiled bitterly, 'if Cockie's out having a ball why shouldn't we? All for one and one for all, after all,' and he drained his own shot glass as quickly.

Victor looked at his watch for the third time, Cockie noticed, in as many minutes. Suddenly he sprang up.

'Cockie, do you mind if I just place a very quick call? I won't be too long, I promise.'

Bemused, she nodded. 'Go ahead, of course I don't mind. Hey, it's your flat!'

'I'll do it from my room so you won't be disturbed. Help yourself to anything – anything at all!'

Left alone, she poked irritably at the remains of her creme brûlée – Marks & Spencer, £1.99 for two pots – she knew it well. What was going on? Mysterious phonecalls? Sudden jumpiness? No. No way. She might watch the damn soaps, but she was buggered if she was going to start thinking like them. Victor hardly had time for her, let alone another woman.

And it had all started so well, she thought manfully – that unbelievable kiss when Victor had more than followed her lead, reducing her to a quivering sex maniac, carrying her – brownie points for physical endurance there – into his flat, slamming the door, then slamming her against the back of it, a display of machismo that she could definitely live with. Then, when they were just getting nicely hot and heavy and Cockie, for one, was thinking of shedding some garments, he had suddenly pulled away, raking his hair back into place with, she was glad to see, unsteady hands.

'Sorry,' he had panted, 'I don't know what came over me.'

Me, nearly, Cockie had thought, luckily too busy trying to find a way of standing up without functioning knees to say anything out loud. Just then she'd caught sight of herself in the full length mirror behind him in the small entrance hall. What a complete tart, she had thought in dismay, skirt askew, glamorous hairstyle toppling to one side, her super-expensive, super-chic voile shirt lurching unattractively off one shoulder, face and chest patchy with the red flush of sexual excitement.

She was disgusted to see that Victor's back view looked

as delicious as his front did – for once he had dressed as sexily as she thought he should. A plain white cotton shirt which screamed designer label was casually tucked into ancient-looking, bum-hugging, loose-everywhere-else, buttery beige 501s, bottomed off by Timberlands, and cinched by a huge, weather-beaten brown leather belt. Gone were the usual Ralph Lauren polo shirts, chinos and deckshoes that she guessed were accepted Silverman Bone mufti. Instead he looked like he'd just walked off the Agnes B catwalk. What oh what was he doing with plain old her?

'Please, come upstairs and have a drink and then we start the evening the way I wanted it – so that the whole thing is perfect.'

'Imperfect is fine by me!' laughed Cockie nervously, wishing that he'd block out the view in the damn mirror.

'No! I want tonight to be perfect – like you,' he added huskily, and that had shut her up.

That had set the tone for the whole evening. From the moment Cockie came back from 'freshening-up' in the loo – she couldn't quite believe she'd said that – she had been pampered, wined, dined – and flattered to within a millimetre of her life. Usually she needed no encouragement to talk herself blue in the face but now, with Victor doling out encouragement by the vatful, she was all anecdoted out.

But he hadn't heard the siren songs from her body, he hadn't seen the come-hither flag waving from her carefully kohl-lined eyes, he hadn't touched her as she squirmed delicately and angled her cleavage for maximum eye-pop potential, hadn't smelt the mounting waves of pheromones breaking out of her every pore, obviously hadn't tasted the same metallic tang of sexual desire that rang against her fillings every time she licked her lips. It was all very well being taken seriously as an intelligent, independent, outspoken woman, but she thought it was about time the budding nymphomaniac got a look in.

What made it worse was that as she gradually stopped paying lipservice to being the life and soul of the party in favour of moving towards a more intimate celebration, he got progressively edgier, looking at his watch, shooting his cuffs, smoothing his hair back; not the hallmarks of your average aroused hot prospect.

Who the hell could he be calling at this juncture, anyway? With him downstairs, she couldn't eavesdrop and she couldn't see any extension, just an empty portable charger. Not that there was much else in the room, gorgeous though its loftlike proportions were. Unadorned, all-white walls and an arched ceiling stretched away above her, the whole room punctuated only by the white leather sofa she was sitting on, a glass console table balanced on a white marble ram's head and an incongruously black Bang and Olufsen entertainment console squatting in one corner. There certainly wasn't any point trying to find any incriminating evidence, the room was entirely clutter-free and, to Cockie, entirely alien.

She glanced over at her handbag, dumped on the console table on the other side of the room. All through supper she had not been able to stop thinking about the condoms placed so hopefully in there. Distracted by the hubblings and bubblings between her legs, she imagined the rubbers glowing like catseyes through the leather, squeaking in a subsonic trill that only Victor could hear, 'She thought she'd get lucky, ha ha ha! She thought she'd get lucky, ha ha ha!' Now she wondered if she should have them closer to hand. She craned an ear down the central stairwell but could hear nothing. Quick as a flash she scooped herself up from the sofa and darted across the pale hardwood floor to pick it up.

'Cockie! Where are you going?!'

Cockie yelped with fright and dropped the handbag with a crash. As if in slow motion its contents fell out, including . . . she looked at Victor, only his head showing incongruously through the hole in the floor, and gabbled for all her distracting worth.

'Oh! You gave me a fright! Nowhere! I wasn't going anywhere! No! I was just getting – I thought I'd run out of cigarettes and I've got a packet of – an extra packet of fags in my handb— gosh, you looked funny like that, just a little disembodied head, quite freaky really,' as Victor climbed up into the room.

She bent down, blushing furiously, and started scooping all incriminating evidence back in.

'Fantastic news, Cockie!' he interrupted her impatiently. 'No, stop doing that – that can wait! You know that share flotation I was telling you about? Well, I've just rung New York – it's close of business there – and I just had to find out how it went. We pulled it off, Cockie! Because of our advice, the client's company is now worth half again what it was this morning! My first leader deal for the London office – and I pulled it off!'

He grabbed her by the upper arms, eyes shining like a little boy's, his perfect teeth gleaming like washing hung out to dry. In the face of such overpowering beauty, Cockie couldn't help but smile back, although she reminded herself to be furious later that he'd had the nerve to worry about a lousy deal rather than pay proper attention to this important date.

'Hey, that's brilliant – what a tycoon!'

Then, seeing an opportunity just begging to be scooped up and wrung out for every advantage, she smiled bewitchingly at him, guile-darkened eyes glowing demurely at him through clogged lashes, swaying pelvis whispering past his.

'So, how shall we celebrate?'

As if by magic, she saw his own green pools of eyes

darken in response, smile disappear behind slack parted lips, his hands grip her arms convulsively.

'You are gorgeous,' he said, so seriously that it sounded like an accusation more than a caress.

Resisting the urge to say, 'So are you,' and not knowing how to react to such a compliment, Cockie just stood her ground.

He stared at her for a heartbeat longer, long enough for Cockie to wonder what was wrong with her that he didn't kiss her when it finally happened. His mouth came down on hers, stubble on his chin grazing hers, signals shooting to every erogenous zone in her body. Just like the first time, several things happened; her knees buckled yet again, her nipples leapt out like darts in a board, the pit of her stomach went into a spin-dry cycle, the sensitive skin on her upper arms shivered under his grasp and her own hands came up to fasten convulsively around his neck.

Their breaths, smelling sweetly of creme brûlée and wine, tied warm aromatic knots together, emerging in little parting puffs as their mouths joined and re-joined, heads waltzing round each other in the ancient dance. With a stifled groan, Victor travelled down Cockie's neck, trailing a daisychain of little kisses down to the highstepping pulse at the base of her throat, Cockie's head tipping back as his hands slipped bracingly between her shoulder blades. As he neared her breasts, it was Cockie's turn to gasp, her hands tensing and spreading in his thick, wiry hair, her head coming forward to clasp his head to her chest so she could breathe in the lemon-touched, herby freshness of his hair. All sensation now, Cockie became only slowly aware that being bent into an S-shape was not the most sustainable standing position and decided dazedly that it was about time she took some of the initiative. Putting her hands on either side of his face, which was nuzzling at the cleavaged gateway of her silver T-shirt, she pulled it up and kissed his mouth again.

As she did so, she angled him round imperceptibly and, judging her moment, launched him back onto the sofa, herself close behind.

Victor's eyes snapped open in alarm. 'Wha –?' he managed, before she shut him up with her mouth. Now it was her turn to explore, overtaken by a languorous urge to dominate the proceedings. Slowly, she pinned him down on the sofa, knees either side of his legs, and leaned forwards, teasingly hollowing her back so that only her face came into contact with him.

She kissed him long and lingeringly, hearing, with a heady glee, his small groans as she caught his lower lip softly between her teeth and darted her tongue between and around his teeth. Finally, it was time to explore the planes of his face with her tongue, feeling out every crevice, every rasp, every fluttering eyelash, like a blind man – except that she had her eyes open, drinking in her fill of his beauty close-up, the tiny vein flickering in his deepshadowed eyelid, the beginnings of a wrinkle above one strong eyebrow – oh, the delicious taste of him . . . soap, the last lingering notes of aftershave, the warm honey-sweetness of a man's skin and, her nostrils fluttering ecstatically, the musky fragrance of his arousal. Softly bringing her pelvis to land on his, she finally swayed back, leaning against the hands around her hips, feeling with a drenching shock the hot roughness of his jeans scratching against the soft skin of her inner thighs. The sudden realisation that her nakedness was only two thin layers away from his, jolted her out of her entranced sensuality into a more urgent pace.

Quickly now, she reached up and pulled her hair out of its folds, feeling every cool strand as it fell onto her neck, wrenching off her blouse with a passionate impatience, her hands going to the hem of her top, before they were stilled by his. He had caught on to the urgency and, as feverishly as she, pulled the T-shirt up and over her head. The cool caress of air on her exposed nipples was the final straw – suddenly she was scrabbling at his shirt, fumbling with his buttons, hesitating only when his sculptured chest was revealed, hard tanned planes glinting through the springy whorls of hair. Her eyes flew up to his, and she leant forward again, their mouths meeting midway for another thrusting, dipping exchange, her chest crushed tantalisingly to his. Trapped in sensation she hardly felt what he was doing with his hands until he stopped suddenly and she froze, realising what he'd discovered.

'You're not—?' he questioned.

Cockie hadn't quite planned how she was going to respond at this point – in a split second, she decided she'd joke her way out of it.

'Would you believe me if I told you that I forgot to put them on?' she smiled teasingly. Then, as he looked perplexed, she changed tack. 'Now you know why I've been acting like a demented sex-toy all night – I was so turned on by the thought of you not knowing,' she purred, fingers knotting themselves teasingly round each hair-strewn nipple on his chest, 'you should try it some time.'

He looked at her disbelievingly. 'My God, you just blow my mind,' he muttered helplessly and, quick as a flash, turned them both round so that she was pinned under him, laid lengthways on the sofa. Soon she was naked. From her prone position, she reached up to pull his shirt off, only to encounter an obstacle when his arm stuck in one sleeve. She tugged at it, anxious for him to be wrapped round her again, and in her awkward impatience, clonked heads with him.

'Ow!' cried Cockie, going off into gales of laughter, and rubbing her head. For a moment, the sheer absurdity of the situation struck her, nervous tension escaping in gusts of hilarity.

Victor, rubbing his own head, frowned.

'Don't laugh,' he said almost sternly, 'why do you laugh?'

Cockie, head lodged into the cushions of the sofa, hair caught in her mouth, starkly naked against his only marginal undress, suddenly felt searingly self-conscious.

'I'm sorry,' she stammered.

Victor's brow lightened, and he swooped back towards her. 'Don't be sorry,' he murmured over her mouth, 'just don't laugh.'

With his free hand stroking steadily up her inner thighs, Cockie was unable to respond, her voicebox paralysed with yet another flood of sensation. Instead, she concentrated what decisive powers she still possessed on getting that arm out of that damn shirt. Fuck it, she thought, I'll just have to rip the bloody thing off.

'Careful, my beautiful one,' whispered Victor in her ear, 'I would hate to tear my shirt – I bought it at Paul Smith.'

Ben could no longer focus on the bottles in front of him. ''S nothing left except ouzo and creme de – creme de – oh, whassitcalled, that minty stuff that tastes like shit. Cockie bought it.' He paused, swaying, 'Bloody typical, silly cow.'

'Be-en,' came a warning croak from under the curtain of blonde hair that was Eva on the sofa. Slowly she pulled herself up, pushing her fringe out of her eyes to give him a long hard look. The effort was too much and she slumped back into the cushions. 'Man, you really need to get your head together about Cockie – I know! Let's meditate – if only I could sit up – oh God, I need toothpaste.'

Ben looked affectionately down at her. 'C'mon, my love, time for bed, before you get us chanting mantras.' He held out a shaking hand. 'Pull you up?'

'Nooo! I don't wanna go to bed,' Eva wailed, 'it's cold

up there.' Without opening her eyes, she fumbled for his hand, tugging blindly at it. 'Let's sleep down here where it's warm.'

Before he knew it, Ben had lost his fragile grip on his balance, collapsing on the sofa beside Eva. Instantly her eyes flew open in alarm, gazing into his grey ones only inches away. For a long moment they stared at each other, momentarily sober.

'Oh dear,' said Ben softly.

'You're quite a talker, aren't you?'

'Mmmm?' Victor mumbled sleepily into her collarbone.

'Well, you're a positive crooner between the sheets.'

No answer.

'Victor! Don't you dare go to sleep!' Cockie drummed her fists and heels on the mattress in giddy frustration. 'How can you possibly fall asleep? I feel grrrrrr-eat!'

Victor groaned and rolled off to lie on the pillows next to her, eyes blinking like an owl. 'That is clear,' he said, and almost split his face in half with a tonsil-revealing yawn.

Cockie laughed. 'Yeah, well I just want to leap about after I've made love – I feel like I could do anything – do you need any mountains moving? Any seas parting? Now's the time to ask – I feel so alive, I feel bloody marvellous!' She raised both arms above her head and punched the air euphorically. 'Maybe this is what coke is like? Tell you what, those City traders should knock off the old Bolivian marching powder and try good old-fashioned rumpy-pumpy to fit them up for their multi-trillion dollar deals? "Make love, make millions!" Hey, not bad! Maybe I should try advertising as my next career?'

'Cockie, before, I thought you were crazy,' said Victor, attempting a bit of sneaky shut-eye. 'Now I know that you are.'

'Victor,' Cockie said suddenly, 'why *do* you like me?'

One eye opened. 'Oh, Cockie,' groaned Victor, 'not now. Please. I beg you.' The eye shut again.

'No, come on, I'm not being paranoid, or anything, I'm just interested . . . Victor! Come on!' She leaned over to tickle him.

Victor swore loudly in his own language, and rolled away from her. 'For God's sake, Cockie! I'm not in the mood – you are acting like a spoiled infant and I've got to get up early in the morning.'

Cockie lost it. 'Jesus, I hate that excuse! Why do bloody men always just want to go to sleep afterwards? Is it some kind of chemical reaction? Hump, pump, slump?! That's all we get? Do you think that just because you fucked me, you can knock off, no questions asked? Well, matey, it doesn't work that way – sex is only half the deal, women like to be spoken to.'

'No, Cockie. *You* like to be spoken to, and you are at best a subjective spokeswoman for your sex. And do not be crude when you speak, I find it so unbecoming.' Victor tapped her on the nose, before presenting her with his back.

Cockie glared at it. How could someone who'd breathed sweet nothings into her ear all night, now be treating her like an odious child? She kicked him sharply, like an odious child, and went to the loo to fume in peace, shrugging on his precious white shirt as she went.

In the bathroom, she pulled the shirt up and looked at herself critically in the wall to wall mirror. She looked pretty damn good, she thought, with some surprise. She'd lost some weight recently without really noticing it until now, and anyway, flab always looked better with the tan that she still had. Her legs were always her best point but for once the rest of her didn't seem so much the poor relation. Hey, why should she be so grateful to Victor for going out with her? Granted, he was the most beautiful man she'd ever seen but wasn't she just a little obsessed with his looks? It seemed to Cockie that whenever she thought about him – or talked about him, which was even more telling – it was always in visual, physical terms. Maybe there wasn't much else to say about a man whose bedroom furniture consisted of a futon, Corby trouser press and a two-foot by four-foot model of his blessed TVR?

Sitting on the loo, she idly picked up a well-thumbed copy of GQ and flicked through it. God, this magazine was just like Cosmo – *'How to Charm the Birds out of the Trees'*, ran one headline, *'Romance your way to the horizontal dance'*. Tacksville, USA, she thought, reading on.

All at once, she frowned, looked closer and laughed out loud. *'Poetry – the Hidden Ace. Byron wasn't Jack the Lad just because of his famous curls and non-discriminatory attitude towards women, men and close relations'*, she read, *'the ability to turn a pretty phrase has turned many a pretty face. Andrew Marvell's "Ode to a Coy Mistress" is just the ticket for blushing maidens, but if you feel that it's all a bit incongruous over your meat and two veg, then plump for the most convincing of the lot – Shakespeare – for a sure-fire hump.'*

Charming, she thought, then, further down, what had actually stayed her eye. *'If there are complaints from 'Er Indoors about the amount of time you're spending at the office, amassing the filthy lucre that keeps her in Lenor, then spout Will's Catch-All sonnet, "When in disgrace with fortune and men's eyes . . ."'*

Sure enough, all written out – even with a bloody pencilmark in the margin – there it was, her poem, the poem that she'd been so touched by, which she'd wasted five good minutes playing and replaying on the answering machine. The cheek of the man! Ben will kill himself laughing when he hears about this, she thought, leaning back on the loo seat and letting the GQ fall to the floor.

Cockie gazed at herself in the mirror, remembering

suddenly that morning up on the hill above Slake, seeing her reflection in Ben's eyes as she woke up. She'd been dreaming – a really hot and dirty dream that she'd always assumed had been about Victor. Now, so recently from his bed, she wasn't so sure. What on earth was she doing here? Was this really as good as it was ever going to get?

Beside her, he stirred uneasily in his sleep, eyelids flickering under her intent gaze, the first tendrils of daylight from the uncurtained window creeping across his face. She braced herself for his reaction when he woke up. Unlike some faces which relaxed in sleep, giving hardened rogues the look of innocent babes, his looked sterner, crueller even, his hair, dark in this light, curling disreputably over his narrow face, his aquiline, bony nose in sharp relief against the dark blue pillowcase, chin jutting at a determined angle. Now, with dark shadows under his deep-set eyes, and the start of stubble picking out the pale gauntness of his face, he looked nothing like the man she knew so well . . . just another wrecked stranger lying next to her after an ill-advised night.

Oh God, what have I done, she thought in anguish, haven't I grown out of the drunken fuck yet? Didn't I swear that these coyote mornings belonged only in my shady past? Now she'd ruined a friendship and . . . for what? A miserable, half-conscious screw, uncompleted and sordid. She knew she should leave the bed, hope against hope that he wouldn't remember what had happened, would think that it had merely been a drunken dream born out of rich food and too much booze. But that was the coward's way out, and being a coward was something she could never be accused of.

Grey eyes opened, gazed blankly at the ceiling for a moment, then swung in alarm from the hand that she was still resting on his chest to meet her own apprehensive blue orbs.

'Hello,' she said, as calmly as she didn't feel.

'Eva,' he croaked, and swallowed hard, his Adam's apple bobbing nervously.

'Well, at least you got my name right this time!' she joked nervously. It didn't exactly break the ice, the look of terror on his face enough to make her laugh in any other situation.

'Ben, Ben, Ben,' she soothed, suddenly feeling a lot older than him, 'don't worry about a thing – we were stinking pissed and like stupid idiots we fell into bed – it was all my fault, I needed to prove something to myself.

'You, my pet,' she reached a hand up to his cheek, immeasurably relieved when he didn't actually flinch, 'were the sacrificial lamb. So, we screwed. So what? Let's rise above this, prove that it doesn't have to ruin our friendship.'

Come on Ben, don't let me down, she pleaded with him silently. I couldn't cope with losing you as a friend when I didn't exactly have you as a lover.

Ben cleared his throat. 'You're wrong,' he said quietly. Then, when he saw her face fall, he rushed on, 'I mean, you're wrong that it was all your fault – it was just as much mine; I needed to drive out a few devils as well and anyway, it's terrifically unfeminist of you to shoulder the blame – don't you know it's fairly tricky to coerce a bloke into sex without, well, some reciprocal interest?'

Eva's eyes filled with tears of gratitude that he could joke, even feebly, at a time like this. Ben, getting the wrong end of the stick, rushed on again.

'Oh, Christ, please don't cry – I didn't mean to tease you about your blasted beliefs.' He gathered her into his arms for a Ben bearhug special. 'Look, I'm not pretending that our friendship won't change because of this, but why do we have to be all sad and gloomy about it? Don't you know that I don't even consider someone a good friend unless I've slept with them? You took your time, I must say, I was beginning to write you off as one of life's acquaintances.' He squeezed her even tighter. 'For a tough little cookie, you can be awful dumb sometimes, you know.'

Eva laughed through her tears. 'That sounds like a line from a movie – a really terrible line.'

'Good on yer, chuck,' applauded Ben quietly, kissing her gently on the cheek. 'Welcome back to the land of the living, fucked-up and hungover as we are.' Then, conversationally, 'Did I really say her name? I'm not usually a talker but that's unforgivable. Why didn't you shoot me then and just drop my body in the Thames?'

Eva smiled at him again. 'Because,' she said deliberately, 'I have a hunch that someone who lives not a million miles away from us, would have my guts for garters if I had done.'

'Well, I should send that hunch back where it came from if I were you,' said Ben drily, 'because even if you were right, my timing, shall we say, is less than good.'

'Hmmm . . . we shall see,' said Eva. 'You forget – I'm an alternative healer – people pay good money for my hunches.'

'Name your price,' he said wryly.

14

Cockie looked up at the little mews house, jade green shutters shining in the sunlight and sighed. It was good to be home. Waking up with Victor, after a few hours of careful rumination in the bathroom, then about an hour tossing and turning on that infernal futon, paranoid that she was going to touch him and disturb him from his precious sleep quota, had not been the stuff of which deep dreams were made. In the morning he had behaved impeccably – had brought her a cup of coffee (which by now he should have known she didn't drink) without even mentioning her tantrum of the night before, but she could tell that he was a bachelor man used to living on his own. She may be that 'special person' he'd been waiting for all this time, but when it came to weekday mornings she just disturbed his routine for getting to work.

The minor embarrassments of the night before – like when they'd moved downstairs from the sitting-room – she feeling her nakedness in dire and wobblesome contrast to his still debonair state of only half-undress, or the inevitably paralysing moment when he had rolled over to get a condom from under his pillow, meaning that after all that, her own condoms had been superfluous – these and a few of the other awkwardnesses of any first-time sexual encounter had been as nothing to when he came downstairs from the loft just before they left, holding out her knickers before him in an exaggerated gesture of distaste and said, 'I think these must have fallen out of your handbag.'

Cockie would have become a lifelong Trekkie if Scottie had been able to beam her away to another solar system at that moment.

She had looked at him – looking exactly the god-like same as the first time she'd seen him that day in the Gallery and then looked at herself, a battered vamp in her creased seductress outfit, makeup rubbed off, her cheeks and chin red raw with stubble rash and to her surprise, the comparison, vast and shaming though the differences were, had not depressed her.

What was crystal clear at that moment was that they were different people beyond just the surface beauty-and-beast imagery. Eva's comment last night about looking like a standard City girlfriend had finally hit its mark then – Victor said that he had fallen for her because she was so unlike the other girls he met, so 'whacky', so 'outspoken', so spontaneous, extrovert and confident, yet at the same time he was gradually changing all these things about her, gradually moulding her into exactly what it was he had apparently been trying to avoid. The only issue now was how much she minded this change herself. Come off it, Cockie, she admonished herself, stop beating about the bush; all that build-up and now you're wondering whether it was all worth it, now that you've had sex with the Perfect Man, are you any closer to the man behind the perfection?

She let herself into the house, looking at her watch. Eight thirty. Upstairs, she could hear a radio on and the sound of the bath running. Good, the others would be down for a good breakfast gathering. As she walked through the hall she peeked into the sitting-room. The carnage there was unbelievable, beer cans everywhere, two empty bottles of whisky, a paraphernalia of silver foil dishes which from the smell and general oil slick impression still contained various curried bits and pieces. I didn't know anyone was coming round last night, she wondered, but it looks like they had quite a piss-up.

She felt a pang. It seemed like a Stone Age ago since they'd last had one of their organic parties, when they started with the three of them, invited a couple of friends round and the night grew from there. Between the Whim and waiting for Victor to get away from the office, she hadn't been able to indulge in that spontaneous kind of night-slacking throughout the summer. Looked like Ben and Eva had done a bit of catching up in her absence. She tried not to feel left out.

Four eggs fried, six sausages grilled, three pieces of bread fried, a carton of mushrooms fried, six rashers of bacon grilled and three tomatoes grilled later, Cockie was one big vat of drool, as she put the trencherful of cholesterol into the oven to keep warm.

'Get a wiggle on,' she yelled up the stairs. While she was waiting, she distracted herself by tidying up the kitchen dresser. Tucked behind a photo of them all at Red's party, she came across the herbal air freshener that Eva had been so keen on at the beginning of the summer. If she remembered rightly, that was the day she first saw Victor . . . what goes around, comes around, she thought wryly and, holding the dusty gizmo in her hand, she knew the answer.

'Cor lumme, this smells bloody great,' Ben bustled into the kitchen, looking more cheerful than he had done for weeks, surprising since he also looked as terrible as Cockie had ever seen him, bloodshot eyes nearly closed under the weight of what was obviously a crusher of a hangover.

'Hello, you dirty stopout, what's the fry-up in aid of?' He squinted at her, then looked away. 'Did you, er, did you have fun?'

'Well, yes, I suppose I did,' Cockie said carefully, quelling the urge to stroke away his pained frown.

'That hardly sounds like multiple orgasms were the order of the day,' commented Eva overbrightly, coming in wearing a startling arrangement of blacks and whites – vertical striped flares, horizontal striped tight T-shirt and a dotted jacket with what appeared to be a rendition of a dartboard on the back, topped off by what looked like a prep school cap in rings of black and white; Cockie couldn't see her eyes under this, but she seemed to be in hardly better shape, her movements nervy and unco-ordinated as she put the food onto the table, her manner forced.

'Heavy night for you two last night, I see,' said Cockie. 'Did you have fun?'

Ben picked up a newspaper. 'Yes, it was, er, good,' he said from behind it.

'Uh-huh,' agreed Eva, trying to connect the coffee with her mug.

'Who came?'

There was a sudden tension in the room until Eva, bright red, let out a bark of laughter. Ben's newspaper shook in harmony.

'What? What's so funny?'

'Nu-nu-nothing.'

'What's going on? Who came over last night?' Cockie racked her brains to think of who could provoke this sort of reaction. 'You didn't have Sam and Esme here did you?' Another, infinitely worse, thought occurred to her. 'Or Annalisa?'

Ben lowered his paper at this. 'God, no!' he exclaimed. 'We didn't have anyone over, it was just the two of us, getting out of our heads.'

'So why all the sniggering?'

'I was not sniggering, thank you very much,' protested Eva, 'no, it's just that, well, I was embarrassed by the thought that we must have totally trashed the sitting-room for you to think that we had people round!'

'Oh right,' said Cockie, tucking into her food now that this had been cleared up. But even as she chewed through her cooked breakfast she was aware that something was up – there were some undercurrents here.

A few minutes later, she was sure of it. Ben hadn't turned the page of his newspaper once and Eva seemed unnaturally preoccupied with her congealing food, not eating it but staring at it as if it were about to come to life.

'OK,' said Cockie, putting her knife and fork together. 'What is going on? You two are like parents in the waiting-room, I've never seen anyone so nervous and conspiratorial.'

'What?!' exclaimed Ben and Eva together.

'My God, you're even speaking together – a sure sign of guilt,' teased Cockie.

'OK, you go first, Ben,' Eva said.

He rolled his eyes at her. 'No, no, you go, I insist.'

'Shit,' said Eva. There was a short pause. 'OK, we drew short straws to be the one to ask you about last night.' She shot a sidelong look at Ben.

Cockie was confused. 'Short straws? What?'

'Well, you can't blame us for wanting to know,' Ben said woodenly, glaring at Eva.

'You always know every step of my lovelife,' added Eva, 'not that there is one any more.'

'Fair enough,' said Cockie equably. 'So who lost?'

'Who lost what?'

'Oh for God's sake,' laughed Cockie, 'sort yourselves out.' She stood up. 'Look, I've got to go and change for work – I'll tell you all about it when I come down and have a fag.'

She stretched hugely and beamed at them. 'As it happens, I've come to a decision about my lovelife, but I'll leave you in suspense.'

She smiled dazzlingly at them and left to walk upstairs.

Because I'm feeling thin, she mused, I'll see if I can fit into that purple suede A-line mini that Ben gave me for my birthday. She glanced into Eva's room, wondering if she still had her purple scarf that went with the skirt. Then she carried on up to her room, something nagging at the back of her mind.

Sure enough, the skirt fitted. Going into Eva's room, she picked her way through the usual fashion minefield on the floor. Suddenly she frowned. When she was getting ready last night, she'd come in here and, in a friendly housematey sort of gesture, had tipped out the contents of Eva's extensive makeup collection onto her bed so that she could pick'n'mix some for herself. Yet here it all was, still strewn all over Eva's immaculately undisturbed counterpane, she being the only person in the Western world who didn't use a duvet. Which meant that Eva could not have slept in her bed last night, so where? Surely she couldn't have been so gross as to crash out in the sitting-room, amongst all the curry and fag butts?

An horrific suspicion was dawning in Cockie's mind. Slowly, scarfless, she picked her way back out of the room and, as if playing Grandma's Footsteps, moved one step at a time up the corridor to Ben's room at the front of the house.

'You slept with each other, didn't you?'

Ben's head shot up from his copy of *Gardening News*. Cockie, in the doorway, gripping the doorjamb, was as white as the shirt she was wearing. His and Eva's shock gave them away.

'You did, didn't you? You!' she pointed at Ben. 'You screwed her?! You actually screwed her twenty-four hours after she splits up with her boyfriend? How desperate are you, Ben? I've never known you take another man's leavings before. And you!' she swung on Eva, open-mouthed on the other side of the table. 'How could you? You knew that I – you knew – you're supposed to be my friend!'

She turned back to Ben, in her eyes an expression that he had seen during one of her panic attacks and had hoped never to see again, like a rabbit trapped in headlights, frozen, immobile and knowing the inevitability of pain.

'You're supposed to be my friend too,' she said quietly, hardly audible over the breaking of his heart. 'I trusted you. I trusted you both . . . with so much of me.' One fist clenched. 'I have so little to give but I gave as much as I could to you both and now . . .'

She stopped, her face stricken, and went on in a tiny voice. 'And you were laughing at me this morning – laughing – conning me into thinking that this was something to do with me and all the time the two of you were laughing up your sleeves at the way I was falling for it, sniggering at my stupidity at not seeing what's been going on under my bloody nose!'

'No, Cockie—'

'Shut up!' she screamed at him. 'Shut up! Shut up!'

'Cockie,' he pleaded, 'please calm—'

'Do you think I'm overreacting, Ben?' she demanded, leaving the doorway to come and stand in front of him. 'Do you think I'm overreacting? Because I probably am. For some bizarre reason I thought that you—' She broke off, her eyes, shining with unshed tears, focused above his head. 'But then again, maybe I shouldn't think, I shouldn't ever think, that's my trouble, I think too much, I'm so busy thinking, that I don't see anything. I'm going to work now.'

Before they had a chance to react, she had rushed from the kitchen. Seconds later they heard the front door slam. Ben got up without a word and punched his hand into the fridge door.

'Idiot,' he moaned, clutching his aching fist. 'Fuckwit.

Wanker. Shitforbrains. Dickhead. Stupid cunt.' He sat down again, burying his head in his hands.

'We were naïve to think that it wouldn't change things, weren't we?' said Eva, in a soft hesitant voice.

Silence. Ben lifted his head from the table and stared at her, wishing that she would just go away and leave him to it.

'Yes,' he said simply.

For the first time ever, I'm having an attack in daylight, in public, on a bus. The core of bitter ice in my chest is expanding, taking away each precious mouthful of air. I am afraid that my fellow passengers will notice my hands already clawlike round the rail of the seat in front of me. I try to focus on the plaid patterns in the shopping trolley held by the woman opposite, but rattling at the bars of the tartan are the faces I have just left, gargoyles leering into my face and deeper, the fetid breath of betrayal coming from carbuncled mouths. Each leery glare and my eyes widen further, dry channels of shame at either side of my eyeballs. Pulling at the impulse to roll them back into my skull to get them away, I close them instead, lids cranking along hinges sandy and forced. But the faces are still there, now so near, so bright that I can feel the heat from them start to blister my burning skin. If I can get away from them maybe I can breathe again, hear something other than this rasping wail I hope to God isn't coming from my own mouth, smell life not snuff this stench . . .

'Are you all right, my love?'

The conductor tapped Cockie on the shoulder. She brought her head out from under her arms. 'You seem a bit flustered.'

'Ju-just a touch of asthma,' she stammered.

He surveyed her tear-stained eyes sceptically. 'Yeah well, whoever he is, he's a bloody bastard. Lovely girl like you shouldn't look miserable, not on a smashing day like this. All men are bastards, you know – my wife's been telling me the same thing every day for the last fifteen years. "Arfur", she says every morning as she's packing my lunch, "Arfur, all men are bastards and don't you forget it, so don't think I don't know what you'd be up to if I gave you half a bleeding chance." Lovely woman, my Debs, best wife a man ever had. So, can I see your ticket please, love? I wouldn't bother you, you see, but they're always inspecting the route, so it's more than my job's worth not to ask you, before they do.'

Cockie looked up at him in despair. What had she done to deserve this man? She showed him her Travelcard.

'Thanks my love. Let me just see the photo – oh, it is you, just with blonde hair. Oh no, you look much better as a brunette, take it from me, my love, my Debbie's got brown hair, so I'm an old-fashioned brunette man myself – yes, give me that Raquel Welch over Britt Ekland any day.'

'Could I just have my card back, please?' Cockie interrupted quietly.

'Yes, of course, don't mind me, I'm such a chatterbox – I say, you don't half look peaky, my love, I bet you could do with a good hot sweet cup of tea – drown your sorrows. Where are you going?'

'Near the end of Fleet Street,' said Cockie weakly.

'Hmmm,' said the conductor, 'only Eyetie cafés up that way if I'm not very much mistaken – you'd do much better getting off at the next stop, just before Aldwych – you'll find a lovely place in Exeter Street—'

'Yes, maybe you're right,' Cockie stammered, seeing that the bus had stopped at the lights.

'Not here, love,' she heard the conductor call out, as she rushed up the side of the bus, 'further up!'

Getting to the back of the bus, Cockie did her usual flying leap from the platform. As she did so – in silent slow motion out of her right eye she saw the lights turn green and out of her left the cyclist bearing down on her at a rushing speed, his mouth open in a yell that she couldn't hear, the wiry muscles on his skinny arms standing out as he leant on his brakes. In a dreamlike flurry of legs, and wheels, and helmets and one staring eye, they collided, the silent thud of the bike sending her body flying through the—

15

So this is dying. The feeling of that first crunch of pain is already fading into a dim resonance and there is no pain, more a spreading feeling of warmth, like the spread of blood from my corpse, and of well-being. Like a television gearing up, the darkness is clearing, light and sounds flooding my senses so that it takes me a moment to focus. The feeling that I am watching the movie of my death persists as I realise I've got a bird's eye view of the scene of the crash. Down below, chaos prevails. Above the hum of the rubber-necking pedestrians, the panic-edged rant of the cyclist soars and dips, slamming into my suddenly acute hearing.

'She stepped right in front of me! Right in fucking front of me! What the fuck was I supposed to do? And look what she's done to my bike! She's a fucking nutter!'

If he looks battered and rattled, his bike will never live to see another courier's day. Like me, it has died; like me, its limbs are now arranged nonsensically, rear wheel wrapping round to kiss the handlebars in a mangled embrace of steel and rubber.

'She'll be a dead nutter soon, so shut your face, and do something useful, my son. Where's that bleedin' ambulance?'

It's my old friend, the conductor, who must have leapt from the bus after me. There's no sign of the bus; I hope it's less than his job's worth for him to have abandoned ship. There's something unreal and definitely undignified about being described as a dead nutter, but I suppose it's what they would say in the movies.

I look at myself curiously. I'm not prepossessing. My left arm is curled over the kerb at a totally unnatural angle and I'm doing a rag doll impression in the gutter. My face looks slack and unfamiliar, bulky even, not pulled into that two-dimensional mirror pose where, without even thinking, I widen my eyes, dip my chin and tip my profile to exactly the angle where it looks best. Dying takes that kind of artistic control away and I'm remotely appalled at the difference it makes. Couldn't someone just be kind and tuck my tongue back into my mouth? There's something odd about my hair too, my parting's no longer on the left but, as I look at it, on the right, which is a faint but unsettling reminder that I'm looking at myself, not at a reflection. The purple mini doesn't look its best either, rucked up round one hip and torn over the other, a dirty smudge of blood spreading through the suede.

I am seeing everything as if through a fish-eye lens, and when I really peer at something, I zoom in on it, too fast, like a child with a camcorder. So I get a faceful of my lower leg, an ugly trifle of bone and blood and white veiny flesh out of which – an urban tomahawk – a bicycle pedal quivers, flecks of mud dissolving in the bright bright blood around it. With a sickening rush, my vision pans back again, just in time to see the ambulance men, all flashing lights and fluoro green jackets, bustling onto the scene. All this fuss over my body, it seems weird, almost amusing . . .

'You're too bloody late,' the bus conductor is shouting at them, as they bend over my corpse, 'she's dead!'

Suddenly it's no longer a movie; the lights go out and I'm flung headlong into a dark tunnel. At least, I think that's what it is; I'm not aware of walking or making any movement and yet there is an intense sensation of speed, air rushing past me, my eyes half-blinded by the cool whoosh of gritty wind, like I'm at the centre of a tornado. Nor am I alone – all around me, there are others, a vast non-jostling crowd all going in the same direction as me. I strain to see through my watering eyes; the darkness is total but I can feel the displacement of air as it goes round all these bodies. I know this isn't a dream, dreams just don't happen this way, so are these dead people too?

It is a moment of time later, and my speed has increased unimaginably. To open my eyes against the wind's velocity is impossible but gradually I am feeling a faint kiss of warmth through the chill of the air, which spreads to a glow across my face, until even through my eyelids, all I can see is buttercup yellow. Suddenly, I stop, immediately, without any lurching or feeling of impact. I'm impressed by the capabilities of my new body and I'm thinking that maybe this afterlife business won't be too bad.

I open my eyes. Like drawing velvet curtains open onto a midsummer's day in full swing, the colours, sounds and smells of this new place burst over me in a fragrant, drenching shower.

Wow! Every cell in my new body is vibrating and my senses wake up and dance – I can see and smell and taste and hear and feel everything – all at the same time! I can hear the buzz of the brilliant brightness, this living light that should blind me but doesn't, taste the tart vanilla of this rustling hedge of a thousand hues of green all around me, smell the character of a hundred scenes I can see through the windows set in the hedge.

Perspective belongs to the old world. Here, I am seeing a whole town of blue, red, purple, yellow, green, orange buildings through one window, where in the next window all I can see are the ends of fingers being drummed onto a small patch of table by an impatient hand. String music comes bursting from a window above me, where a band of men and women in wigs and livery are entertaining a middle-aged lady in a nylon housecoat; next door, a youth flies through endless clouds, face split by an enormous grin, as he rolls himself like a seabird and streaks through the sky, a yellow streamer billowing from his foot. It is MTV gone mad, a kaleidoscope on LSD, but alongside my live and kicking faculties is a clear-sighted certainty that this is all real, that I am in full control and that I can do anything I want to. Are my helpers here? Is there a bus passenger here? A pilot? A child?

I crane out of my window. I feel almost dizzy with all the different levels of activity going on within me, a babble of voices questioning, probing, judging. Slowly I filter everything else out until I can hear one last voice clearly, a low, slow murmur asking one question over and over again. It is my voice.

'Where are you?' it is asking. All my frisking, gambolling, tingling senses come together, fused by this one demand. I am not afraid of being dead, sometimes I have longed for it, felt that I deserved it but if I am dead, where are you, Mum and Dad? Where are you, Gus?

I bend my new hearing, my sharpened sight, my exfoliated touch to the task of finding you all, but every nook and cranny of this bright world within me is swept clean as I look, and the hedge in front of me yields up no more secrets.

There's no door to the room I am in, so I turn to the window again, clasping my hands over the marble of the window sill. Even this has life – each warm molecule vibrating through my sensitised finger tips. As nimbly as any gymnast, I spring onto the ledge and balance there. If my family won't come to me, I'll come to my family.

I step off the ledge. There is no fear, not even any adrenaline; I am confident that since I've already died, I can't die again, I can only fly. Fly like the boy through his clouds except that I shall swirl and soar around this infinite tube of life and light and mystery until I find you . . .

But I don't. When I step off the ledge, nothing happens. If I dip my toe I can feel a cushiony nothingness below me, but I'm not moving, not even floating, because my arms are still by my side. I'm just . . . there, suspended in the mysterious time of this place.

For the last time, I ask the question, the words bubbling out of every pore – springing from my fingertips, cartwheeling from the tip of every hair and exploding from my mouth, quivering with the anticipation of finally getting that longed-for answer.

'Where are you?'

And as the words leave me, you leave me. All of you. I am

not conscious of saying goodbye but within me the last bond is broken and I come away free, resonating with a new note. For the first time since I can remember, I am neither daughter nor little sister nor girlfriend . . . I am totally and completely me, Cockie.

And then I stop looking within and look across, and I see . . . myself.

This is my answer.

Perhaps there never were any helpers, any handy guardian angels. Perhaps that whole conspiracy theory came out of my head. I was looking for guidance, for help, for an explanation for the swings and roundabouts of my life and, all along, the answer was within me.

Now I can make my own destiny. I don't need to have panic attacks any more: I no longer need to play up to the abscess of grief within me; I have lanced that boil. I don't need to look for help around me, I can help myself. I am me, Cockie.

The relief makes laughter flood through me with the clash of cymbals, the swilling, swirling whirl of this world's liquor, every particle inside me twisting into a gaily coloured fandango, every giddy breath a honeysuckled rainbow of life. Sweet tears giggle and teeter on watery high heels along dipping lashes, euphoria is a candied delight on my jigging tongue.

This is my answer, just an ordinary mystery, nothing special, nothing to panic about, a shaggy dog story, a joke! Maybe now I can be like everyone else. Maybe I don't have to be a marked card. Maybe I can just be me, Cockie, having a laugh.

Ben looked at his watch without letting go of Cockie's hand. It was after eight o'clock, yet that damn surgeon hadn't reappeared yet with the results of the latest test.

For the umpteenth time he prayed that they would be the same as they had been before.

'There's no sign of any bleeding in, or bruising to, the brain yet,' the surgeon had said then, 'but sometimes it doesn't appear on the X-rays for quite a while. ECG and other activity scans appear to be normal so if no blood clots form, there is a fair chance that there will be no permanent brain damage at all.'

'But when will she come out of the coma?' Ben had wanted to know.

'Now that, I'm afraid,' the man had smiled gently, 'is where science stops and fate takes over. When the patient is ready to wake up, she'll wake up, believe me.'

Please, he prayed silently into Cockie's sheets, his left hand holding her right hand, please wake up. Why did you have to go flinging yourself off a bus anyway? Please don't let it have been deliberate, please don't let me have done this to you. Please come back, Cockie. Please let me explain.

'Gosh, it's drab here,' said a clear voice above his head. Ben's head shot up to see two familiar enormous amethyst eyes gazing sleepily down at him, the light of the setting sun refracting glitteringly in her dilated pupils.

'Hey dude,' said Cockie.

'Hey,' whispered Ben, hardly able to speak for the lump in his throat.

Cockie continued to stare at him, a wide shaky grin wandering across her face. 'You look like dogbreath.'

'Y-y-you can't see dogbreath.'

'When it looks as bad as you do, you can.'

'Welcome back anyway.' He looked at her curiously. 'Are all recovered coma patients meant to be this lucid?'

'I don't know, do I? I presumably slept through the peptalk – why? How long was I a' – her eyebrows danced – 'coma patient?'

'A day and a half.' The longest thirty-three hours and eighteen minutes of my life, he added silently.

'A day and a half! Bloody hell!' Cockie exclaimed. 'That's wild!'

'I can think of better words,' Ben said darkly. 'Anyway,

why aren't you saying things like, "Where am I?", "Who am I?", "How did I get here?" and the like?'

'Simple,' she said calmly. 'I just took stock of the situation when I opened my eyes and saw that this was a hospital, surmised, when I saw the bandages and that thing' – she gestured to the tented bedclothes over her leg – 'that I had been in an accident, and when I saw you sleeping on the job—'

'Hey!'

'Well, you were looking a bit slack! Anyway, I knew who you were immediately, so it came as no great surprise that, having remembered your name, I remembered my own.'

'Smart-arse.' Ben looked at his watch, and reluctantly let go of her hand. 'Look, I promised I'd ring your brother as soon as you woke up and I suppose the nurses will want to know as well – do you mind if I just nip off and tell them?'

'Not at all,' Cockie beamed at him, eyes dancing. 'I'm feeling a bit sleepy actually, I might grab forty winks.'

Ben grabbed her hand again. 'Don't you dare go back to sleep! Do you hear me?'

'Kidding! Only kidding!'

Within seconds he was back. 'I met Nurse Donnelly in the corridor and she's going to get in touch with Robert.'

'Great,' she smiled dozily. 'Come back here, boyo,' she waggled her free hand lazily at him and he came back to sit at her side, nonchalantly holding her hand again.

'So have they got me on some major league drugs or do all coma victims feel as bombed as I do?'

Ben laughed out loud. 'God knows, although I think you're on painkillers for your' – he mugged dramatically – 'grievous wounds.'

'Cool – I can recommend them. So what is this thing?' She pointed at the tent over her leg.

'That's keeping the bedclothes off your plaster cast. You got smashed up by a flying pedal which stuck in your lower leg and broke your shinbone.'

'Oh, that's right, I remember.'

'What do you mean?' Ben stared at her. 'How would you know?'

Cockie narrowed her eyes at him. 'Of course I don't know – you just told me, therefore it's right. Anyway, why am I in a private ward?' She beetled a suspicious brow. 'Did you pull rank?'

Ben smirked. 'No sirree bob, I did not. Mister Ben Milton at your service, ma'am.'

'I'm definitely high,' she told the air above her head. 'What did you say?'

'Well, how the hell do you think I'm in here with you? Only relatives are allowed in to sit with you, and Robert couldn't get here until late last night and can't be with you all the time so he agreed to confirm that I was your brother.'

'Oh! Brother!'

'Yes,' he looked at her curiously, 'what else could I have been? So anyway, plain old Ben Milton couldn't have pulled rank for you even if he'd wanted to, but I did ask Nurse Donnelly quite nicely.'

'I bet!' said Cockie drily.

'And they were pretty quiet at the time, so she moved you in here until Robert arrived and then he paid for a private room anyway.'

'Robert?' she asked, flabbergasted. 'Pay extra for something? Wow. He must have been worried!'

'He was, and is,' said Ben agitatedly, 'and no wonder – at one point, for no real medical reason, you were apparently technically dead for thirty seconds!'

'Only thirty seconds!' Cockie interjected, then, seeing Ben's surprised look. 'Never mind, go on.'

'Well, then no-one knew when you were going to

wake up – everyone was worried – Drew's been here, pacing outside the door, looking through the window and saying that he was going to redecorate this room if you were going to be under for much longer.'

'That's so sweet,' murmured Cockie.

'Yeah, I think the hospital staff will be a bit pissed off that you've woken up.' Ben started to tick off on his fingers. 'Mel and Rowena have rung – separately – about five times, as has that girl from the Gallery, and Victor, and Ravi and a whole host of other people. You have no idea how fast news travels in this place. And last but not least, the whole bloody Whim team – Patrick, Flo, TJ, Fred – even Felipe braved being busted – came here this morning and have promised to deliver hot lunches and dinners straight from the Whim for the rest of your stay here. You are one spoilt little Miss Popular!'

To Ben's amazement, two large tears fell from each of Cockie's eyes and plopped down her cheeks.

'Hey, what did I say? This is flattering stuff here.'

'They're tears of happiness, you jerk,' she said, sniffing. 'So, carry on with the list, if you're up to it.'

'Well, that's about it, but look at all your flowers.'

'Wow!'

'Yes. The hospital florist loves you to bits.'

'Who on earth sent that revolting bouquet pushed to the back – that huge one with a bit of every colour in the world thrown in?'

Ben tried not to let his smirk show. 'That one is from Victor,' he said pokerfaced.

Cockie laughed again, and Ben's heart leapt up. 'Ye-es, enough said. And what about those gorgeous lilies – wow, get a niff of those!'

'Those are from Eva.'

'And why hasn't Eva been to see me, eh? Don't tell me she won't enter the portals of conventional medicine?!'

Ben looked serious. 'No, actually Eva's had some bad news of her own, and she's gone home.'

'What? Eva? Home? Parents' home?'

'Yes, her mother's got cancer and get this – that bitch of a sister knew all along and didn't breathe a word to Eva – Eva only found out by chance, when she decided yesterday, for one reason and another,' Ben faltered slightly, 'to re-establish touch with her parents.'

'What a cow Laura turned out to be! Who would have thought it? How bad is the cancer?'

'I don't know. Her dad didn't really want to discuss it over the phone. She was really sorry that she couldn't come to see you.'

'Don't be silly!'

Ben paused. 'Cockie, I'm not sure you should be talking this much anyway but the doctor thinks—'

'I've been out of action for nearly two days – I've got some major catching-up to do!'

'Hey, be serious for a sec. The doctor thinks that you will have probably forgotten the twenty-four-hour period immediately before the accident – now, quite a few things happened in that twenty-four hours and although I really don't want to, I think I'm going to have to tell you—'

'Ben,' Cockie said softly. 'Don't put yourself through this – I remember everything as clear as a bell and it's OK, do you understand?'

She looked thoughtful. 'There's just so much bullshit floating around about how we're all supposed to conduct ourselves in our relationships with other people, don't you think, Ben? We spend ninety per cent of the time talking about sex and relationships, but we can never quite bring ourselves to say anything that is actually true to the most important people, can we?'

She smiled woozily. 'I mean, I'm a case in point: I'm probably only saying all this because of the drugs and because I've been having some extraordinary . . .

conversations myself lately but don't you think that life would sometimes be so much simpler if we just said what we felt? I'm always told that the game is half the fun – and I suppose that life would be just too simplistic without all the shenanigans, but still, when I think how I've faffed around in the last few months . . . how much quicker and easier all round would it have been if I'd just said, "Look, I fancy you but I'm not sure I like you – do you like me and, if so, why?" or "I like you, I think I've always fancied you – you like me, you fancied me once, do you fancy me now?" I mean, wouldn't that just cut out the crap? And another thing, why isn't there an acceptable word between "fancy" and "love"?'

'I – I – I—' stammered Ben, hardly daring to hope.

'I might have known the peace would soon be over!' boomed a voice from the doorway. 'Nearly two days of blessed silence, but as soon as I came down the corridor what did I hear? Yak yak yak yak – same as bloody usual. Wotcher sis, how the hell are you?' He bent down to kiss her cheek, and looked at her penetratingly. 'Back with us for good, I hope.'

'I'll stick around as long as you keep me in this private room,' Cockie joked. 'It's very good to see you, Robert.'

'It's only three days since the weekend, you ninny – are they dosing her up on drugs or is she being this horribly sentimental for real?' he asked Ben, sticking out his hand for him to shake.

Ben grinned. 'Haven't a clue, guv, I'm just the loving next-of-kin.'

'So I see,' said Robert pointedly, looking down at their clasped hands. So quick that Ben thought he must have imagined it, the other man flashed him a wink before turning back to Cockie. 'Did you have good dreams while you were down under, Cockie?'

She looked at Robert curiously. 'You could say that.'

'They tell me that for a while there you were actually stone dead – so, give us the scoop – is there an afterlife?'

'I'd love to tell you that I saw Mum and Dad and Gus and that we had a little tea-party over there but I'm afraid that would be telling too many porky pies.' Cockie's eyes twinkled blindingly.

Ben nearly gasped out loud – never had he heard her mention her family so jokily. What had gone on inside her head while she was in the coma?

'Well, these are from Ariana,' Robert said, holding up a brown paper bag, 'where do you want them?'

'Oh, over there with the flowers, I suppose. What are they?'

'Bananas,' said Robert, utterly straight-faced. 'Ariana insisted.'

There was a small silence, then all three of them laughed out loud, Cockie weakly, Robert boomingly, Ben's edged with the sharp taste of relief. She's OK, he thought, she's really OK. The lifting of that worry, which had weighed so heavily on every fibre of his being, left him feeling light-headed and giddy, almost uneasy. Now there was the other matter to worry about . . .

'Bloody awful flowers!' Robert was exclaiming.

Cockie shot an amused glance at Ben. 'They're from Victor, Robert.'

'Victor? Ohhh, *the* Victor! And,' he said archly, 'will we be meeting *the* Victor for a touching reunion at the hospital bed?'

Cockie plucked at her sheet, not meeting their eyes. Ben found himself holding his breath. Eventually, she looked up.

'Well, he's hardly a close relative, is he?' said Cockie blandly. Ben's heart went stratospheric as she squeezed his hand. 'No, I don't think we'll be seeing much more of Victor Landis.'

16

From the plane's tiny window, London dwindled into a far-stretching circuit board below her. Despite the discomfort of sandwiching her plaster-bulked limbs into her seat, Cockie could feel only relief that she'd got away. It seemed to her that since coming out of her coma, she had not been allowed a single moment on her own to reflect on everything that was going on, both inside her head and outside. The days up to her release from hospital had been a kaleidoscope of tests, interviews and visits from an ever-inflating pack of friends. Then, when she'd got home, the intimacy she and Ben had shared in the hospital was suddenly translated into the mundane business of being flatmates again. Without the chaperonage of nurses and the neon lighting of the hospital, those talks they had had, stretching through the night, were suddenly a little dangerous. It seemed to Cockie that they had said everything, sorted everything out, declared all their feelings, short of the three-word cliché – but in laboratory conditions. Once back at Ebury Mews, an uncomfortable Cockie was clumsy and helpless with leg and arm still in plaster. Ben was obsessed with looking after her, with keeping Eva's spirits up as she battled with a decade of distance between herself and her parents and trying to clinch a new contract for Hyde Landscaping. Unable to keep their hands off each other but unable to explore past the chastity belts of Cockie's injuries, the tension was soon making them both edgy. Finally, Ben took action.

'OK, here are your plane tickets,' he announced one breakfast. 'You leave in three days. I've checked it all out with the doctors and they think it's a great idea. Don't even think about arguing,' he added, seeing Cockie's face. 'I know I'm being bossy and dictatorial – but you need to get your head in order, not to mention the rest of you, and you can't do that with me around. I'm giving you until after Christmas. This isn't a holiday, by the way, you're damn well going to finish that book of yours – and think of a bloody title – or write another one. I don't care, just go and heal yourself. There, I've said it all – and you didn't even get a chance to interrupt! Now, what do you say?'

Just in case she hadn't told herself a million times since her accident, at that moment Cockie realised just how much she loved Ben. One of these days she might even be able to tell him so to his face, his beautiful, ugly face now looking expectantly at her, waiting for her response.

'OK,' she said meekly.

17

Tradewinds
St Kitts

Thursday

Darling Eva,

A thousand homages, my sweetling, for driving me to the airport the other day – I still can't believe that Ben had stressed the invalid thing to British Airways so much . . . your face as I was whisked off on the electric buggy was a picture, my dear, an absolute picture. On the flight, I couldn't have been more toadied to if I'd been wearing mink pyjamas and had had eight husbands (bit of a *Hello*! reference there, I'm afraid, so you may be playing catch-up) – we had *Shadowlands* as the movie and – you know me – when I'd got to the choked-up, heaving chest, swollen-eyed, second tissue box stage (so, about half an hour into the film) one of the flight attendants (is that PC enough, sweetie?) came up to me and said – with such a concerned expression that I thought she had to have painted it on – 'Oh, Miss Milton, are you in a *lot* of pain?' Pain? Well, yes, I suppose seeing Anthony Hopkins cry is a sort of pain . . .

This is actually going to be a shortie because Eli

(caretaker and general dude) is taking the jeep away in a few minutes and – given that it's at least a half an hour crutch hop into the village (hey, it's hot out here!) – has offered to post this for me so I'd better be Speedy McSpeedy from the Clan Speedy. The house is un-be-fucking-lievable – this beautiful octagonal design, perched on top of a hill with the most jaw-clanging views to the bay below – and just ever so slightly run-down at the same time, which actually makes it even more romantic. I haven't had a chance even to *see* if I would rattle around it like a pea yet, because Ben seems to have alerted the entire island to One's Arrival . . . there has been a constant tramp through, of visitors who each treat me as if I'm wrapped in just a little bit more cotton wool. I mean, I am meant to be convalescing and I know I'm good at playing the invalid card but it's all getting a bit ridiculous – when I stood up to offer Patsy (owner of best bar, dontcha know) a drink, I could see that she was about to run down the hill screaming, 'It's a miracle! Lordy me, it's a miracle! She threw away her crutches and she walked! It's a miracle!'

Now I know you gave me strict instructions not to talk about you in my letters but, guess what? I'm going to ignore that (heh heh). I've got my fingers crossed for you and Mike, and am waving my magic wand (Eli is, shall we say, a good provider of life's essentials) furiously to get you two back together again. I feel it in my bones – even the broken ones – that you're meant to be together, so don't start getting paranoid on me, babe, and start thinking that he's only talking to you again because of your mother.

It's strange, isn't it, that *we* all thought of you as the hard-nosed, pragmatic one when all along, *you* were waiting for your prince to come, thinking that Mike just wasn't quite royal enough? Well, as you said to me about ten times in the last few days, he *is* the one for you, so no shilly-shallying, woman, get to it.

Please send my love to your mother – it was so sweet of her to come and see me in hospital when she must be so sick of the places herself – and tell her that I've got everyone out here saying some major league prayers for her, whether voodoo or herbal or good old-fashioned holy. I still can't believe that you can be so polite to that bitch of a sister of yours but I can understand why you're doing it (spike her tea from me, anyway). Why didn't you tell me your dad was so good-looking? Terry, the male night nurse, nearly passed out when your dad walked in, and proceeded to wait on me hand and foot for the duration of your parents' visit, with much fluttering of eyelashes.

Eli – in a sort of Caribbean, time-goes-slower-out-here kind of way – is looking a tad impatient so I'd better finish now. Keep in touch – you know where I am.

Yours brown-ly
Cockie

Patsy's Bar
St Kitts

Tuesday – 18 shopping days till Christmas!

Drew-baby,

I know I only wrote to you two days ago, but I got your letter this morning and you'll never believe who 'dropped in' yesterday? Do you remember Emma from the Gallery – the one who was measuring you up for size that day you took me out to lunch? Well, right from the word go, she had her hooks into Victor – even accusing me of stealing him from her, which was a little premature if memory serves me right – and practically as I was still flying through the air and landing in the gutter, was working on getting him back . . . well, all credit to her, she did it, she snagged him, persuaded him to take her on holiday to the Caribbean and had the cheek to drag him to St Kitts to see me! There was I, still enjoying my blissful isolation, putting in some really steamy penmanship on the Mills and Boon, (getting almost hot and bothered, I have to confess – well, have you ever tried writing a sex scene?!) and in walk these two blasts from the past. It was all rather bizarre – apart from anything else, it must have taken some serious sleuthing for Emma to have found me because as far as I can remember, Ben only told the Gallery that I was going to St Kitts – no address, no telephone number, nothing – and I had my head so full of Luca and Allegra and throbbing malenesses and hot little pants that I could hardly see straight, let alone cope with the fact that my inspiration for Luca was actually in the room. He did look rather uncomfortable – not entirely surprising considering the end of our relationship . . . no, no, don't chuck someone, that's the dull way – no, just hurl yourself from a bus and spend the next few weeks hiding out in hospital! Not that he really tried to stick around – I suspect that he's one of life's health fascists: he looked rather distastefully at my cast and asked me what on earth I found to do on St Kitts if I couldn't do any watersports. Egad, that was a narrow escape – to think how closely I nearly screwed up my chances with Ben, for a dweeb like our Victor – hoo-whee! On the subject of Ben, your letter was even more abominably smug than you have been in the flesh;

anyone would think that you set us up, instead of Not Telling Me What Was Going On Like A True Friend. But we've been through that, haven't we, my sweet, and anyway, the cat's not quite in the bag yet (is that the expression? It looks odd.) – the dirty deed has not yet been done – another reason why I was getting so hot under the collar when writing yesterday; I'm just hot diggedy damn horny: this place is one walking advertisement for sex but, much as I adore Eli, he's not quite Ben-like enough (and that's as mushy as you're going to get, slush-hound!) and I suspect, anyway, that he may be slightly more up your street. Talking of which, I'm glad to hear that you're getting over Jonathan . . . Carl sounds lovely and I'm not even going to start teasing you about how serious it already sounds, it just wouldn't be like me.

Will write again in a few days' time; glad to hear that the Grand Opening of No. 42 has been delayed until New Year's Eve – I think it'll be a much glitzier party on that date, *and* there's a chance I might be back by then. The photos of the Trompe L'Oeil Room look stunning, by the way – by golly, you did it, didn't you?

Proud of you, honeychile.

Cockie

To: Ben Hyde, Master of the Universe
At: Hyde Landscaping (44) 171 233 3037
From: Cockie Milton, Drooling Slave
Date: December 10th
Pages: Two in total

Not that I can be bought or anything, but this fax is the business! I'm feeling too lazy even to think about how you managed to organise it – and I've got a busy day ahead . . . Patsy has found me the groovicst physio called Sy (Cy? Psi?) who can only function on a beach, at a certain time of day, with a certain (large) amount of grass in his spliff. We do yoga and, like, get inside our heads, man, and it's all just so cosmically entertaining . . . he reckons that I can take my cast off earlier than the London doctor said, because I've been giving the bones such happy, like, healing vibes since I've been here. Hmmm, we shall see.

In the meantime, it's full steam ahead (quite literally) on the Mills and Boon (still title-less, I'm afraid) which looks like being finished well in time for Christmas – oh, what am I going to do then? All festived-up and no-one to play with? I can think of one person who should, as he is reading this, be checking his passport details, getting on the phone to Trailfinders and getting his ass out here pronto onto Toronto, Tonto. Not that I'm hinting, or anything. No, no.

What the heck. Yes, I am hinting. I miss you horribly and am feeling unconscionably horny. I see your photo all over the house – you have to have been the ugliest ten-year-old I've ever seen, but just the cutest eighteen-year-old – and I want you here! Now! I'm banging my knife and fork on the table and I'm going to scream and scream and scream until I'm sick, or until you bring yourself to me.

Fax – Urgent – Fax – Urgent – Fax – Urgent – Fax – Urgent
Attention: Cockie: 001 809 465 6572
One page in total

Bugger this – the garden business is snowed under, literally not metaphorically, so I'm on the next plane out. Keep your bandages on until I get there so that

I can admire the tan lines. With my heart in my mouth – Ben.

Dear Whim-lings

Haven't seen Rudolph yet, but there are lots of tourists with red noses at the other end of the island; we're dreaming of a white Christmas but are settling for grim reality: deserted beach (see front of postcard), waves trying to lap but finding it all very hard work, and a turkey which Eli, in his infinite wisdom, has called Prince Charles. It's tough at the top: see you all in January if we ever come back . . . happy festives in the meantime and big kisses, Cockie and Ben

PS: **Now then, TJ – Who's Dale??? You're meant to be broken-hearted, you tart. XXXX**

PPS: A title for the Mills and Boon – at long last . . . how about 'Know Me Now'?!

Cockie stretched out against the wiry length of Ben, yawning luxuriously.

'Ohhhhh, I—'

'Don't you dare go to sleep on me, you abandoned woman. I haven't finished whispering sweet nothings to you,' he growled into her ear, hands rippling lightly up and down her back.

'If you'd let me get a word in edgeways,' she teased him, 'you'd have heard three little words that would have been sweet little everythings. Hmmm, what could possibly go, "I mmm mmm"?'

Ben looked intently at her. 'If you're joking, I will have to kill you – you know that, don't you – ve-ry, ve-ry slowlee . . .' He paused a mere inch away from her mouth.

'Well, look forward to a long and happy life with me pestering you, babe,' Cockie whispered, her hands doing X-rated things to him, 'because you're not going to be killing anyone.'

Ben groaned ecstatically. 'If we keep up like this, hussy, I'm going to die from exhaustion.'

'Just lie back and think of England, old man. Yup, the cold, the wet, the rain, the Regent Street lights – hey!'

As Ben grabbed her, Cockie's heart took a photograph. Here was her Imperfect Man, doing Perfect Things to her, and she wouldn't have it any other way . . . well, maybe this way, she giggled to herself, as Ben lifted her on top of him, oh, and that way, as he kissed her, oh, and that . . .

Much later, she woke to find Ben looking intently down at her.

'Mmmm?'

'You know,' he mused out loud after a moment, 'I was reading that book on Near Death Experiences and some pretty weird things have happened to other people, so why not you?'

'Why suddenly bring this up?' smiled Cockie.

'Because your eyes do have this sort of sparkling look about them.'

'It's called the look of love, dumbo, and I really am out of my head crazy about you,' said Cockie, kissing him.

'No, let me finish, temptress! Don't forget that I was with you that weekend when you were describing the eyes of the child at the wedding – before you even dived into the afterlife – and now, that is how I would describe your own eyes – young and old, wise but not weary, I can't really describe it.'

'No,' agreed Cockie laughing, 'you can't! Anyway, I thought I was being set up with Victor, don't forget – and I would have been truly off my head to have ended up with him.'

'No arguments from me there,' said Ben ruefully, giving thanks for the thousandth time that all those mix-ups were, if not forgotten, then consigned to the out tray of history.

'Basically, I agree with you – it all seems too vivid and extraordinary just to be out of my head, but if there's any celestial wisdom I did absorb, it's that life's too short to worry about conspiracy theories, supernatural or otherwise, and that – at the end of the day it's up to little ole me to put my life on course, I can't blame anything on anyone except myself, or wallow in a self-perpetuated sea of troubles!'

Cockie gazed at Ben in a haze of love, focusing dreamily on his lower lip, truly a wondrous feature of anatomy – tender now, plumped and rosy – especially from her point blank range. TJ was right, such a lip was worthy of poetry. Now that she'd finished the first draft of the Mills and Boon, perhaps she should distract herself by writing eulogies to every part of his body. Doing the research would be fun, that was for sure.

Ben stretched, and gathered Cockie into his arms for another bone-crushing hug, his hands sliding luxuriously from her nape to her waist and meandering tantalisingly up her front again. With everything tightening inside her once again, Cockie could hardly move her love-drugged limbs in response. She felt saturated by sensuality, a lioness lolling ecstatically in the sunshine of sex.

'Oh God, we have to get out of bed before I'm tempted to do us some serious damage . . .' Ben cupped her flushed face in his hands and kissed her tenderly. 'Talking of wallowing in seas, let's go and have a swim – it's too hot in here, and God knows I should have worked it off by now, but I'm still full of turkey dinner.' He rolled out of bed, laughing at the sound effects as their sweat-licked skins separated from each other.

'Christmas in the Caribbean! What a totally, like,

weird concept,' giggled Cockie as she stood up unself-consciously, proud of her body at last, and stepped into a swimsuit.

'Cockie,' said Ben, on their way to the beach, 'you say you'd decided to stop going out with Victor before the accident and before you even came back to the house that horrendous morning?'

'Uh-huh, that's right.'

'What made you take that decision? I mean, I know your reasons now, but what actually spurred you into making that decision at the time?'

'Do you really want to know?' Cockie grinned at him. 'You won't believe me!'

'Try me.'

'OK.' She peeped over the top of her sunglasses at him. 'He wore Y-fronts.'

'What?!'

'I'm not kidding – it's a real problem – I just can't fancy anyone who wears Y-fronts, briefs, whatever, and – well, you've got to draw the line somewhere – and I decided that this was—'

'No! Don't tell me—'

'The bottom line!' they chorused together.

FIONA WALKER

KISS CHASE

Felix Sylvian is as irresistible to women as melted chocolate on a ripe strawberry but he has one nasty habit he can't seem to break: a sadistic tendency to ride rough-shod over any girl foolish enough to fall for him. Is Phoebe Fredericks the girl to take on Felix and beat him at his own game . . .?

'Walker has a nicely epigrammatic turn of phrase and she understands how love can make normally sensible adults behave like imbeciles'

Daily Express

HODDER AND STOUGHTON PAPERBACKS

PHILIPPA TODD

BLIND DATE

Would you accept a job as a researcher on a TV programme about dating agencies? Would you set off on a round-the-world voyage of discovery and embark on a series of blind dates with men you'd never met before?

Camilla Cage does.

Little does she realise what she's let herself in for.

Because that marks the start of a series of sometimes hilarious and often hair-raising adventures as Camilla finds herself trapped in a hot air balloon in Australia, attending the Oscars ceremony in Los Angeles, and held in bondage in a plush Park Avenue establishment, faced with a terrifying predicament.

But, as she says, it's a living. Certainly not a way to meet one's ideal mate.

Although true love does have a way of creeping up on a girl just when she least expects it . . .

HODDER AND STOUGHTON PAPERBACKS